The Fire Lord's Lover

"Enthralling... combines magic and realism as its excellent plot reaches out with great depth of emotion, heart-stopping action, and characters easy to care about wrapped in a passionate love story."

—*RT Book Reviews*, 4½ stars

"The unique world Kennedy has created and the underground rebellion of humans against their cruel magical rulers is enticing. Readers will be eagerly anticipating the sequels to experience the other six unique realms and follow the epic conflict between humans and elves... as well as enjoying the sexy romantic intrigue."

—*Booklist*

"Not only did this book exceed my expectations, it blew me away. Kennedy's novel is so well written and her characters are so rich and captivating that I simply could not put it down."

—*The San Francisco Book Review*

"Kathryne Kennedy pens an ambitious tale of love, romance, and sacrifice against the fantastic background of magic in an alternate reality of eighteenth-century England... *The Fire Lord's Lover* is an amazing start to what promises to be a wonderful series. You can't miss this!"

—*The Romance Reviews*

Also by Kathryne Kennedy

My Unfair Lady
Beneath the Thirteen Moons
The Fire Lord's Lover
The Lady of the Storm

Praise for Kathryne Kennedy's
Elven Lords series

The Lady of the Storm, a *Booklist* Top 10
Romance Fiction of 2011

"Kennedy's exquisite world building and terrific plotting make this a must-read for fantasy fans as well as readers who like sizzling romance. Kennedy creates a satisfying, fully realized world where adventure abounds and conflict and relationships are consistent and believable."

—*Booklist*

"Mesmerizing… Kathryne Kennedy crafts a glittering historical romance, greatly enriching it with a splash of fantasy. Her imagination knows no bounds… I was completely addicted from the first page… *The Lady of the Storm* casts a magical spell, conjures a passionate romance, and beckons to be enjoyed over and over again."

—*Fresh Fiction*

"This is much more than a romance novel—it is a nail-biting, action-packed page-turner!"

—David Benz, Edgar-nominated novelist

"Kennedy mixes the fantasy and romance genres in a very rewarding manner, which will please fans of both."

—*RT Book Reviews*, 4 Stars

THE LORD OF ILLUSION

KATHRYNE KENNEDY

sourcebooks
casablanca

Published by Sourcebooks Casablanca, an imprint of Sourcebooks,
Inc.
P.O. Box 4410, Naperville, Illinois 60567-4410
(630) 961-3900
FAX: (630) 961-2168
www.sourcebooks.com

Printed and bound in Canada
WC 10 9 8 7 6 5 4 3 2 1

～

The link between the world of man and Elfhame had sundered long ago, the elven people and their magic fading to legend. Tall beings of extraordinary beauty, the fae preferred a world of peace. But seven elves—considered mad by their own people—longed for power and war. They stole sacred magical scepters, created their dragon-steeds, and opened the gate to the realm of man again and flew through.

Each elf carved a sovereign land within England, replacing the baronies that had so recently been formed by William the Conqueror. They acquired willing and unwilling slaves to serve in their palaces and till their lands. And fight their wars. Like mythical gods they set armies of humans against each other, battling for the right to win the king, who'd become nothing more than a trophy. They bred with their human slaves, producing children to become champions of their war games.

The elven lords maintained a unified pact, using the scepters in a united will to place a barrier around England, with only a few guarded borders open to commerce. Elven magic provided unique goods and the world turned a blind eye to the plight of the people, persuaded by greed to leave England to its own, as long as the elven did not seek to expand their rule into neighboring lands.

But many of the English people formed a secret rebellion to fight their oppressors. Some of the elven's children considered themselves human despite their foreign blood and joined the cause. And over the centuries these half-breeds became their only hope.

One

England, 1774

DRYSTAN HAWKES WOKE IN A COLD SWEAT, STILL seeing visions of fire and blood and death. He blinked his eyes to dismiss them, but as usual, he had also been sent another image and he could never banish this last one so easily. A young woman, beautiful beyond his wildest imaginings, with the most startling multi-colored eyes. Elven eyes.

Drystan untangled himself from his bed linens and raked back his pale hair, knowing he could not ignore the summons, for it was more than a dream or nightmare.

The three stolen scepters of the elven lords called to him.

His bare feet touched the cold flagstone floor and he suppressed a shiver, reaching for his stockings and boots, his own elven eyes quickly adjusting to the gloom of midnight.

"I would like to sleep through just one night," he muttered as he finished dressing, crossing the room of his bedchamber with nary a whisper from the soles of his boots. He had learned to be quiet on his nightly excursions. His fellow orphans already thought him strange enough.

Drystan carefully opened his chamber door, causing only a slight squeak from the old hinges, and peered down the long hall of Carreg Cennen castle. One lone candle shone near the privy, but the rest of the passage lay shrouded in shadow, not even a mouse astir this late. He had taken this same route every night since he had ceased fighting the summons, so he strode confidently to the stairs, thinking he could now manage it with his eyes closed.

He found it easier to answer the call of the scepters at night, than to suffer the fits brought on by their visions during the day. He only wished he had conceded sooner. Perhaps then the other half-breed children would not have come to treat him like an outcast. Because of the fits brought on by the visions, Drystan gained the reputation of being cursed, or mad, or at the very least, physically abnormal. And any offspring of the elven lords rarely suffered from lack of physical perfection.

Drystan never knew when the scepters would send him a vision. He would fight it until the world went black, and he would wake in the middle of the school-room—a meal—the play yard—surrounded by horrified faces and children crossing themselves against evil.

Yes, when the scepters sent him a vision, it was better to answer the call and find out what they wanted. And as a man, he'd gained some control. But the damage had already been done, and Drystan lived his adult life almost as isolated as he had as a child.

Drystan shrugged, discarding his loneliness the same way he removed his greatcoat. He'd learned to be content with his own company, had even turned it to an advantage. And he had his books.

His stories transported him beyond the walls of this old castle. Novels where he became a hero who rescued the fair maid. Where he sailed the high seas, fought against the armies of the elven lords. Became a secret spy for the Rebellion.

And inside his stories, he had many friends who did not fear him. Indeed, they admired his strength and cunning and bravery...

Drystan reached the last flight of the circular stairs and entered the kitchens at the bottom of it, slipping past the cook whose bed nestled up amongst the brick ovens, and silently made his way into the cellars. Past the barrels of corn and turnips, behind the wine racks, to the enormous oak door. He fished out his key from his left pocket and unlocked the chains, careful to keep them from rattling.

Not many of the castle residents knew about this chamber, and Drystan had become privy to it only because of his... connection with the scepters. An old prime minister for the king, Sir Robert Walpole, created this storage place for the Rebellion years ago, when he began to smuggle the children who escaped from the trials of the elven lords to this old castle in Wales. The once-leader of the Rebellion thought it safer to store records and enchanted artifacts beyond the barrier of magic that surrounded England. He thought they could be kept more safely here, where their magic would be inactive.

Sir Robert had been wrong, at least where the scepters of the elven lords were concerned. They may not have the power they would possess within England to enhance each elven lord's magic, but they still retained a certain amount of dangerous awareness.

Drystan made his way down the earthen stairs into the castle dungeon—which thankfully had been cleared of torture devices and heaped instead with crates and barrels holding artifacts and the private journals of spies, historical accounts of England, and secret correspondences between the leader of the Rebellion and his allies.

He strode past it all without a glance, straight for the small cell in the back of the room. Drystan withdrew another key and opened the door. Bare earthen walls, stone floor. Nothing to indicate the malignant treasure it harbored within.

Drystan collapsed on a square of stone in the center of the room and pounded it with his fist. "All right. I'm here. What the hell do you want?"

The air shivered. The hair rose on the back of his neck. When he had been a lad and the scepters first called to him, he thought it was God sending him a vision. How very wrong he had been.

Drystan pounded the ground again. Buried beneath the stone lay the stolen scepters of three of the elven lords. The blue of the elven lord of Dewhame, Breden. The lavender of the elven lady La'laylia of Stonehame. The silver of Lan'dor, the elven lord of Bladehame. Drystan knew the story of the theft of the blue scepter, for the two who had stolen it, Giles Beaumont and his lady Cecily, lived in the castle of Wales. They had taken over the running of the sanctuary and the children who sheltered here.

The two half-breed elven who had stolen the lavender scepter, General Samson Cavendish and Lady Joscelyn, had returned to Firehame to continue to aid the Rebellion. And Alexander and his warrior-lady, Wilhelmina, had returned to Firehame as well, after they delivered the silver scepter into the keeping of Carreg Cennen castle.

Drystan did not know all of the details about their adventures in stealing the scepters, although he'd read about them, and more importantly, had seen glimpses of them in his dreams. Dreams he did not welcome.

Except for the lady in his visions. He could still see those rainbow-colored eyes staring at him with such loneliness, and hidden fury. Large faceted elven eyes that seemed to echo the very feelings within his soul. Those haunting eyes possessed all the colors of the scepters within them: lavender, silver, blue, and green, with flecks of brown and black and gold. As if her elven blood held a mix of all seven of the elven lords and their sovereignties. And perhaps each of those powers?

Drystan spread his fingers over the cold stone. "Where is she?" he whispered. "I have searched and searched to find any record of her…"

The ground shivered. Another vision sprang into his head with enough force to make it pound in fury and Drystan clutched at his temples. Seven dragons flew in a maelstrom of color above the swirling blonde hair of a black-clothed woman. The air sundered with a violence that tore apart the very fabric of the universe and the lady watched it all with mouth agape in horror. Then blackness, and another scene. The same woman casting her hands over the head of a child, a flash of a symbol that Drystan could not quite make out branded onto the child's skin. And then a vision of another child, and another, each of them passing along the birthmark.

"I have looked for any reference to the descendants of the white witch of Ashton house," he said to the empty cell. "The records of the family disappear with the elven wars of the fifteenth century. The family was captured and enslaved…"

Another vision assailed him. This time of an ivory-haired child that grew into the beautiful woman with the multicolored eyes. Her delicate face so pale. So vulnerable. She wore a dress of white that billowed around her thin frame, and she ran from something hidden in shadow. Something that threatened her. And he knew he must save her. He held her only hope and salvation.

Her eyes kept him spellbound until the vision finally faded.

And then the scepters spoke to him in words he could comprehend.

The descendant of Ashton House holds the key to the doorway to Elfhame. Find her.

Drystan jerked at the unholy voices in his head. Fire screamed through his every nerve, like knives shearing open each vein and filling it with acid. The agony grew until spasms racked his body, until anguish beat at his mind and misery filled his heart. Whatever awareness the scepters held, those alien thoughts were not meant for mankind to endure.

But they had spoken this message to him before, and Drystan managed to hold onto consciousness. A grown man of five and twenty years now, he did not collapse into convulsions as he had done as a lad.

It took him some time to find his voice.

"I have tried."

Although it had not been for their sake. Not just because they tortured him night after night. Not just because they would not let him sleep until he answered their summons. But for his own sake. For the lady who spoke to his heart with those unusual eyes. For the sheer desire he had to protect her. To hold her in his arms.

He had barely looked at another woman since she began to haunt his visions.

"I will not stop trying until I find her."

Seemingly satisfied, the tug on Drystan eased, as if the compulsion that the scepters used upon him to draw him into this chamber relaxed enough to allow him his own free will.

He rose, a bit unsteadily, but with purpose. As he did every night, he locked the cell behind him and made his way across the dungeon to the heavy oak table that served him as a desk. He lit the candles, throwing a halo of light around him, casting eerie shadows beyond that circle. He opened the journal that recorded the contents of the storage room and noticed a new entry, written in Giles's sweeping hand. A shipment from Dreamhame, procured with the loss of life of one of the Rebellion's most precious spies.

Drystan felt a shiver of anticipation from the direction of the barred cell, although he hardly needed the inducement. He blinked his golden elven eyes, a testament to his ancestry from the elven lord Roden of the gold scepter, who ruled the sovereignty of Dreamhame with his magical gift of glamour and illusion. Outside of the barrier of magic, Drystan could not know the strength of his own powers within England, but he often wondered. He held the looks of the elven lord in abundance, from his white-blond hair to the extraordinary strength and grace in his limbs. Despite the disdain of the other orphans, Drystan fancied his powers would put the rest of them to shame.

And he often wondered how he managed to blend into the background at will. How he could charm someone when he set his mind to it. These were instinctive gifts, surely, remnants of the power that awaited him in England.

Not that he would ever know. Unless…

He stood and searched the room for the new shipment. There, next to the stack of journals from Terrahame. A wooden crate that Giles had yet to open and catalogue. The master of Carreg Cennen castle would not mind that his curator opened and recorded the contents. Indeed, only Giles and his lady Cecily knew of Drystan's connection to the scepters, and his search for the lost key to Elfhame. They kept his secrets and shielded him from the curiosity of the other castle residents.

Like most of the other orphans, Drystan considered Cecily and Giles his adoptive parents.

He dragged the crate over to his desk and pried off the lid. A small box sat on the top of mounds of loose papers and books, and when Drystan opened it, a flash of gold winked in the candlelight. A slip of paper described the enchantment of the coin within: it would appear as several coins, fooling any merchant who possessed less than a healthy share of elven blood. Drystan duly recorded it in the catalog, despite the hum of anticipation he felt from the scepters.

This crate contained something important.

Something that would finally help him discover the whereabouts of the descendant of the white witch. Drystan knew it as surely as he knew that snow fell beyond the thick walls of the castle.

He'd felt the scepters' compulsion grow stronger over the years. Drystan was dismayed to think it meant he'd succumbed to their combined will. Perhaps it had only been because he was close to solving the mystery of the white witch?

He slowly removed the first stack of documents from the crate. He would not rush. He would not give *them* the satisfaction.

But the thought of finding the lady in his dreams made his hands tremble.

He read the first packet of papers. Reports from a man named Mandeville to Lord North—the current prime minister and leader of the Rebellion. North came to the position as a member of the King's Friends, George III's attempt to gather control of his government. A government which held little actual power. The elven lords must be laughing at such antics.

They considered humans as little more than animals. Playthings to use in their elven war games, a pastime that cost the lives of thousands of Englishmen. Just to keep them entertained.

Drystan set aside the packet, recorded the contents, shrugging off the impotent rage that accompanied his thoughts. Despite all of the Rebellion's efforts, they still had not come any closer to freeing England from its slavery to the elven lords.

Although they managed to save countless children. This was not the only castle in Wales that harbored orphaned fugitives. Lady Cassandra of Firehame discovered that the trials—the magical tests of power the elven lords put their half-breed children through— were a subterfuge for certain death. That the lords did not really send the children who showed exceptional magic to the fabled land of Elfhame. The tests were a ruse to weed out those who might possibly grow into enough power to threaten an elven lord's rule.

Most of the children weren't truly orphans, for most had families in England, but they all felt and referred to each other that way.

Drystan had parents in Herefordshire County, although he could no longer remember what they looked like. He occasionally received letters from them, and knew he had a brother who strongly resembled him, but apparently Duncan did not possess enough elven magic to be a threat to the elven lords.

Would he ever be united with his family?

Drystan rubbed at his eyes.

If this key truly existed… if this brand the white witch emblazoned on all of her offspring held a clue to opening the door to Elfhame… Would the Rebellion be able to send the elven lords back where they came from? Perhaps humans did not have the power, but by all accounts, the elven lords were considered mad by their very own people. If the door between the two worlds opened, would their kinsman come through and take the lords back home? Drystan did not know. He only knew the scepters wanted to return to Elfhame, and this key might accomplish that.

It might be England's only hope.

Drystan squared his shoulders, feeling the weight of his task, wondering why he had been chosen for it. And then remembered the girl and knew.

He felt he was the only man who could save her. Because he was the only man who knew her torture as his own.

Drystan picked up another sheath of papers and began to read. And then another, and another. Like every night for the past decade, he read until he exhausted even the strength of his elven eyes, until they burned and drooped and he could barely see the words on the page.

It lay at the bottom of the crate, of course.

He opened the leather journal, sighed when he realized it was just a household inventory of Dreamhame Palace from years ago. But the quiver he felt from the direction of the cell made him squint to focus his eyes on the entries. Linens, silver, candles. Gold plate, crystal glasses, silk cloth. And then in the kitchens: caskets of gin, bottled wine, sacks of wheat, cooking pans.

And a scribbled note at the bottom of the entries: three scullery slaves: M. Shreves, A. Cobb, C. Ashton.

Ashton.

Drystan's eyes watered and he closed them, felt them throb in time to his heartbeat. How many times had he come across this name in various records? Hundreds. And each time it failed to lead him to the line of the white witch. His dreams of blood and death would become more violent, as if the scepters punished him for that failure.

Such an impossible task, since Ashton House had fallen in an elven war game between Dreamhame and Terrahame centuries ago, its inhabitants scattered across the seven realms when their ransom was not met.

Had some of them become enslaved in Dreamhame Palace?

He opened his eyes, stared at the entry. Blinked. *Witch* had been messily scrawled near the edge of the paper.

Had he indeed found the white witch of Ashton House?

"Yes!" screamed the scepters in his head, rocking Drystan backward in his chair, the journal falling with a thump upon his battered desk.

And then he gracefully slumped forward, blackness overwhelming him from that final blow to a mind exhausted by years of sleep deprivation.

～

A callused hand gently shook Drystan awake. "I'm sorry, lad. We have a very important visitor."

Drystan blinked up into the light of a lantern, and then farther upward into the face of the master of Carreg Cennen castle. Drystan did not mind being called "lad" by Giles Beaumont, for the elven warrior was *old*, in his sixties at least, with a spattering of gray in his long blond hair and through his dark brows. But his elven blood gave him the carriage of a younger man, and Drystan knew from painful experience that Giles still wielded the battered blade at his side with the vigor of a human half his years.

"What time is it?" Drystan mumbled, sweeping his own white-blond hair away from his face. His hand came away with a smudge of ink on his fingertips, and the awareness that he had a crease across the skin of his cheek from where it had lain on the edge of the journal.

"'Tis early," replied Giles. "If we hurry, no one will notice you—us."

Drystan stood. He must look worse than he felt, if Giles sought to shield him from curious eyes. "That bad, eh?"

The other man smiled. "You look as if you've been up all night for the past ten years... which I suppose you have. It's sorry I am to wake you, but Lord North has arrived."

"The Prime Minister? Here?"

"Aye. I wouldn't have woken you otherwise." Giles studied him with the ordinary-shaped human eyes that defied his otherwise elven looks. Concerned, worried eyes. "Sorry, lad. You look particularly hellish today."

Drystan straightened the sleeves of his coat, quickly buttoned the front of his shirt when he noticed it hanging open. He looked hellish because... Drystan glanced down at his desk, his heart giving a leap in his chest. Because he had finally found *her*. But the news that Lord North himself, the leader of the Rebellion, had traveled to Wales to see them personally gave him pause. "It's not good, is it?"

Giles shrugged. "Is it ever?"

Drystan picked up the journal. "No. Perhaps I can change that."

"What do you—you found her?"

Drystan nodded, feeling a tingle from the direction of the cell. He did not wonder that Giles did not feel the scepters' eager reaction. Apparently, only Drystan possessed that connection to them.

"Are you sure, lad? 'Tis like finding a needle in a bottle of hay."

"I am sure." Drystan glanced at the cell. "They are… eager."

Giles frowned. "For some reason that gives me little comfort. And yet, perhaps now they will leave you be. There are few men I know who would endure what you have without complaint. I wish we could reveal your work, but the safety of the Rebellion is in the secrecy of the whereabouts of the scepters, not to mention the rest of the contents of this room."

Drystan laid a hand on Giles's shoulder. "Do not apologize, Father. I'm well aware that you could not share my secrets with the others. I do not blame you for the shape of my life. The scepters chose me for this task, not you."

Giles let out a sigh. "Well, lad, it's over with, at least. We can give the information to Lord North and you can live a normal life from here on."

Surprise held Drystan speechless. Did the other man truly believe this meant the end of his task? Did Giles think he would give over the information and let some other fellow find the descendant of the white witch? Perhaps Giles's reaction was Drystan's own fault. He had told Giles of the lady with the strange eyes, but had not confessed his feelings about her. He would have sounded like a fool. Yet now…

Now he would have to convince Giles, and Lord North, that he must be sent on this mission. A young man with little training, and no experience as a spy. Who had spent most of his life doing nothing more than reading about the exploits of the Rebellion.

Giles turned and made his way back up to the cellar, and Drystan followed, stuffing the journal in his coat pocket. Drystan felt surprised that Giles did not ask for further information about the witch. His foster father's gaze was turned inward, apparently too worried about the visit of Lord North and what his news might portend. Giles locked the door behind them, and waited until the kitchen emptied before stepping within.

One of the maids entered from a door on the opposite side of the kitchen and let out a squeak, dropping a bowl of eggs at the sight of them. Another two maids appeared at the open kitchen door, a light dusting of snow drifting into the room. A bit broader, a bit taller, Giles should have commanded their attention. Instead all eyes went to Drystan, who quickly stiffened and tilted his chin slightly upward. Arrogance and indifference were his only weapons against their rudeness.

The lady who had dropped the eggs crossed herself, and the two in the doorway leaned their heads together and passed a whisper, which made them both titter. Drystan had grown up with the two young women, and knew them to be particularly silly. Each resident of the castle took on the chores of what suited their skills, and if they lacked any, usually were put to chopping wood or vegetables.

Drystan guessed them to be vegetable choppers.

But at their whispered exchange, Giles glanced over at him. "Perhaps you should wash a bit? We wouldn't want to concern Lady Cecily."

Drystan sighed, did as he'd been told while the girls continued to giggle. The older orphans filled in the younger about his odd fits, his screaming nightmares, and lurking about the castle corridors. He suspected the stories had grown with the telling, for the girl who had dropped the eggs actually appeared frightened of him. He gently apologized to her with enough enthusiasm to pink her cheeks before he left the room.

Perhaps if he had not been obsessed with finding the white witch's descendant, he might have been able to charm them all out of their foolishness. He had not wanted to waste the time.

As he followed Giles up the stairs to the second floor, Drystan's heart beat a bit faster. He had found her! The woman of his dreams. He would rush to her rescue and she would welcome him with open arms, and they would decipher the meaning of the brand on her skin and save the world...

Giles strode past what had once been a guardroom and now served as a dining hall, the voices of the residents within growing silent as they passed. Drystan followed his lead, giving the room nary a glance, his attention focused on the button just above the skirt of Giles's coat.

He could not wait to leave Carreg Cennen castle.

They entered the formal withdrawing room, which

had once been an armory and still displayed medieval weapons along the walls. The metal had been polished to a high sheen, reflecting the firelight in the large hearth, the myriad tables scattered about the room, the velvet-upholstered chairs and cushions. Giles's wife, Lady Cecily, had decorated this room, as she had renovated most of the castle, calling the enormous pile of stone her "little cottage by the sea." Drystan never understood what she meant, but her comment always made Giles smile with tenderness.

She sat near the fireplace now, a silver-laden tea service at her elbow, the gray in her hair made more obvious because of her black locks. Drystan always thought her one of the most beautiful women he had ever seen: with her large blue faceted elven eyes, her red lips, and heart-shaped brow. The fine lines about the corners of her eyes and mouth served only to enhance her loveliness with character.

Those lines deepened as she turned to smile at her husband and Drystan. Giles beat him to her hand by a hairsbreadth, falling to one knee.

"My love," he murmured, kissing the top of her lace glove. She smiled even wider, not in the least embarrassed by her husband's display of affection in front of her guest. Once Giles rose, Drystan bent and kissed her cheek. She smelled divinely of lavender and mint tea.

Then they both turned and faced the man who sat in the chair across from her.

Lord North studied them in turn. He had come to Wales once before, when Giles reported of the strange connection Drystan had to the scepters. A large man with a cherubic face and a sharp wit. Drystan had immediately liked him. But wondered how such an affable soul had become the leader of the Rebellion.

Giles reminded him to never judge a man by his looks.

"Giles Beaumont! You still look half your age, damn that elven blood of yours. And Drystan Hawkes, is it not? You have grown since I've last seen you." The gaze within Lord North's protruding eyes sharpened. "Although I must say, lad, you look as if you could use a fortnight's sleep or more."

Drystan bowed. "It has been to good purpose, my lord." He would have blurted out his discovery right then and there, but Giles cleared his throat and when Drystan rose, Giles nodded at a leather chair next to Cecily. Drystan took his cue and sat, watching Giles take a seat next to the prime minister. So, he would have to wait and hear the other man's news first.

"What brings you back to Wales, Lord North?"

"Ah, Beaumont. Never one to mince about, eh?" Then his smile faded, and he glanced at Cecily. "I'm afraid it's dire news, my lady."

She met his gaze with aplomb. "I had no doubt of it, my lord. Despite your pleasantries over tea." She set down her cup with a rattle. "Please tell us the worst. My patience has been worn by the wait."

Lord North nodded, setting his white wig slightly askew. A novelty to Drystan, who lived amongst those who possessed the natural color. Giles had explained that in England, humans imitated elven locks by wearing the wigs. The prime minister had added a dash of silver sparkle to his hair as well, which Giles said the elven lords themselves possessed... and even some half-breeds. Drystan idly wondered what cosmetic Lord North used to copy it.

The prime minister settled back into his chair, calmly folded his hands in his lap, the lace of his sleeves falling across his knuckles as if artfully arranged on purpose. "A half-breed has killed the elven lord Mi'cal, and taken over the sovereignty of Verdanthame."

Cecily gasped.

Giles sucked a breath through his teeth. "Is he one of ours?"

North shook his head. "No. We became aware of this half-breed—Dorian—only recently, following the rumor of a man the locals called 'the forest lord.' We sent Aurelia, one of our best assassins and a most skilled spy, to seek out the half-breed. She now stands at Dorian's side."

"Then we have an advantage," said Cecily.

"Perhaps. But of what use? The Rebellion did not plan this takeover. We wouldn't have. Too risky. And we were right. The elven lords have gathered together for the first time in our history. They suspected the theft of the scepters. They suspected that one of their own, Lord Mor'ded of Firehame, was in truth a half-breed. Now they know for certain."

Lady Cecily and Giles looked horrified. Drystan only felt confused. "Should we not be celebrating? With half-breeds on the thrones of Firehame and Verdanthame, and the possession of the scepters of Dewhame, Stonehame, and Bladehame here in Wales, only two scepters remain within the elven lords' hands. Surely the might of five will conquer the two?"

Lord North rose one heavy brow, and Giles quickly

answered. "We wish it could be that simple, Drystan. But the Imperial Lords still retain their powers, even without the scepters. And we have only three half-breeds who can wield them."

"Four," murmured Cecily.

"I forbid it."

"Giles. If I am needed to wield it, then I must."

"You are too o—"

"Oh, you wouldn't dare say it!"

Giles lapsed into disgruntled silence.

Lord North cleared his throat. "I am afraid it may be our only option, Beaumont. The elven lords are gathering an army to lay siege to Verdanthame. Lord Mor'ded—or should I say, our half-breed General Dominic Raikes, who has assumed the disguise of Lord Mor'ded—refused to join the war. His neighbor, elven lord Breden, who lost whatever wits he might have had, has longed for an excuse to invade Firehame. With the elven lords' suspicions about Mor'ded confirmed, they have given their blessing. Since Firehame shares a border with Verdanthame, the eastern half of England is in chaos."

Drystan glanced at Cecily. Her skin looked as white as parchment. Breden of Dewhame was her father, and he'd been rendered completely insane when Cecily had stolen his blue scepter. He knew she did not regret it, but it crushed a part of her soul when the madman she hoped to love as a true father had tried to kill her, and forced her hand to retaliate against him.

Her voice did not betray her inner feelings. "What would you have me do?"

Lord North leaned forward. "Return with me to England. With the scepter."

Giles made a strangled noise.

"You can at least hold Breden of Dewhame at bay, for without the scepter his powers might not prevail with your use of it against him."

"I forbid it," said Giles once again, but this time without any hope in his deep voice.

"She should be safe," continued North, "with the scepters returned to Firehame."

"Until Verdanthame is overrun. Then there will be five elven lords who will march against the sovereignty." Giles stood, unable to contain his agitation any longer. "Admit it, Lord North. Our tactics were wrong. Stealing the scepters was not the way to free England. They do not hold as much power as we hoped. We will lose this confrontation and set our efforts for freedom back a hundred years."

Drystan tried to keep up with the numbers the men threw about, then decided not to bother. This war would not be won by numbers and armies. It would be won with a key. He spoke into the heavy silence following Giles's prediction. "I must respectfully disagree, Father. The scepters hold more power than anyone could have guessed."

Giles strode over to the window, staring at the scattering of falling snow, his breath frosting the glass. "I do not have as much faith in your visions as you do."

Drystan frowned. So, that's why Giles did not question him about his discovery. After all these years, he had only been humoring him? Did he even believe that the scepters spoke to Drystan?

But apparently the leader of the Rebellion did, because he turned to Drystan and pierced him with that intent gaze. "They still send you visions of this white witch?"

"Yes, my lord. And at last, they have helped me to find her." He pulled out the journal, opened it to the proper page, and showed it to North. "I believe this is her descendant, who carries the birthmark upon her skin."

Lord North took the book, staring intently at the entry. "A slave? Hmm. And this mark, you say it is some sort of key to Elfhame?"

"My vision shows the white witch witnessing the arrival of the elven lords through the gateway between our worlds. And then she brands something on her child. Some clue to what she had seen. If there is a way to open that gate, I believe it exists in that birthmark passed down in the Ashton line. And I intend to find this woman."

Giles spun. "You? No. We need an experienced spy for such a task."

North ignored him. "Ever since Lord Thomas Althorp found the source of magic and the doorway to Elfhame, we have tried to find a way to open it. The elven lords' dragon-steeds have always referred to their masters as mad. They profess that the elven are generally a peaceful people. We hoped if we could open the door, we could send them back where they belong."

"Or release a scourge of them into our world to conquer the whole of it."

"Giles," interjected Cecily. "Must you anticipate doom with every breath?"

"It has kept my loved ones alive."

Drystan heard the scuffling of feet through the hall as

background accompaniment to their words. He leaned forward, his attention focusing on the man who could grant his wish. "That is my same thought, Lord North. Based on my research—the thousands of records I've read long into the night, I believe the key to our freedom may lie within the opening of that doorway, and may rest upon the clue this girl can provide."

The leader of the Rebellion absentmindedly rubbed his chin, the lace of his sleeves waving to and fro, staring at Drystan as if truly seeing him for the first time. "You are a bookish lad. And you look as if a stiff wind could knock you off your feet."

"You aren't actually considering sending him to England?" said Giles. "The lad has barely slept in the past ten years! At last he has found what the scepters wanted, and now that he has an opportunity to finally lead a normal life—"

"Do you truly believe that?" interrupted Drystan. He spoke calmly, quietly, for despite Giles's protests, it appeared Lord North was seriously considering Drystan's proposal. "They will not allow me to rest. I can feel them even now, pushing me... prodding me to find this girl. And I swear to you all, I am the only one who will be able to manage her."

"What do you mean?" asked Cecily.

Drystan colored. "It is not just a matter of finding this brand and deciphering it. Indeed, the mark may mean nothing to us, and the girl may hold some clue to it. I can't... I can't explain any more than that. I do not understand it all myself, for the scepters have never made it clear. But I know I am the only one who will be able to reach her."

Cecily's faceted blue eyes probed Drystan until he had to resist the urge to squirm. "She is the girl of *your* dreams," she whispered, her words laden with understanding.

Drystan nodded abruptly.

She picked up the rose-patterned teacup and took a sip. "You must send Drystan, Lord North."

Giles looked ready to tear his hair out. "I cannot allow you to go to Firehame and Drystan to Dreamhame. I cannot be in two places at once. How will I protect you both?"

Lord North grunted. "You have an extraordinary sensibility about your loved ones, Giles Beaumont. Haven't you taught the lad to protect himself?"

"He knows how to use a pistol and a sword, if that's your meaning."

"Good. It's decided then. You will all sail back with me on the morrow. And we shall bring the scepters with us, Beaumont, for although they have not won us our freedom as we hoped, at least they might help us in this war. We are setting in motion plans to search the orphans for those who might possess enough power to wield them." North turned and studied Drystan again. "Without the bruises beneath your eyes and that haggard face, you would look very much like your brother. Hopefully once you are on your way to England, the scepters will allow you to sleep."

Drystan blinked. To have this man refer to his brother aloud somehow made Duncan seem more real. "My lord?"

"We must have a disguise for you at Dreamhame court. You will arrive under the banner of Viscount

Hawkes. As the eldest brother, the title should have gone to you anyway."

Cecily reached out and clasped Drystan's hand. "I am so sorry, my dear."

Drystan froze. The news should not affect him this strongly. He did not know that man… and now he never would. "My brother holds the title? My… birth father is dead?"

"My apologies," said Lord North. "I forget how slowly news travels to you. Aye, your father died last year, passing on the inheritance. I do not think your brother will mind your borrowing the title for a time, since he knows it truly belongs to you."

"My… mother?"

"She is alive and well, although I cannot allow you to return to your home, you understand. As it is, Duncan will have to go into hiding for a time. You would not want to endanger them, would you?"

Drystan scowled. "I am not a fool. Indeed, you will not find another man as learned. I have been *forced* to that occupation, my lord, with a daily ritual of mental torture."

Giles strode over to Drystan and laid a hand upon his shoulder. "You have endured more than any man should. And you have always been a son to me. You know that."

Drystan could only nod. What kind of man would he have become without the love of Giles and Cecily? Probably one as mad as an elven lord. His throat tightened and he stood. "If you will excuse me, I have much to prepare for the morrow."

And before anyone could utter another word that

threatened his mettle, he left the room, closing the door quickly behind him. Drystan leaned against it for a moment, closing his eyes as he swayed on his feet. He prayed North was right, and that the scepters would allow him to sleep once he was bound for England. Otherwise he did not know how he would manage the journey.

Then a face formed in his mind. A lovely woman with thick, flowing ivory hair and elven eyes that sparkled with the colors of a rainbow. Eyes that held more loneliness than his own.

He would find her. If he had to walk through fire to accomplish it, he would find her.

Two

CAMILLE ASHTON SAT ON A STOOL NEXT TO THE dowager duchess of Pembridge, near the fireplace within the golden withdrawing room of Dreamhame Palace. Camille loved this particular room, with its gilt walls and gold-upholstered furniture and golden candle stands. Although the ceiling had a tendency to sparkle, and occasionally shower down flecks of gold dust, at least it did not actually move. And even though the walls flickered and shifted, they did not try to close in on one.

There were worse places in the palace to mingle with the court.

Camille quickly tapped Lady Pembridge on her silk-gloved hand, startling her from a snore. The duchess gave her a brief smile of gratitude and ordered her to fetch some more tea. Camille kept her eyes averted as she threaded her way through the groups of courtiers, who treated her as one of the invisible servants, so she did not worry about their notice. But when she went to the sideboard to fetch a new kettle, she could feel the malicious stares of the other servants.

Camille had usurped her place. Not once, but twice. A slave should not be allowed to dress as a servant, to learn to speak even better than one, and to attend the gentry. If they had their way, she would be clad in rags again and sent back to the kitchens where she came from.

Camille had worked too hard to gain her current position. She tried equally hard to forget when she first came to Dreamhame as a captive of war. At first she had been treated gently, but when no ransom appeared forthcoming, she had been sent to the scullery to toil for long hours in the damp and heat. She would not have minded the work. But when the soldiers discovered that she had been designated a slave—

Camille cut off the thought, brought the kettle back to Lady Pembridge, ignoring the servants, maintaining a blank expression that had taken her years to perfect. Damn them to Elfhame and back. She would never allow another man to use her. She was no longer a frightened young girl. She knew the ways of the world—that life was nothing more than a precarious existence between one danger and the next.

She cared only for the opinion of those who offered her protection.

"My lady, may I pour for you?" she whispered.

The duchess blinked owlishly at her. "Of course, my dear. Do you know where I put my spectacles? I seem to have misplaced them again."

Camille poured a spot of tea and then gently removed the glasses from the lady's high white wig and handed them to her. Lady Pembridge liked to dress in the height of fashion. Camille attended to all that her costume required. She shaved the lady's head in preparation for her wigs, ground the stone that provided the silver sparkle in them—although Camille did not see how humans thought it imitated the elven lords' own magical sheen.

Lady Pembridge had a whimsical streak, however, and her wig did not imitate the straight locks of the elven. The wig spiraled upward from her brow like a column of cloud, flowers and stuffed birds and glass fruit twisted among and between the locks. The lady loved her rouge and patch-box as well, often requiring Camille to place more than one black beauty mark upon that wrinkled face.

She often looked ridiculous. Camille loved her for it.

"Can you compress my hoops again, my dear? They seem to have sprung back up and keep poking my elbows. It is quite distracting my attention from my neighbors."

The duchess enjoyed nothing more than watching her neighbors. And gossiping about them. Camille surmised that Lady Pembridge knew more about what went on in the palace than the elven lord himself.

As if she had conjured him with a thought, Imperial Lord Roden entered the room, frighteningly resplendent in cloth of gold, the skirt of his coat swirling about him as if caught in some invisible wind. Gold thread had also been woven in the lace at his throat and sleeves, even finer strands creating the design of a dragon in the clocks of his hose. His long white hair flowed down his back like a river of sparkling silver, his pointed ears peeking through the strands of it. Large golden faceted eyes surveyed the room, only the malignant expression on his face robbing it from glorious beauty.

Silence enveloped the room at his entrance. He appeared to enjoy it.

Camille quickly stuffed Lady Pembridge's hoops into the sides of her chair and hunkered back down on her stool. Besides gracing his palace with illusions that terrified and trapped the unwary, Lord Roden liked to play with his courtiers. He held the golden scepter of glamour and illusion, and enjoyed using it to torment and humiliate random victims.

His games had become especially malicious since a half-breed had killed the elven lord of Verdanthame and stolen the green scepter.

"I am bored," he announced to the room in general.

Men paled and women swooned.

The duchess muttered something that Camille couldn't quite make out.

"Lord Berkhamstead." Roden turned toward a bear of a man who wore his black hair in a natural queue down his back, defiantly wigless, although he dressed as lavishly as his companions. "I understand your wife has recently given birth."

Up to this point the man had refused to show any sort of reaction toward the elven lord's presence. Now his face quickly paled to the same shade of the others. "I… uh…"

"Come along, man. Surely you don't believe the rumors that I kill off your young? If your daughter has the requisite power, she will be sent to Elfhame." Roden smiled, a perfect display of even white teeth that made Camille shiver with dread. "Magical, beautiful Elfhame. Where rivers flow with honey and diamonds are as common as gravel."

"She will be sent to you for testing, my lord."

"See to it, Berkhamstead. And none of this sneaking off into the night with the infant. Or some malady overtaking it so a quick burial is necessary. The ingenuity of your race is impressively unimaginative."

Roden's golden gaze roamed the room. "Although I must say, our elven blood has infiltrated your species to an astonishing degree. Whence all our troubles come, methinks. We would not be marching to war if it hadn't been for you half-breeds."

His eyes fixed upon a young girl, barely past her teens and dressed well enough to meet even Lady Pembridge's standards.

"Is that a wig upon your head, girl?"

"N-no, my lord."

He strode over to her, taking a lock of hair between his fingers. "No sparkle though. But your eyes. They remind me of Lady La'laylia's, glittering like amethyst jewels. I wonder how much of her blood you carry within your veins. You are new to my court?"

Camille held her breath. Although everyone at court had been tested for magical ability and proven harmless as a threat to the elven lord, a newcomer would be tested again. And Roden had a… taste for new blood.

"Yes, my lord," replied the young girl. "I am visiting my cousins."

"Odd time to visit, with the war and all. You humans wander like nomads. And who is this, one of your admirers?"

The girl blushed to the roots of her pale hair. "No, my lord. I mean, we have just met, my lord."

The young man in question colored almost as red as the girl.

Roden raised his scepter, aiming the triangular-shaped head straight at the girl.

Lady Pembridge muttered something and Camille quickly patted her hand to shush her. The elven lord could swallow them all with a thought, which the old lady knew perfectly well. But her outbursts had grown more voluble lately, rising in proportion to her inability to remember the latest gossip, or when she had last eaten.

Only someone addlepated would seek the elven lord's attention. One did not *mutter* every time he spoke.

A flash of gold light sparked the tip of the scepter and swelled to surround the girl. She still had a half smile on her pretty face, her hands demurely folded at her waist beneath an embroidered stomacher that boasted rows of ribbons to match the ones tied in her hair.

The ribbons disappeared first. Then the stomacher. Then her pale pink dress and bodice, until she stood in nothing but her stays, hoops, and chemise.

Camille let loose a sigh of relief. He would not truly harm her, then.

The court gasped and the girl turned startled eyes on them. Then the rest of her clothing disappeared, with the exception of her stockings and gold-buckled shoes. Her clothing still covered her of course. The elven lord had just turned it invisible, so the poor thing realized her position only when she glanced down.

Her stays pushed her small breasts up into a position that looked quite odd without the covering.

She gasped and covered herself with her hands, turned a horrified glance at the young man beside her, and began to cry.

The court grew deathly silent.

Roden laughed, a musical sound that belied the cruelty within it. His loyal followers echoed his laughter, although most just turned their heads away in sympathy.

The young man finally gathered his wits and threw his coat about the girl, scooping her up in his arms and carrying her from the room.

Camille knew the girl would survive the humiliation. There were so many other things the elven lord could have done to her, which she would not have survived. The girl had been lucky, but Camille imagined her own perspective might be twisted from experience.

A sparkle of gold dust fluttered down from the ceiling, covering the elven lord's hair and shoulders, making him glitter in all his handsome elegance.

Living at Dreamhame Palace taught Camille to never trust in appearances.

Lady Pembridge muttered yet again, this time loudly enough to capture the elven lord's notice. He turned toward her, one pale brow raised in interest. "You did not enjoy the entertainment, madam?"

Devil take it! Camille hunched her shoulders and tried to make herself as inconspicuous as possible. She should not have allowed her sympathy for the young girl to distract her from the duchess. Now it was too late. The old woman blinked in surprise at first, then realized she held the attention of everyone in the room.

She removed her spectacles, a stubborn look crossed her face, and Camille felt her heart drop.

"Certainly not," replied the dowager duchess. "Humiliating such an innocent thing. It smacks of a bully, my lord."

Those faceted golden eyes glittered and that handsome mouth twisted. "Ah, but don't you see it is a harmless way to test her? If she held enough magical ability to counter my power, she surely would have used it to save herself from—as you call it—such humiliation."

Lady Pembridge humphed.

"Tsk, tsk." He stalked toward them, a cat playing with a mouse. Camille tried very hard not to shiver. "Such censure. I cannot bear it, old mother. And yet, we must have some amusement. Since you did not enjoy mine, perhaps you would be willing to provide some yourself."

Camille's hand still rested on the arm of the duch-ess's chair from when she had last tried to stop the lady from muttering. Her fingers curled into a fist. The movement caught Roden's attention and those golden eyes captured hers briefly; a flash of memory shone within them, and then he dismissed her.

With his uncanny elven memory, he must have recalled her as the slave girl who held not a whit of magical ability, despite her elven eyes and features. Most people found it difficult to forget her odd multi-colored eyes. Roden had tested her more than once, certain she held some powerful magic with eyes that carried colors from all seven scepters.

But time and again she had proven to carry no magic whatsoever. She did not have the power to enchant gems, as Lady La'laylia of the lavender scepter did. Camille could not cast an illusion as Roden did with his gold scepter, or conjure fire as Mor'ded did with the black, or command the earth as Annanor did with the brown, or craft metal as Lan'dor did with the silver, or control sea and sky as Breden did with the blue. Or enthrall a forest, as the elven lord Mi'cal had once done with the green scepter, until the half-breed killed him.

"Come now, my lady," purred Roden to the dowager duchess. "Do not demur. I recall you have some magical ability for illusion. I see some golden color in those hazel eyes."

Lady Pembridge finally seemed to realize her predicament. She had become the elven lord's new entertainment. She stubbornly refused to play along.

"You must know I carry little magic to speak of, my lord, or surely I would have cast an illusion to erase the wrinkles from this old face."

Chuckles scattered about the room. Camille glanced at all the fine lords and ladies, in their silk skirts and velvet coats and golden jewelry. How much of it was real? Most of them carried enough elven blood and power to cast such harmless spells, and Camille had none of her own magic to counter it and see past the illusion. Roden, of course, could see through such weak enchantments with little effort, as could those with enough of the elven blood. So Camille guessed most of what they wore to be real. But human blood still dominated the room, and not a crooked tooth or blemish could she find. Illusion perfected their features, no doubt.

Except for the half-breed elven. Such beauty needed no magic to enhance it.

Roden turned, flipped up the back of his coat skirts and sat on a chair slightly across the room from them. "You are being too modest, Lady P— something-or-other."

"Pembridge. Dowager duchess from the house of—"

Imperial Lord Roden waved her to silence. "It hardly matters. What shall your illusion be? A prancing unicorn? A garden fairy to delight the ladies?"

The duchess humphed again. "I am not some young girl, my lord, to enjoy such amusements."

"Excellent! Some sophistication is in order, then! We sit all atremble, Lady P, awaiting your creation."

Camille uncurled her fingers and edged her hand atop the duchess's, squeezing those old bones lightly in warning.

But the lady ignored the touch, her brow furrowed in concentration, those weak eyes staring at a spot on the solid gold floor halfway between her and Roden. "I have tried," she said, "to perfect the illusion of Grimor'ee."

A hazy golden dragon took shape upon the floor.

"But I can never quite get it right," finished the duchess, blinking her eyes at the illusion. "I told you, my lord, my powers are weak, barely worth your attention. This is the best I can manage."

Camille gently squeezed Lady Pembridge's hand again. This might not be such a disaster after all. If the lady insisted that this was the best she could do, the elven lord might humiliate her as badly as he had the young girl—but that would be all.

Roden looked scornfully at the illusion of his dragon-steed. "The scales look like fur and the eyes are all wrong. And it is barely two hands high. Surely you can produce better than this? Why, Grimor'ee would be insulted! He has been known to eat men for less."

The duchess gaped. Camille knew the lady feared the dragon more than she did the elven lord himself. Indeed, that's why she worked on her illusion of the dragon, to try and mitigate that fear. Camille also knew Grimor'ee did not eat humans, had tried to reassure her mistress that the dragon was certainly not the raging beast the court made him out to be.

But Camille could not reveal how she knew this for a fact. Could not repeat the story of how she'd been mishandled by soldiers, crawled to the tower to escape them, and for the first time had been met with concern. In the golden eyes of a dragon.

The duchess stared at her illusion in horror. "I… I meant no disrespect to Grimor'ee. Perhaps I can manage… yes, I shall try harder…"

Her frail body vibrated with intent. Camille squeezed the lady's hand harder in warning. But she already felt the thrumming of the elven blood within those old bones, gathering whatever power the duchess possessed in an attempt to strengthen the illusion.

The hazy dragon-shape solidified and grew to the size of a small pony. The outline of golden scales became bright and sharp. The eyes blinked, now looking as real as Grimor'ee's own, the irises separated by lines of red which made those golden orbs resemble a sliced pie. Wings delineated with ridges of muscle began to beat the air, fanning the silver-white hair of the elven lord.

Camille huffed and glanced at her mistress. Most half-breeds could create a realistic illusion. It took stronger power to add sound, touch, taste, smell… and only the elven lord himself could add them all to create illusions realistic enough to completely fool the senses.

"Who knew the old hoyden had it in her?" whispered a man to their left.

Imperial Lord Roden narrowed his eyes. "It appears that you have been withholding the true extent of your powers, Lady P." He lifted his scepter. "I wonder what else you might manage given the proper incentive."

"No, my lord," blurted Camille. "She has very little power, I assure you. It's just that she fears Grimor'ee."

The court gasped as one that a mere servant had the temerity to speak within their presence. Worse, a servant who had once been a slave.

Roden ignored her, his attention completely fixed upon Lady Pembridge.

"I… I am astonished, I assure you," said the duchess. "I have never held any power beyond a wisp of illusion."

The dragon threw back his head and roared, streams of mist issuing from the cavernous maw. Several members of the court held their hands over their ears at the swell of sound, but Camille continued to hold onto the duchess's hand, as if she could somehow stop the woman from embellishing the spell.

To no avail. A thin stream of gold issued from the tip of Roden's scepter, heading directly for the wigged head of Lady Pembridge. Her illusory dragon doubled in size, lunged in front of that threatening beam of magic and snapped at it, dissolving the golden mist into shreds. And then turned upon the elven lord.

Women screamed. Tables toppled.

Roden raised a brow and instantly created his own golden dragon. This one from the stuff of nightmare. Jagged teeth, elongated claws, barbs along the golden scales. It hissed at Lady Pembridge's illusion and pounced.

Several members of the court tried to leave the room. The enchanted walls heaved and swelled. Doors slammed and windows collapsed, preventing any escape. The more savvy of the aristocrats took refuge behind velvet couches and overturned tables.

Camille could only stare in horror as the two dragons rolled about the room, tails slamming into mirrors with a shatter, growls piercing the air, teeth snapping on golden scales.

She could not lose another employer. Not again. She would never manage to climb her way out of the destitution of slavery for a third time. Camille gritted her teeth and squeezed the duchess's hand once more, but this time not in warning. This time she willed the old woman to fight back with everything she had. For if her illusion faltered…

Imperial Lord Roden smiled. Lady Pembridge stared in stupefied fascination at the two dragons.

Roden's illusion clasped the other about the throat and sunk its teeth into the smaller scales there. Blood as red as the finest claret began to ooze from scale and teeth. The duchess's dragon writhed about, finally managed to break that hold, and bit down on its opponent's wing.

Roars shook the room.

Another tumble of scale and wing and teeth. Blood now covered the golden floor. It soon became apparent that Roden's illusion would prevail.

A ghastly sound of flesh ripping. A clawed arm flew across the room to knock the wig from the head of a lady in white, who promptly screamed and fainted.

Camille now began to pray that Lady Pembridge would allow her illusion to fade. But her mistress no longer seemed to have any control over her creation. It bled and screamed and scattered shiny guts about the room as Roden's dragon tore it slowly to bits.

Tears tracked a path down the duchess's wrinkled cheeks.

With a final roar, her illusion finally winked out of existence, leaving not a single stain upon the palace floor, although Camille still held the shadow of grisly death within her eyes. As she looked about the room, she realized that others did as well.

"Well done," said Imperial Lord Roden. "I underestimated you, Lady P. That was more entertaining than I had ever dreamed." He tapped his beautifully sculpted chin with the golden scepter. "But it does leave me with a dilemma, my dear. In light of the developments at Verdanthame, I fear I must make an example of you."

Camille's heart raced. Lady Pembridge did not react at all, her frozen eyes still tracing tears down her face.

Roden's dragon turned its red eyes upon the

duchess and approached her chair, talons screeching jagged gouges into the floor. Camille wanted to scream, wanted to fling herself over her mistress's body to protect her. But she could not move. Her legs would not listen to her commands. Her arms shook as if the muscles had been fatigued beyond endurance.

"You see, my dear," continued the elven lord while his dragon took one long sniff down Lady Pembridge's frozen body. "I cannot allow my subjects to hide any of their powers from me." He turned to the courtiers, who still crouched behind whatever barrier they managed to find. "Get up, the lot of you. From this moment forward, you will report anyone who shows the slightest increase in their powers. If you do not…"

The dragon hissed, his nose inches from Lady Pembridge's face. The sound finally broke the spell of terror that held her frozen, and she looked up, up into those cruel red eyes.

"No," growled Camille.

"No," said her mistress at the same time. But that maw opened, wicked sharp teeth glittering in the firelight, and engulfed the old woman's head so swiftly Camille barely had time to blink.

"It cannot truly harm you," insisted Camille. "It is only an illusion." But she knew that unless one possessed enough elven blood to see through it, it held more reality than the stool she sat upon. And her mistress held little elven blood within her veins. Yet, surely the lady could use whatever power she managed to conjure today to fight the elven lord's own?

But the duchess's dragon lost the battle, had he not?

A grinding sound followed as the dragon worried at his prey. Then the loud snap of bone.

Lord Roden waved his scepter and his illusion disappeared to reveal Lady Pembridge's head tilted at an odd angle, only Camille's grip on her arm keeping the old woman upright in her chair.

"This will be your fate," pronounced Roden. "Now, I will take your petitions for testing at dinner this eve. I cannot seem to bear your faces for another moment. Such surprise! Did you think you would not suffer the same doom as my champion if you over-stepped yourselves? I had thought to make an example of him, but it appears you needed more proof of my intentions. Do any of you still doubt your peril?"

A whisper of denial rushed about the room.

Roden smiled. "Excellent. Oh, and send that damn slave back to the kitchens where she belongs. Those mottled eyes are disgusting to look at."

❦

The kitchens looked exactly as Camille had left them two years ago, from the dried herbs hanging from the ceiling to the enormous oak table where most of the staff took their meals. No magical illusions had been wasted on this part of the palace. The reality of soot-stained fireplace, worn stone floor, and blackened walls stayed the same.

In many ways, Camille preferred the battered decor to the illusions of upstairs. At least she knew her surroundings would not change from one moment to the next.

"Sent ye back, eh?" said Cook, glancing up from

the mound of dough he'd been folding. "Can't say as I didn't warn ye."

Camille nodded. Cook told her she could not fight fate, yet she had stubbornly refused to listen, using every opportunity she could to find another way out of slavery. She thought she'd found a home with Lady Pembridge...

"Go on with ye, now. The slave master is waitin' for ye."

He sounded almost... sorry for her.

A few soldiers already sat at table, drinking their nightly ration of gin, and they all turned to stare at her. Camille glared back at them, feeling as if they stripped her naked with their stares. Damn this slave clothing. It marked her as a nobody, lacking even the rights that servants were entitled to.

She turned her head away and pretended to ignore them as she walked carefully to the cellars, wincing at the sharp cracks in the stone floor. After two years of wearing shoes her feet had grown tender, and it would take some time for them to toughen up again. She did not miss the trappings that came with the rest of her servant's uniform: the hoops and tight stays. But she did miss her shoes, and the feel of softly brushed wool against her skin.

And she already missed Lady Pembridge. Her kindness and humor and even her absentminded ways.

Camille's eyes burned although they did not water. She couldn't remember the last time she actually cried. She had realized quickly enough that it did little good.

She hoped to reach the little closet she and Molly had once shared before the slave master spotted her.

But he stood in the hallway, waiting for her. A smile of anticipation on his pockmarked face. Slapping a whip into the palm of his hand.

"Ye didn't learn the first time, did ye? Couldn't pass yerself off as a nursemaid, and now the ole lady dies and yer back again, ain't ye?"

The large man who resembled a hairless ogre took a step forward. Camille fought the urge to flee and held her ground.

"And now I got to teach ye a lesson again." He leaned closer until she could smell his rank breath. "Ye is a slave, ye will always be a slave, and it's best ye remember it from now on, girlie. I'm doin' this for yer own good. Unbutton yer dress."

Camille could run. But the soldiers would catch her and be driven to a sexual frenzy by watching her beating and she'd never escape them tonight. And the slave master would add twenty lashes for her efforts. If he had to tie her to a post, he would beat her until she could no longer stand. She learned long ago that fighting the lash would only make the beating worse.

She reached behind her and struggled with the buttons.

The master's eyes glittered like a beastly predator. "I went easy on ye the first time ye thought to rise above yer station. This time I'm thinking ye need a more severe lesson."

Camille's mouth went dry and she fumbled at the buttons.

"Devil take ye, girl. Get it off or I'll rip it off for ye and then ye'll have to work nights to earn a new one."

She just managed to unbutton them before he yanked

her arm and spun her around, shoving the bodice over her shoulders to expose her back, kicking her to the ground with a well-aimed boot to her bottom.

The whip cracked and sliced open her skin, the blood running hot down her back. Camille tried to distance her mind from her body, but it had been too long since she'd felt the lash, and she had forgotten the trick of it.

The whip cracked again and she grunted. The slave master turned beating into an art form with his magic, somehow imbuing the whip with a spell that made it sting as if salt had been rubbed into the wound. Presumably he had been chosen for the position because his welts also healed by the next day, offering no permanent damage besides the light scarring. A damaged slave could not work or pleasure the soldiers.

But from the first strike of the lash until the morrow, the wounds would burn and ache with magically enhanced pain.

Camille soon lost count of the number of times the leather struck her skin. Soon lost her vision to a red haze. She did not cry out, did not plead for help. There would be no point to it—and she would not give the slave master the satisfaction.

He gave her a final strike with a grunt of pleasure and left her where she lay.

Camille had no idea how much time passed before she managed to rise to her feet and stagger down the hall, holding her bodice over her breasts, unable to pull the cloth over her back.

She ducked through the door of the closet that

she and Molly once shared and met the eyes of her fellow slave.

"Lud, how bad did he beat you?"

Camille turned and showed her back.

Molly hissed and led Camille to her old bed of straw and woolen blanket, disappeared for a time and returned with a bucket of water and a pot of salve. She tended Camille's back with gentle fingers and not a word between them, until clean bandages covered the salve and she buttoned up Camille's frock.

They never discussed the beatings. Had long ago ceased crying and flinching while they tended the wounds. Camille did not know why, but pretending the beatings did not happen somehow made them more bearable.

The same way that pretending they would have a normal life someday, with a proper marriage and a household of children, made the knowledge that the elven lord had made them sterile easier to bear. Although in truth, Camille could only be glad Roden set the enchantment upon her. She did not think she could bear having a child by one of the soldiers.

"Fie, I heard about the duchess." Molly settled next to Camille on her own bed of straw. "You want to talk about it?" Molly must have come from a good family, for she had always spoken almost as well as Camille, although she often lapsed into the soldiers' jargon, while Camille had cultivated her speech upstairs.

"No." Camille shifted on the itchy wool blanket. Straw stuck through the thick weave and poked her legs. The salve would prevent the wounds from festering, but held no magical powers within it to stop the agony. When she spoke, she could barely raise her voice above a whisper. "The elven lord... it was too horrible. Tell me what you have been doing."

Molly shrugged, the black shapeless slave's dress revealing little of her figure, which Camille knew was shapely and lush, unlike her own thin frame.

"Just the usual. Scrubbing. Chopping. Copulating." She flashed a toothy grin at the look on Camille's face. "But I want to thank you for the presents you sent."

Both of their gazes swept briefly to the corner of the room, to the loose brick behind which they stored their treasures. Slaves were not allowed to own property. Even the clothes on their backs belonged to the elven lord.

"Especially for the candles." Molly lowered her voice. "I have written several stories since you left."

Camille nodded. Sometimes she thought the only thing that kept her sane had been Molly's stories. She had snuck the other woman as many journals and quills and ink pots as she could without the duchess taking notice.

She knew Molly would delight in them. And although Camille loved the stories of lands far away, she had hoped never to be in a position to listen to them again.

"Will you read one of them to me tonight?"

Molly nodded. "If they let me."

"The soldiers still come?"

"Fie, and why wouldn't they? Honestly, Camille. If you wouldn't fight them, you might learn to manage—"

"Never."

Molly sighed, giving up the old argument. Camille

could not understand how Molly had adapted to slavery, while she continued to fight against it. They had both been forced to service the soldiers as soon as they became women. Molly recovered from those first initiations, finding ways to use her charms to cajole the men who had once treated her so harshly. A lovely girl with elven beauty and grace, with a hint of gold in her hazel eyes a testament to her small and often erratic gift of illusion, she had no need of using her powers to alter her appearance to please them. But she cast her features into an image of their heart's desire, and they treated her more kindly as a result.

Camille found ways to discourage them.

She rose and fetched the bucket of water, scooped up some dirt from the floor, and used what was left to mix a heavy batch of mud.

"No, Camille. You look so pretty with your hair combed and your face clean."

Camille slapped her muddy palms against her scalp and began to rub. "All the more reason for me to sleep in the kennel tonight."

"Lud! We'll have fleas in our beds again! Truly, Camille, I don't mind the dirt so much, nor the stink, but the fleas bite."

Camille shrugged, winced from the pain still burning her back. "Then I'll just stay in the kennels. The master won't mind." Indeed, the slave master had a taste only for the young kitchen boys. So if the girls did not complain or bother him or try to run away—or seek to rise above their status—he left them to their own devices.

And perhaps she would visit Grimor'ee. On that

first day the soldiers used her body so cruelly, she had crawled up to his tower to hide from them. The one place she knew they'd never pursue her. But Camille feared the dragon much less than she feared rape, and for his part, Grimor'ee had not eaten her. Since then she'd been able to slip away to the tower. Unlike the elven lord's illusion of him, the beast appeared to possess a peaceful soul, and sometimes even seemed to enjoy her visits.

"No," said Molly, her mouth a stubborn line. "You will come back here to sleep once you think you have enough stink to keep the men away from you. Some of them aren't so picky, you know, and you might need my help."

Camille hid a grim smile. She might not have any magic, but she had managed to fight off more than one soldier over the years, and the slave master never punished her for it. Indeed, it seemed to amuse him.

But for some reason Molly felt it her duty to protect Camille.

"Because you're thin enough to be blown away by a stiff wind," said Molly, as if reading Camille's very thoughts. "Didn't that old woman feed you?"

"Of course she did."

"You missed a spot on your nose."

Camille quickly spread some mud over the curve of it. "Better?"

"Yes. You look perfectly ghastly."

Camille set down the bowl and gingerly lay sideways on her pallet with a groan. The dogs would be overjoyed to see her again. She would bed down in their dirty hay pile in the stables, and by morning she would smell of manure with a spice of urine, and her clean dress would have a wealth of stains to cover it.

She quickly banished the memory of Lady Pembridge's rose-scented toilette water and sighed.

How quickly she had fallen back into her old role. She could suffer the hard bed and endless toil—even the occasional beatings. But she could not suffer a man's hands upon her body ever again.

"I am cursed, Molly."

"Don't be a goose. The entire land is cursed by the elven lords. Do not think it is all about you."

Camille propped her now rather crusty head in her hand, caught a breath from the pain of the movement. "I am serious. First the Ailesbury children and now the duchess."

Molly pushed her pale hair behind elegantly pointed ears. Camille envied her those ears. Despite all of her otherwise elven looks, she had rounded human ears.

"You cannot blame yourself. The elven lord killed them, not you."

"If only I'd had the power to stop him. To be given eyes speckled with every color of the sovereignty, and to hold none of those powers, seems like the cruelest trick of nature."

"Fiddle. No one can stop them! And don't you dare feel sorry for yourself. You were given a will of iron and I envy you that more than you know. Did you not raise yourself up to a servant, not once, but twice?"

Camille's gaze drifted upward and she stared at the cobwebs strung across the wooden beams of the blackened ceiling. Several years ago she had met the Ailesbury children, Rufus and Laura, who loved dogs and stumbled upon Camille asleep in the kennel. They struck up an immediate friendship. Their tears and combined temper tantrums won her as their nurse-maid, and she had spent several contented years with the family. Until the children had been tested by the elven lord...

She could still feel them within her arms as the elven lord sent a monster from a nightmare toward them. Neither of the children showed much affinity for magic, but suddenly they created a shadow that swallowed Roden's monster as if it were an insect.

The children had been ripped from her arms to be taken to Elfhame. Although by then, the entire court knew that the rumors were true. That the children were murdered behind closed doors. Camille—nor the children's parents—could do anything to stop it. And Camille was sent back to the kitchens.

And now, with a half-breed murdering the elven lord of Verdanthame and taking over his sovereignty and scepter, Roden looked as if he would no longer bother to do his killing behind closed doors, despite his continued lies about the fate of the children.

Poor Lady Pembridge.

Camille frowned and the mud cracked, a chunk of it falling on her blankets. It would stay trapped in her hair for months, but she needed ashes to wipe across her smooth face instead of mud. "This won't stay on for long. I must go, before any more soldiers come for their ration of drink. They will not care that I have been beaten."

Molly stood up, brushing at her skirts. "It would go easier with you if, like me, you would just use your charms on them. I'm sure *I* shall find a proper husband from the lot one day."

Camille stood. "Ha. My charms! I have missed you, Molly."

"I missed you too. Although I wish you had not come back. You gave the rest of us slaves hope."

"Did I? How odd, to think I can give anyone hope, when I have to fight for it myself."

Camille left their little closet, Molly trailing right behind her. They peeked around the corner into the kitchen. The servants had all left for the evening, abandoning the room to the soldiers and their drink. Most of them took their ration and left, but many of them stayed. And kept their eyes on the slave quarters.

"I shall distract them," whispered Molly, careful not to brush up against Camille's back as she passed her and sauntered into the light surrounding the table in the room. She put her hands on her hips, outlining the curve of her waist, and tossed back her ivory hair. "Well, gentlemen. Who will be the first to offer me a drink?"

While the men fell over themselves to bring Molly a tankard, Camille crept to the fireplace and rubbed ashes where the mud had flaked off. She hadn't realized the lateness of the hour, for Cook had banked the fire for the evening.

Molly did an excellent job of capturing the soldiers' attention, for not one of them glanced up at Camille's silent shadow as she opened the door into the courtyard.

Devil take it. The sun had fallen, a light dusting of snow still hovering in the clear air. The night brought more soldiers for their ration of gin. And to the doors of the slaves' quarters.

A group of them made their way across the cobblestones to the kitchen.

Camille fought down panic. She could not return to her closet, for that would be the first place they would look for her. She could not run to Molly, for the girl might get hurt trying to help her. And the pain of the beating had sapped her strength. Her elven speed and agility would not help her this night.

She was right back in the position that she swore she would never be in again.

Camille sidled over to the oven and reached for the herbs, sniffing at them, hopefully to find the ones that smelled the most foul. Garlic. Dried Onion. She quickly rubbed them against her neck. This would not do. She now smelled like Cook's favorite roast. And then her eye saw the slop bucket. She opened the lid and the stink made her eyes water. Thank heavens the lads had forgotten to dump it.

She had her hands half-buried in the mess by the time the soldiers entered the room. Camille tried not to imagine what might be in the refuse as she smeared it over her black gown, into her hair, down her naked legs. Along with shoes, slaves did not warrant stockings.

The men stomped through the door, bringing cold and wet and terror with them. A few joined Molly's group, but the rest headed for the back cellars of the slave quarters, and Camille could hear Ann's voice yelling at them to enter her room only one at a time.

Camille closed her eyes and swallowed. She hadn't

had time to give a greeting to her other fellow slave, but then again, she couldn't be sure Ann would care. The half-breed spent most of her time absorbed in her tiny golems, creatures that she made from stick and mud with the magic she inherited from Terrahame.

The golems were generally harmless, unable to sustain animation for long with Ann's weak magic, although they could be a nuisance if she let them, crawling into clothing and pinching sensitive places, poking tiny pointed sticks deep into skin.

The soldiers muttered, but did as Ann asked.

Camille wished again for some magic. Just a tiny bit. Anything that might keep the soldiers from her. She had only her wits and stealth, and for the moment it worked, for she managed to slip out the door into the courtyard without any of the men taking notice.

The frosty cobbles stung her feet and the snow swirled about her shoulders as she raced across the courtyard, gritting her teeth against the pain, determinedly heading for the stables. It would be too cold tonight to make her way to the dragon's tower, especially without shoes or cloak. She had looked forward to telling Grimor'ee about the illusions made of him, and wondered what he would think about the elven lord killing a member of his own court right in front of everyone.

And she wondered if sadness would touch those golden eyes when he saw she had once again resumed the wardrobe of a slave...

Faith, what did it matter? She learned long ago that Grimor'ee would do nothing to help her. He had this philosophy that one must take care of oneself, earn his place. That humans must fight for their freedoms; for something that was easily gained could not be appreciated.

Camille reminded herself that she could not judge the dragon based on her own concepts and values. That he had a mind as alien and mysterious as the elven lords themselves.

A beefy hand reached out from the darkness and snatched her arm, spinning Camille about to slam up against a hard body. Ugh, he smelled worse than she did.

"Let me go."

"Now, now, ye little hoyden. Where ye off to in such a rush—?"

Her back burned in agony and Camille reacted to the pain, raised her leg and kneed him in the groin. He let out an "oof" of surprise but kept a firm grip on her arm.

"What ye got there, Cuthbert?"

Cuthbert made a strangled noise.

At that moment, Camille decided she could bear this life no longer. She would not endure another rape. She did not have her usual elven physical strength to fight them. She drew the pistol tucked into Cuthbert's sword belt and pulled back the hammer, pointing it at her captor's belly. "Let me go."

This time he did.

She backed away, pointing the weapon between one man and the other. Cuthbert glared at her, but the smaller man with the elven-shaped eyes smiled. "They kill slaves for touching a weapon."

"But I will have the pleasure of killing you first."

"Indeed. No, old boy." He turned and caught at Cuthbert's arm. "Do not draw your steel. We don't want to hurt her—there's not enough doxies to go around as it is."

"I am not—"

"No offense, my dear. I detest labels myself. Now, are ye going to hand me the weapon, or must I take it from ye?"

Camille glanced wildly around. A group of soldiers approached from the left, and oddly enough for this time of night, a carriage rumbled down the service road at her right.

She had no hope of escape. But this time… if she fired a weapon they could have her put to death. Despite everything, she had always wanted to live, had always thought she could climb her way out of misery once more. Despite her pain and exhaustion her hand held steady, and her resolve to refuse to face another day as a slave only strengthened. She fired the pistol.

It lit with a brief flash and the sharp whiff of gunpowder, the recoil tearing it from her hands. Instinct urged Camille to run, but for some reason the snow eddying about her ankles suddenly felt thick as molasses.

The smaller man had magic.

Cuthbert howled, clutching at his leg and jumping up and down.

"Now look at what ye've done," drawled the other man. "He will really want to hurt ye now, and it would be such a waste."

"I'm gonna kill her, Joseph."

"Pshaw, ye'll do nothing of the sort. *I* shall punish her. Ye would like that better, wouldn't ye?"

Cuthbert suddenly stilled, a gleam of maliciousness lighting his ruddy face. "Ye'll use yer magic, Joseph?"

"Oh, aye. And by the looks of her, she has none of her own to counter it with."

Several gray shapes began to take form around Camille. Shapes with sharp fangs and jagged claws. She told herself they weren't real. They couldn't hurt her if she didn't believe in the illusion.

But that never worked, did it?

Camille screamed.

Three

DRYSTAN SAT INSIDE HIS BROTHER'S BORROWED COACH and scowled at the empty seat across from him. The past few days had stripped him of any romantic notions he harbored from his novels about England and the life of a spy. Chaos ruled his homeland, from brigands on the highway to soldiers at every crossroads.

He mentally thanked Giles for having the foresight to provide him with an armed escort, for viscount or no, they might never have made it to their destination. Indeed, you either joined the elven lord's army or were shot on sight, and more often than not, the soldiers didn't bother to check papers first.

And Drystan's hope that his own magic would prove powerful enough to vanquish any foe shattered as soon as they entered England. Lord North had been the one to provide him with a tutor aboard ship, to help him master his power of illusion. Drystan quickly realized harnessing his magic would be no easy task, and his conjurations proved too weak and erratic to maintain the shape he tried to craft.

North had been pleased, for he vowed he would

not have sent Drystan to an elven lord's court if he'd held enough power to get him tested and killed.

Drystan still felt deprived of yet another of his expectations.

But if his magic had been a disappointment, at least his journey allowed him to recover from years of abuse. He could still feel the scepters' connection to him, but it felt like little more like an annoying itch. And he could ignore it at will. He slept. He ate. His body filled out in places that astonished him. In a relatively short time he changed him from a skinny young man to a full-bodied half-breed in prime form—

A feminine scream pierced the dark night and Drystan jerked upright, pressing his face against the frosted window. He had heard many screams since entering England, but this one made his heart race, made him pound on the carriage wall. "Faster!"

He could hear disgruntled shouts from his men as they pressed the tired horses faster. His guards had shaken their heads when he ordered them to drive around to the back of the palace, instead of taking the front entrance. Only one of the men, Captain Edward Talbot, knew of Drystan's true identity and purpose in coming to Dreamhame Palace.

Slaves were quartered near the kitchens, which lay at the back of the palace.

Had that scream truly sounded familiar? With all the disappointments he had faced in coming to England, could it be possible he had found the white witch's descendant so easily?

Drystan wiped the window with his gloved hand but it did little to help him see out into the snowy night.

Another scream rent the air and he could bear it no longer. He flung open the carriage door and leaped from the still-rolling coach, landing lithely in a drift of snow. Thank the devil for his elven strength and speed, for it had not failed him in his homeland—indeed, the magic in the air appeared to enhance it. And thank Giles for his constant training in swordsmanship, for it had been his primary defense on his journey.

Drystan drew his sword and ran, leaving the coach behind him.

Snow crunched beneath his feet on the golden road, and the castle turrets wavered in the air before him. From a distance, the palace looked like some mythical creation from medieval times, albeit one made of solid gold. And it appeared to hover above the city, on a cloud of shifting shadow. But the road had been solid enough, and although the gargoyles and statues adorning the stone walls appeared alive, flapping golden wings and growling warnings with open mouths, they offered no true harm.

Drystan narrowed his eyes and tried to focus his sight, as his tutor had taught him. Tried to discern the difference between illusion and reality. He still hadn't quite managed the full knack of it, and saw the court-yard ahead of him as a wonderland of golden arches and flowering trees. In winter.

A knot of soldiers stood within that grand open space, looking incongruous in their worn uniforms and unkempt hair. They formed a circle around dark struggling shapes, and hooted and called, occasionally shouting out wagers.

Another scream, this time much weaker than the

ones before, as if it had been issued with no hope of an answer to the plea within it.

"My lord," called out Edward. Of all his men, the captain held the most elven blood and had followed him. "Wait… this might not be wise…"

Drystan had no thought but to reach the woman who had made those screams. Even if it wasn't the woman he sought, the soldiers had no right to treat anyone so poorly, much less a lady who did not have the strength of a man to fight back with.

Drystan used his full elven strength to leap over the circle of men, landing in the thick of…

Within seconds he took in the sight of a dark-haired woman clothed in the black rags of a slave, her face nearly the same color as her garments. Drystan had only a moment to register his disappointment that she wasn't the ivory-haired girl from his dreams, for the creatures she fought against turned on him quickly enough.

They had been surely crafted from illusion, for God would not have created such twisted monstrosities. Dark wraiths with jagged claws and pointed teeth, their bare breasts and flowing hair grossly exaggerated their gender.

Drystan hesitated.

The girl struggled with two of them, crying out obscenities whenever they managed to rake their claws across her arms or her face, her blood bright against her exposed flesh. He admired not only the ingenuity of those obscenities, but the young woman's fierce determination in fighting off her attackers. As if she held a wealth of experience at both.

Claws pierced Drystan's shoulders from behind, a foul stench accompanying the weight of a body suddenly on his back. He flipped backward to the ground, a grunt of surprise behind him as a result, and when he twisted upright once again, the weight had left him.

The soldiers shouted out new wagers.

Drystan enviously admired the strength of the illusions. Not only sight, but feel and smell as well. He could not hope to cast an illusion strong enough to prevail against them.

With a growl of irritation, he lay in with his sword.

It did not take long. Soon, the creatures lay maimed and bloody at his feet.

Drystan wiped down his sword and sheathed it, shrugged his tight shoulders. He held enough magic, at least, for his body to know the wounds inflicted on him by the creatures were just an illusion. The slave girl had not been so lucky. She huddled in a ball beside him, her garments torn to shreds, blood flowing freely from multiple gashes on arms and legs.

Drystan lowered his head at the crowd, his golden-brown eyes narrowed to slits. "Who is responsible for this?"

Several men backed away, but a beefy soldier and a smaller man held their ground. The smaller man spoke with a negligent toss of elven white hair. "We was having just a spot of fun, guvner. She ain't nuthin' but a slave."

His words appeared to have given the larger man some courage. "Ay, and who are ye to be spoiling our fun?"

Drystan ignored them and turned to the girl, bowing low over her bent head. "Viscount Hawkes at your service, my lady. May I help you rise?"

He held out his hand to her. She ignored it, looking up at him with what appeared to be genuine shock upon her face. Although Drystan could not be *quite* sure, for he could not make out her features for the dirt that had been smeared across them. Had she gotten it in the scuffle? No, too much of it. As if she had slept in the warm ashes of a fireplace and not washed in months. And she smelled worse than the wraiths.

He resolutely continued to hold his hand out to her.

She blinked. A spot of moonlight penetrated the drifting snow, and Drystan caught his breath. Those eyes. Despite the dark hair and unidentifiable features, he could not mistake those eyes.

They held within them all the colors of the seven sovereignties.

A flush of heat spread through his body, and it took all of his willpower not to snatch the girl up in his arms. Filthy or no. He realized in some distant part of his awareness that as soon as he had mentioned his title the soldiers scattered, that his carriage had finally entered the courtyard and his men now surrounded him. The maimed creatures at his feet had disappeared.

He could see nothing but those eyes that had haunted his visions for years.

She glanced at his outstretched hand as if it offended her and rose to her feet with elven grace.

Drystan took a step back, reality once again crashing about his head like a tide of water. Except for those multicolored elven eyes, she looked nothing like his dreams. Scraggly hair, dirty face, ragged clothing. Her head barely topped his shoulders and only the memory of her beauty allowed Drystan to glimpse it.

C. Ashton. He had wondered what the *C* might stand for.

He bent down a bit to appear less threatening and tenderly whispered, "What is your name?"

With a speed that rivaled even his own, she drew his pistol from his belt and aimed the barrel at him. "Get back."

Drystan obliged, although more from surprise than anything else. "Damn, woman. I just saved your life."

The naturally sweet tone of her voice contrasted sharply with her surly growl. "Unfortunately, they would not have killed me. And I'll be damned if I shall let you touch me any more than I would allow them to."

"Touch you? Have you looked in a mirror lately? Have you smelled—do not flatter yourself, lady."

"I am not a lady. I am a *slave.*" She spit out the last word. "And now that you have proven yourself a gallant, kindly allow me to leave."

Damn, she was starting to annoy him. "And go where? Back to your quarters to shoot another soldier or two? I think not. Give me the gun."

Her lips firmed and she planted her feet, hands steady on the pistol.

Drystan had reached his limit. He should have listened to Giles when he warned him about reading poetry. About gilding his visions of England. Nothing had been what he expected. Magic produced too many horrors and not enough beauty. Battle consisted of little more than hacking your opponent before he had a chance to hack you. And Drystan's own magic had proven too weak for him to master.

Now he had rescued his beloved, and she not only refused to thank him and fall into his arms with gratitude, but stood there pointing his own gun at him with every intention of killing him on the spot.

Drystan ignored the pistol. The smell. The filth. He closed the distance between them, forcing the hand that held the gun to shift to the side, and clasped her shoulders, giving her a little shake. "What is your name? And do not make me ask you again."

She trembled violently, as if his touch terrified her more than the creatures that had attacked her. He loosened his grip, worried his frustration might have made him clutch her too hard. He stared deeply into those faceted varicolored eyes, and recognized she had reached a breaking point. She no longer cared whether she lived or died. Exhaustion lined her face; hopelessness shadowed her gaze.

Perhaps only Drystan would have recognized the signs, for he had experienced a moment in his life where he had felt the same.

Before the scepters sent him the dreams of the white witch's descendant, he had become infatuated with a local village girl and had done his best to compete for her attentions against the other lads, and to his surprise, she actually started to respond to him. But then the lavender scepter of Stonehame had been delivered to Carreg Cennen castle to join the blue of Dewhame's within the vault in the dungeon, and his fits had worsened. The lack of sleep started to take its toll on his young body, for he still fought against nightmares.

He'd had a convulsion at a festival within the village square, and awoken to a ring of people staring down at him, signing the cross against the devil. He would never forget the look of disgust and fear on the girl's face.

At the time, he had not realized the scepters were causing his fits. He had discarded the notion that God spoke to him, for *He* would not have sent such unholy visions. Drystan became convinced he was truly cursed by the devil. He returned to the castle that day knowing he would never live a normal life. And that he could bear the visions of blood and death and fire no longer. He refused to eat, determined to end his tortured existence.

Cecily and Giles fought to discover his malady, and had pieced together that his illness was connected to the scepters, which served only to make Drystan more determined to deprive the magical artifacts of their victim. He wanted nothing more than to end his misery.

And then the scepters sent him the vision of the lady with the rainbow eyes. And he knew he must live to save her. To claim her as his one true love.

She made his life worth living again.

But she couldn't know he came to save her in turn.

She had reached her own breaking point. And he could not explain that a vision sent him. Indeed, she would think him mad.

But at least he had a chance. At least he had reached her in time.

Drystan continued to stare into her eyes until she finally answered his question.

"Camille. Camille Ashton. Will you kill me now?"

"Camille," he breathed. At least her name did not disappoint. It sounded enchanting on his lips. And then her words penetrated and his confidence that he would be able to save her wavered. Shook him. "Hell no. Why would I rescue you only to kill you?"

"But you must. Slaves are not allowed to touch weapons, much less fire them."

Drystan dropped his hands from her shoulders, quickly reclaimed his pistol.

"They will whip me until I die. It… will take a long time."

He felt sure that was an understatement. Her words—the furious acceptance in her voice—touched off too many emotions within Drystan for him to acknowledge them at the moment. He straightened, putting all of the confidence and reassurance he could summon behind his avowal. "No one will touch you, or they will have to answer to me. Do you understand?"

Drystan did not wait for her to reply, making sure that she understood he did not need her acceptance. That he had stated a fact. He spun and leveled a gaze at his captain. "She is under my protection. Make that clear to the rest of the men."

Edward nodded, understanding flashing within those silver eyes. Drystan knew the man did not understand at all. Yes, they had been sent to Dreamhame to find the descendant of the white witch, to discover the birthmark and unravel the mystery of a key to a doorway into Elfhame. But the captain did not realize Drystan had come to save the lady herself. Any other man could have forced her cooperation, found the birthmark, and then left her to continue her existence as a slave in the elven lord's household. Drystan had other plans.

He would have to gain this abused woman's trust before he could gain her heart. Before she would allow him to save her. He would not leave Dreamhame without her, damn the key and the Rebellion spy... and whatever reasons the scepters had for sending him to England.

He did not want his captain to read any intentions in his expression and quickly grumbled, "She could have shot me, you know."

Edward's mouth curved. "You did not appear to need my help, my lord. With her, or the wraith creatures. You may not be an expert with your magical skills, but your sword work is not lacking."

Drystan tried not to let the compliment affect him too strongly. It had been a pleasure to be surrounded by people who did not consider him mad, or cursed by the devil—who treated him as a normal person. As soon as he had started on his journey the dreams ceased, and he no longer feared a fit would overtake him.

He turned back to Camille and saw the fire leave her eyes as she shuddered and swayed on her feet. He cursed himself for not seeing past her belligerence. The night had turned frigid and even if the frock she wore had not been sliced open in several places, it still would have done nothing to protect her from the cold. Drystan quickly removed his fur-trimmed cloak and wrapped it around her shoulders. She did not protest until he enfolded her in his arms as well, flinching at his touch.

What had they done to her, to make her detest the touch of a man, when he intended only to warm her?

"Let me g-go," she whispered.

"I fear that if I do, you will fall."

"I do not f-faint, my lord. But my back——" Her eyes closed and she proceeded to do the very thing she had just denied. Drystan swept her up in his arms. She weighed next to nothing. And he realized she wore no shoes, that her toes looked blue with cold—and what had she meant about her back? The injuries from the wraiths looked superficial, scratches that tore cloth and drew blood but should not cause her such pain, illusion or no.

His instincts told him something might be seriously wrong with her. "Edward, get me another cloak. And a fur to wrap about her feet."

His captain followed orders, and as soon as they had Camille wrapped to Drystan's satisfaction, they entered the palace by the back way, passing a group of drunken soldiers, and surprising a grumpy kitchen boy into summoning the palace steward.

Drystan found the woman's small hand within the folds of her wrappings and clasped it gently. He spoke as soon as the old man came down the stairs. "I need a physician."

The steward looked down his nose at the bundle in Drystan's arms and sniffed. "Slaves are treated by the soldiers' physician, who is rather deep in his cups at the moment."

"I don't want a damn surgeon! I want the palace healer."

The steward took a step backward. "My most humble apologies, my lord. But even if I summon him, he will not treat a slave. His magic is limited, you see, and he saves it for the gentlemen and ladies of the palace who can—"

Drystan cut him off with a growl. "Take me to Viscount Hawkes's—*my* rooms, and then find someone who can heal her or I swear I will have your head, man."

The steward appeared quite used to receiving threats and odd requests from the aristocracy he served, for his face took on the patronizing look of a man well trained in patience. "But, my lord, the girl. She belongs in the slave quarters."

Drystan's temper flared. The most important person in the world to him lay still as death within his arms, and this insufferable little man had the audacity to stand here and argue with him. He suddenly felt his magic, his unpredictable uncontrollable magic, well up from deep within him. When he had practiced his illusions aboard ship, his magic always felt weak… and scattered. As if it lay fractured inside of him, not knowing how to coalesce to his commands.

But at the moment it gathered like a storm cloud, building within him until it burst with a flash like that of lightning. A queer smell permeated the air, similar to the stifling aroma of sulfur.

Brimstone?

Drystan felt his body change. He had filled out quite nicely, yes, but the shoulders in his arms suddenly appeared twice as large; his height grew beyond his six foot to over seven.

Drystan did not know what illusion came over his features, but he glanced at Edward, and realized his spell had overtaken Captain Talbot as well, and had a feeling his face reflected the same changes. Edward's skin had turned a bright crimson; horns sprouted from his forehead, and pointed fangs hung from the corners of his mouth.

Ah. When Drystan spoke, he felt those elongated teeth rub his bottom lip. His words took on a volume that shook the stone walls of the room. "She stays with me."

The raucous soldiers froze in sudden silence, turned to stare at Edward and him. Captain Talbot gifted them with a smile and a swish of his sharply pointed tail, causing several of the men to tremble in their boots.

The steward fell to his knees. "Of course, my lord. I meant no disrespect."

Edward could not stop grinning. He spread his fingers, and claws the length of his dagger sprang from the tips. He raked them against a stout wooden chopping block and sliced it into four neat chunks.

The steward hastily pulled a leather journal from his pocket and offered it to Drystan in supplication. "I-I will add the slave to your list of inventory, Viscount Hawkes. Will that be satisfactory?"

The man spoke as if Camille had no identity as a person and could be appropriated along with the furniture and candlesticks. Drystan tamped down his anger, for Talbot kept glancing around the room, looking for something else to try out his claws on. Several soldiers crawled under the table.

"Quite." His voice did not boom as loudly this time. "Get up and lead on, man."

The steward rose on unsteady legs and led the two demons up the stairs. Drystan's men would be directed to the barracks, but as captain of his personal bodyguard, Edward stayed with him. By the time they reached the ground room of the palace, the captain's fangs and horns disappeared, and Drystan felt his own body return to normal. He still could not believe he had managed such a compelling illusion, and wondered if he might be able to do it again.

Exhaustion made him almost stumble, and those of elven blood did not stumble.

"How did you do that?" murmured Edward.

"I have no idea. You saw me try to use my magic before... it was so weak I could not call up a decent wraith. Perhaps it is the magic that permeates the air of England, and it will make my own grow stronger."

Edward shrugged. "Pray that it happens slowly, so the elven lord does not catch wind of it."

Drystan felt so drained of energy from that brief show of illusion that he did not fear growing in power as quickly as all that.

"The tail was a bit much," mused Edward. "But couldn't you have left me the claws?"

Drystan ignored him, intent only on Camille. Her lashes fluttered. She sighed once, and it lifted his heart. She would recover. She must. Drystan still could not believe he had found her. That she was real. And despite the glory of the palace they strode through, it

paled next to the dirty, smelly bundle of womanhood
in his arms.

Above the basements, Dreamhame Palace had as
much gold within as it did without. The walls had
been gilded with it, the floors paved with smooth
blocks, the doors patterned with golden swirls.
The rooms beyond those doors held illusions that
surpassed Drystan's imagination. He caught only
glimpses of what lay inside: a yellow plain of grass
with a glaring sun upon it, a snowcapped mountain
peak with humped animals nosing through the drifts,
a jungle of twisted trees and diaphanous vines strung
from limb to limb. Some of the rooms appeared quite
normal, with chairs and fireplaces and tea tables… but
he noticed the walls occasionally moved; the chairs
morphed into flower petals; the fireplaces belched
curious golden sparks.

They ascended two more flights of stairs carpeted
with designs of dragons in the weave, to the second floor,
which consisted of a maze of hallways and numerous
doors presumably opening onto guest chambers. The
ceiling soared above them into infinity, sprinkles of
illusory stars glittering like diamonds, shooting across
the darkness in glowing arcs. Along the walls, amber
statues of nymphs danced upon short fluted columns;
a Pegasus reared and fanned the air with yellow-
feathered wings; a centaur played a mournful tune on
a pipe.

Large tapestries had been woven with equally
fanciful creatures, and they had been spelled to move
just as lifelike as the statues… but they acted out
hideous roles. A mermaid sang a sailor to his death,

embracing him while he struggled to regain the surface of the sea. A griffin pounced upon a maiden and proceeded to tear her apart with his jagged beak. Several harpies teased and tortured a man in turn, until they finally feasted on his remains, fighting each other for the choicest morsels.

Other creatures Drystan could not name performed even worse acts of torture and degradation, presumably repeating the scenes again and again.

Drystan averted his eyes and focused on the shiny bald spot on the back of the steward's head. The elven lord of Dreamhame had an effective method of warning his guests that his magic could be fearsome as well as beautiful.

The steward stopped before double doors gilt in an odd sort of reddish-gold, and swept them open with a flourish.

Drystan stepped into the room, quickly took stock of his surroundings, trying to discern illusion from reality. Again, his magic responded to an astonishing degree. The golden tables had actually been crafted of oak, the marble floors of plain flagstone, the velvet settees of sturdy wool. The walls held moving tapestries, but unlike the ones in the hallway, they depicted soothing landscapes of waving heather and rippling waters, and with a bit of concentration, Drystan saw the real embroidery beneath.

"Your chambermaid," said the steward, indicating a woman standing across the room. "Augusta. If you should require another…"

"No. Just fetch me the healer."

Moving nimbly for such an old man, he quit the

apartments, while the maid stepped forward, smiling coyly at Drystan. When his eyes passed over her, she quickly turned her attention to Talbot, and a saucy smile lit her mouth. She obviously had no elven blood gracing her features, but a lovely girl nonetheless.

Drystan brushed past her to the open door across the room, skirting tea tables and potted palms and overstuffed chairs. He laid Camille on the enormous bed and began to unwrap her from the furs.

Edward appeared at his elbow.

"Tell the maid to build up the fire," said Drystan. "And fetch a bucket of water—make that two. And soap. And cloths. As many as she can gather."

Captain Talbot repeated the orders to Augusta, omitting the part about the fire, for he proceeded to take care of it himself. In a short time the maid returned, panting and weighted down with buckets and cloth.

Drystan wrinkled his nose as the full force of Camille's smell hit him. "What the hell did she do, bathe in rancid pig suet?"

"Sheep, I think," answered Edward.

"But why?" He did not receive an answer, and did not expect one. He had his own guesses… which would have to wait until Camille recovered.

Drystan soaped a cloth and began to gently clean away the crusted blood from the cuts of the wraiths. As he suspected, the wounds were superficial. He took a deep breath, and gently, gently, rolled Camille to her side and unbuttoned the ugly black gown. Bandages covered her back, and she groaned as he peeled them away; fury welled within him at the sight of the bloody mess.

"Lash," hissed Edward through his teeth.

"I shall kill the man who did this to her." Drystan spun and glared at the maid, anger making his voice sharper than he intended. He did not want anyone else touching Camille, but he would not subject a lady to the embarrassment that may come from tending her personally. He knew Camille. She knew nothing of him. "Cut the gown off of her to avoid her any further pain. Clean her from head to toe. Gently. I will stand just outside the door, and if I hear a breath of pain from her…"

Augusta's gaze went from him to Camille, confusion crinkling her smooth brow. "But my lord. She is a slave. She should not be here."

Talbot stepped forward before Drystan throttled the maid. "His lordship saved the girl's life and therefore has a sense of responsibility to her. He is a man of… unusual honor."

"How strange," murmured the girl, and then shook her head. "Pardon me, my lord. I did not mean any disrespect."

Drystan shrugged off her words. "Do you know who did this to her?"

"I-I'm sure 'twas the slave master, my lord. But the whippings are not usually this bad. They do not like to damage the goods permanently, ye see. Methinks she may be the slave Lady Pembridge took a liking to. I have only just been elevated upstairs meself and am not familiar with—"

Drystan slashed a hand through the air. "Enough. Just see to her." He strode from the room, Edward hard on his heels, just as a knock sounded on the outer door. Drystan took up a stance just outside the wall of the bedroom, so he could not see her, but could hear every movement within.

Talbot answered the knock, and a diminutive woman stepped into the apartment, cricking her neck to look up at Edward with the blackest eyes Drystan had ever seen. Large faceted elven eyes. "Where is the patient?"

Drystan immediately liked her. A woman of action and few words. Captain Talbot led her across the jumble of furnishings to Drystan, and she cricked her neck just a bit higher to look up at him.

"I sensed tainted magic within her wounds," he said without preamble. "Do you have healing magic to counter it with?"

The tiny woman twitched her rather large nose. Other than her eyes, she didn't appear to carry any elven blood at all within her homely features. "I am a humble servant, lacking the mighty powers of the palace healer." Her voice dripped with sarcasm. "But my ancestors hale from Firehame, and I have a bit of the blue healing fire."

"Then—" A shout from within the bedroom, in a voice already dear to Drystan, made him bolt through the door, damn propriety and a lady's sensibilities.

Augusta stood with soapy wet cloth in hand, her green eyes wide with annoyance and a touch of fear. She held her other hand over her reddened cheek. Camille sat up in the bed, those astounding eyes wide open, flashing with multiple crystalline colors in their depths. She held the edge of his fur-lined cloak over her breasts, her smooth, long legs pale against the dark cloth.

"Come any closer and I shall slap you again."

Augusta turned to Drystan, her gaze sliding quickly to Talbot in appeal. "I swear I did not hurt her. I tried only to wash the soot from her face—"

"You," snapped Camille, her gaze finding Drystan's and not wavering from it. "Where am I?"

"In my apartments, my lady. Did you not understand when I told you that you are now under my protection?"

"I am in your *bed*."

"Aye. And you are smelling it up, my dear. Captain Talbot, escort Augusta from the room for the nonce. It appears that Miss Ashton and I must discuss a few things. And tell the healer to wait."

"Yes, my lord." He put his arm about Augusta and led her out into the withdrawing room. A tear slid down her cheek, but Drystan suspected it a ploy for his captain's attentions rather than any true pain from her reddened skin.

Drystan closed the door behind them and took a step toward the bed. She flinched. But only slightly. She had become adept at concealing her fear, hiding behind a fierce scowl and fingers curled into fists.

Just as he had become adept at hiding his fear of the alien mental touch of the scepters.

Drystan did not come any closer. Instead, he pulled up a stool and brushed back the skirt of his coat before he sat, adjusted the lace at his sleeves with a casual air in perfect imitation of Lord North. He had been tutored in the affectations of the gentry by the ultimate personage of the prime minister. He had adjusted to velvet instead of wool, a lace cravat instead of his worn cotton handkerchief. Tight breeches instead of well-worn leathers.

He had put his foot down, literally, at the heeled shoes with sparkly buckles. A pair of polished knee-high black boots covered his silk stockings.

Camille's hands relaxed upon the crushed fur as he continued to sit there and just smile at her. Those eyes—Drystan thought he could gaze into them the rest of his life and never tire of it. Augusta had managed to remove most of the soot from her face, and Camille had more than her fair share of elven beauty. From sculpted cheekbones to full lips that begged to be kissed, his dreams had not deceived him. Her beauty left him breathless.

"Are you mad?" she whispered as he continued to stare at her.

Drystan wished he could tell her the truth. His dreams of her loving him at first sight, of rushing into his arms, had shattered the moment he met her. She would not believe he loved her, even if he confessed his visions of her, his connection with the scepters. She would not know about the plans of the Rebellion. And even if he explained it all and she managed to believe him, she would suspect he had come for the brand upon her skin and nothing more.

He would have to make her fall in love with him first, and did not have the slightest idea how to go about it. "You have been abused by men. You hate the thought of any man touching you."

She did not need to answer.

"Allow me to relieve your fears, madam. I did not acquire you to warm my bed."

She frowned at him in disbelief. "Then why am I here?"

He leaned back in the chair, choosing his words carefully so she might believe them. "I had the misfortune of saving your life."

Her chin rose. "And that means?"

"Why, my dear, it means I am responsible for your welfare from this moment on. The Hawkes family has always prided themselves on their honor, and it is a custom in my family that has survived over the years. It works in the reverse as well. If you had saved my life, I would be just as bound. Indeed, we flaunt the ancient system of honor as a silent defiance of the elven lords' occupation and slavery of England."

She still frowned at him with suspicion. "It is not possible that I have been saved a third time."

"My lady?"

"I am not a lady—oh, never mind." Camille stared into his eyes, as if she tried to see the man beneath the velvet and lace. "I have risen above my station as a slave, you see. Once as a nursemaid, another as a companion, and now… I draw the line at becoming a mistress, my lord. I… I could not bear it."

She could not know that she probed a tender spot, that in spite of his elven good looks, women had avoided him due to his odd behavior. She would not be the first who could not bear to touch him. But he reminded himself that her reasons differed. Greatly.

The damage that had been done to her might even be greater than his own.

"I assure you, I do not lack for women willing to warm my bed."

Her face altered for a moment, roaming his features, his body. Damn, she believed him.

"Then what shall you do with me, my lord?"

Drystan rubbed his chin. "That is a quandary, is it not? I have neither a need for a nursemaid nor a companion. I suppose you may assist Augusta in whatever tasks she may have. Is that amenable to you?"

"I… yes, my lord."

That desperate look in her lovely eyes faded, and Drystan breathed a sigh of relief. She would not attempt to leave him. For the moment, he would be content with that much.

He stood, smoothed the front of his coat. "Now, you will allow the healer to tend you, and Augusta to wash you. Thoroughly. Perfume bothers my nose, and I have found a bath is more purposeful to noxious smells than layering oneself with scent. Then you shall rest—with Augusta in the servants' quarters—and take on your duties when you feel able. If you have any questions or other needs, you will direct them to me. Is that clear?"

"Yes, my lord."

Drystan turned and opened the door. Glanced over his shoulder one more time to convince himself that he had found her. That she was real.

She looked bewildered, and still rather a mess, but so lovely his heart turned in his chest.

"Camille?"

"Yes, my lord."

"I vow you will never be mistreated again."

Before he could see the expression on her face, Drystan left the room.

Four

CAMILLE WOKE THE NEXT MORNING FEELING SURPRISINGLY well. She sat up without a wince and suspected the official palace healer had less talent than the little old woman who had tended her last night. She glanced around, still in a dreamy haze over the events of the last four-and-twenty hours.

Augusta had already risen, her bedding still rumpled but empty. The fire in their grate had dwindled to glowing coals, and Camille's breath frosted the air. She fought the temptation to snuggle back underneath the down-stuffed coverlet. Similar covering graced Augusta's brass bed, only her coverlet had a woven design of wildflowers upon it. Even when Camille had worked for Lady Pembridge, she had not been given such luxurious bedding.

Nor such a large room, even if she shared it with another servant. A washstand stood between the beds, a ceramic bowl painted with cherubs and a matching pitcher beside it. Two small tables with beveled mirrors perched above them sat across the room from the beds, Augusta's covered with papers and bottles of scent and ribbons and heavens knew what else. It appeared she had used both tables, and cleared the other for Camille, dumping her own things in a rather messy pile.

An enormous wardrobe carved with elaborate designs of scrolls and Gothic arches stood between the tables.

Camille rose and opened it. Half of it had been emptied, Augusta's things once again tossed into a haphazard pile on the other side of the wardrobe. Presumably, the other woman expected Camille to fill it with her own clothing, but she must know slaves possessed only the frocks upon their backs. And the last time she had seen her only one, it had been ripped to shreds.

Camille sighed and glanced down at the borrowed nightgown she wore. It must be Augusta's, for it lay loosely upon her shoulders, and the hem ended too high above her ankles.

Despite Lord Hawkes's instructions to ask him for whatever she might need, Camille knew she could not. Would not. She did not trust him or his motives. Why had he bothered to rescue her? Why would a lord care about a slave? The aristocrats cared only for themselves, for their comforts and luxuries and their false allegiance to the elven lords.

She had always been beneath their notice. No more important than the hounds in their stables. Less so, for the dogs routed the birds in hunting season, providing them entertainment.

Slaves entertained only the soldiers.

Camille shied away from the thought, and began to rummage through Augusta's clothing, hoping the other woman would not mind if she made use of her castoffs. She found a gown worn at the elbows and torn at underarm and hem, stays with frayed eyelets, a tattered chemise, and thick wool stockings with multiple holes. She dared not touch Augusta's extra set of hoops, for they looked new, but found an old petticoat that could be repaired, and since Augusta seemed to be a few inches shorter than Camille, it should suffice in lieu of hoops so the outer gown would not drag along the floor.

Thank heavens Augusta kept a sewing box in her quarters.

Camille built up the fire, lit a candle against the gloomy day outside, and spent the next few hours bent over her needlework, ignoring the growling of her stomach.

She would not dare venture out of these private chambers in a nightgown.

As she sewed, she tried not to think of her rescuer, so naturally, she spent the better part of the time thinking about him. She did not believe for one moment that he did not have some sort of ulterior motive for his actions last night, despite the story about his family honor. Camille had learned from painful experience that kindness did not come without some cost. But she could not imagine what he might have gained from saving the life of a mere slave.

With the holes in the stockings repaired, she uncovered her legs from the bedclothes and pulled on the heavy warmth. She hunted for a smaller needle and finer thread for the chemise, and started to repair the thin tears.

She just wished he wasn't so handsome. He stood tall, not as tall as the elven lord Roden, but taller than his guard. He had the same colored eyes as Roden, faceted golden jewels that had glowed like amber last night. He must possess some power of illusion; indeed, he could be a direct descendant of the elven lord, for they looked very much alike.

Except…

Except Viscount Hawkes's eyes glowed with warmth and compassion. And although his voice did not have the musical timbre of Roden's, it held a deep throaty quality that for some reason soothed her. His pale blond hair lacked the silver luster of the elven, but it looked thicker, with an unusual natural wave to it, with small curls at the ends and about his pointed ears. His brows were brown and not white, his lashes thick, making his eyes appear a paler gold.

If she had not been so abused by men, did not fear to touch them, she would have been tempted by this one.

The abrupt thought confused her. Those golden eyes of his indicated a blood connection to Roden of Dreamhame. How much magical power of illusion did he possess? Had Lord Hawkes managed to cast a glamour for him upon her?

"Ouch." Camille sucked the blood from her pricked finger.

He had promised she would not be mistreated. She might question his motives, but she believed he meant those words. He looked at her as if… as if he could not believe she existed. As if she were the most precious thing in the world. She could not mistake the tenderness in his eyes, in his voice when he spoke to her.

No man had ever looked at her like that before.

He puzzled her.

Faith! She needed to stop thinking about him. She had been thrice saved and could not count upon such luck again. When the viscount left Dreamhame Palace, she would be back in the slave's quarters once again. If something dreadful did not happen to him first.

A man of true honor did not last long in the palace of an elven lord.

Camille chose a larger needle and a thimble to push it through the stiff fabric of the stays and repair the eyelets. The lacing had been so worn in places she would have to try to repair it as well, but even so, she would have to lace it loosely.

She must look to herself. She would never go back to being a slave again. So she must...

She steadied the shaking of her hand.

She must plan an escape. A woman on her own would never manage it. But a woman disguised as a man. A woman who had pistols for protection. It had not been as difficult to fire one as she would have guessed. Yes, she might manage to make it to another sovereignty. She just wished she knew which one of the seven her family hailed from. If she could find kin to take her in... but no, she could not count on that. Roden would soon have enough soldiers trained to march upon Verdanthame and the usurper. Surely she could blend amongst them for a time. Many of the men possessed an elven beauty similar to a woman's.

And she knew soldiers. Knew their habits and mannerisms.

Camille realized her upper lip had curled in disgust at the mere thought of them. But she could endure it.

She would no longer seek protection from others. She would protect herself.

Her heart felt suddenly light as soon as she made the decision. Her fingers flew through the rest of the sewing, and when she finally put on the clothing, it did not fit her as badly as she feared.

She padded the toes of a pair of Augusta's old leather slippers to make them fit, shuffled to the door, and peeked into the outer room.

The large withdrawing room took up most of the living space, along with the master's bedroom. A dining room lay across from the main room, with a cozy parlor next to it. A water closet sat on the other side of the main entrance. She did not dare enter the master's bedroom, but still, the silence told her she had been left alone in the apartments.

Camille opened the door to the outside hall and jumped in surprise at the guard standing there. "Who are you?"

The grizzled old warrior gave her a lopsided grin. "Arthur Drinkwater, miss."

"Am I a prisoner here?"

He frowned. "Why, no, miss. Ye are free to go about whatever business ye may have. My orders are to make sure ye are not molested by anyone. I'm to protect ye, miss."

The viscount wasted one of his men just to protect her? A man of his word, indeed.

"Where is Viscount Hawkes?"

The old man scratched his cheek. "Well now, him and the captain don't bother to keep me informed of their whereabouts."

"I see. What about Augusta?"

"The maid? Not my concern either, but I believe she went to oversee the washing of his lordship's bedding. The coverlet belonged to his great-great-grandmother, ye see, and it is old and might easily tear from the boiling and whatnot."

Camille tried not to look guilty. It might take Augusta all day to get the smell out.

Her stomach suddenly growled.

Arthur smiled. "Perhaps we should visit the kitchens."

And face the other slaves? And the soldiers? Not yet. "No, I think not. I shall just wait here until she returns."

The old man narrowed his eyes, eyes that held the same silver sparkles as the captain's. Not surprising, as the best soldiers hailed from Bladehame, where the elven lord Lan'dor ruled with his power over metal, and turned the north central part of England into a land of mines and forges. And warriors skilled in battle with enchanted weapons.

"Ye need not fear going anywhere, my lady."

Perhaps. But even this hardened soldier could not withstand the magic of Roden of Dreamhame. She wondered what his response might be if she requested he follow her to the Imperial Lord's private chambers. And then chided herself for her lack of graciousness, when the man sought only to offer his protection.

"I would rather wait for Augusta to return. Yet I would ask you a question, sir."

"Aye?"

"Would you… could you… is it possible for a woman to learn how to use a sword?"

His gray eyebrows rose. "There are many female warriors trained in Bladehame. The Imperial Ladies hire most of them for their bodyguards and army, so few make it into the ranks of the five male elven lords' sovereignties."

"I see. But they are trained from birth, are they not?"

"Indeed."

"Then… then I imagine it would take a long time to train a woman who has never held a sword."

He shrugged. "Well, now, that depends. On her stature and strength… most of the women fighters rely on speed rather than strength, so their swords are magically crafted differently anyway. I suppose a woman who held an enchanted sword might be able to defend herself against an ordinary weapon in a short amount of time." He suddenly scowled, transforming his grizzled features into a man who may be old, but had the hardened experience of battle to make up for it. "If ye doubt my ability to defend ye, lady, ye may ask the viscount for a new man."

Camille backed up a step, his anger uncoiling the constant knot of anxiety she held within her. She had not meant to offend him, and now she owed him an explanation. She lifted her chin and curled her fingers into fists. "I do not doubt your skills, sir. It is just that… I have resolved not to rely on others for my protection anymore. It has not served me well."

His face softened, a touch of sadness in his

silver-speckled eyes. "I know a little of your lot, and I think I understand. Ye might be better off learning the pistol."

Camille breathed a sigh. "I have managed to shoot one."

"So I have heard." His voice held a hint of lightness to it now. "But half the time a pistol don't shoot where ye aim it. We use it for the first volley in battle, but in close quarters, we must rely on the sword. It takes too long to load the pistol, ye see, and that is the knowledge ye would need. How to care for the weapon, I mean."

"Ah. I don't suppose... well, do you think you could teach me?"

He shuffled his feet, his worn-polished boots the only sound in the empty hallway. "Ye would have to ask Viscount Hawkes such a question, my lady. I do not have the right to answer such a request."

He truly looked saddened by his admission.

"I understand. Please forgive me for asking."

Camille gently closed the door behind her, so he would not think her angry. In truth, she had hoped to find someone to teach her. There must be another way to gain such knowledge. Still, she had to get a weapon first! She'd been a fool to think she could plan an escape.

No, she would not think that way. Perhaps Molly. The slave girl might be able to steal a soldier's uniform. And she had such a way with the men. Perhaps she could talk a soldier into teaching her how to shoot...

The thought of one of Roden's men standing that close to her made her shudder.

Well, then, she would just have to give this more thought.

Camille stared around the empty apartments. She must take advantage of this opportunity the viscount provided her. Time to make plans. And perhaps she had been too hasty in thinking to refuse his offer to ask for what she needed, although she doubted that extended to uniforms and pistols. But besides providing Molly with ink and paper, she could also offer coins for bribery.

If Viscount Hawkes had some ulterior motive for acquiring her as his slave, then she now had her own secret motive for staying in his household.

But slaves were not paid for work.

Servants were.

Camille passed a finger along the mantel, across the delicate tables gilt in gold, atop the vases crafted with golden-etched scenes of hunting and flowers. Not a spot of dust anywhere. Apparently Augusta earned her place here. Plenty of coal stocked near the fireplace. Water full in the pitchers and buckets.

Oh, and joy! The sideboard in the dining room held two rounds of cheese, some hard loaves of bread, and candied fruit. Camille ate a hasty meal, still feeling like an interloper in this place. She defiantly drank a tumbler of warm port, and immediately felt better. A bit bolder.

She sucked in a breath, made her way to the viscount's bedroom, and opened the door. Surely she would find much to clean within. But the bedding she had soiled had already been changed to a different coverlet, the floor cleaned, and the dirty cloths cleared away.

Camille sniffed. She could not smell a trace of the suet that had coated her body last night.

She frowned in dismay until her eyes lit upon the trunks. Viscount Hawkes's trunks. He had not brought a valet with him, and Captain Talbot did not look like a man who could serve in that capacity. She would wager nothing had been unpacked as of yet. The dressing table looked bare, and when she opened the wardrobe door, it rattled with a hollow sound.

She had found a useful occupation.

She would not think about the opportunity it gave her to find out more about Lord Hawkes. It would not be prying. He would expect someone to unpack his things for him.

Camille ignored the leap in her belly as she opened the first trunk. Clothing. Mounds of velvet, silk, and damask coats. Brocade and embroidered waistcoats. Silk stockings and lace-trimmed cravats. Breeches of matching material and soft leather. White shirts edged with lace. And near the bottom, polished boots. Judging by his attire, Viscount Hawkes was a wealthy man, although singular in the color of his clothing. Unlike the vibrant colors of the court, he preferred browns and blacks edged with gold and silver.

She hung up the coats, laid out many garments in the clothespress drawers to smooth the wrinkles, and reminded herself to ask Augusta the whereabouts of a flat iron to press the most wrinkled of the cravats. Camille would not consider actually dressing the man, but perhaps she could lay out his clothing of an evening. She would make sure to create appealing ensembles of tidy appearance.

Most gentlemen of the court considered it of utmost importance.

Camille opened the next trunk. Unlike the careless way his clothing had been packed, the contents of this chest had been lovingly arranged, with white sheets of paper separating the books.

Books.

What kind of man went to the difficulty of lugging about his book collection?

Camille picked up the first leather-bound volume and read the title gilt in gold, *The Unfortunate Traveler*. She resisted the temptation to open the pages and read. She had missed Molly's story last night, and did not know when the next opportunity might arise to hear another… although Camille heartily prayed it would not be anytime soon, no matter how much she longed for a whimsical tale.

She rose with book in hand and glanced about the room. A set of shelving sat next to the bed, currently occupied by a few artful boxes of gold, a clock with sculpted angels surrounding the face, various other items obviously left behind between visits so the place would not look bare. She took down the pieces and arranged them on a table, and set the book upon the first shelf.

It looked as if it belonged there.

She imagined a man so enamored of his book collection would prefer to have them easily at hand, and hoped to please him by arranging the entire contents of the trunk upon the shelves.

He had saved her life, after all.

Camille had half the contents emptied before she

could resist temptation no longer. The clock told her the noon hour had passed, and Augusta had not appeared. Nor anyone else, for that matter.

It was not necessarily forbidden for slaves to know how to read, but their time and duties certainly made it unlikely. If not for Molly, Camille never would have learned.

Still, she held her breath for a moment, listening for any sound, and could not stop the feeling of guilt that arose when she opened a volume titled, *Mr. William Shakespeare's Comedies, Histories & Tragedies*, and the book fell open to the play, *Much Ado About Nothing*. Despite having to puzzle over some of the words, she soon became absorbed in the story, a smile playing about her mouth at the banter between the hero and heroine.

Molly wrote charming stories, about a world that had never been invaded by elven lords, an England gay with parties and debutants and admiring beaus. But this story, which she first thought to be a frivolous love story, involved complexities that lay beneath the surface, deceptions that reminded her strongly of those used by the elven lords.

Camille did not hear anyone enter the apartments. Indeed, when she looked up and saw him standing at the door, it gave her such a start she dropped the expensive book.

"Where is Augusta?" asked Viscount Hawkes, one arm across his chest to grip the other, his face paler than usual.

"I... I do not know, my lord. I haven't seen her since last eve."

He slumped against the door frame, exposing the

frowning face of Captain Talbot just behind him, and glanced over his shoulder.

"You shall have to fetch the healer," Lord Hawkes told his man. "And twice bedamn what the court fools say, fetch that old woman, not the palace healer."

"Aye, sir. Perhaps I should see to the bleeding—"

His lordship shook his head. "Camille will tend me."

Captain Talbot gave her a doubtful look, one that made her bristle with indignation.

"I am not unfamiliar with the sight of blood."

"I should rather think not," answered Lord Hawkes. "Go on, Edward."

Without another word, the captain turned and quit the apartments, leaving Lord Hawkes standing there with his gaze fastened upon her once again. The tender way he looked at her made her feel peculiar inside.

"As much as I would enjoy standing here and looking at you forever, I'm afraid I might fall over if you do not help me to the bed."

Camille quickly stepped forward, and just as quickly came to an abrupt halt.

"Come now. You do not truly think I am in any position to molest you?"

She shook her head. But he stood so tall, his broad shoulders barely fitting through the doorway, or so it seemed to her. He exuded that masculine aura of strength and dominance, and despite the blood seeping between his fingers where he clutched his arm, that well-earned knot of warning rose to strangle her.

The frown of pain etched on his mouth gentled into a half smile. "I understand it will be an odious chore to touch me. I fear you shall have to bear it."

Camille's aversion to men mostly extended to soldiers, for the other men she met usually just ignored her. This man fit neither mold. Still, he had the look of a warrior, and she could feel he *wanted* her, but chose to deny himself.

She had thought him a puzzle. Now, she feared to solve it.

He cocked a brow. "Will you truly stand there and allow me to bleed to death?"

"No, I..." Camille stepped forward, held out her hands. He did not reach out to her in any way, just stood there, waiting. She closed the distance between them and grasped his uninjured arm, allowing him to lean on her as she led him forward.

"You may not have any magic," he said, "but you have the elven strength in plenty." He sat on the edge of the bed and looked up at her. "And the grace, and more than the fair share of beauty."

Camille flushed. No one had ever called her beautiful, not with her odd eyes that seemed to take up most of her face. The compliment made her feel even more peculiar, so she chose to ignore it. "How do you know I haven't any magic?"

"My dear, you would have used it to save yourself last night."

"Of course."

"Can you help me off with my coat? I shall have to release my hold on the wound, which means it will spout more blood, so you shall have to try to be quick in the removal of it."

"I understand."

"Jolly good then. On three. One, two, three."

He let go of his wound and Camille tugged the coat over his shoulders. It had not been her imagination. He had very broad shoulders. She thought of the blood gushing down his arm, heard him mutter a curse beneath his breath, and quickly jumped on the bed behind him, yanking at the collar, pulling the coat down his back.

Lord Hawkes quickly grabbed his injury again.

"Camille?"

"Yes, my lord."

"The room is spinning."

She scrambled off the bed, tugged off his boots. Folded his ruined coat with the wet part inside and placed it on the bed. She would not allow his bedding to be ruined two nights in a row. He started to fall over sideways, so she picked up his legs and heaved, allowing him to collapse on his back.

Camille leaned over and positioned the coat a bit more securely beneath his injured arm. It brought her too close to him. She could feel his heat, smell the spicy scent of his skin, and wondered what cologne he wore.

He inhaled deeply, echoing her thoughts. "You smell wonderful, Camille. Like sweet wine... and something else. It is a vast improvement over the scent you wore last night."

He made her smile. And she did not feel afraid to be this near to him, even though she could tell he desired her, injury notwithstanding. His voice had such a deep, tender quality to it, a teasing note she could not take umbrage to.

She pulled away, stared into those faceted golden brown eyes, and then blinked. "I shall fetch some soap and water." With a swirl of her borrowed skirts she ran from the room, returning with a bucket she had noticed in the wash closet, and cloths and soap.

Lord Hawkes captured her with his gaze yet again. "I am afraid I cannot let go of the gash in my skin. Parts of me will be liable to spill out. If you would grant me the boon of washing the rest of the blood off of me, Camille, I would consider it a personal favor."

She glanced at his bloodstained shirt. Went into her room and fetched the scissors from the sewing box, and promptly went about cutting off the shirt. She ignored the contours of his chest as she went about the task. Ignored the ridged muscles in his abdomen. The bulge of muscles standing out in shoulder and arm. The smooth, nearly hairless expanse of his skin, testament to the elven blood running through his veins.

She set cloth to soap and plunged it in the bucket. Wiped down his arm, his chest, his belly, always careful to keep the cloth between the touch of her fingers on his bare skin. His eyes closed, and she thought he might have lost consciousness, except for the sighs that occasionally escaped his lips.

He had extraordinarily full lips for a man.

Camille found herself breathing hard. Too hard to account for the small labor of washing him. Heaven help her. She had never desired a man before this moment. But she recognized the feeling. Because sometimes her traitorous body gained pleasure from the soldiers, and she could not stop it. And this had disgusted her most of all.

Lord Hawkes had lulled her into a false sense of security. He made no movement to touch her. Had made no advances to threaten her, to weaken her guard. But how much magical glamour had he cast over her?

Tricky bastard.

Camille jerked away from him and abruptly flung the reddened cloth into the bucket.

He opened one eye. "What is wrong?"

"Nothing, sir. You are as clean as I can manage at the moment."

"I see." He shifted on the bed. "What is taking Edward so long? Even a good healer cannot stop the fever completely if the wound festers."

Camille sniffed, refusing to be put off her guard again with sympathy. Besides, he had probably acquired the injury by flirting with some man's wife and being taken to account for it. The scenario happened all the time with the aristocracy, much to the amusement of the elven lord. She sometimes wondered if they did it just to please him.

"How did you come by your injury, sir?"

His other lid flew open, and the color of his eyes darkened to a smoky gold. Those lips narrowed, and his face hardened with a mask Camille somehow thought familiar to him. As if he had adopted the wearing of it over the years.

When he spoke, his voice vibrated with some deep emotion. "Let us just say that the slave master shall never beat another woman again."

Camille gasped. Swayed on her feet. She remembered something he said last night, but the pain of her back had made her only half-aware. She thought she had misheard him, or that his vow had been spoken only in the heat of the moment. Apparently, Viscount Hawkes could be taken at his word. "Did you kill him?"

His smooth chest rose and fell on a great sigh, and when he spoke again, he used the same gentle tone she had grown accustomed to. "I have killed men only in self-defense. I certainly could not kill one who wept at my feet, despite the temptation to do so."

The master had wept? She always suspected him to be a coward. Lord Hawkes only confirmed it.

But she must be mistaken. Surely the viscount had not fought the man just because he had beaten a mere slave. The slave master had been employed for that very task. There must be more to the story.

"Did he insult you?" she inquired, although she could not imagine a man foolish enough to do so.

"Yes." Those golden eyes glittered.

"What did he do?"

"He dared to harm someone I care about. And if you insist on keeping me distracted by talking until the healer comes, I need a glass of port. No, brandy. The pain is getting annoying."

A rush of shame made Camille flee the room again, this time knocking over a tea table in the process, scattering golden teacups about the room. She did not stop to bother with it. Within a moment she returned to his bedchamber, decanter of brandy and glass in hand.

Her hand shook as she poured. Surely he had not challenged the master to a duel because of her? No one ever bothered with Camille Ashton. This honor he spoke of extended beyond the realm of anything she'd ever heard of before. She could perhaps believe saving her life gave him some responsibility for her. But to challenge a man for beating her? When his lordship knew naught of her until last eve?

When she neared the bed with the glass, he gifted her with another of his smiles. She wished he would quit doing that. His smile did not leer or demand or taunt. It spoke of a gentleness she could not afford to believe in.

Lord Hawkes glanced down at his arms. "I fear I shall need more of your help in order to drink. Can you bear to touch me again?"

Camille did not answer. She set down the glass, pushed some pillows beneath his head, brushing his wavy white hair out of the way. It felt like thick silk. Then she perched gingerly on the edge of the bed and held the glass to his lips.

He took a sip. The brandy glistened on his lips and he licked it away, making her wonder what it would be like to kiss him.

She had never kissed a man. Most of the time, the soldiers did not bother with it. And when they did, she always moved her face away. A small power of denial—but one that made her feel less impotent.

Her hand shook, and brandy spilled down his chin. "I am so sorry, my lord."

"It is all right, Camille." His voice lowered to a whisper. "I understand. More than you know."

What was it about this man that rattled her so? What did he think he understood? He lived a life of luxury, and could not imagine the despair and torture she had lived through. And yet…

She found a clean cloth and wiped the brandy off

his chin and neck, again being careful not to touch his bare skin.

She feared she would enjoy the feel of him.

"Did you truly challenge the master to a duel because of me?"

"Yes."

"But why? I am only a slave, no one of great importance."

"I told you. You are my responsibility now. This will set an example to all others that I will allow no harm done to you without repercussions."

Camille fought down a helpless feeling of frustration. "I still do not understand—"

A cough from the doorway made her jump up from the bed, as if she had any reason to feel guilty.

Captain Talbot looked at her. Then at Lord Hawkes. And had the audacity to give him a cheeky grin. "The healer, my lord."

The small woman entered the room, and Camille backed into a shadowy corner, for Talbot blocked the doorway.

"Now what?" snapped the healer, bending over Lord Hawkes to peer at his wound. She sniffed. Loudly. "Well, no magic here to blight it, leastways."

Camille watched with fascination as the little woman's hands began to glow with unearthly blue fire. She almost jumped forward to stop the healer when that magical force made its way toward Lord Hawkes's arm, then chided herself for being a goose. She had seen such power before, although never this strong, but knew it would do no harm to him.

After a few moments of that fire licking its way

around his arm, the viscount leaned back with a sigh. "I was right to send for you."

"Of course you were," replied the healer. "But mark my words, I cannot stop the fever from over-taking you. There are times when the body is best left to heal itself, without the interference of magic. You shall keep to this bed for several days."

Lord Hawkes did not appear offended by the woman's authoritative tone; instead he smiled and thanked her. She immediately turned and looked up at Captain Talbot. "He needs rest tonight, broth tomorrow, solid food the day after. And as much port as he can drink. Can you manage it?"

Talbot bristled. "Of course."

"Good. Then pay me and let me be on my way. There's a baby to be delivered, and I refuse to waste any more time on the injuries of fool men who resolve their grievances with a sword."

Lord Hawkes barked a laugh at the look on his captain's face, and then his brow wrinkled with pain. Talbot led the woman from the room. Camille stayed in the shadows, watching his lordship. Had the healer done enough? Would he truly recover? Why did it worry her so?

Because she felt guilty for having been the cause of his injury. Because she must have time to prepare her plans for escape.

She would make sure he recovered, but that did not mean she trusted him or his motives. Camille had quit trusting in people a long time ago. It would take more than gentle smiles and a cut to the arm to even remind her of the concept of it.

Talbot returned soon enough, gave his lordship three glasses of port before his eyes finally closed and he fell asleep. Then the captain turned to the shadow she hid in. "I suppose you will watch over him all night?"

She did not answer.

Even so, Augusta appeared a few moments later with a dinner tray for Camille and set it down beside her without a word.

Camille ate automatically, her eyes fixed on the sleeping man, and afterward curled up in an overstuffed chair and continued her silent vigil until she nodded off to sleep herself.

Five

CAMILLE WOKE TO THE SIGHT OF LORD HAWKES sitting half-upright in bed, his brow furrowed in concentration at a spot near the foot of it. A shape hovered just above the bedding, a swirl of colors that danced haphazardly to and fro, coalescing for a mere second into what might have been some sort of flower, before shattering apart into another merry dance.

"What is it supposed to be?" asked Camille.

He smiled, but kept his concentration fixed upon his illusion. For just a moment she glimpsed a bouquet of flowers: orchids, iris, bellflower, primrose, and other blooms she could not identify. Then the yellows and pinks and blues melted into a brownish spot at his feet, and disappeared.

His lordship collapsed back against the pillows. "It was supposed to be for you. Flowers in winter. Faith, I just cannot understand how to harness this magic. One moment I can turn Talbot into a demon, and the next I cannot even conjure a decent posy."

Camille suppressed a smile. She did not think it

would take too great of a spell to turn the captain into a demon. But she wondered at Lord Hawkes's frustration, for his family had little talent for magic, despite the hue of gold in his eyes, or the elven lord would have sent them to Elfhame.

And if she feared he had put a glamour upon her, his display this morning caused her to doubt it—although perhaps he had done it for just that reason. She did not know which should concern her more. For if magic had *not* been at work to make her think of him so often, what had?

"Surely this is not your first visit to Dreamhame, my lord?"

"Err—*I* came once with my parents, long ago. To be tested." He sighed. "I suppose it is best I have little knack for it."

He sounded most annoyed, and she felt compelled to ease him. "It takes a great amount of energy, or so I have heard. And if you don't mind my saying so, it is best to reserve your strength to fight the fever. You are still flushed, my lord. And you spent a restless night." She scrambled to her feet.

"I cannot imagine that chair was too comfortable," he said.

She shrugged. "I have slept in worse places, my lord."

"I imagine you have. And last night, ah, last night! At least I managed to sleep through the whole of it yet again."

Camille did not quite know what to make of that statement, but before she could ask, Captain Talbot entered the room, his muscular arms laden with a gold tray topped with steaming cups.

He set it down next to Lord Hawkes, who grimaced. "What is that?"

"Broth, my lord. On the instructions of the healer. And damn me if I would challenge that little lady."

"Indeed."

Talbot shoved more pillows beneath his master's head—a bit too roughly, Camille thought—and picked up a bowl and spoon.

His lordship scowled. "Just what the hell do you think you are doing?"

"Feeding you, my lord."

"Hell no. I still have one good arm."

"You are so weak, you are liable to slosh hot broth all over you."

"Then Camille will care for me."

Captain Talbot looked over to the corner, as if he hadn't known she had been there the entire time. "Your attentions toward the girl are… alarming."

"And none of your business."

Talbot's lips curled. "Mayhap, my lord."

"Oh, devil take you, Edward. Get out of here. I am sure you would much rather break your fast with Augusta."

The silver specks in the captain's gray eyes sparkled at the words. Then he glanced at Camille again and the excitement faded. "If you are sure, my lord. This… whatever is happening here. It goes beyond the bounds of our… visit."

"I know what I am doing, Captain Talbot. And you will not question my actions again."

The guard stood at the tone of voice his master used, carefully set down the bowl and spoon, and stiffly bowed. "As you wish, my lord. Forgive me, my lord. I am a buffoon, my lord."

Lord Hawkes rolled his eyes. "Just bring the lady a tray, so that she may eat with me."

Talbot grinned and left the room.

Camille did not know what to make of either of them.

"That broth actually smells good," said Viscount Hawkes, looking at her with such hopeful entreaty she could not help but smile as she stepped forward and then perched on the edge of his bed.

The intimacy of being in the same bed with him no longer made her uncomfortable. Nor did the act of spooning broth into his mouth. Nor wiping the corner of his lips. But she avoided looking into his eyes. And at his naked chest.

When he professed to be full, Camille sat at a small table next to the bed, where Augusta had set another tray a few moments ago, and began to eat the poached eggs, cold toast, and sliced mutton.

She could feel his eyes watching her every move. It made her uncomfortable. It somehow made her feel important.

"I fear I make a terrible invalid," said his lordship. "I will be restless with nothing to do."

Camille nodded.

"You know how to read."

He made it a statement, and she remembered when he had entered the room last evening and caught her in the act. Her gaze traveled to the volume still lying open upon the floor.

"Is it forbidden for slaves to read?"

She shook her head.

"But unlikely. How did you learn?"

She shrugged.

"Faith, woman. Why are you suddenly so quiet? You stayed with me all night as if you cared for my health, and now you will not speak to me. Nor look at me."

The bedding rustled and she looked up in alarm, afraid he had managed to gain his footing. He had managed only to sit upright again, swaying a bit; his perfect skin now flushed an even-brighter red.

Camille looked into his eyes. Caught her breath at the beauty of the golden color, the way the facets reflected the weak sunlight filtering through the windows. "Please do not upset yourself, my lord. I still do not understand… I have still not become accustomed…" and she threw her arms wide, encompassing him, the room, her place in it.

"Ah, Camille, Camille. You still do not trust me. You are so unused to human compassion it confounds you when you find it. Do you not realize that I know you?"

"You speak as if we have met before. But I swear I would remember if we had. And I cannot understand why you think you would know me—would know the life of a slave, when you have been surrounded only by power and luxury."

Lord Hawkes clutched his arm, which held only a trace of his wound, the skin healed together but still red with fever. "You are right, of course. I have been surrounded by love, and you do not know the meaning of it. And although I could explain many things to you, I fear it would make things complicated between us. And I would like to start simply."

"Simply?"

"Aye. I know you, you see, because I have dreamt of you."

"I do not believe in dreams. Or stories. I believe in the reality of staying alive."

"But… do you believe this much, at least? That I have dreamed of you for years, and those dreams led me to find you?"

"It smacks of magic, my lord. And that is something which has been used to hurt me more times than I care to recall."

"But this time it brought me to you, Camille. Surely you cannot regret that, despite whatever other reasons I was sent dreams of you."

So, she had been right. He had other motives for becoming her protector. Camille almost asked him about it, but knew he would not reveal them to her. He wished to start "simply," whatever that meant. And she had as little right to question his actions as Captain Talbot, even less so. Lord Hawkes kept making her forget her status, and a slave who did that suffered for it. "You should beware these other reasons you speak of, my lord."

"Believe me, they are not as important as you." He leaned closer to her, white hair falling about his angular cheeks, the tips of his pointed ears revealed within the mass of it. "If you believe nothing else, I beg you to take my words to heart. There is nothing in this world as important to me as you."

Camille feared the fever had made him distraught, to think the opinion of a slave mattered a whit. Yet he spoke so earnestly, his face so intent upon hers that she feared he might do himself some harm. She glanced toward the door, also fearing Captain Talbot's return and his anger at his master's upset. "Please, my lord, do not fash yourself. Lie back down before you make yourself more ill."

"I shall. But only if you make me a promise."

From the other room she heard the faint sound of Augusta's laughter, the answering deep reply of a male voice. Despite her anxiety that the captain would return and blame her for Hawkes's upset, she would not readily make a blind promise, and suspicion laced her voice. "What is it?"

"Will you read to me?"

The request took her aback.

"It will relieve my boredom. And perhaps teach you of love and faith and honor."

She gave him a scornful glance. "They are only fairy tales."

"Written from the heart. Based on imagination, yes, but with truth at the core of them. Come, I will show you."

"If you will lie back down."

He sighed and did as she bade him. "There. Now tell me the books you have unpacked."

She listed a few of the names, and he made her stop when she read the title, *Robinson Crusoe*."

"Ah, Defoe. A good place to start."

He turned as Captain Talbot entered the room, Augusta in tow, and asked him, "You will handle the matter we discussed?"

Captain Talbot bowed. "It will be my pleasure, my lord."

Augusta exchanged a glance with Camille, who shrugged her shoulders. She had no idea what they spoke of. But that Augusta would treat her as if they would exchange a confidence to one another made Camille feel warmly toward the other woman for the first time.

And the maid had not said a word regarding the clothing Camille borrowed.

Augusta cleared the trays, and Captain Talbot bowed out of the room. Camille pulled up a chair next to his lordship's bed and opened the leather-bound volume. She tried not to betray her excitement at the task. She never imagined she would be given the opportunity to read a real book. The children she had taken care of, Rufus and Laura, kept a governess, and Camille had not been allowed in the schoolroom. And Lady Pembridge had no desire for books, only gossip.

Camille read slowly at first, afraid her skills might embarrass her, but Lord Hawkes did not show any signs of frustration if she struggled with a word or two. Indeed, he would help her to decipher it, then praise her as quick-witted when she did.

She soon found herself engrossed in the story, the world of the author vivid in her mind's eye, shuddering at the black magic of the natives when they tried to sacrifice the slave. She glanced up at his lordship when she read how Crusoe had rescued Friday. Glanced up again when the perils of their life on the island strengthened their relationship to a deep friendship—when the line between slave and master disappeared.

"You see?" he said, when she paused at the end of the chapter, a smile tugging at the corner of his handsome mouth. "Others may define us by our circumstances, but in truth we are all equal as human beings."

Augusta entering the room saved Camille from a reply.

"There is a messenger at the door, my lord. You have been extended an invitation for tea."

Lord Hawkes appeared confused. "Reply that I am indisposed."

"Yes, my lord."

Camille picked up the story only to be interrupted again a short time later.

Augusta held a silver tray in her hands, heaped with cards and letters. "I am most sorry, my lord. There is another person at the door. A Lady Hensby, who insists on seeing you. She says she will not leave until she has assured herself of your good health." She held out the silver tray. "And these are all inquiries and invitations from members of the court."

Lord Hawkes still looked confused. Camille hid a smile. Apparently he had charmed the court—and she imagined most especially the ladies. It was endearing, the way he could not quite comprehend it.

"Tell the lady I am indisposed." His eyes fell upon the pile of notes. "And throw those things away."

"But—but, my lord." Augusta set down the tray and proceeded to wring her hands. "The lady is *quite* insistent. She had a fit of vapors when I refused her entrance. And the letters must be answered, or it shall only get worse. They will come themselves, you see, if they do not receive a reply."

He scowled. "You don't say?"

"Indeed, my lord."

Then his expression changed, became calculating.

"Lady Hensby, you said. Styles her hair in a tremendous heap, with hoops nearly as wide?"

Augusta swallowed. "She is, uh, quite elegant, my lord. And very pretty."

"Indeed."

Something twisted in Camille's chest at his lordship's agreement. Something odd, a feeling she could not identify.

"Very, well. Then send her in."

Augusta nodded with relief and retreated, and Hawkes turned to Camille.

"Can you write as well as read?"

"Yes, my lord."

"Good. Then you shall answer all these notes"—he looked at them in disgust—"and give your voice a rest from reading. Return to me as soon as Lady Hensby leaves."

Camille rose. "Yes, my lord."

"And do not look like that, Camille. I have eyes for no woman but you."

He took her breath away when he said such outlandish things. And yet, she suddenly felt lighter, and when she saw Lady Hensby enter the apartments in all her silk and lace and rouge, she did not feel dowdy by comparison, even when the lady glanced at Camille's refurbished clothing with a sniff of distaste.

Lady Hensby closed the bedroom door behind her.

"Well," announced Augusta. "This shall make my duties more difficult."

"May I help?"

The maidservant looked at Camille for the first time. Really looked at her, from head to toe. "It seems his lordship has acquired an attachment to you, and far be it from me to complain. He should have hired at least several more servants, yet refuses to do so. And I am not so proud as all the rest to deny help from a slave."

A knock sounded at the door.

"Lud, I have broth to reheat for his lordship, but nothing fancy to serve the ladies, and I will lay odds it is another woman who has set her cap upon him."

"Her cap?"

"Oh, aye. Viscount Hawkes has not been to court for years and has taken the ladies quite by storm. There is naught a servant I know who has not heard of how handsome, noble, and charming he is from their mistresses. And although many of them seek marriage, there are more than a few who will gladly settle for his bed."

Camille colored.

The knock at the door sounded louder.

"We need a footman! Lud, Camille, will you run to the kitchens while I answer the calls, and fetch something fancy from the cook? Tell him it is for Viscount Hawkes and his lady friends."

"I… yes, of course."

"No, wait! You cannot go looking like that. You will embarrass the house. Fetch a new gown from my wardrobe; although you were right not to borrow my hoop-petticoat, for they shall all be too short otherwise. You are so tall and thin."

A tiny man suddenly materialized before them, complete with red pointed hat and a beard that reached to his toes. He bowed. "Excuse me. Lady Windthrop is at the door and requests to be allowed entry."

Augusta clasped a hand over her large bosom.

"Now they are sending in illusions. Quick, Camille, be off with you." And the small woman hurried to the door while Camille ran to their room and did as Augusta asked, choosing a serviceable brown serge with a white apron to cover the front of it.

By the time she entered the main withdrawing room, several ladies sat upon the velvet settees and gilt-edged chairs, eyeing one another jealously, uttering false compliments on each other's appearance. Augusta's thin brown hair had escaped its bun and hung about her cheeks as she bustled around the room, setting pots of tea on lace doilies.

Camille escaped into the hall with a sigh of relief. Even the dreadful tapestries woven with death scenes seemed tame in comparison to the feminine vultures within Lord Hawkes's apartments.

He said he had eyes for no woman but her.

Camille stalked through the hallway, ignoring the dancing of the nymphs and the glorious flapping wings of the Pegasus. She had grown up in this palace of illusion. Why would she believe in the even stronger one Hawkes offered her?

What type of man would fall in love with a dream?

She took the servants' stairs down to the kitchens. At least they offered no glamour, for the elven lord did not waste his talent upon the staff. That knot of fear that always sat coiled within her breast began to tighten. There were always soldiers in the kitchen. Her gown declared her new status, but would they honor it? Everything had happened so quickly—from misery to hope yet again—that her head still spun with the thought of it.

She stifled her fear and marched onward. She must

see Molly today. Although she had nothing to pay her with as yet, she felt sure Lord Hawkes would allow her the same wages he paid Augusta, and she would soon be able to repay her fellow slave any costs she might incur. And she dare not waste any time in planning her escape.

Robinson Crusoe had liberated his slave Friday, making him an equal. And Lord Hawkes had looked at her as if she should believe in such a thing happening.

Such an altering of circumstances did not occur in real life so easily.

Still, she could not wait to go back and finish the book.

The kitchen bustled with activity, scullery maids and serving boys rushing about. A few soldiers sat at table, but when they caught sight of her, they quickly glanced away.

The knot of fear lessened.

Camille stopped to talk to Cook as he chopped onions. "Viscount Hawkes is entertaining ladies in his room. He requests luncheon for them." She could not keep the scowl from her face at the thought of his lordship feeding the vultures, smiling that gentle smile of his all the while.

"So, ye managed to find a place upstairs yet again," said Cook, eyes watering from his task. "Wouldna' believed ye could do it thrice."

"I scarcely believe it myself."

"Well, there's no accounting for the odd ways of the gentry. Some like ta skim the edges of society. Thrill for them, it is."

Camille bristled. "I am not his whore, if that's what you are implying."

Then Cook surprised her. He actually looked

frightened that he might have given offense. To a slave. "Nay, Camille. I know how it's been with ye." Cook briefly turned and smacked a girl for putting a finger in the pudding, then said, "We have a new slave master. Ain't as good as the old one. Slaves don't fear his lash as much without the magical taint of pain that used to come with it."

So, Cook knew Camille had been the cause of the old master's dismissal. No wonder he looked so frightened. She changed the subject, nodding at the empty table. "Where is everyone today?"

Cook jerked his head in the direction of the court-yard. "Another fight. As usual. Sounds like a good un, and I wished they'd waited until after the noon meal rush so I could watch. Ah, well. I'll have a girl set up a tray for ye in a few minutes."

Camille almost smiled. She had just been given the perfect opportunity to visit Molly.

But when she reached their little closet, it lay empty.

When she turned to go, Ann opened the door of her own closet and poked her head out. "Camille. If you are looking for Molly, she is out in the courtyard."

Camille should have known. Molly never missed a good fight.

Ann's dark brown elven eyes sparkled. Eyes that proved her link to the sovereignty of Terrahame, to the Lady Annanor with the brown scepter of the power of earth. "I heard you had come back, and then"—she snapped her fingers—"you're right up the stairs again." The little golem that sat on her shoulder snapped its twiggy fingers in perfect imitation of its mistress.

"I am sorry I did not get a chance to visit you,

Ann. How have you been? Is there anything I could bring you?"

Ann shook her head, thick white hair sparkling with silver. She rarely left her rooms, and seemed to require nothing more than her stick-and-mud creations to keep her company. "They have nothing up *there* that I desire."

Camille glanced at the golem on her shoulder. "Perhaps some bits of cloth to dress them? Or tiny buttons to use for eyes?"

"La, what a famous idea!" She turned her head to peer at her little man. "Would you like that, Sir Mudwise? We shall dress you up like all the fine lords of the court. How grand you will look!"

The creature could not portray an expression, but it did clap its twiggy hands, a portion of mud flaking away to fall upon Ann's shoulder.

"I promise to bring you scraps from the sewing box the next time I come, but I do not know when that might be. Do you think you could manage to give Molly a message for me?"

The other woman nodded.

Camille huffed a breath. She would be taking a risk, but she felt the urgency to plan for her escape as quickly as possible. She feared Lord Hawkes. His gentle smiles. His talk of dreams that portended more than he would admit.

Besides, Ann could not read, nor could most of the soldiers. Still. "It is a secret message, Ann. It cannot fall into the wrong hands."

Her eyes widened and then she... saluted. The little golem mimicked her.

"I shall be right back," said Camille, wondering about Ann's peculiarities, and not for the first time. The girl had escaped the cruelties of her situation by retreating into an often childlike world populated by her enchanted creations.

Camille removed the brick from the wall and took out quill, pot, and parchment, and scratched Molly a hasty note.

I need a soldier's uniform that will not be noticed missing. I will pay. Do not take any risks. C.

Molly was too smart of a girl not to understand the implications in the message. Perhaps it had been an advantage that Camille could leave her only a letter. There would be no arguments about the foolishness of her plans.

Ann took the folded paper and handed it to the golem for safekeeping, then retreated into her room, immediately admonishing another of her creations for making a mess in her absence.

Camille entered the kitchens just as two soldiers escorted another man from the courtyard toward the stairs. She froze in place, for the man screaming curses at his escorts looked familiar. Flashes of magical illusions scattered about the heads of the soldiers: small winged creatures with jagged fangs and wicked claws, daggers of smoke and shadow, keening wraiths dancing in frenzy. But the escorts were the elven lord's personal guards, and they possessed enchantments to protect them.

"Look, see?" screamed the man. "My magic ain't

strong enough to get past yer barriers. I tell ye I ain't no threat to his lordship! Let me go, devil take ye!"

Camille could not remember his name, but she recognized him as the man who had set the wraiths upon her the other evening. She waited until the three of them and their magical maelstrom went up the stairs before accepting the tray of pastries and sweetmeats from Cook.

"Everybody's scared to show a whiff of their magic," he muttered, "since that half-blood killed the elven lord Mi'cal and stole the green scepter of Verdanthame."

"It has made Roden of Dreamhame cautious."

"Ha! Cautious, she says. More like a madman—go off with ye, Camille. Yer partly to blame for *that* one." And Cook gestured toward the now-empty stairs.

"What do you mean?"

"Go ask yer new master."

But Camille did not need to. She carried the tray slowly up the stairs, making sure she did not encounter the man and his guards again. Roden had told his court to report those who showed a marked increase in their talent, so anyone could have reported that man for testing, but Camille knew Lord Hawkes had taken revenge for her sake yet again.

He would make those who harmed her pay, trying to ensure her safety. Did he not realize what would happen when he left court? That those who suffered because of her would exact revenge?

She had made the right decision to escape as soon as possible.

By the time Camille reached the apartments, she had made another decision. Tonight she would visit

Roden's dragon, Grimor'ee. She would tell him of this strange man, and of her plans for escape, and perhaps it might help.

Not that the dragon had ever shown any interest in helping her directly. But talking with him always allowed her head to clear, to strengthen her resolve to help herself.

Grimor'ee had the oddest way of giving her courage by goading her to it. Camille had not quite decided if the dragon's perverse nature rankled, or if he just brought out her own obstinate nature in response.

She could be sure of only one thing: the dragon kept her secrets.

At her knock, the door of the apartment flew open, and Augusta frowned at her. "Where have you been?"

"You know perfectly well—"

"Oh, aye, I'm sorry; here, let me take that." Augusta took the tray, eyes widening as it sagged in her arms from the weight of it. She lacked the elven strength and seemed to forget Camille held it in plenty. "He has been asking for you."

"Where are the other ladies?" asked Camille as she stepped into the now-empty apartments.

"He made them go. Well, Lady Hensby did, when she finally emerged from his room. She has a will of steel, that one. Told them all that his lordship needed his rest to recover from his 'valorous wound,' and if she heard of a one of them pestering him within the week, she would take them to account. None of the ladies seemed inclined to challenge her."

Camille rather thought not. Rumor had it that Lady Hensby held the ear of Roden's inner circle of admirers.

She half-smiled at the thought of Lady Pembridge and her gossip. It came in handy more often than not.

"Well *you* might smile," said his lordship when she entered his bedchamber. "You did not have to spend the last half hour listening to the idle chatter of women. How can they manage to speak so many words while saying nothing at all?"

Camille did not reply, but her smile grew wider. "It is called flirting, my lord. And you should be flattered by the attention."

"Should I?" His golden eyes took on a calculating glitter. "Does their interest make you jealous?"

Camille's smile disappeared. She would not admit the truth. Even if she had known what it might be. "Certainly not. You are an exceptionally handsome and charming man, and it is natural for the court to be drawn to you. Do not be surprised if your circle of admirers grows to include a few men."

He sat up, pale hair curling across his naked shoulders to spill down his chest. "Men? Ah, wait, no; do not distract me with that comment. I wish to hear more about the *exceptional* part."

"My lord?"

"Well, it is one thing to be handsome and charming. But quite another to be thought exceptionally so. Do you not agree?"

Camille caught herself from wringing her hands like Augusta. This man had the oddest way of setting her heart beating with thoughts she never contemplated before. "Was there something you needed, my lord? Some broth, perhaps."

He flopped back against the pillows. "You are a

tough one, Camille. I vow you have every right to be. But I am just as stubborn, you know."

She held her face carefully neutral.

"Ah, well. There are those notes to answer. I think... I think it would amuse me to have you read them aloud. And then you may write my reply."

Camille nodded, picked up the silver tray, and sat in her usual chair. Only by sheer force of will did she not betray herself by glancing at the book of *Robinson Crusoe*. They had been very close to finishing.

She set down the tray and picked up the first of the notes, layered heavily in scent, and began to read. Her voice lowered to a halt halfway through. "My lord, this is highly personal. Perhaps you would like to read the rest of it yourself?"

His gold eyes had been fixed on her face as usual. Outside the windows, clouds covered the skies and candles had been lit throughout the room as a result, the gentle glow highlighting the angle of his cheekbone, the ridge of his jaw. The sensual curve of his mouth. "No, I like hearing your voice. It soothes me."

"As you wish." Camille took a deep breath, her face coloring as she read an intimate and detailed account of all of Lord Hawkes's attributes. From his flowing white hair with the unusual waves at temple and brow, to his faceted golden brown eyes, to the width of his shoulders and the curve of his... bottom. Guesses could only be dreamt of as to the breadth of his member, but the writer managed to hazard a description in glowing detail. Of its size and strength and feel. And to please quench this longing that kept the lady awake at night, thinking of him, aching for him, imagining them together and how he would touch her...

At last, Camille read the flowing signature at the bottom of the letter. She could not speak, could not look at him for embarrassment. What this lady described did not resemble what she remembered of the sexual act. Indeed, it appeared to be an entirely different portrayal than she might ever have thought.

"How shall I answer, Camille?" His deep voice soothed, while the sound of her name excited.

"Firmly, my lord."

"Firmly?"

"Indeed. But gently. For she must be discouraged without offending her. She is a great lady at court."

"I see. Then I suppose I shall not take her up on her offer?"

"No, my lord."

"Why not?"

"I..." Camille did not know. But the thought of her lord in bed with this woman made her want to scream.

"Then you shall have to devise an appropriate reply. My writing box is over there, with quill and ink. Read it to me when you are finished."

And with those words he closed his eyes, and she did as he asked, only the sound of his deep breathing accompanying the scratch of her quill across paper.

When she read her reply, he pronounced it satisfactory, and bade her read another of the missives.

Camille sighed. The next note was of a more flowery nature, speaking of moonlight and stolen kisses and the meeting of eyes across the room. When she reached the signature, she recognized the name of the young lady of the court.

"You should dissuade her in a fatherly manner, my lord."

He opened one dazzling eye. "I am not so old."

"She is very, very young."

"I see. Write the reply."

After Camille read and responded to several more letters, Augusta entered the room, built up the fire, and brought them hot tea and a portion of the iced cakes Camille had fetched from the kitchens for the ladies.

Camille breathed a sigh of relief. Each letter made her feel hotter and hotter, as the thought of one of these women in his lordship's arms set a blaze inside of her, until she finally recognized the emotion.

Jealousy. For the attentions of a *man*.

She set aside the letters and picked up a cup and saucer, the china so delicate it looked nearly transparent. She bent forward to place the cup against his mouth.

"You are an excellent nursemaid, but I think I can manage on my own this time," said his lordship. "Please just fetch me some more pillows to prop me up. This way we can sup together."

Camille did as he asked, pushing her chair closer to the bed, the tray between them. She sipped her tea, watching him do the same, the way his throat moved as he swallowed, admiring the breadth of his chest in much the same fashion as the ladies in their letters. It felt peculiar to view a man so differently.

"You are not eating, Camille."

"Slaves are not often given such sweets, my lord."

"Then it is high time you had them."

Camille picked up a cake. Not a partial crumb of one, or the day-old remains that filtered back to the kitchens. But a freshly baked, sweetly delicious, mouth-watering confection. It tasted like a bit of heaven.

She did not hesitate when Lord Hawkes urged her to eat another.

"So, am I to reject all of my admirers?"

Camille froze in the act of choosing another treat. "I thought that was your wish, my lord."

"And it seems to be yours, as well. I detected a certain… enthusiasm in your replies. Am I wrong?"

"You did not seem interested in anyone—"

"But you," he finished.

"Because you dreamt of me."

"Yes."

"I fear your dreams, my lord."

"As did I. Until they sent me you."

Camille wondered who had sent him these dreams, for his words indicated he knew. She did not have the time to ask, because he reached out and touched her hand.

She knew snow swirled outside the palace windows. She knew Augusta had stoked the fire high to ward off the winter chill. But suddenly she sat in a meadow of wildflowers, surrounded by apple trees in full glorious bloom. White petals fluttered down around them, blossoms filling the air above her. Bees buzzed about fallen fruit, the ripe sweet scent filling her nose.

Without intending to, Camille curled her fingers around his lordship's.

He still sat opposite her, minus bedding and pillows, his legs clad in loose breeches and his chest still bare, his skin glowing in the sunshine. His eyelids drooped lazily beneath his light brown brows, the golden color of his irises near yellow in the light.

"Your illusions are improving, my lord."

His lips curled. "My magic is too erratic. It seems to respond only to my strongest emotions. And for *some* reason, my strongest emotions all center around you."

Camille smiled. Truly smiled at him for the first time. Her memories of abuse suddenly faded to the back of her mind, as if they had happened to an entirely different person. She could picture only the visions of courtly love his letters invoked.

He caught his breath for a moment, held her gaze with his eyes, as if he sought to discover the truth of her heart in that bold look. When he leaned forward, Camille did not pull away. She did not have to fight the urge to do so. Faith, she found herself leaning toward him, meeting him halfway.

A gentle wind rustled in the apple blossoms and blew their sweet scent about them even stronger.

She could see her reflection in his eyes.

And then she closed hers, for he came so close she could no longer focus on his handsome face. On his dark brows and thick lashes, on the smooth sweep of his nose or the bottom curve of his mouth. She could not see his beauty.

But she felt it.

Six

AT FIRST SHE COULD NOT BE SURE HIS MOUTH HAD EVEN touched hers, for it felt as gentle as if one of the petals dancing on the wind had alighted on her lips. And then she felt a light pressure, a warmth that spread through her entire body.

And then a withdrawal.

"Camille," he whispered. "I would not do anything you do not wish for. I—"

She leaned forward and silenced him with another kiss. A kiss. She had never had one before. Oh, they tried, when she had been that other person. But most of the soldiers had not bothered, and when they did, she turned her face aside, a defiant gesture to control the situation in the only way she could.

But this… this warm touch of mouth upon mouth, this quiet exchange of tenderness, made her almost want to weep. Made her understand the letters she had read to him this eve. Letters of a different sort of passion.

Lord Hawkes groaned and she felt his hand in her hair, his mouth press harder against hers, as if her silent permission released a wellspring of desire within him.

He angled her head, bringing their mouths closer, until she could taste the salty-sweetness of him.

His tongue swept across her lips, and she opened her mouth, granted him access, bringing them closer together. She still held his hand with hers, but the other sought the thickness of his hair, ran fingers through the silky strands and gloried in the feel of it.

Then she traced a path down his neck, to the smooth skin of his chest she had always avoided looking at in fear… yes, in fear of this buried desire to touch it. He felt so warm and hard at the same time, the muscle beneath his skin as taut as if he held himself in check with rigid restraint. His heart beat fast, a pounding rhythm that seemed to echo her own.

He groaned, the sound vibrating against her lips, across her fingertips, which still explored his chest. Camille felt lost in a dream, a wonderful dream of desire and tenderness and of being truly wanted for what she could offer, and not what could be taken from her.

A woodpecker knocked against the trees.

"Lord Hawkes?"

Captain Talbot's voice made Camille start, as if a bucket of ice water had been dumped upon her head, waking her back to reality. She had kissed him! Willingly! What sort of enchantment had he put upon her to break down her defenses so? She abruptly pulled away from his lordship.

Sadness flared in his eyes when she did so.

And then irritation quickly replaced the emotion. "Damn it, Edward, what is the meaning of this interruption?"

The vision of the apple orchard surrounding them slowly faded, to be replaced by the gilt-paneled walls of Viscount Hawkes's bedroom, the frosted windows gloomy with dusk, the smoky smell of the roaring fire replacing the sweet scent of the blossoms.

Captain Talbot stood in the doorway, appearing not the least bit discomfited. "You told me to report to you immediately upon the completion of my task."

"Ah, yes." Lord Hawkes ran a hand through his pale hair, collapsed back on his pillows. "Did you have to kill him?"

Talbot shifted his feet, this time looking a bit chagrined. "I'm afraid so, my lord. He would have done *me* the favor, otherwise."

"Outmanned, were you?"

"Devil take it. He was a *big* mean bastard."

Camille glanced from one man to another. "Who?"

Talbot looked affronted by her temerity.

Lord Hawkes just shrugged his shoulders.

"The fight in the courtyard this afternoon," whispered Camille. "You dealt with both of them... both of the men you rescued me from. And the slave master, as well. Do you not understand the danger you are putting yourself in on my behalf?"

"Don't look at me," said the captain. "I warned him."

"I would have personally taken care of that other bastard too," said his lordship when her gaze switched to him. "Except for this damn wound. I wanted retribution administered quickly, so there would be no doubt what it was for. *Whom* it was for."

Camille knew she should feel grateful. But instead, anger overcame her. "You will bring yourself to the attention of the Imperial Lord, and you do not want Roden's notice. He could destroy you with a flick of his scepter!"

Lord Hawkes reached out to her. She flinched away from his touch. "Do not worry. If anything should happen to me, my men have orders to protect you."

He thought she worried for herself. And he should have been right. But Camille realized her fear stemmed from some harm being done to him. Because of her. What had happened? What had this man done to her? Slaves could not afford to worry about anyone other than themselves. They did not last long, otherwise.

Camille abruptly stood, swayed a moment, before clenching her hands into fists. "If you will excuse me, Lord Hawkes. I am afraid I do not feel well."

He glanced at his captain. "Call the healer."

"No. It is not necessary. My head aches. A bit of rest is all I need." And Camille flew from the room, Captain Talbot barely swinging aside as she brushed past him through the doorway.

Camille went to bed, feigned sleep when Augusta entered the room, and waited.

When the palace felt quiet, she put on her borrowed dress and shoes, found a warm mantle in the wardrobe, and pulled the hood low over her head.

She quietly left the apartment, and this time took the servants' stairs upward, past the floor where the permanent court and the Imperial Lord resided, to the attic. She stood for a moment in the dust and darkness, gained her bearings, and crept across the timbers, the chill making her shiver. She had visited Grimor'ee along this path when she started to care for Rufus and

Laura, a more secretive way than the one to be had from the slaves' quarters.

Grimor'ee had told her of it.

When she opened the door to the roof, the cold took her breath away, but she resolutely crossed the narrow bridge to the dragon's tower, and found him waiting for her, eyes open and back covered with a light drifting of snow.

She had forgotten the sheer size of him. The illusion Lady Pembridge created for Roden had been miniscule by comparison. Even curled up with his wings tucked to his sides, and his tail wrapped about the lower half of him, he loomed like a snowcapped hill above her.

His eyes had been crafted rightly though, those golden orbs separated with lines like a pinwheel. And Lady Pembridge had done justice to his golden scales, for they shone even in the darkness of night with a light of their very own.

He opened his massive jaw and yawned, making Camille hesitate.

"Must we go through this every time?" he asked, his voice like the rumble of a waterfall laced with the hiss of steam from a kettle.

Camille shivered, despite her borrowed mantle and stockings and shoes. She could not stop her teeth from chattering. "I am not af-afraid of you. I am f-freezing."

"You humans are so delicate. It's a wonder you survive to adulthood." And with that, he breathed a stream of mist, and a fireplace appeared near his snout, a cozy settee with a down blanket atop it near the hearth.

Camille immediately dove for the seat, scrambled

under the blanket, with only her head appearing above it. With a breath of mist from his cavernous maw, Grimor'ee could create illusions almost as powerful as the elven lord himself. She had heard the dragons of the six other sovereignties had different powers associated with their elven lords: the black dragon of Firehame could breathe fire; the blue dragon of Dewhame, lightning; the green dragon of Verdanthame could breathe a mist that grew tangled briars and enormous trees. The silver dragon of Bladehame spat molten metal, the brown dragon of Terrahame emitted a roar that cracked the earth, and the violet dragon of Stonehame could turn anything to stone with his breath.

Camille decided she liked Grimor'ee's magic the best.

The dragon twitched a wing, shifting some snow off his back. "So, he has finally come for you."

She blinked. "What do you mean?"

"I feared he might be too late, but I saw him save you in the courtyard below." He sniffed, a whoosh of roaring air. "He is not bad with a sword, but his magic is pathetic."

First this mad talk of dreams, and now this. "How do you know of Viscount Hawkes?"

"Ah, my dear. We dragons are... attuned to the scepters, for lack of a better word—the human language is much more limited than the elven." His golden eyes seemed to twirl for a moment, making Camille dizzy. "This affinity for the scepters means we dragons know things others do not."

"Even more than the elven lords?"

"Bright girl. Yes, even *them*."

Camille scowled. She had grown used to the dragon and could anticipate that he would not answer, yet had to ask anyway. "Who sent him? He said he dreamt of me. Who would send him such dreams?"

"Ah, little human. So full of questions. I could tell you, but then you would not have the adventure of finding out for yourself now, would you?"

Fie. Just as she had suspected. "All right then, what *can* you tell me?"

"A more astute question would be: What can *you* tell *me*?"

Grimor'ee could answer one question with another for hours. Camille huffed a breath that the cold turned to white mist, and just gave up and answered him.

"Lord Hawkes is strange," she began, her gaze straying to the blazing fire. "It is as if he has known me his whole life, and yet I met him only a few days ago. And he will tell me only that he dreamt of me, and these visions brought him to save me. But why? I am just a slave, with not a speck of magical power, despite these odd eyes of mine."

"Did you ask him that question?" rumbled Grimor'ee.

Camille scowled. "He says it is complicated, and he would like to start things simply between us."

"I see. He is either very clever, or very much a fool. Events progress too quickly for him to indulge you."

She did not bother to ask him what events he alluded to. But this time, it was because she feared the answer. Feared she might play a small part in something on a much grander scale than... than the viscount's feelings for her.

Camille shook her head. How could a mere slave

be of such importance? No, there had to be something more to Lord Hawkes's interest in her.

And yet…

"I think…" she whispered to herself. "I do believe the viscount cares for me. And he is making me feel things… making me care for *him*." She raised her voice. "I fear Lord Hawkes has put a glamour upon me, or at the very least, is starting to infect me with his mad talk of love and faith and honor." Her hand crept to her lips. "But he has shown me there is a difference between lust and love, and now it has made the thought of a soldier's hands upon me even more unbearable. Yet I cannot stay with him much longer, either. He is a dangerous man." She raised her chin. "I had thought death would be preferable to becoming a slave again, but now… now I have discovered a new resolve."

"Ah." If he had not been a dragon, but a human, Camille would have thought that one word vibrated with intense curiosity. "You have a plan?"

"Yes. I shall escape Dreamhame Palace."

"And why do you think you shall succeed this time?"

Camille scowled. She had tried to escape several times over the years. She had always been caught. Had been lashed until she thought she would rather die than continue to suffer with the pain. She then decided to rise above the station of a slave, instead. But fate kept interfering with her plans. Perhaps this time she would be luckier. "You have heard of this half-breed, Dorian? That he has killed Mi'cal of the green scepter and taken over Verdanthame?"

"Yeeeesss." Was that sarcasm in his reply?

Camille ignored it. "The elven lords are gathering vast armies to march upon Verdanthame—"

"And Firehame."

"Indeed? I did not know they continue their war games for the king as well."

The dragon did not reply, and Camille suspected more to a unified invasion of Firehame than the usual game of "capture the king," who had become a mere trophy to the elven lords, an excuse for them to pit their human armies against one another for amusement. Firehame had held on to the king and his court far longer than any other sovereignty in history.

But these things were far beyond the concerns of a mere slave.

"Well," she continued, "there are men conscripted into Roden's army every day. So many that they cannot be kept track of properly. So would another be noticed when they march?"

Grimor'ee made a sharp grunting sound, like a knife smacked upon a stone. "So that is your plan? To disguise yourself like a man? Like the soldiers you so despise?"

"Why not? I should finally gain some advantage from my knowledge of them. And the army will be crossing several sovereignties. I can choose which one to run to."

"If they don't shoot you for desertion first—no, do not make that human face at me. I think your plan might actually work, even though a soldier is as much a slave to the elven lords as you. But it requires you to use a sword. And at least be able to fire a pistol without it flying from your hand."

Camille colored. He had been watching closely the night Lord Hawkes saved her. "I know. It shall be easy to acquire a uniform, I think. But it takes years to learn to wield a blade, and I do not know how I will manage to acquire a pistol. They are too dear."

The dragon seemed to consider a moment, his tail rising to swish against the night sky, sending the falling snow into a frenzy of movement. "Have you asked your rescuer?"

"Lord Hawkes? But why would he...?" And yet, perhaps he would. He might be willing to teach her, since he seemed so concerned with her safety. He could not always be at her side to protect her. "Why, Grimor'ee, that is a famous idea! And here I have thought you would never help me."

His head slumped down upon the ground. "I have aided you as much as I can, within the limitations set upon me."

"By whom?"

He surprised her again by answering.

"By the enchantment set upon me long ago by the elven lords."

"I see." But she did not... not truly. His sadness touched her, and she rose from the settee to put her arm about his cold snout.

Camille tried to smile. "You know, you could make this all so easy for me if you would just fly me far away from here." The mere thought of actually clambering onto his back and flying so high above the earth made her cringe, but she would do it, to escape this life. And she did not want him to think she feared it.

"You would likely just fall off," he grumbled.

"I have faith you could maneuver to catch me. I have seen you dance with the stars."

He sighed, a great heave that shuddered the stones of the tower and wrenched his snout from her arms. "You cannot escape your destiny so easily, lady."

Camille could not suppress a shiver, and felt tempted to go back to the fire. But she might fall asleep—she could feel the heaviness of her eyes, and could not risk being caught by the elven lord with Grimor'ee, his own dragon.

She walked back to the settee, picked up the blanket, and wrapped it about her shoulders. It would not last beyond Grimor'ee's sight unless he spelled it to, and she doubted he would bother. But it would see her across the cold bridge and into the attic.

"I will come again soon," she said over her shoulder.

Grimor'ee did not answer, his gaze fixed upon the star-studded sky.

Over the next few days Viscount Hawkes requested her presence in his rooms to read to him, until she became quite comfortable with being near him. Oddly enough, familiarity did not lessen the excitement she always felt with him, and she grew accustomed to that emotion. Indeed, she began to welcome it, for it made her feel a peculiar sort of anticipation that left her deflated when she left him.

She tried not to think about the kiss they had shared.

Camille read *The Unfortunate Traveler* by Thomas Nashe, recounting the horrifying adventures of a lowly page, which held so many similarities to her own life that she often found herself scowling as she read.

"Well," she muttered upon finishing it, "at least this book is based upon reality."

"Ah," replied his lordship, amber eyes glittering, "then you do believe stories may hold some truths."

"I suppose so."

Camille sat in her usual chair next to his bedside while he lounged atop his cushions. His arm had healed enough so that he managed to put some clothing on his upper body, which she felt extremely grateful for.

Lord Hawkes had not attempted to touch her again, much less to kiss her. He pretended nothing had happened between them, but she often felt him studying her intently.

Which made Camille feel alternately relieved and frustrated. And shy and insecure about her new position in his household.

But she found the courage to at least ask to read a book of her preference, and he allowed that Shakespeare's comedy of *Much Ado About Nothing* would be a welcome contrast to *The Unfortunate Traveler*. Camille finally had the opportunity to finish the play, and she could not help the smile that stayed on her lips throughout the reading of it.

They were not interrupted except for mealtimes, and once when the healer came to his apartments and insisted she check on her patient. Lord Hawkes commanded that Camille leave the room while the healer looked him over, and he did not say a word regarding his health when she returned. Instead, he bade her read an epic poem titled *The Faerie Queen*, which involved knights and virtues and sorcery and love and betrayal. It all seemed so very real to Camille, who found herself praying for the knights to complete their quests, and more surprisingly, sympathizing with their love stories. Hoping true love would win. Especially when the poor squire, Timias, began to waste away for love of his beautiful Belphoebe.

"It's about time," she muttered when Belphoebe finally returned to Timias.

She looked up from the book when Lord Hawkes shifted on the bed, his injury now appearing not to bother him in the least. His pale hair spread about his pillows like a wavy halo, his strong arms folded across his chest, his handsome mouth curled into a smile. Sunshine flooded the room for a change today, dust motes sparkling in the rectangular beams of light.

Camille could not forget the delight of the warm apple orchard and suppressed a sigh.

His lordship eyed her closely, tossed back the bedding, and rose in one lithe movement. "I think we both need to get out of this stuffy chamber."

"Are you sure you are well enough?"

"The healer suggested it, and damn if I will cross that little old woman." He strapped on his sword belt, pulled on his boots and coat, and grasped her hand, pulling her from the chair and tugging her out into the withdrawing room before she could say another word.

"Augusta," he commanded. "Fetch Camille some outerwear."

The maid appeared from the dining room, a dirty cloth over her arm, and quickly did as her master instructed.

He tapped an impatient foot while Camille pulled on boots, gloves, and a thick cloak that looked new enough to be Augusta's best.

Before she knew it, they had left the apartments, strolling arm in arm down the corridors, Lord Hawkes ignoring the odd looks thrown their way from gentry and servant alike. He took the main stairs as if he didn't care a whit that he would set tongues wagging, but when they reached the ground floor, he entered an empty hallway and left the palace out of a side door Camille wasn't familiar with.

She blinked at the glare of sunshine on snow, and took a deep breath of the crisp air. They stood in an enclosure of ice statues shaped in the forms of fairies and tiny gnomes and hobgoblins with mischievous smiles. Camille wondered which courtier had crafted the charming beings, for they contrasted strongly with Dreamhame's usual decor, but Lord Hawkes pulled her so quickly across the space she focused her attention on her footing.

The sun had packed the snow so they did not fall through the crust, but it also made the surface slippery enough that only her elven grace prevented her from falling. She wished she had stuffed the toes of Augusta's boots, for they wobbled on her feet.

Lord Hawkes opened a gate and stepped through and halted, a slow grin spreading across his face. Camille followed his gaze to a steep hill where several children clustered, sliding down the packed surface on sleds, only to trudge up it again and repeat the process.

He led her toward the sound of their laughter.

"The stories have changed you, Camille."

It took her a moment to pick up his thoughts, and then she shook her head. Nay, *he* had changed her with his magic.

"You professed not to believe in love," he pressed. "But now I think you feel sorry for Timias and annoyed with Belphoebe."

"It is almost as if the writer has cast a spell upon me," she admitted. "Sometimes the characters in your books seem more real to me than you and I. Are the books enchanted?"

He threw back his head and laughed. He had an easy laugh, deep and resonant. She liked it.

"Nay, they are not. Nor have I cast any glamour upon you."

She started and looked up from her boots. "Have you not?"

"Ha. I was correct. You suspect I have cast some spell upon you."

"Your magic seems strong enough."

He grimaced. "I have managed only two decent illusions since arriving at Dreamhame Palace, although I assure you I have tried—to work an illusion, that is. A glamour is a much more difficult task, I assure you."

"Is it?"

"Indeed." His eyes gazed intently into hers, and he lowered his voice to a husky whisper. She barely heard his words over the squeals of the children. "Besides, why would I use glamour to make you fall in love with me? It would not be real."

"And you wish it to be real? But why?"

"When someone is in love with another, Camille,

they would like for that love to be returned. Would they not?"

Camille took a breath. She did not know if her next words were mixed with an odd sort of hope. "But you do not need it to bed me. You have only to order it to make it so."

He came to an abrupt stop. An errant breeze made his hair fly over his cheeks, curl artfully across his forehead. Drat the man. How could she want to be close to him, and run away from him, all at the same time?

"Is that what you think? That I wish only to bed you?"

"Perhaps you like your women willing. Perhaps all of your actions are designed to make sure I do not resist you the next time."

"The next time."

"The next time... you kiss me."

He arched a pale brown brow at her. "I do not recall you resisting the first time."

"You put a glamour upon me."

"Which I have just assured you that I did not. That I cannot. Egads, you are a stubborn woman, Camille."

He dropped her hand and walked away from her, approaching the cluster of children, bending down to speak with one of the older boys before reaching his hand into his pocket. He turned and strode back toward her, dragging a sled behind him.

She frowned. "What are you doing?"

"Taking you sledding."

"We are not children."

He shrugged, his shoulders appearing broader in his greatcoat. "And yet I think we have both missed out on our childhood... you even more than I."

Camille shifted her gaze to the children, who had halted their play to watch them with curious eyes. "We are liable to break our necks."

He laughed. "Then we shall have a jolly good time doing it. Here, you get on first, and I'll sit behind you."

The contraption did not look big enough to hold them both. And the skinny runners would surely sink in the snow from their combined weight. She had often watched Rufus and Laura go sledding, but having no experience with it as a child, it had never occurred to her to join them.

She gave Lord Hawkes an entreating glance. His golden eyes sparkled with determination. Camille sighed and clambered onto the small platform, scooching up to the front as close as she could, the lower half of her legs hanging over the front of it. He pulled her toward the edge of the hill, and the drop looked much steeper from this new vantage point.

He settled behind her and draped his legs on either side of her, anchoring them against the wooden steering bar. She flushed as all that male warmth and scent surrounded her, and realized she liked the sensation. The muscles in his arms bunched as he pushed them toward the precipice, and Camille clutched his thighs. She felt him suck in a breath.

"My lord," said the boy who had given them the sled, "with all that weight upon it, you are likely to go pretty fa—"

Lord Hawkes gave one mighty heave and threw them over the brink, but Camille could guess the last word. They slid down the hill with a whoosh of cold wind, the scenery blurring around them, the runners barely touching the snow. Camille's stomach flew up into her throat, and she would have screamed if she had been able to.

The children had built a stop of sorts, a mound of snow designed to keep their sleds from continuing their slide across the meadow of snow at the base of the hill. Their sled hit it with a spray of snow, not slowing their progress a whit. Instead, their sled went up the mound and launched into the air, sending them flying for a few, brief, glorious moments.

And then they hit the ground.

Camille parted from the sled and rolled a few feet, landing on her back, the world tilting crazily for a moment.

"Camille?" said Lord Hawkes. "Are you all right?"

"I—I think so."

His beautiful face appeared above hers, and he half-lay over her, concern and delight warring across his features. "Are you sure? That was a bloody fast ride!"

She nodded, and he brushed some snow from her cheeks while she felt her lips curl into a smile. "It was... it was... exhilarating. But what of your injury?"

"The healer must have been right about the fresh air. Not a twinge."

"Then let's do it again."

"Of course." He blinked at her. "You look so lovely right now. I—I'm sorry, my dear."

"For what?"

"For calling you stubborn. I would rather think you had to be, to survive all you have been through. Sometimes I forget you do not know me as I know you. Sometimes I think I shall waste away from want like poor Timias."

Camille searched his face. She could not bear the thought of his lordship wasting away. Could she?

"How does one explain oneself," he continued, "when they cannot be sure of their own worth?" He frowned, his pale hair curving about his angled cheekbones, his gaze downcast, those thick, dark lashes shadowing his brilliant eyes. "We are not so different, my dearest Camille. For I have also been a slave most of my life."

She raised a brow. She could not help it. "A slave to your social position, perhaps? To the demands of your tenants, or the time you must spend relieving the boredom of the idleness of a gentleman?"

He glanced up, and the expression in his eyes made her ashamed of her words, and held her transfixed, even as the coldness of her snowy bed crept through her cloak. "Perhaps G—my father, or my mother, could explain my circumstances to you. For many years, starting as a young lad, I was afflicted by a... condition. One that set me apart from others—caused me to have fits, until I came to understand what brought them on."

"Your dreams," breathed Camille.

"Again, my dear, your wits astound me. Yes, my dreams. Dreams of blood and fire and death. Voices in my head that paralyzed me, that caused me to black out at times. That made my life a living hell of solitude. I retreated from the world, and in so doing became somewhat of a scholar, absorbed in my books and poetry."

Camille nodded. Perhaps this was why he had come to court only once for his testing and not returned since—if she remembered rightly the rumors Lady Pembridge once mentioned of the Hawkes family.

"The voices retreated for a while, but…" He shook his head. "Sometimes I fear I am just as much a slave as you."

She could swear he showed her his heart with the look in his golden eyes.

"But my dreams of you saved me, Camille. You stood among all the death and chaos in a center of calm, like an angel in a gown of white, offering me hope in a way I still do not understand. But I recognized the need in your eyes, for it matched my own, and I knew I must save you. And it filled me with purpose. To find you. To protect you."

Camille knew he meant every single word. She thought of his poetry and his stories and his sense of honor and bravery, and knew he believed in them as well.

And somehow, he had made her believe in them, too. Had made her believe in *him*.

"But we do not truly know one another, my lord."

"Do we not?" He cocked his head. "I feel as if I have known you forever, so it is easy for me to forget you met me only days ago." He shifted with a crunch of snow, his voice suddenly deepening. "Damn, I wish we had more time… but I have learned patience the hard way. And you are more valuable than anyone may guess."

Camille narrowed her eyes. All his talk of loving and protecting her hid a deeper motive. But before she could ask him what he meant, he lowered his head, sweeping his mouth across hers, the firm warm feel of it chasing away her thoughts.

His kiss started to deepen when the crunch of boots, and the sudden shout of a young boy, made him pull away from her.

"See? I told you they weren't dead." The voice held a note of disappointment.

"Aww, they're just kissing," whined another. "Let's go back."

Lord Hawkes sat up and brushed snow from his sleeves. Camille did the same, glancing back at the hill. They had landed several feet beyond the mound of snow.

"Bet you never saw anyone go that fast," boasted his lordship.

The boys turned back around, the taller one shrugging. "Never saw anyone land a sled like that before." A snicker. "But I've gone faster."

Lord Hawkes stood and helped Camille to her feet, his gaze going to the sled. "It appears to be in one piece."

She smiled. "'Tis a miracle, I'm sure."

He echoed her grin. "Shall we take the challenge, my lady?"

"Yes, let's. Will it be as fun the second time?"

He grasped her hand. "I will avoid the mound this time, so I promise we will not have such a rough landing."

The boys looked a bit disappointed by this statement, but they turned and whooped nevertheless, shouting out to their fellows about the impending race.

Camille followed Lord Hawkes up the hill, basking

in the pleasure of his company. In the anticipation of the race. In the memory of the sheer fun of that wild ride. And then wondered what on earth had come over her. The man always stirred up emotions within her that she thought she could never possess. She pushed them back down where they belonged. She would be a fool to trust him so easily. Wouldn't she? Surely he had cast some sort of enchantment upon her, to make her feel the way she did at this very moment. Her sense of self-preservation warred with the fragile sense of trust he had begun to instill in her.

The boys patiently waited while Camille settled on the sled again. A small girl with freckles on her nose held a red kerchief in the air while the contestants maneuvered the noses of their sleds to the very brink of the drop. More than half the children lined up with them.

"This is quite a competition," said his lordship while he settled closely behind her, and suddenly the scene changed. A throng of spectators appeared around them in balconies of colored snow, waving banners and cheering. The young girl's kerchief changed into a brilliant red flag, and the slope of the hill now sported lines of red to separate the sled lanes, each with a grand finish line at the bottom with golden arches and crowns of roses.

The children gaped at the illusion, which wavered slightly yet appeared quite vivid. Camille could not resist testing him yet again. "It is probably a good thing you cannot cast a glamour upon me, Lord Hawkes."

He bunched his shoulders and pushed them forward as the girl lowered the flag with a snap. "And why is that?"

"Imperial Lord Roden would kill you for having such strong magic."

He appeared to choke a bit, but she couldn't be sure as they swept down the hill again, and the rush of their slide made her squeal with excitement. They won the race, Lord Hawkes telling the children they had done a fine job, and that surely one of them would win the next.

Or the next.

Until the children finally gave up and went home, and the illusory stadium disappeared. But Camille and Lord Hawkes continued to sled down the hill in the gathering twilight, their laughter ringing out across the empty meadow.

❧

Camille awoke the next morning to an imperious rap upon her door. She glanced over at Augusta's bed, but the maid had already risen. The other girl never woke her, as if she had strict instructions not to disturb Camille. And Camille had the luxury of sleeping late most every day, something she never had before and certainly needed, what with her late-night visits to Grimor'ee.

The dragon continued to be obstinately unhelpful in her requests for help in her rescue plans, and Camille had not found an opportunity to see Molly during the day to pursue them further. Viscount Hawkes kept her by his side every day, and she would not visit Molly at night, when the soldiers came to the slave quarters.

This time her door shook a bit from the pounding.

Camille scrambled out of bed, gathered a shawl about her shoulders, and opened it.

It took her a moment to recognize the elegant lady who stood before her. "Lady Hensby?"

"Regretfully, yes." The lady stepped aside and ushered in two servants and Augusta, each of them holding piles of garments in their arms. They carefully laid out each piece upon both of the girls' beds.

Camille could only gape at the elegant dresses of pale lavender silk, creamy satin, burgundy velvet.

"Well, girl," said Lady Hensby, tapping a diamond-buckled shoe against the floor, "Get undressed and let me see if I guessed correctly. I pride myself on my eye for figures, you see."

"Figures?"

"Quite." The lady pursed her rouged lips for a moment, and then continued, "I do not understand what his lordship sees in you. By my estimation, you possess a stick of a figure." She patted a laced-gloved hand upon her generous bosom. "Clever of you though, to deny him your favors for so long. But I do wish you would get along with it. There are several of us ladies waiting, you know."

Camille scowled. "I do not know what you mean."

"La! Of course not. After being a slave for your entire life, I am sure you are quite innocent of what goes on between a man and a woman."

Camille eyed the lady and the door, calculating her chances of dashing past the woman.

"Oh, how droll." Lady Hensby rolled her blue eyes. They did not have the facets of an elven, but she surely possessed a healthy degree of the blood. For the skin of her face lacked any imperfection whatsoever, and her features looked so even she surpassed beauty and missed the realm of ethereal gorgeousness of the elven only by a mere fraction. "Do not tell me you are shy about undressing? Very well then, I shall leave the room, but you have my strictest instruction to let your maid dress you quickly, so I can judge the artistry of my wardrobe selection."

"Augusta is not my—"

The lady spun in a swirl of silk, the scent of roses wafting behind her, and left the room with her two servants.

"What is happening?" demanded Camille.

Augusta brushed back a straggling lock of her brown hair. "It is Viscount Hawkes. He ordered you a complete wardrobe." She eyed the clothing heaped across the beds with a bit of envy.

"Well, I do not want it."

"Lud, hush! Lady Hensby might hear you and be offended. Do you have any idea of her position in the court?"

Thanks to Lady Pembridge, Camille most assuredly did. She began to undress.

"Oh, try on this one," said Augusta, choosing a soft linen chemise heavily embroidered with white roses. "And the matching stays. How lovely."

"She does have good taste," agreed Camille with a grimace. "And I will show her their fit, but I cannot wear them."

Augusta handed her the chemise. "Why on Elfhame not?"

Camille held the linen in her hand for a moment, marveling at its softness before slipping it over her head, the material sliding down her body with a whisper like a rippling sigh. "Because I shall look like his mistress."

The other girl paused in the act of wrapping the stays around Camille's torso. "Well, aren't you?"

"Certainly not!"

"Lud, everyone thinks you are, so what's the difference?"

She had a point. Camille doubted if Augusta would believe she did nothing more behind closed doors than read to Viscount Hawkes, especially given some of the conversations the maid had overheard. And a mistress stood quite a notch above a servant on the social scale. No soldier would dare to touch her. Faith, she would even be allowed into the court withdrawing rooms as a little bit less than an equal.

How astonishing.

She wished she could believe his lordship had ordered this new wardrobe just to ensure her safety. Fie! Did he truly think her so shallow that he could buy her into his bed with silk and lace? A frisson of anger replaced Camille's confusion, and she immediately felt much better. Some of the accessories in the wardrobe would fetch a nice price, and allow her to escape sooner.

She realized Lord Hawkes had distracted her from her plans for escape. She must make more of an effort. But she enjoyed their time together, the books and conversation they shared. She must resist this glamour he had cast over her and continue with her plans in earnest.

But she held no magic of her own to counter his enchantment, and as she donned the gown Augusta handed her, a creamy satin with a pattern of pale pink roses, her chin unconsciously lifted. She felt like a lady, for although the gown had a ridiculously large oblong hoop beneath it, it was in modest taste and impeccable design. Her satin stockings made it easy to slide into the pink satin shoes, and the silk scarf wrapped about her shoulders matched the pinner Augusta put upon her head after doing up her hair. The lace lappets attached to the cap had tiny pink roses sewn onto them, and they trailed about her shoulders like a miniature garden.

Viscount Hawkes made her an equal with clothing. But when Camille glanced at herself in the mirror, the safety the costume granted her no longer seemed so important.

She could think only about the look on his face when he saw her.

Lady Hensby had apparently grown impatient, and another sharp rap on the door preceded her entry.

She folded her arms. "Faith, I have an accurate eye. Tall and thin, with a tiny bosom. Still…" She let loose an elaborate sigh. "I am too skilled, and I fear it may be several months instead of weeks before he tires of you."

Camille raised her chin.

Lady Hensby scowled. "He said he wants to see you right away. Something about his correspondence. La! But I have patience, my dear. And with this little favor, I shall be first in line."

She left the apartments as abruptly as she entered them, trailing her servants and perfume behind her.

"Dear heaven," said Augusta.

"Quite. She spares no illusions, does she?"

"When have those of the court ever done so? You had best go to his lordship." She lowered her voice. "You do look lovely, Camille. Enjoy it while you can. If you can."

Augusta surprised her yet again. The other woman sensed more than she let on.

Camille picked up her satin skirts and carefully walked to his lordship's room, unaccustomed to balancing in such high heels, the clack of them across the floor a perfect accompaniment to her pounding heart.

How dare he try to buy her!

What would he say when he saw her?

Viscount Hawkes sat in a leather chair. He held in his lap a silver tray of invitations, frowning as he rifled through the pile of them. He had braided the hair at the sides of his face, with the plaits pulled backward and gathered behind his head, making his cheekbones stand out even more prominently. He wore black velvet from head to toe, with naught but a golden cravat about his neck to relieve the color. And bring out the golden sparkle within his eyes as he looked up at her standing in the doorway.

Time suspended for a moment as they gazed at one another, something crackling between them that pulled Camille into the room toward him, her hoops barely clearing the door frame.

Seven

DRYSTAN BLINKED AT THE VISION BEFORE HIM, UNCER-
tain for a moment of the reality of the woman. She
looked exactly as she had in his dreams. He took a
deep breath, the scent of her overwhelming his senses,
and realized the descendant of the white witch did
indeed stand before him.

He held out his hand to her. "You look beautiful."

Her arm rose, as if to take what he offered. But those
multicolored eyes suddenly clouded, and she stopped
advancing toward him. Drystan tried not to scowl.

"Do I look the part?" she demanded.

"What do you mean?"

"For the role of your mistress. Surely that's why
you bought me this new wardrobe."

She confounded him at every turn. Drystan knew
she wanted him, her kisses confirmed it more than her
words ever could. But still she held herself aloof from
him. What would it take to tear down those walls she
had built around her heart?

And yet, he knew those very walls had allowed
her to survive her years of abuse. The woman of his

dreams was nothing compared to the reality of her. Over the past few days he had come to understand her inner strength, and often glimpsed the core of softness that lay buried deep within her. Captain Talbot's discreet inquiries on his behalf revealed the harshness of the life she had led, so like his own, and yet so very different.

That she stood so defiantly before him made his admiration for her soar to new heights.

"Would it be so terrible to allow me to love you?"

She gasped.

Drystan rose, scattering the tray of invitations onto the floor with nary a care. He closed the distance between them, until he fancied he could feel the beat of her heart in time with his own.

"I don't understand," she whispered, tilting her head to look up at him.

Drystan drew a ragged breath. "What have I not made clear?"

"Who sent you the dreams of me? And why?"

She had every right to be suspicious of his motives, and deserved to be told it all. But Drystan still feared to tell her. Feared she would not believe that his only purpose in coming had been for her. Unless and until he managed to make her fall in love with him first.

He could not allow himself to doubt she ever would.

"You have asked me for nothing," he finally said, changing the subject. "I thought you would be pleased with the clothes."

"I—" Her eyes suddenly became calculating, and Drystan wondered what went through that beautiful head.

"I am sorry if I seem ungrateful. I should be thanking you for your generosity instead."

Drystan frowned. Perhaps she should, but he knew her too well. "But?"

"Oh." She gave him an artful smile, something he had *not* known she might be capable of. "It is just that if you had asked me…"

"Yes?" Drat his heart. He could not suppress his eagerness to find out a way to please her. "There is something you would desire even more?"

She nodded, a lovely flush to her delicate cheeks.

"Then name it, and it shall be yours, my lady."

"You might think it rather odd…"

"Camille!"

"I would like a sword," she blurted. "And a pistol. And I would like to learn how to use them. To defend myself."

Drystan could have smacked himself over the head. Of course she would care little for the fripperies of a normal woman. She had not led a normal life. Survival had been her only goal for so long, he should have realized she would not abandon it so easily. Especially when she could not trust in his protection.

He would change her mind on that. But in the meantime…

"Of course you shall have a sword. And it must be enchanted, to allow you to wield it without too much training. And a pistol, yes. They defy elven magic for enchantment, as do so many of our human inventions, so you will need extensive training in the use of it."

"Your man, Arthur, might be willing to teach—"

"I shall see to it myself," he interrupted.

She gazed at him, and damn if he still didn't see fear in those amazing eyes. Perhaps she did not trust him fully yet, but he had given her no reason to fear him.

He brushed the back of his hand across her cheek. Ah, Gods. Softer than a rose petal. "You have been so brave your entire life, Camille. And yet you fear me. Why?"

Drystan suddenly smelled the sweet scent of apples. He did not know why that vision had sprung to his mind when he thought to first kiss her days ago. He supposed the orchard came from some long-ago memory as a lad. The surroundings just seemed to fit his desire for Camille.

She backed away from him, a rustle of lace and silk. "I fear the glamour you have put upon me, my lord—despite your denials to the contrary. My desire for a man died years ago, and yet your magic brings these unbidden feelings within me."

Her honesty shook him to the core. And her words made such a joyful hope flare within his heart. The pitiable amount of magic he seemed to possess could not cast such a glamour over her, even if he tried. And he had not tried. So these feelings she feared... ah, those came from no unnatural source. It could only be her true heart opening to him. His courtship had not been in vain.

He needed only to figure out a way to combat her fear of wanting him.

"Lord Hawkes," said Captain Talbot, suddenly appearing at the door.

"Damn it, Edward, I told you to never interrupt—"

"Unless it is urgent. This is urgent, my lord."

"What is it?"

"A messenger from Imperial Lord Roden. Err, he is more harmless than he looks," he warned.

Captain Talbot stepped aside. Camille started, and Drystan unconsciously put his body between her and what now stood in the doorway.

A large golden snake. With a fat sinuous body risen to rival a man's height, black glossy eyes staring unwaveringly at him. A black tongue flicked out to test the air. "You have been absssent from court for too long," said the thing. "So I have sssent my messenger to order you to come."

And after speaking those few words, the snake slowly dissolved into thousands of sparkling golden flecks.

Talbot reappeared in the doorway, a smile on his face. "Scared me at first, let me tell you. But Augusta said it's a common enough messenger the elven lord uses when sending a polite invitation."

"I wonder what he sends with an impolite one? No, never mind. And stop laughing, Edward. You have an odd sense of humor."

Captain Talbot shrugged. "It has managed to keep me sane. Will you go?"

"How can I not? To ignore such a summons will only make him suspicious, and it seems I can no longer use my injury as an excuse." Actually, he had used it only as a ruse to spend time with Camille.

"I would go with you, my lord."

"Can't resist some more fun, Captain?"

"It appears not."

Camille suddenly scrambled from behind Drystan,

her new skirts almost tripping her up. "You cannot go, my lord!"

Talbot sighed. "I will await you in the hall." And disappeared from the bedroom doorway.

Drystan looked down at Camille's pale face. She had never looked so frightened before, even when she had been faced with a pistol, several wraiths, or the prospect of his naked chest. "Do not worry, Camille. It is high time I met with the elven lord."

"But you do not understand. Since the overthrow of Verdanthame, Roden has been suspicious of all half-breeds, especially those who possess magic. If he thinks you might be the slightest threat to him…"

"But I am not—"

"I have seen what you can do. I have felt the glamour you have cast upon me. I assure you, weaker mages have died for less."

"Camille, Camille." Drystan took her in his arms; he could no longer fight the urge to do so. He could not bear to see her in such distress. She trembled within his embrace, and he smoothed her silken back. "I assure you my magic is no threat to the elven lord."

And damn if that apple orchard did not suddenly spring up around them again. Drystan could smell the ripe scent of apples warmed by the sun, feel the slight breeze that swished through the brilliant green of the grass now surrounding his boots.

"See?" she muttered, her forehead crinkling at the soothing scenery. "Only someone who possesses strong magic can create an illusion with such vividness."

"But only sometimes. I can rarely do this, and I doubt I shall be able to envision apple blossoms in the presence of the elven lord." Drystan did wonder about his erratic magic, and he admitted that although he appeared to have no control over it, he had taken a risk by staying in the palace longer than necessary with Camille. Although he could not regret it.

"Will you kiss me good-bye? Just in case, mind you."

"You cannot jest at a time like this."

"I do not jest, my love."

She caught her breath. Tears glistened in her eyes, and Drystan could only hope they were for him. And not from her fear of being abandoned to slavery once more.

"I told you," he murmured, lowering his head to hers. "My men have instructions to take care of you in the event of my death."

She made some sort of strangled sound in the back of her throat, and then threw her arms around him, pulling his face all the way to hers, covering his mouth with her sweet lips. He lost himself for a time in the feel of it. In the feel of the woman of his dreams.

When she broke away, her breath came in little pants. "Please don't go. I will do anything. Anything to make you stay."

Drystan straightened. Stepped away from her. His illusion faded once again, the world quickly turning back to the rather gloomy morning.

"That is not the way I would have you, Camille."

He walked stiffly to the door, glancing back at her small form still trembling in her new lace and satin.

"I cannot fault you for not believing me," he added, "but when I return, you will have proof that I do not have the power to cast any glamour upon you. You will be forced to acknowledge what you feel for me is real. Are you sure that is not what you truly fear?"

Her mouth opened as if in denial, but Drystan did not give her the opportunity to speak. He strode through the luxurious rooms and met Captain Talbot in the hall, the dark-haired warrior giving him a crooked grin as Drystan slammed the apartment door behind him.

"I would not have thought it possible, my lord. I do believe the lady actually cares for you."

"I never doubted it," replied Drystan, in no mood to reveal his insecurities to the other man. He spun to where his house guard had managed to hide within the shadow of a golden pillar. "Arthur."

The old soldier stepped forward.

"Do not let anyone enter or leave these rooms until I return."

"Aye, my lord."

Drystan walked down the hall, ignoring the tapestries of death and animated statues. Odd, what one could get used to. His captain followed him in silence, his mouth still twisted in a half smile, his callused fingers caressing the hilt of his sword. They did not speak a word to each other until they descended to the ground floor, and heard the noise flowing through the massive doorway of the great room.

"It appears your summons has caused quite a stir, my lord."

"They probably think the elven lord will kill me."

The flecks in Talbot's gray eyes sparkled, the metal color a testament to his elven blood. "He'll have to get past my sword first."

Drystan appreciated his captain's bravado. But no mere sword could defeat an elven lord, not even one enchanted and wielded by one of the most expert swordsmen Bladehame had produced in some time.

"Stay behind me," he commanded as he stepped into the doorway. Silence slowly rolled across the gathered throng at his appearance. Drystan lowered his voice to a mutter. "If the worst happens, flee with Camille to Bristol. I have a ship waiting there to take her to Wales."

"Aye, my lord."

"Protect her with your life. She might be England's only hope."

Drystan strode boldly forward, looking neither left nor right, his eyes focused on the golden dais at the end of the great hall.

"You have discovered the birthmark, then?" whispered Captain Talbot.

Drystan would not admit that he had yet to find a birthmark on Camille's body, although he had surreptitiously looked. He regretted he had not had the chance to explore all of her soft skin, and now might not have the opportunity to be the one to find it and unravel its meaning. If the mark did indeed have a meaning.

But Camille's safety lay within her importance to the Rebellion. So he left Edward to wonder at the answer to his question as he neared the elven lord's throne.

From the corner of his eyes Drystan glimpsed the people of the court lining the sides of the hall like sentinels, the gay color of their clothing swirling together into one silk-and-satin garden. He recognized a few faces of the ladies he had met, but they avoided his gaze.

Not a propitious sign.

Drystan ignored the soaring columns that sported marble statues of creatures cavorting up and down the length of the supports. After glancing briefly upward at the nonexistent ceiling, the heights to infinity making his head spin, he ignored that illusion as well.

But he had difficulty ignoring the floor beneath his boots. *Things* moved under the transparent solid surface. Things with fins and jagged teeth and razor-sharp scales. Orbs that glowed, swimming forward with long tendrils. And once, the face of a woman smiled up at him, green hair the color of seaweed swirling about her face.

Drystan could hear Talbot breathing heavily behind him, and wondered if his captain still retained the smile upon his face. He kept his own gaze fixed upon the elven lord, the walk toward the dais seemingly longer than the room should allow.

Imperial Lord Roden wore enough golden thread in his clothing that he should not have been able to move. But when he shifted on his chair, the magical qualities of the fabric became apparent. The cloth flowed like water down his shoulders and arms, the glitter and gleam of it near making him glow. Despite the overcast morning Drystan had glimpsed through his window, a skylight above the dais shot down rays of golden light that surrounded the elven lord, and if possible, made him glow all the more.

All illusion, to be sure. But quite impressive.

Drystan finally neared the throne and swept Roden

a low bow. He looked to be in his midthirties, although in truth, Drystan knew the elven lord to be hundreds of years old, although no human could actually say his true age. Half-breeds did not inherit that longevity, although they kept their youth and vigor longer than the average man who lived to the same age.

"Ah," said Roden, his voice low and more musical than a song. "Viscount Hawkes has finally chosen to grace me with his presence."

"Forgive me for my tardiness, Your Most High. My injury prevented me from visiting you earlier."

"Hmm, yes, I heard about that. Such a fuss for a mere slave girl. But rumor has it that you've taken her as your mistress, so perhaps I can allow you the passions of youth as an excuse, although I'll be damned what you see in the girl. Those eyes of hers are repulsive, and she hasn't a whit of magic to improve her appearance."

Drystan flushed, then quickly buried his anger. He must appear as a fop to the elven lord, a simple young man with only pleasure to occupy his mind. And he did not want Roden's attention fixed upon Camille for any reason. "I have not been to court since a lad, Your Most High, and have forgotten the protocols."

Roden snorted. Elegantly. His handsome features froze into a mask of indifference, so at odds with his words. "You had little regard for them then, if I recall." He leaned forward in his chair, and for the first time, Drystan glimpsed the golden scepter.

He ignored the alien voice that suddenly whispered unintelligible words in his mind.

"You grew into a more handsome man than your

boyish features once suggested. Have your powers altered as well?"

Drystan lifted his chin. Ah, now, the elven lord did not waste any time getting to the point of the visit. And he could only marvel at the elven lord's keen memory, for Roden had met his younger brother years ago. He felt grateful the lapse of time allowed him his charade. "I have advanced little since my testing."

"Indeed? I have heard a story of demons in my kitchens."

"A childish illusion."

"Perhaps. But one with enough reality that the soldiers complained of the smell of brimstone for days." Roden continued to wear his mildly placating expression as he lifted the scepter and pointed it at Drystan.

The crowd gasped. Heels clacked as feet shifted, skirts swished, and a wave of perfume wafted over him. He had nearly forgotten the court. Indeed, he barely managed to acknowledge them now, for the scepter's whisper grew louder in his head. Although different in tone from the three that had invaded his dreams for so long, he recognized the sheer alien sound of it.

He had glimpsed the scepters at Carreg Cennen castle only once, before they had been buried beneath the stone. The golden scepter resembled them all except for the color. A round cylinder with a triangular pointed head, elven runes carved along the length of it. Nothing to suggest the deadly power it could wield.

But Drystan had never touched one.

Roden stood, and with that eerie elven grace, stepped down from his dais.

A deathly silence swept the room, allowing the whisper in Drystan's head to grow in volume by comparison, until it took all of his willpower not to cover his ears. Captain Talbot made a strangled sound and stepped closer to Drystan, but he held up his hand to stop his man from advancing any farther. Camille would need him to escape.

Roden raised a pale brow at the both of them, appearing not in the least perturbed by what he would consider their antics. "Perhaps it would be… easier for you," he said, "if you just showed me your talent."

Drystan tried not to shout his reply, knowing that only he could hear the humming in his head. "I shall try, Your Most High. What little magic I possess is erratic at best."

The elven lord negligently waved his scepter. "Get on with it, man."

Drystan remembered how his anger had called the illusion of the demons. How his love had called an orchard for Camille. How his excitement had formed a stadium. He ignored the noise of the scepter that tried to form words in his head and concentrated on how it felt when his magic had come to him, as if it lay within his very blood, scattered but taking a thought of will to bring it to his fingers.

But his memories did not help him.

And he must show the elven lord something, anything, for he knew what the other man intended to do.

Drystan could barely manage the sound in his head. He shuddered to think what actually touching a scepter might feel like. Cecily had once told him it felt like holding lightning within her hand. But Cecily had enough elven blood to possess it. The scepters would kill any other human foolish enough to touch it without the power to wield it.

Drystan knew he did not possess such power.

And damn if he could access any of his magic despite the threat before him.

"I am sorry, Your Most High. It appears I cannot even conjure an illusion of a flower."

"A flower?"

"Indeed. I tried to present one to my lover…"

The elven lord's impassive face suddenly shifted. Suspicion warred with contempt, and Drystan prayed the latter would win.

It did not.

"You need an incentive," sighed Roden, "but I regret that I do not have time to play this morning. There is a war I must prepare for, you see."

He reached out to touch Drystan with the scepter.

Drystan did not blame Talbot for taking a step backward, in spite of his earlier show of bravado. Nor did he think less of the other man for doing so. Indeed, he might have shrunk back himself, if not for the fact that he could not move.

He watched the angled tip of the scepter draw near the front of his black velvet coat, just beneath the dangling tip of his gold cravat.

Several women in the audience screamed, and Drystan thought a few might have fainted, based upon the cushioned thumps he heard. It seemed the entire court knew full well what happened to a man when touched by the elven lord's scepter.

The growling of the golden scepter grew louder in his head. Beneath it he could hear the other three scepters, clearer than they had been since he'd arrived in England. And once again, he found he could not stop the visions that sprang in his mind. Visions of too many deaths, too much suffering. He could not bear the pain he felt, as if each death destroyed a part of his own being.

The golden scepter brushed against his cravat.

Drystan could no longer resist the impulse to cover his ears with his palms, although he knew it would do little to stop the sounds. His sight grew blurry. He could not breathe. Tremors of pain wracked him. Drystan thought he had left his fits behind him in Wales. He struggled against the blackness that threatened to overcome him.

"You are killing him, Your Most High."

Talbot? Yes, the voice sounded near enough.

"Can you not see he lacks the power to touch the scepter, much less to use it?"

Talbot again. Brave man, to speak up so. He may be the scepter's next target.

Drystan felt the tremors overtake him, and he fell sideways. Such a long way down to the floor. Perhaps if he hadn't been so tall…

Blackness. The realization of it coming upon him only as his brain started functioning once again.

Talbot's face coming into focus. And Lady Hensby. And several other ladies whose names he could not remember at the moment. Drystan flashed to his memories of his life in Wales. The times he had succumbed to the fits in public. But the faces looking down upon him now reflected entirely different expressions.

Of course. They did not think him mad or possessed. They thought only that the nearness of the scepter had overcome him.

Drystan felt grateful it had just swept against his cravat. Had it touched him in truth, he did not think he would be wakening now.

Damn. The scepters had saved his life. Their voices managed his collapse before the golden one could touch him. He could only wonder if it had been by accident or design.

"Thank God," breathed Lady Hensby, "he did not have enough magic to threaten the elven lord."

Drystan did not dispute her words. Indeed, he swallowed several times, wondering if he could yet speak.

"My lord," said Edward, the specks of silver in his eyes as flat as hammered metal. "Can you rise?"

"Roden?" Ah, his voice did work.

"Gone. Along with most of the court."

"G." All he managed for the word "good." Perhaps it would take a bit longer for him to recover after all.

Captain Talbot held out his hand and hauled Drystan to his feet, shouldering most of his lord's weight in the process.

Legs appeared to work fine. Although a bit wobbly.

"Allow my friends to assist you," said Lady Hensby, waving her gloved hand at several lords surrounding them.

"Nay," replied Talbot. "I will take him to his rooms."

She stepped forward, a frown on her beautiful face as she looked up at his captain. Drystan idly wondered what she truly looked like without the enhancements of her magical skills.

"Then you will allow us to accompany you. To show our sympathy and support." She turned toward Drystan and placed her hand on his coat, just above his heart. "I have never witnessed such bravery, my lord viscount. Never has a man stood his ground when faced with the threat of a scepter. Only the nearness of such sinister magic forced you to weaken."

"As you wish," muttered Edward in answer to Lady Henby's request, leading Drystan forward, their entourage surrounding them all the way back to their rooms.

Lady Hensby insisted on seeing his lordship to bed. Drystan felt too tired to argue. He allowed the woman to make a fuss over him as he collapsed on the bed, aware that Camille sat in the shadowed corner of his room.

He could feel her eyes upon him.

"We must all leave him to rest," said Lady Hensby, imperiously ordering Captain Talbot and the others from the room. She then tucked a blanket about him and softly said, "Sleep, my lord. You are lucky to have survived such a close brush with death... no, *we* are lucky you survived. I look forward to seeing you amongst the court tomorrow. You shall be hailed as quite the hero."

Drystan did not care what the court thought of him. Only one person's opinion mattered, and she sat watching him with nary a word. He stared at the shadowed corner, wondering what Camille might be thinking of all of this.

Lady Hensby frowned, turned toward the corner he studied so intently. "Faith, I suppose you shall care for him? Should he need anything?"

"Of course," answered Camille.

Lady Hensby sighed in resignation and left the room, closing the door softly behind her.

The fire crackled in the hearth; the wind cried eerily beyond the frosted windows. Exhaustion overcame Drystan, as it always did after one of his fits. He fell into a heavy slumber and did not wake until Augusta knocked at the door with his dinner tray.

Camille rose from her corner and took the server from Augusta—who left without a word—and placed it carefully on the golden table. Then his lady stood by his bedside, just as quietly as she had sat during the entire time he slept.

"What happened?" she finally whispered, her impatience at having to wait for hours to ask the question clearly apparent.

"Brandy," replied Drystan. Ah, his voice seemed to be working correctly again.

He heard the rustle of her skirts, heard liquid pour from pitcher to glass. He rose up on one elbow and drank her offering. Looked up into those luminous, multicolored eyes. Something had altered her appearance. Not the new clothing; she looked as lovely to him in coarse wool as she now did in silk. Her expression just seemed somehow softer, her eyes gentle upon him, her face glowing with some inner light.

"Lady Hensby said you almost died."

She still spoke in a whisper. Drystan lowered his voice to match hers. "I could not create an illusion. The elven lord thought I hid my powers from him. So he tried to touch me with the golden scepter."

"Tried?"

"I... collapsed before it could touch me." He would not tell her that the scepter had spoken to him. Nor that the other scepters had reached out from as far away as Wales to cause his fit. For he sensed he was close. So very close to gaining Camille's love. And would not such a revelation make any woman fear him?

"You could not produce an illusion?"

He half-smiled. "Not even with the threat of death, my lady. I told you my magic is erratic."

"Then you cannot have cast a glamour upon me."

"No."

Drystan watched her struggle with that knowledge. And waited in turn.

She set down the glass of liquor, her back to him. "Then these feelings I have for you. They are truly mine. I think of you all the time, not just when I am with you."

His heart leapt at her words; strength flowed back into his body, his encounter with the elven lord all but forgotten in the sudden joy of her confession.

She turned and faced him. "You have seduced me with your stories and poetry. With your kindness and concern. For the first time, I yearn for a man's touch. I cannot sleep for thinking of you."

Tears glistened in her eyes with the battle that waged within her. She wanted him, yes, but still feared him as well.

Drystan held out his hand to her.

She stared at it in alarm.

"Will you come to me, Camille?"

She shook her head, but reached out and clasped his hand.

Drystan did not want her to fear him. Did not want her confused or reluctant. He wanted to erase all of the memories she had of abuse and replace them with the joy of physical pleasure that two people could share when they loved each other. He wanted to show her the power she held over him.

Her memories would fight her body's inclinations until then.

And above all else, he desperately wanted intimacy between them, and wished fervently he could somehow gain it.

The room shimmered, a golden haze replacing the gloomy winter evening.

Ah, at least his unpredictable magic would not fail him now.

The illusion he conjured surprised him, though. It must have come from his collection of stories from *Arabian Nights*, for suddenly a tent surrounded him, his bed replaced by a large round cushion, gauzy drapes comprising the walls of the tent.

Incense spiced the air; small braziers burned beyond the cocoon of the tent. Smaller pillows of bright-colored silk lay scattered about him, and intricate woodcarvings comprised the ceiling above. He lay completed naked, but the air felt warm to his skin, as if desert heat had replaced the chill of winter.

The bindings around his wrist and ankles surprised him most of all.

Drystan glanced above his head, where Camille still gripped his hand, then down at his feet. The silk ropes had been secured to iron posts firmly planted into the ground. He tested them, muscles bulging at arms and legs. He could not escape them to save his soul.

He smiled.

Camille gasped. A thin veil covered the lower half of her face, so he could clearly see only her lovely eyes. They widened with surprise, and then her gaze traveled down his body, studying him for a very long time.

"You are beautiful," she finally whispered, the veil moving with the breath of her words.

Drystan felt his shaft harden as he studied her new outfit. Her gown of pink roses had been replaced by a strip of sheer cloth about her breasts, long silk pants down her legs, leaving her torso bare. The lacy cap she'd worn over her coiffure had been changed to a golden string about her head, small round coins dangling from the ends of it over her forehead. Her ivory hair lay loose about her shoulders and fell down the length of her back.

"What story are we in, Lord Hawkes?"

He shifted, aware that her gaze had fixed upon his groin and the growing proof of his desire for her. "*Arabian Nights*. It is a collection of stories from Islam."

She trailed her fingers down the inside of his arm, making his skin tingle. "I would like to read it, sometime."

"Not now," he groaned.

"No." Camille smiled beneath her sheer veil. A radiant curve of her lips that for the very first time reached her eyes. She stared at him boldly as her fingers trailed down his chest.

"I would pay a fortune if you would kiss me," he whispered.

She looked into his eyes. Drystan struggled against his bindings in genuine frustration. He wanted to touch her, to hold her in his arms. But his magic knew what she needed, even if he did not like it.

"I have to beg, you see."

"I see."

She leaned forward, placed her mouth upon his, the thin fabric between them making him long for the softer skin of her lips. Camille reached up, removed the silk string from about her forehead, the attached veil sliding off her face with it. She stared at the coins, jingled them in her hand, then tossed the headpiece aside. "The book will be interesting, I think."

Drystan smiled. She caught her breath, and after a timeless moment, leaned down once more. Her lips felt as warm as sunshine, tasted like honey and dark wine. He tried to deepen the kiss, but she pulled away. Letting him know who had control.

As if he needed the reminder.

She continued her exploration of his body, fingers touching him in places that made him groan, made her smile. Thank heavens she did not touch his shaft, for surely he would splinter into a thousand pieces.

"I would..." Drystan caught his breath. "I would like to touch you as well. Since that is beyond my ability at the moment, I would see you, Camille."

She raised an ivory brow, as if considering his request as a favor she would grant in her own time.

His magic would kill him.

Camille slid her leg over his hips, sat gently on top of him. Drystan gritted his teeth as her weight added additional pressure on his shaft. It took all of his willpower not to buck against her. But she easily distracted him as she untied the laces of the cloth covering her breasts, allowing the small garment to slowly fall off her shoulders, revealing portions of her skin so slowly Drystan felt transfixed.

Her breasts were more perfect than he could have imagined, small and firm, with nipples the color of pale roses. He wanted to touch them. The ropes tightened about his wrists as he tried to match thought with action.

Camille smiled, and he watched with avid fascination as she ran her hands over her breasts. He imagined his own following the same path. Drystan groaned, and she seemed to take pity on him, leaning forward to press her upper body against his chest, allowing him to feel the taut nipples, the soft warmth of them.

He angled his head down to kiss her, relieved when she decided to allow it. She stretched out fully on top of him, somehow sliding off the loose coverings on her lower body with one hand.

The feel of her skin covering his made Drystan long to hold her closer. To never let her go. When she pressed her tongue into his mouth, he suckled it, showing her the pleasure he could bring to her, if only she would undo his bindings.

But Camille appeared to be enjoying herself. And she did not fear him. His desires would have to wait for another time.

When she broke the kiss, Drystan took a long, arduous breath. "I love you."

She frowned. "I believe you."

"Then make love to me, Camille. Allow yourself to

feel the pleasure I can give you. Take what you want of me, freely given."

She pushed herself slightly upward. Her pale hair flowed across his chest, tickled his sensitive skin. She spread her legs, knees beside his hips, and opened herself to him. He felt the inner folds of her against his shaft as a hot, pulsating wetness. Slowly she began to move up and down, rubbing her most sensitive area against the full length of him.

He lost himself in the rhythm of Camille building her pleasure to a peak. Drystan needed no encouragement of his own, for he had felt poised over a precipice from the moment she slipped her body over his. Instead he strove to hold himself back, to allow her the time to take what she needed.

He felt her tremble. Watched as she threw back her head, the beat of her heart pulsating in her throat. She slid swiftly against him now, slick and smooth, her breath coming in pants that near matched his own.

He knew when she reached the beginning of her climax, for she slid herself over him then, fully encasing him inside of her as tremors wracked her body.

And he could not hold back any longer. He did not want to. For they came together as one, Camille grinding against him as deeper tremors shook her, Drystan unable to tell whose pleasure shook him the most.

Hers, or his own.

Camille collapsed on his chest, her head tucked beneath his chin.

They lay together for a timeless moment, Drystan daring not to move. Not to speak. He had dreamed of making love to Camille for so very long, his mind conjuring different scenarios until his need overwhelmed him. But he had never imagined such a scene. Had not realized how truly glorious it would actually be.

Then the tent began to shiver, the bindings on Drystan's hands and feet disappearing, until he could finally lower his arms. His shoulders ached and his fingers tingled, but it had been worth it.

When he wrapped his arms around Camille, moving as slowly and tenderly as possible, she did not flinch. Indeed, she burrowed even closer to him.

"What happened to the illusion?" she asked, a shiver accompanying her words as the chill of an English winter crept over their naked bodies.

Drystan hauled his bed coverings over her. "You do not need it anymore."

She glanced up at him, smoothed his cheek with a confident hand. "No. I suppose I do not. Lord Hawkes—"

He took a breath. He wanted her to know his true name, damn it. "Drystan. Faith, I think you can call me by my given name now."

Her head snapped up, a frown marring the tranquility of her delicate features. "Drystan? But many of your letters refer to your given name as Duncan."

He shifted, moving one hand down to her bottom, exploring the smooth perfect roundness of it. Their closeness made him feel confident enough to reveal this much, at least. "That is my younger brother's name. I assumed his identity, you see, to gain entry to the palace."

"But why? And if you are the elder, why do you not rightfully hold the title?"

"Because I do not exist."

She rolled off him, and he allowed her to go, knowing he could never force Camille to do anything she did not wish to. Above all considerations, he must prove that she had rights and freedoms of her person.

She sat up and held the blankets to cover her chest, much to his dismay. He enjoyed looking at her body. Indeed, he rather thought he could spend the rest of his life filling his eyes with the resplendent sight of her nudity.

"What do you mean?"

"Mean?"

She huffed. "That you do not exist."

"Ah." Drystan reached out and gently stroked her hair, lowering his voice to a whisper. "Apparently I showed promise of too much magic, and fearing my testing, my parents hid the fact of my birth and sent me to Wales."

Her rainbow-colored eyes widened as she realized the trust he had just placed in her by revealing such a secret. "So that's where you get that odd accent. But why Wales?"

Camille might care for him but had not resolved herself to loving him. Yet she trusted him with her body, and he owed her the truth. He would not withhold any answers to her questions, even if it meant losing what little ground he had gained.

"It is where the Rebellion sends the children to hide them from the elven lords. Perhaps it is the natural barrier of the mountains, but the elven lords' magic does not extend into Wales."

He watched her face as she worked through the

implications of what he told her. "But that means you must have shown the promise of great magic."

Drystan scowled. "Apparently my parents were mistaken about the strength of my elven blood. I was told by… my tutor that I have the capability for strong magic, but without the training—or perhaps because I've been so long parted from the magic that flows within England—I may never gain my true potential. It does not bring back my missing childhood with my family, however."

"No. I suppose not. But… you have not lived the life of an aristocrat, then? That would explain much."

He folded his arms behind his head. "Meaning?"

"You are not so involved with your own interests. You do not toss orders about as if you expect us lesser beings to obey. You are a scholar with interests beyond gaming and drinking."

He cocked a smile at her, enjoyed her reaction to it. She unconsciously leaned closer to him.

"Thank you," he said, and sat up, unable to resist the impulse any longer. He covered her mouth with his, and she eagerly returned his kiss, breathing a small sigh of delight into his very lungs. Drystan wished he could make her a part of him forever. Indeed, he vowed to do so.

He broke the kiss to allow her to breathe but did not pull away from her. Instead he laid his cheek next to hers, enfolded her thin shoulders in his arms, and whispered in her ear. "I have shared one of my secrets with you, Camille. Now you must share one of yours with me."

She stiffened. "What do you mean?"

He hated himself for his insecurities. She could not possibly have another lover. And yet... "Tell me where you go at night."

Eight

SHE DID NOT ANSWER HIM IMMEDIATELY. INSTEAD SHE pulled away, and Drystan let his arms fall, studying her face intently, trying not to be distracted by the delicate beauty of it.

"You do not trust me enough to tell me?"

Confusion warred with fear on her delicate features. "I have never told anyone about him."

He squelched the immediate jealousy her response provoked. "So, it is a man you visit, then. I did not think it possible... no. There must be some other explanation than what I am thinking."

She arched a delicate brow, some inner humor lighting up her multicolored eyes until the facets appear to glow. "And what are you thinking?"

"Stop teasing me, Camille. This is no light matter you speak of. Do not make me regret revealing my heart to you."

She immediately appeared contrite. She lowered her head, ivory hair cascading down to hide her face. "I have no experience in matters of the heart, Lord Haw—Drystan."

Drystan put his hand beneath her chin, raising her face, revealing the tears in her eyes. Lud, what this angel did to his soul. "Who is this man?"

"He is not—it is not what you think. Besides Molly and Ann, he is the only one I can talk to."

The two women she had named must be her fellow slaves. But they did not inspire the wrath in him that this blackguard did. He wanted to see what sort of man Camille would choose as a confidant.

"Indeed?" Drystan got out of bed, began to pull on his clothing, which lay neatly folded upon a velvet chair. What accommodating magic he had. "I should like to meet this friend of yours."

"He is not really a... friend."

"Still. I would see what his intentions toward you are."

"I don't think he has any *intentions*."

He glanced at her, chagrined by the amused look on her face. Did she realize he spoke from jealousy? "We shall see. Do you need help dressing?"

"You cannot mean to meet him tonight?"

"I do. At this very moment."

"But, Drystan—"

"I suppose you shall have to call me Lord Hawkes," he muttered, picking up her delicate chemise while he searched for her stays. For some reason, his magic had not piled her clothes so neatly. Erratic, as always. He handed her the items. "But only when we are *not* in bed together."

She flushed and took the clothing, pulling the chemise on over her head before rising from beneath the covers. She wrapped the stays about her and presented him her back. Drystan threaded the laces through the holes, a bit clumsily, for he had never done up ladies' underclothes before. He kept feeling the warmth of her skin through the thin chemise and could not help wondering what madness had over-come him. He should have kept her in bed.

The gown turned out to be more difficult than the hoops, which she insisted she must wear to prevent her skirts dragging along the floor.

He regretted buying the new wardrobe for her. The clothing of a slave would be much less complicated to put on. But when he finished and she turned to him in all her finery, he chided himself for the selfish thought. She held her chin higher, moved more confidently in her new clothes. They represented far more to her than mere cloth. They represented a rise above the status of slave, a symbol that no man could molest her without penalty.

"I must get my cloak," she said, walking out the door with that elven grace of hers. "It will be cold."

He nodded, strapping on his sword belt. If he did not like this other man's *relationship* with his Camille…

She returned in a moment with a hooded cloak of black velvet lined with white fur, the hair near the tips shaded to a dark black. He had been right to take Lady Hensby into his confidence for Camille's new wardrobe. The lady had excellent taste.

"You look like a snow queen," he said, taking her hand and leaning toward her. He waited a moment, and when she did not back away, he lightly brushed his lips across hers. "I could get used to kissing you all of the time."

She gave him a smile and handed him a lantern,

which he took without question as he followed her from the room. The Camille of his dreams had been wondrous, but the real breathing woman made his dreams pale by comparison.

She halted at the door to his apartments while he put on his greatcoat, uncertainty lining the smooth skin of her face. "I—I am not sure this is such a good idea."

"Camille." He kept his voice low. "I would know all of your secrets… as I would have you know all of mine. We must start somewhere."

She sucked in a deep breath, and then nodded.

Arthur bowed his head to them as they left his apartments, the old man's face wrinkled with curiosity by their departure at such a late hour, but he wisely kept his questions to himself.

Camille took Drystan up several flights of stairs. It must be later than he thought, for they encountered only a few servants, who glanced at them with interest, but like Arthur, asked no questions. When they reached the third floor where the permanent residents of the court kept their apartments, including Imperial Lord Roden himself, she continued on to another set of stairs, these old and worn and obviously rarely used.

An oak door that looked centuries old opened with a creak, and she crept into the dark recesses of the attic.

"I did not even know the castle had an attic," whispered Drystan, finally understanding the need for a lantern. He held it up and peered through the gloom. The dust of ages covered odd humps of cloth-covered furniture, and boxes, and what appeared to be suits of armor.

Camille strode forward, certain of her path. She must have brought the lantern for him, for it looked as if she had come this way many times before and could find her route among the jumble of debris with her eyes closed.

Drystan shivered, his breath frosting the air, but found the chill journey through the attic nothing compared to the blast of icy wind that assaulted him when she opened a door at the far end of the chamber. A blizzard had sprung up during the night, the howling winds across the towers of the castle and through the eaves of the attic sounding like the screams of some panicked animal.

Drystan could see nothing except a white swirl of snow, and when Camille stepped forward off the roof, he shouted and sprang after her into nothingness.

His boots met a solid surface, which swayed with the wind and made him wonder who had built this bridge between the castle proper and what looked to be one of the towers. Made of rope and wood, it might have been a temporary scaffolding that had never been taken down, perhaps when the castle had been constructed long ago.

Drystan did not trust it. He would have grabbed Camille and dragged her back into the attic if it had not been for her elven speed. She moved faster than he did, disappearing into the whiteness, the bridge swaying with her movements as well as the battering of the wind.

He cursed under his breath and followed, wondering whom Camille intended to visit, for unless his sense of direction failed him, they now headed for the tower that housed the dragon. Grimor'ee. Perhaps she knew one of the slaves that tended to the dragon's needs?

Drystan knew about the dragon-steeds of the elven lords from the castle records—which meant he knew nothing at all. For they were mysterious beasts, spell-bound to serve the elven lords, and connected to the scepters in ways even the imposter Mor'ded could not understand. The elven lord Mor'ded's half-breed son, Dominic Raikes, had killed his father and taken over the sovereignty of Firehame long ago, and the black dragon, Ador, had helped him accomplish the task, but in a way that could have been disastrous for the Rebellion. Dominic knew the dragons the best, and he did not trust in them at all.

By all the reports he had read of them, Drystan could only heartily agree.

The bridge finally ended at an opening between the merlons of the tower. He could see only the vague outline of the rounded structure through the flurry of snow, but glimpsed a hill of golden scales toward the far end of it. When his feet met the solid surface of the stone floor he leapt forward toward Camille, grasping her gently about the waist, pressing his mouth to her ear.

"Be quiet," he said. "We do not wish to wake the beast."

She gave him that amused look again. "But that is why we are here."

The wind threw her words away from him and he felt sure he had heard wrong. "What do you mean? I thought your confidant was a slave who tended the— surely you do not mean that you visit the *dragon*?"

The wind had scoured her cheeks to a rosy flush, so he could not be sure of her reaction to his words. But she looked... annoyed.

"You may find it strange," she replied, "but Grimor'ee would listen to me when no one else would."

"He listened?" The thought still boggled his mind.

"Yes, Lord Hawkes. And he has kept my secrets. There is naught for you to fear."

The swirl of snow cleared a moment, and Drystan caught an unobstructed glimpse of the golden scales at the far end of the tower, snow capping the top of them like some enormous golden mountain. But he did not fear the beast. He feared what the beast might know. "My concern is only for you, Camille. Do you not know how untrustworthy the creatures are? They serve the elven lords, and the scepters. A human's life is insignificant to them in their grand schemes—of which we have no inkling whatsoever. I do not think a relationship with such a creature is wise."

She scowled at him, tugging her arm from his grasp. "I am aware of his... limitations. And I have known him longer than I have known you."

Drystan winced at the well-thrown barb. He had not been forthcoming with his information to Camille, although he had every intention of revealing all to her in time. He just wasn't sure if this was the right time yet. And Drystan could not know what knowledge Grimor'ee might possess. With his connection to the scepters, the dragon could know more about Drystan and his task than he wanted to reveal yet. She had just begun to trust him...

The mound of golden scales shifted, sloughing

snow off that massive back in thick clumps. The head rose, and golden eyes so very like Drystan's own stared at him. But these eyes had lines separating the irises like a sliced pie, and they appeared to twirl in a hypnotic pattern.

"Camille," said the beast, in a voice that sounded like a rumble mixed with the hiss of steam.

She turned and cast a glance at Drystan. "You are the one who insisted on meeting him." And then strode confidently forward through the falling snow.

Drystan could do naught but follow. He had underestimated the size of the tower, for it took longer to reach the far end than he would have imagined, and the beast rose up before him to an astonishing height.

That massive jaw opened and breathed a white mist, which slowly coalesced into the illusion of a roaring fireplace with two chairs set before it, the snowfall now blocked by some sort of invisible shield above the area.

How cozy.

Drystan grimaced and strode forward, not surprised to feel true heat from the fire. The dragon possessed a skill with illusion matched only by elven lord Roden himself.

"It is about time you brought Viscount Hawkes to see me."

Camille sat in one of the chairs, as easily as if she sat within Drystan's room. For just a moment he saw through the illusion, to the mound of snow Camille truly sat upon. But the clarity from Drystan's erratic magic quickly faded, and he took the other chair, feeling a cushioned surface behind his back, the soft velvet beneath his hands.

"He insisted upon meeting you," she replied, giving Drystan an arch look.

"Indeed," rumbled Grimor'ee. "You have dallied too long, Drystan of Carreg Cennen castle. The elven lord will march his army upon Verdanthame soon, and you have yet to discover the key."

Drystan mentally groaned. Just as he had feared. Grimor'ee knew too much.

He felt Camille's eyes upon him. "What key?"

Drystan could only glare at the dragon. Let the beast swallow him in one bite. That would be better than what he tried to do now.

If those golden eyes had been even partly human, Drystan would have sworn he saw amusement in their depths.

The wind abruptly died as the storm passed, and snowfall no longer obscured his vision of the dragon. The golden scales glowed with a light of their own, massive wings nestled at his side, eyes still steady upon Drystan's face.

"If you do not tell her," said Grimor'ee, "then I shall."

"Tell me what, Lord Hawkes?" demanded Camille.

He swept his gaze to hers, seeing the distrust in those rainbow-colored eyes once again, and ignored the dragon for the nonce. The beast did not matter.

Drystan leaned forward, but did not dare touch her. "I wanted only to give us a chance to know each other first, before I involved you with the interests of the Rebellion."

"The... Rebellion? What have I to do with the Rebellion?"

"You have... damn, let me start from the beginning. My dreams of you were sent to me by the scepters. The three scepters which were hidden within the stronghold of the castle in Wales. The Rebellion thought they would be powerless beyond the barrier of magic, but they did not account for the supernatural forces of our world that would keep them sentient."

"The Rebellion has stolen the elven lords' scepters? Which ones?"

Drystan did not think it truly mattered to her. She just tried to make sense of what he told her. "The blue scepter of elven lord Breden of Dewhame, taken forty years ago by my foster-mother, Cecily, and her husband, Giles. The lavender scepter of La'laylia of Stonehame, stolen by her once lover, Samson, and his true love, Lady Joscelyn, five years later. And Lan'dor's silver scepter of Bladehame, stolen by his own champion, Wilhelmina, with the help of Alexander—son of Dominic Raikes... they took it over twenty years ago now."

Camille held a hand to her temples, as if her head ached. "How has this been kept a secret?"

Drystan shrugged. "Breden went mad, and La'laylia and Lan'dor have been secretly searching for their scepters for years. Neither of the rulers wanted the populace to know their scepters had been stolen. It would make them vulnerable, and perhaps they feared to look foolish. Who knows? But it has aided the Rebellion—although the elven lords' lack of scepters has not diminished their power as much as we hoped."

"It has weakened the magical barrier," interjected Grimor'ee. "But unless and until you humans produce half-breeds who can wield the scepters, it will make little difference in your battle for freedom."

Drystan threw the dragon a glance of disgust. They knew that already, which is probably why Grimor'ee offered up the information. He trusted the dragon even less now than before he had met him.

"I am only a slave," muttered Camille. "I am not privy to the Rebellion's secrets, nor do I think I want to be. For it means..."

"Do not fear, Camille. I will not allow you to come to harm."

She drew up a skeptical brow. "Forgive me, Lord Hawkes, but I trust less in your assurances with each passing moment."

Drystan felt his heart drop. When she knew the entire truth, the ground he had gained in winning her trust might be entirely lost. He regretted not telling her the whole of it already, and yet, doubted it would have made a difference. He had needed more time to reveal the truth slowly, damn the interfering dragon.

Camille shivered in her fur cloak. "So the Rebellion took these scepters to your castle, and they somehow sent you dreams of me?"

"Yes." Drystan clutched at a thread of hope. "And I fell in love with a vision, and vowed to find and rescue you."

"But you had to have help in finding me."

He held out his hands. "As you know, I am some-what of a scholar. We house more items in the castle than just the scepters. I searched the records for years, seeking a hint of your identity and whereabouts."

"But the Rebellion found me important for other reasons."

Ah. At least she admitted that his reason for searching for her might be for his own purposes. He laid out the rest of it bluntly. "The scepters told me you hold the key to opening the door to Elfhame and sending the elven lords back where they belong. We cannot completely trust in the truth of this, but the Rebellion thought it worth the gamble, and agreed to finance the search for you."

"Yes, this key. But I am a slave and have no possessions."

"It is not a true key, but a clue, a birthmark… upon your skin."

She held her hand up to her left ear, then her eyes slowly narrowed. "Did you find it tonight?"

Grimor'ee snorted, a white mist spouting from his round nostrils. "So, Lord Hawkes, you do not move as slowly as I suspected."

Drystan spared him a glare before turning back to Camille, lowering his voice for her ears alone. "I was not looking for it, my love."

She snorted, rather in the same manner as the dragon, but much more elegantly. "But you would have, eventually. And then what?"

"I would have taken the information back to the Rebellion. And would have sent *you* back to Wales to wait for me."

"Ha. Despite Roden's distraction with the coming war, I doubt he would let you take one of his slaves so easily."

"I don't see why not. The steward included you in my household inventory—but it does not matter. I already have plans in place to steal off with you once Roden marches to war."

She stared into his eyes, and he tried to show her the truth of his words within their reflection. She did not trust him fully. She did not disbelieve him, either. He held onto that hope.

Camille looked up at Grimor'ee. "You are awfully silent. Does he speak the truth?"

"I do not know the hearts of men," replied the dragon, twitching a wing in disdain. "I only know the scepters want to return to Elfhame, mad elven lords or no. And unless you two discover this key very soon, the chances of that happening dwindle."

Camille's eyes sparkled, the flecks of silver and gold within them twinkling in the firelight. Drystan suspected she considered more than the scepters' wishes, more than his love for her. "If this key opens the door to Elfhame and the elven lords are sent home, then I might have the means to free all of the slaves within England."

"Yes," growled the dragon.

"Not just me," she murmured.

"Yes," agreed Drystan.

She looked up at the dragon. "Why did you not tell me this before? Did you laugh at my foolish plans to escape, knowing I might hold the freedom of all slaves within my grasp?"

Drystan fought down the urge to ask her about these escape plans, but could only watch in astonishment as the dragon lowered his head in what appeared to be shame. Perhaps... perhaps the beast might be a true friend to Camille after all. There had been rumors that a dragon had fallen in love with Lady Joscelyn before she stole the lavender scepter...

"It was not my secret to reveal," said Grimor'ee.

"It never is," snapped Camille.

The dragon tucked his head under a wing, curling his tail even more tightly around his body, a picture of sadness and resignation. Camille ignored him and turned back to Drystan.

"I have a birthmark behind my left ear, but it is nothing unusual."

"It has more meaning than you might know. The scepters sent me a vision of the white witch of Ashton house, who witnessed the coming of the elven lords. She then branded a mark onto her child, which has been passed down for generations. I suspect it is a clue to the doorway to Elfhame, or her interpretation of it, leastways. May I see the mark, Camille?"

She hesitated, her mouth pinched in thought, then she finally nodded. "If it does not aid the Rebellion, will you still promise to help me escape from Dreamhame Palace?"

"I have told you..." Drystan took a deep breath. Damn Grimor'ee for pushing circumstances too soon. Camille had suffered a lifetime of abuse, and he could not expect to earn her trust so easily. Now Drystan would have to be even more patient and gentle than he had been before. "I vow on my honor, my lady, to see you freed from slavery, whether the mark proves useful to the Rebellion or no."

She slowly brushed aside her pale hair and leaned toward him, bending back the top of her left ear. Despite her otherwise strong elven features, she lacked the pointed ears of a half-breed, the tops rounded and delicate. Drystan balanced on the edge of his chair and pressed his face close. Ah, she smelled heavenly, and he could not help inhaling her scent deep into his lungs.

"It is the shape of a star," she said a bit breathlessly. "Molly described it so, for it is difficult for me to see it in a mirror. I have not thought much about it since she pointed it out long ago."

Drystan saw the dragon's eyes peek over his wing, those glowing orbs casting a gentle light on the snowy ground between them. Then Drystan focused on the spot behind Camille's ear, gently spreading her pale hair so he could see the entire mark, for half of it lay buried under the hairline. The fire flared, as if the dragon knew Drystan would need the additional light to make out the shape of it.

"It is indeed a star," he said, "but an odd-shaped one, in truth. Grimor'ee, may I have paper and quill, or is that helping us too much?"

A small golden table appeared at Drystan's right, with the requested items and an ink pot. He quickly began to sketch the star, putting all of the detail in it he could. When he finished, he showed it to Camille, and they both lowered their heads over the paper to study it.

"I do not see how this can be a key," she murmured.

"I do not know if it is. But it could be a clue to the key, if we could decipher it. Remember, this is only a representation of what your ancestor witnessed."

"You are smarter than you look," rumbled the dragon. Drystan glanced up into the cavern of a snout, and jerked backward. Despite his size, Grimor'ee moved with deadly stealth.

Camille did not appear the least disturbed by the dragon's proximity. "I do not suppose *you* could tell us what it means?"

Grimor'ee backed away, once again appearing contrite, as if she had hurt his feelings. Drystan could not believe a dragon had any feelings, at least in the same way a human did.

"How would I know," said Grimor'ee, "what a human might mean with a scribble? I know only the runes of the elven, and this picture does not resemble any of them."

Drystan swore he heard a note of apology in that hissing voice. He glanced at Camille. At the sorrow permanently etched on the delicate beauty of her face. At the hard-won strength in the firmness of her mouth. At the vulnerability she tried so hard to hide. Did Grimor'ee see the same? Had Camille enchanted him the same way she had Drystan?

He shook his head. Such foolish thoughts. Many humans tried to sense some humanity within the elven lords, and they had all failed to their peril. It would be doubly unlikely their beasts would possess feelings. Would it not?

"Perhaps it is a star in the sky that appeared when the elven lords came to our world," suggested Camille.

Drystan focused on his drawing. "Then it would be of little help to us, unless we consulted an astronomer. And even then, I do not see how it would open the door to Elfhame."

"Then you already know where the doorway is?"

"Indeed. One of the most daring of our spies, Lord Thomas Althorp, gave up his life to discover the opening between the elven world and ours. He was father to my foster mother, Lady Cecily."

Drystan could not keep the sorrow and admiration from his voice. Of all the stories he had read, the sacrifices that Lord Althorp made impressed him the most. And although he had no blood connection to the man, he had felt Lady Cecily's loss every time she spoke of him.

He started when Camille touched the back of his hand. "I am sorry."

"I did not even know him… but I wish I could have. Because of his bravery, the Rebellion discovered that the opening between the worlds has not fully closed. That magic leaks through from Elfhame within the juncture of the chaos of the seven sovereignties, in a mad forest called the Seven Corners of Hell."

"An apt name.

"Indeed."

"So this clue is not to a location."

"No. I am sorry, Camille. I should have explained more. When I say key and doorway, I use human terms to describe the inexplicable. Even Thomas's description of the door to Elfhame is phrased in words we can understand. He says the opening is a collection of stones, with magic pouring from it in small rivers of water."

Drystan rubbed his forehead in frustration. How could they understand the meaning of a star? When a door is described as a waterfall, and magic as rivers? His head spun with all of the research he had done on the subject, much of it only conjectures by scholars. Even Cecily, who had been near the doorway with Thomas, could not describe it in clearer terms.

"These lines," said Camille, tracing a finger along the inside of the star. "They appear to separate each point of the star."

Drystan focused again on his drawing, a half smile curving his mouth. Camille apparently did not bother with obscure meanings. Her mind had a more practical bent. "They were not clear within the birthmark, but distinct enough that I drew them."

"There are seven points," she murmured thoughtfully.

She picked up the quill and dipped it into the ink pot, and drew out individually one of the seven shapes that formed together to make up the star.

Drystan blinked. Somehow that shape looked familiar. His mouth dropped open. Indeed, he had seen the like this very morning. "It is the shape of a scepter."

"And there are seven points," she repeated.

"And they are joined using the triangular heads of each scepter, here in the middle, to form this star shape. Camille"—Drystan's voice deepened—"can it be that simple? That the doorway will be opened if we join all the scepters in such a way?"

"I do not see how this is simple at all. First, you

must possess all seven scepters, and then a half-breed strong enough to use each one."

Drystan frowned. "And it may be that the scepters have to be wielded by an elven lord, and two of them are dead."

Drystan rose to his feet, paced the small area of illusion, now outlined with banks of piled snow. "But we know half-breeds can wield as much power with the scepters as the elven lords themselves. Dominic of Firehame, and now Dorian of Verdanthame, are both testament to that." He passed by her chair, absent-mindedly brushed his hand across her cheek. "My dear, the scepters told me you held the key. I believe that not only do you carry the birthmark, but that somewhere within you lies the buried memory which will allow you to decipher it."

She did not shy away from his touch. Instead, she looked up at the silent dragon. "You were there, when the elven lords came to our world. You know how they opened the gate. Are the joined scepters the key?"

Grimor'ee lifted a claw, scratched at a golden scale, the sound like knives raking across stone. He then studied the sky, idly twitched his tail at a mound of snow, sending it scattering in all directions.

"He does not answer, which means I am right."

Grimor'ee's massive maw lifted in what might be a smile. "Well done, Camille Ashton, descendant of the white witch. I have hope for humanity's future after all."

Drystan began to pace again. He had not truly believed he would find the key to Elfhame. And now that he had, he dared not imagine what might happen next. The scepters had sent him hunting for it, after all, and he trusted their motives less than he trusted the dragon.

"I will take this information to the Rebellion, Camille, while I send you somewhere safe. It is up to the Prime Minister to decide what the Rebellion does with it, and how the task might be accomplished. My main duty is to protect you."

"No."

The single word brought Drystan's pacing to a halt.

Camille hugged her shoulders, her face a study of mixed emotions. "I am coming with you."

"You cannot," replied Drystan. "The Prime Minister resides in Firehame, and that sovereignty is currently besieged by Breden of Dewhame. Not to mention that Firehame borders Verdanthame, and Annanor has already engaged her troops against it. Once Roden marches—no. The land is awash in war and magical chaos. I will see you safely away from it, Camille."

She set her mouth in a stubborn line. "And I will see myself in the midst of it. I would help England fight for freedom."

Drystan suddenly sympathized with Giles. He felt like tearing his hair out. "But you already have! This key to opening the door is the closest we have come to finding a way to defeat the elven lords. At the very least, it will bring hope to the Rebellion at a time when they shall need it the most."

"Perhaps it is my ancestry with this white witch, but I feel I am needed." She dropped her hands, shrugged with a rueful smile. "I know I am only a slave and may make very little difference. But for the first time in my life, I have an opportunity to do so. I will not turn my back on it."

The dragon shifted, scales screeching on stone. "She is right, Drystan of Wales. You must take her with you."

"Stay out of this," snapped Drystan. Monster-size beast or no, he would not allow the dragon to interfere more than he already had.

"I have killed men for less," remarked the dragon.

Drystan ignored him. He feared nothing except the loss of Camille. He knelt at her feet. "Do not do this to me, my love. My sword arm is strong, but my magic is weak. I do not know if I can protect you."

"Then teach me."

"Teach you?"

"As you promised. Teach me how to defend myself. With sword and pistol."

Drystan gathered her hands in his, her fingers so cold within his grasp. Despite the strength of Grimor'ee's own vision, he suddenly smelled apple blossoms. "To defend yourself, yes… but not to have you join the Rebellion. I would rather send you somewhere safe. Do not ask this of me."

She twisted her hands from his hold. "For the first time in my life, I have the ability to act upon a decision of my own. Indeed I ask this of you."

He knew what it felt like to be subjected to the will of others and had vowed to give Camille her freedom. He could not go back on his intentions just because he did not like the cost to himself.

Drystan rose. "I had intended to send you to Wales with Talbot, while I joined the rest of the court marching with Roden of Dreamhame to war. When his army reached Firehame, I planned to sneak away, which will involve crossing battle lines. It will not be an easy journey, my lady. It will not be like the books we have read, for there will be little glory, and mostly privations and horrors."

Her full lips curved in a smile. "I am used to such things."

"I know. And I hoped to make it otherwise."

"You do not have much time," interrupted Grimor'ee.

Drystan spun. "What do you mean?"

"The elven lord marches in two days."

Worse and worse. How could he teach Camille to wield a sword and pistol in two days? "I will consult with Captain Talbot tonight. Beg, borrow, or steal, I will get you an enchanted sword that requires nothing more of you than to hold on. I just wish pistols did not resist spells, but I suppose teaching you to shoot will not be so difficult. It is not as if guns are known for their great accuracy."

Camille smiled at the resignation in his words. Such a brilliant smile that Drystan felt his legs go a little weak in the knees. He wondered if she realized how much power she had over him, and then realized he did not care if she knew.

It might cause her to trust him more.

She rose from her illusory chair, away from the real heat of the illusory fire, and did a most astonishing thing. She approached the dragon, wrapped her arms around his great snout, and hugged him. "I do not know if I shall be able to speak with you again," she said. "My dearest Grimor'ee. I do not know what enchantments bind you, but they must be very dire. I know you have done for me all you can. I just want you to know I understand."

Drystan watched in amazement as a rosy hue flushed the dragon's golden scales from snout to tail. Great wings rose and covered Camille for a moment, apparently the version of a dragon's hug.

"You humans," he rumbled, "have such capacity for greatness within your concept of love." His golden eyes glanced at Drystan, who stood with arms crossed, watching the beast with as much obvious distrust and skepticism as he could display with a raised brow and a sneer.

"And weakness," added Grimor'ee, removing his wings from around her and pointing them skyward. "We will speak again, Camille. You must promise to visit me tomorrow evening. Will you do so?"

"Yes. Yes, of course, if you wish it."

Grimor'ee gazed at her silently, the smaller scales covering his forehead folding together as if contemplating a serious and disturbing matter. "I do so wish it." He stretched out his wings to their full length, easily twice his own height. "Now get the man from my sight before I turn him into a frog. He annoys the human hell out of me."

She backed up as the dragon stroked the air with his wings, the cozy fireplace Grimor'ee had conjured disappearing as if washed away by the breeze he created. Drystan leaped forward and shielded her body with his as the dragon took to the air, his golden scales shining against the night sky as brilliantly as the stars twinkling above.

"You hurt his feelings," said Camille.

Drystan sighed. "Dragons have no feelings, Camille. At least, none that remotely resemble a human's. It is a grave mistake for you to think so."

"Is it?" She pulled away from him, heading back toward the bridge between castle and tower. "*He* has never lied to me."

Drystan scowled, trudging after her through the freshly fallen snow.

Devil take it. Could he be jealous of a dragon?

Nine

WHEN CAMILLE AWOKE EARLY THE NEXT MORNING, she chose the least elaborate of the gowns Lady Hensby had designed, for she had every intention of pressing Lord Hawkes to keep his promise to teach her sword and pistol.

She sighed as she looked in the mirror. The least elaborate costume consisted of a quilted petticoat instead of the wide elbow hoops, a jacket bodice, and a closed skirt. The dark gray silk petticoat had been stitched to create layers of puckered fabric from waist to hem, accented with tiny silver beads that sparkled even in the dim light of her room. It would have been a shame to cover such elegance, except the silk jacket and skirt matched the petticoat, although the fabric was of a lighter, dove gray color.

Camille pinned up her hair and covered it with a ruffled mobcap. She settled a tucker over her shoulders and pinned it across her chest with a diamond brooch, then slipped into leather boots instead of the matching silk-covered shoes, before leaving her room.

Augusta did not glance up from cleaning the

drawing room hearth when she told Camille that Lord Hawkes still lay abed, having been up all night in consultation with his captain. Camille wondered how far the relationship between Augusta and Talbot had gone, for the other girl looked annoyed by the captain's late-night meeting.

But Camille had enough problems of her own and did not ask Augusta about the matter. Instead she made an excuse to visit the kitchens to replenish their sideboard, and darted out of the apartments, giving a nod to the old guard who stood next to the moving picture of an ogre chasing a maiden. Today might be her only opportunity to see Molly before she left Dreamhame Palace.

As Camille made her way down the stairs, she could still not quite believe she would be free of this dreadful place. Drystan Hawkes offered her more hope of doing so than she ever had before, and she prayed he would keep his word and take her with him.

She wished she did not still doubt him. But so many lies surrounded him she could not decide how much might be the truth.

But she thought… having no experience, or any expectation of such a feeling, she could not be quite sure of what it might feel like to love a man. She only knew he made her feel things she never felt before. Like gratitude for saving her, and then continuing to protect her. Although he might have done it all to discover this key for the Rebellion, she still could not banish that feeling.

Nor could she seem to stop replaying the images of their lovemaking. She had never been made love to before. It felt sublime and overwhelming, his tenderness in just one night almost replacing years of abuse. And for him to tie himself up that way to make her feel in control… ah, what sort of man would do such a thing?

Fie, her head felt all muddled. Because she had begun to care for him, did it follow she should trust him as well? Despite his avowals, she knew the Rebellion and its quest to earn England's freedom held equal importance in his heart. Otherwise, he would have stolen her away the moment he found her, regardless that she held the key to Elfhame.

She could not blame him for his loyalties. The very thought that she could make a difference to England, as well, had consumed her with more purpose than she ever felt in her life.

And that purpose made her feel powerful.

Camille shook off the confusing thoughts as she entered the kitchens, the aroma of grilling bacon making her mouth water. Her new status gave her the courage to swipe a piece off the counter as she walked by, and Cook did not bat an eye.

She unconsciously lifted her chin a few degrees while she ate the savory meat, licking her fingers when she finished. Astonishing, what new clothing could do.

Several soldiers looked up from their plate as she walked past, but quickly turned back to eating. Not a one of them shouted out a ribald comment, tried to catch her about the waist, or stuck out a foot to trip her. Even the new slave master, who sat just outside the hall to her old quarters, did not demand to know her business as she sauntered by.

Despite her show of confidence, Camille heaved a great sigh of relief, allowing the tension to flow from her as she opened Molly's door.

The slave girl lay sound asleep on her cot, her clothing rumpled and her pale hair spread about her face like some wild hoyden. Camille leaned down and regretfully shook her shoulder.

"Give it a rest, lad," Molly mumbled.

"It is only I," Camille said.

Molly opened one hazel eye. "Lud, Camille. It's about time you came to see me." Then both eyes sprang open wide when she noticed Camille's gown. "It's true then! You have become Viscount Hawkes's mistress."

Camille glanced down at the beaded silk and collapsed on her old cot. She realized she could not deny it. The memory of her night with Drystan swept over her in a rush that heated her face.

"I would not have believed it," said Molly as she sat up, smoothing back her hair. "He must be an extraordinary man to have seduced you. Or…?"

"No, Molly. I went to him willing enough."

The other girl shook her head. "Well, that's a relief then. Will you tell me how he managed it?"

"Certainly not."

"I do not know how I have put up with you all these years. You are no fun at all."

Camille smiled. Molly's brashness and sense of humor had saved their sanity more often than she cared to remember. "He says he loves me."

"Lud, they all say that." She waved her hand dismissively. "But this Lord Hawkes is a strange one. Perhaps he will marry you and take you away—"

"Impossible," snapped Camille, not in the mood for pretending.

"Is it true he maimed the old slave master, and had two men killed for your honor?"

"I… I think so."

Molly huffed a breath. "Not a man to take lightly, then." She stood and pulled out a wrinkled garment from beneath her bedding. "I don't suppose you shall still be needing this?"

"How did you manage…? No, I do not want to know." Camille took the soldier's uniform from the other girl and began to bundle it up. "I hope I did not put you at risk."

"You still plan to escape, then?"

"The less you know, the better."

Molly's pale brows rose. "That's the way of it? No, no, you are right. It is better I do not know what you are about, for I have already guessed too much. Lud, Camille, just be careful. I fear I may never you see again."

Camille unpinned the brooch and handed it to Molly, along with the tucker. "Take this as payment, Molly. And give the kerchief to Ann to make clothing for her golems."

"I would have done it for nothing," she replied, her hand reaching out for the sparkling jewelry with mindless desire. "But it is a pretty bauble, Camille. I could never wear it, but…" She stood and removed the brick from the wall and put the jewelry with the rest of her treasures. "But I know it is there, and it is a wonder to think I own something so grand."

"I am glad it makes you happy. I have come to

say farewell, you see, and the thought of giving you something as a parting gift pleases me."

Molly blinked rapidly. "I hope you are doing the right thing. You have ever gone your own way, Camille, and I suppose you always shall. I wish I could go with you to help you, but I cannot imagine leaving my home, as horrible as it is. The evil you know is always preferable to one you can only imagine. Can you forgive me?"

"There is nothing to forgive. You have managed to find some happiness here. I must go and seek it."

"And this viscount of yours? Has he not brought you some—?"

A knock at the door made them both jump, and as one they turned to stare at the flimsy wood. Normally they listened for footsteps in the hall to protect their privacy, for no one bothered to knock on the door of a slave's room. No one would, that is, except for...

"It is Lord Hawkes," whispered Camille, rising in one smooth movement. Molly quickly replaced the brick in the wall and smoothed out the wrinkles in her black dress.

Camille opened the door to reveal the man himself, dressed in soft buckskin breeches and coat, with tall boots, and a greatcoat covering the lot. He held a bundle in his arms and stared about the room with an expression of dismay on his handsome face, which he quickly erased as Molly bobbed him a curtsy.

"Miss Molly, I presume?"

She flashed him a cheeky grin.

He returned it in kind. "Pleased to meet you."

"What are you doing here?" interrupted Camille, suddenly comparing the small quarters to his richly appointed apartments. He did not belong here, and it brought the differences in their stations grossly to light.

But Lord Hawkes did not appear to notice her chagrin, acting as if he called upon some fine lady in her grand suite, rather than a slave in her hovel. "Looking for you. You promised me an outing today."

"I did not think you would seek me out *here*."

"And why not? Look, I have a gift for you." He glanced at the bundle in her hands, his golden brown eyes lighting up with understanding. "Allow me to trade your burden for mine, my love."

Molly sucked in a breath at such a boldly spoken endearment.

Lord Hawkes's sudden appearance and familiar attitude flustered Camille, and she handed him the soldier's uniform with nary a thought. He gave her a leather girdle in return, with a holster and scabbard attached. She could only stare at it in wonder for a few moments. The reality of what she held suddenly overcame her. She stood in the room that represented a lifetime of slavery—not in Lord Hawkes's apartments where he had made her believe in the fantasy of freedom. It was illegal for slaves to use weapons, much less to own them.

"You should put it on," said Drystan.

Molly flinched, and Camille swept a glance at the girl, who shook her head, an expression of horror on her face. Molly knew the consequences of Camille's actions. There would be no turning back this time.

But Camille truly did not want to, for although Molly did not know it, within Camille's hands might lay the first step in freeing them all from slavery.

Camille buckled the belt about her waist, the weight of it a comfort, not a burden.

"Now, then," said Lord Hawkes. "I must teach you how to use the weapons so you do not injure yourself." He gave her a small grin, one that altered his face from handsome to breathtaking, then turned to Molly, whose mouth had fallen open. "Miss Molly, I don't suppose you know of a private place on the palace grounds where we can practice unseen?"

Her gaze flitted from Camille to the girdle of weapons, then back to his lordship. "I do not think... I am not sure..." She let out a breath. "Within the forest bordering the south of the palace is a garden where even the soldiers dare not enter, for they swear it is haunted. It is said to be a creation of the elven lord to remind him of his homeland, but Roden has not entered it in decades." She gave a graceful shrug. "Besides the dragon's tower and the elven lord's private chambers, it is the only place I know of where no human dares to enter."

At the mention of the tower, Lord Hawkes raised one dark brow at Camille but did not comment. Instead, he handed Camille her cloak and gloves. "I had the foresight to bring these along." He crooked his arm in offering. "Shall we, my lady?"

Camille pulled on the fur and covered her head with the hood, tugging on the warm tight-fitting leather gloves. "Good-bye, Molly."

"Do not speak as if this is the last time we shall see

each other," she replied. "I shall bid you farewell only if you promise you will come visit me again soon."

Camille shrugged, and then left the room with Drystan, unwilling to make a promise she might not be able to keep. Molly stood at the door and watched them walk down the hall, an expression of hope and dismay on her pretty face.

Lord Hawkes led her through the kitchens and out to the back courtyard, where a stableboy stood with the reins of a small brown mare and a black stallion. The sun chose that precise moment to peek through the leaden skies, lighting up the newly fallen snow on the ground and atop the flowering trees and golden arches to a glowing white. Camille squinted against the brightness, following the path Drystan broke through the drifts, grateful that the courtyard appeared deserted.

The ground near the stables had been turned a mushy brown by hooves and boots, so Drystan took her arm again to prevent her from slipping, and then helped her into the saddle of the mare. He stuffed the soldier's uniform in a sack attached to his saddle and swung up onto the stallion with one graceful leap, his elven strength making the boy blink stupidly after them as they galloped away.

Camille held on to the pommel of the saddle with a tight grip, the reins an afterthought in her hands. As a rule, slaves did not ride horses, but fortunately her time as governess and companion provided her with an opportunity to learn how. But she did not have the skill that Lord Hawkes did, and could only be grateful the little mare followed the stallion without any guidance from her.

After a few miles the horses slowed, hampered by the thickness of the snow, and Camille managed to relax enough to appreciate the morning. The sun hid behind the clouds yet again, but the sky had turned from gray to a brilliant blue, and the snow still sparkled with tiny dots of light. A stillness lay about the landscape, as if the morning held its breath.

The snow also helped to hide most of the ghastly illusions Roden had created around the palace, for which Camille could only feel grateful. An arbor with climbing black roses sheltered an ogre molesting a nude slave; a frozen waterfall shivered above a beast with horns and claws sucking the marrow from a child's bones; jagged crystals surrounded a miniature battle of humans tearing each other to pieces in homage to the elven lords.

She breathed a sigh of relief when they reached the southern forest, for Roden had not bothered to touch it with his magic, other than twisting the trees into abnormal shapes.

Drystan slowed the horses to a walk and allowed his stallion to choose his own path between the drifts of snow that collected beneath the trees through the spiky canopy.

Camille's heart started to pound again. Somehow it felt *wrong* within this forest, the deformed shapes of the trees throwing odd shadows upon the ground. And a strange sort of throbbing noise had started as soon as they entered.

"Well," said Lord Hawkes, the sound of his voice nearly smothered in the suddenly thick atmosphere, "I doubt anyone will follow us in here."

Camille shivered. "I imagine not. Perhaps we should turn back. Who knows what sort of a garden would grow within these oppressive woods?"

He turned his golden gaze on her, and she felt her blood heat in response. "How badly do you want to learn to defend yourself?"

Camille stiffened. "Lead on, Lord Hawkes."

He gave her a wink, which she ignored, and urged the stallion deeper into the woods where conifers overtook the oak and elm, blocking the snowfall and creating an easier path. The throbbing sound grew louder, until Camille imagined she could feel it within her very bones.

They came upon an enormous wall surrounded by bare bushes, looking like some skeletal hands protected the stone. They rode around the perimeter of the wall until they came to a gate, which stood half-open, as if someone had fled the garden in such a hurry they neglected to close the door behind them.

The top of the gate had been capped with wrought iron, shaped into odd figures that Camille could not identify as man or beast.

Drystan dismounted and quickly helped Camille do the same, and she followed him to the gate, the untouched snow proof that no one had gone before them.

He did not hesitate, but boldly walked through the gate, Camille a step behind him. The throbbing turned into a pounding the moment they stepped inside the garden.

"Damn," he shouted, "what is making that noise?"

Camille shook her head, gazing around at the enclosed space. Swells and valleys of snow stretched before her, broken by clumps of trees that looked similar to the conifers of the forest, until she realized the leaves ranged in color from crimson to indigo, with shades of yellow between. The smooth bark of the trunks appeared to undulate with the same colors, as if alive and flowing, like blood through a body.

Drystan's amber eyes brightened with interest, just as they had when Molly had mentioned the garden. Just as they did whenever he opened the pages of a new book.

The pounding changed to a clattering of sound, and he seemed engrossed in kicking at the snow to reveal the ground beneath it.

"Ha," he shouted.

Camille glanced down at what he had revealed. A path of gravel, the stone unlike any she had ever seen before, rounded pebbles that glowed with some inner light. Drystan continued through the valley of snow, stopping occasionally to clear the humps edging the walkway, revealing odd plants curled in upon themselves, as if hiding from the winter instead of going dormant like any decent growth would.

The clatter abruptly stopped, and they both froze, their breath frosting the air in little pants.

"It is asleep," said Lord Hawkes. "I would give much to see this garden in spring."

"Do you suppose these plants are indeed a copy of those in Elfhame?"

He turned and grinned at her, pleased by her question. "I imagine the elven lord drew them from memory, wanting a touch of his homeland. But I would not doubt that he might have altered them with his own perverted magic. We must tread carefully."

"It would be wiser to just leave."

"Perhaps. But each discovery about the elven lords serves only to give us the knowledge to better oppose them. I have dreamed of making discoveries instead of reading other's accounts of them—"

The ground rumbled yet again. Drystan turned and looked for the source, and Camille gave up trying to discourage him. She knew he would let nothing come between him and his dreams.

They reached another clump of trees, turned a corner, and stepped beneath the roof of a round building open on all sides, the roof supported by tall columns carved from rose-colored crystal, clear icicles hanging from the eaves. Camille would have studied the stone closer, for it undulated with color the same way as the odd trees, but the structure topped a small rise, and Drystan pointed down into a shallow valley.

She looked in that direction and felt her mouth drop open. An entire clump of snow suddenly rose to a great height, revealing green and yellow tubers, which sprouted enormous crimson petals that fought against the weight of the snow smothering them. They stretched to reveal hairy maws glistening with sap, and then suddenly collapsed upon themselves once again with a clatter of sound and a quake that shook loose several icicles.

The plants struggled for freedom several more times before collapsing once again.

"I am tempted to free them of their burden of snow," Drystan said. "For I imagine it would lessen the racket. I shudder to think what they hope to catch in those sticky mouths."

"They are big enough to swallow a horse."

"Ah, well. Good thing we left our mounts outside then. And this is as good a place as any…"

Camille caught the barest whisper of steel being drawn and suddenly found her sword in hand, her cloak thrown half off her shoulders, the blade waving defensively in front of her.

If her jaw had not already dropped at the sight of the odd plants, it surely would have done so as she stared at the weapon.

Drystan laughed. "Talbot did well! Just hold on, Camille, and let the sword defend you." And then he lunged at her.

Steel met steel with a ring that rivaled the racket of the crimson petals. Camille held on to the hilt and tried to keep her legs from getting tangled as the sword pulled her about the enclosure, swiftly blocking each of Drystan's thrusts, allowing his larger and heavier blade to slide off instead of absorbing a direct blow.

Camille's arm began to ache and her brow to sweat before Lord Hawkes pulled back.

"You need to watch my eyes, not the tip of my sword."

"Nay, I need to watch my feet," she replied. "I almost fell over myself more than once."

"But you did well." His pale hair curled damply on his forehead, his face glowed from exertion, and he curved his mouth in a sensual smile. "If you watch my eyes, however, they will tell you in which direction your feet should go next."

Camille nodded, leaned against a pillar, and held

the sword before her gaze, allowing herself a clear look at it for the first time. The blade had the silvery sheen of a weapon forged in Bladehame. Plain of hilt and pommel, with faint runes etched within the metal. "Where did you find an enchanted sword? Especially one made for a woman's hand?"

"Let's just say I had to do all three: beg, borrow, and commit a bit of thievery. I doubt if the owner even knows it's missing, for it has been tucked away in a vault for longer than I could guess. But keep it hidden within your cloak, just in case the owner may remember it."

The plants set up a racket again, and Camille sheathed the sword as she shook her head. Stolen or not, she would be put to death if anyone saw her carrying it. "You keep forgetting I am a slave." She said the words without rancor. Indeed, the fact that he kept doing so pleased her in an odd sort of way.

He cocked his head, apparently unable to hear her words over the clamor of the garden. She just shrugged and drew the pistol, studying it closely. Finer than a soldier's, but just as plain as the sword. She then raised her eyes and gave him a questioning look. The plants would help cover the sound of gunfire, just in case it carried beyond the walls and forest. Drystan apparently realized the same, for he nodded and stepped to her side, positioning her hands on the handle and trigger, his body so close she could feel his warm breath on her cheek. Could smell the spicy scent of him.

He kept his hands on hers while she pulled the trigger. It did not frighten her this time, nor did she reflexively loosen her grip. She felt him grunt with approval, then he handed her a tin box of powder, patch, and bullets, and proceeded to teach her how to load the weapon.

She fired, loaded, and repeated the process several times, until her arms began to ache again. Drystan seemed to sense her exhaustion just as he had before, and stepped away from her to stare out over the garden. Camille holstered the pistol, put the tin in the inside pocket of her cloak, and joined him.

The plants collapsed with a resounding clatter, shoring up their strength for another try at shedding the snow from their tops.

"You did not teach me how to aim it," she whispered into the silence.

"You're not likely to hit a man who stands more than ten paces from you. Point, shoot, and pray is the best you can do with a pistol, and it takes too long to load, so your sword is your best defense."

"I see."

He turned to her, gripping her shoulders and staring into her eyes. "No, you do not. If I had more magic… if I could control it… Damn, Camille, how shall I protect you against the magic of the elven lords? I wish you would allow me to send you to Wales, away from danger. I wish—" He swept his mouth over hers in a suddenness that took her breath away. The contrast of his warm mouth against the chill cold made her want to melt against him. Indeed, she found herself leaning into him, her arms wrapping about his broad shoulders, smoothing the silky hair tied back from his face, tangling her fingers in the loose fall of it beyond the leather string that held it.

His lips traced a path to her ear as he folded his arms about her, and then gathered her close to his chest, until she could hear the beat of his heart.

"Teach me more."

She felt his sigh shudder through his lungs.

"Drystan. For some bewildering reason, you think that because you love me, then you must protect me. Have you ever considered a different purpose to your dreams?"

He loosened his grasp to hold her by the shoulders so he could look down into her face. "What do you mean?"

"Just that... perhaps you were not sent just to save me. Perhaps I was meant to save you. No, do not doubt me so quickly. You might need me on your journey. Perhaps the two of us are stronger than you alone could ever be." She reached up and touched his sculpted jaw. "Could you not at least consider the possibility?"

He frowned. "I cannot risk losing you when I have waited so long to be with you. I love you more than life itself, or have I not made that very clear?"

Camille could not help returning his frown. Perhaps Molly was right, and men bandied about words of love until they tired of a woman and moved on. Perhaps he had come to find her for the key. Perhaps he had saved and protected her because he thought she held the means to decipher the clue of her birthmark. But now he had what the Rebellion needed, and still kept his word to her and given her the means to defend herself, when he clearly did not want to. He had proven she could trust him with her heart.

But did she have any heart left to give him?

"Drystan, I—what is it?"

He had looked away from her, his golden eyes wide, the facets glittering in the sudden burst of sunshine. A bird chirped, and a warm breeze caressed Camille's cheek. She turned in his arms and stared out over the garden.

A riot of color had replaced the blanket of white snow. Rays of yellow sunlight streaked down from the bright sun of a lazy summer sky, making the color of those odd trees seem twice as brilliant as they had a moment ago. Without the layer of snow hampering their movements, the crimson petals of the yellow and green tubers opened and closed with a light clap of sound, catching slow dragonflies and an occasional unwary bird within their giant mouths. Tall fronds of lavender swayed in the gentle breeze, and the tall blue tubes, capped with small crystal-like blossoms growing within each one, chimed like bells with the flowing movement.

Grass that could not be so—with its pink color and crown of glossy berries—shook with movement as some furry creature with bright eyes and bushy tail reached up with extraordinarily long arms and fingers and plucked the fruit, stuffing it into already bulging cheeks. Flowers of red and gold fluttered their petals while trailing long stamens of orange, leaving behind stripes of fluffy pollen that stained the ground with patterns of color. Birds with crests of feathers like ladies' veils sported tails of a brilliant hue as they floated on a pond of liquid silver within the distance.

"The elven lord is here," warned Camille.

"No," said Drystan, holding onto her more tightly. "I have brought springtime to the garden. It is my magic. I can feel it. I do not know how I am doing this, or how long it will last, but come, Camille." And he loosed her enough to clasp her hand and pull her from the shelter of the gazebo.

"But, Drystan," she panted, her legs scrambling to keep up with him, "We do not know if any of these… things are dangerous."

He laughed, tugging her along the path of glowing stones. "But I have you to protect me, do I not?"

"Hmph. That is very unfair of you."

He laughed again, and this time infected her with his boyish enthusiasm. Camille smiled at him, and he squeezed her hand, leading her through a maze of wonders, stopping occasionally to poke and prod at some strange specimen while never letting loose of her, as if afraid she might run away. Which she felt tempted to do after hours of exploring.

"If this is a copy of Elhame," he said much later, pulling open the black leaves of a spiky plant to reveal a pod covered with blue hairs, "I wonder what the entire world must be like."

Camille's feet had started to ache, and even though she had already shed her cloak and gloves, her thick winter underclothes began to itch from the warmth of the summer sun. "I would not want to find out."

"Oh, it is rumored to be a peaceful place. The elven that broke through the barrier to our world are considered mad by their own people. I imagine that's why they left Elfhame in the first place… perpetual boredom for those who lust for war and glory."

"It is hard to imagine a kind elven lord."

"Well, we might see for ourselves, if our key does open the doorway."

He stood up, frowned at whatever expression had crossed her face, and tugged her along. "Do you hear water falling?"

Camille cocked her head. What with the birdsong—and the clapping, whistling, ringing plants—she could not distinguish any particular sound within the cacophony. But as they rounded a low hill she saw the waterfall, felt the cool spray across her face. The clear water tumbled over smooth white crystal stone and emptied into a shallow pond. A thick carpet of moss led to the water, and they both dropped their outer coats and sat, shoulders touching while they removed boots and stockings, then dunked their feet in the water.

"Aaah," breathed Camille.

Drystan shed his coat and waistcoat—tossing them on their pile of outerwear, and flopped backward, crossing his arms behind his head, his hair a curly tangle of pale silk on the dark moss. Camille angled her head so she could look at him, admiring the broad chest outlined beneath the fine linen of his shirt, the fit of his buckskin breeches, the strong line of his jaw, the smooth fullness of his mouth. He crooked a grin. "I would like to kiss you, right here, right now. What say you, Camille?"

She caught her breath. "I would say you are too bold with your thoughts, sir."

He leaned up on an elbow. "Are you frightened?"

"Certainly not."

"Then come here."

A shadow of snow shimmered around them.

"Quickly, my love, before my unpredictable magic fades and we are lost to winter once again."

Camille leaned down and covered his mouth with hers. Faith, she could get used to kissing him. He tasted rich and salty, the skin of his mouth like the finest satin, his tongue like smooth velvet. He let her lead, and it gave her the confidence to press for more, wrapping her arms around his shoulders, melting down beside him in the moss.

His shirt had come untucked from his breeches, and she bunched up the fabric in her hand, then slid her palm beneath it, allowing her the wicked delight of touching the bare skin of his back. He groaned and pulled away to stare into her eyes.

"My arms and legs are not bound this time," he said.

"I know."

The look he gave her made her senses come fully alive. The shadow of snow receded as the illusion of the summer garden solidified once again. Dragonflies buzzed on the surface of the pond. A warm breeze blew the spray of the waterfall over them, a cool mist that bathed her cheeks and lips. She could not tear her gaze away from his golden brown eyes, for they shimmered with desire and intent and love.

Without even glancing at his hands, he slowly removed her belt of weapons. When she did not protest, he grinned, crinkling the skin at the corners of his eyes. Drystan guided her upright as he rose to his feet, and then began to slowly unbutton her bodice. Camille looked up at him, and his gaze still did not waver as he smoothed her top off her shoulders, allowed it to fall at her feet. His fingers did not fumble at the ties of her stays, and when that garment dropped as well, her breath hitched, and he covered her mouth with his.

It seemed an eternity, or perhaps just a moment, before he removed the last of her clothing and clasped her hands, stepping back to allow his gaze to roam over her body in the bright sunlight. Camille felt her face heat—not from embarrassment, but hope. Hope that she pleased him.

"You are beautiful," he said, his voice deep and husky.

If she could have spoken, she would have told him the same, but his own beauty left her speechless. His pale hair had loosened from the leather tie at the back of his neck, wavy strands curling about his high cheekbones and smooth forehead, the tips of his pointed ears parting the hair at the sides of his head. His dark brown brows and lashes made a startling contrast against his pale skin, making his eyes appear even larger than his elven blood already made them. A straight nose, a full mouth...

And as her gaze slid lower to the pulse at his throat, she realized he also stood naked before her. He had used magic to remove his clothing.

He might have also have made her clothing disappear, but instead chose to reveal her body a bit at a time.

Most unfair. For it took Camille several moments before she could fully take in the sight of Lord Hawkes's naked skin in full light. Smooth and unblemished, with a sprinkle of hair at chest and... below. A testament to his elven blood. Broad shoulders of muscle, a tight stomach, lean hips, and muscular legs.

Camille would have liked to gaze at him longer, but he groaned and enfolded her in his arms, and the feel of all that bare skin against hers overwhelmed her every thought. His hands roamed her body, as if he sought to touch every inch of her, and she could only hold on to him, his desire leaving her breathless and her body trembling like a leaf in a gale.

The world spun a moment and she found herself on her back, the fur of her cloak beneath her, Drystan above, his lips following the same path his hands had already taken. Her eyes closed as she focused on the skin he suckled, licked, and stroked, not knowing where he would explore next, not really caring.

And then he spread her legs, his breath hot against her thighs, and continued his tender assault at her core, until she arched her back and cried out his name. With elven swiftness he moved up her body, caught the last of his name with his mouth, plunging his tongue between her lips at the same time he entered her.

Camille filled herself with Drystan.

He said her name again and again as he moved inside of her with a feverish intensity that made her wonder at his patience when they had made love the first time. For he held nothing back—his heart, his soul—within every thrust.

He threw back his head and arched into her, his body hot and pulsing against her. Inside of her. And she found a deeper pleasure that matched his own, until their pleasure became one, and they flew together for a timeless moment across a wave of ecstasy, tumbling down to earth with mingled sighs of complete fulfillment.

Drystan rolled over, taking her with him, their bodies a tangle of legs and arms, and he stroked her back, whispered his love for her, until Camille's eyes threatened to water.

"I am hot. And hungry," he said after a time, his stomach rumbling to punctuate his words.

"I am too content to eat."

"Are you?" He rose abruptly, with her in his arms, amazing Camille again with his elven strength. Then he walked straight into the pond and sat, adjusting her on his lap, while cool water splashed over them, just beneath her breasts. She had not realized how heated she had been until he scooped up a handful of water and trickled it over her head. He leaned forward and licked a drop that trembled on the tip of her nose.

Camille cupped her hands and scooped water over his head, then licked the drops from his lips.

"Easy, my lady," he breathed, "or you will find yourself back on the fur."

"It is a good thought, my lord."

"Shameful minx."

And then he splashed her face with water.

Camille blinked, entirely taken aback, and stared at him. "Why did you do that?"

His lip quirked, and he splashed her again. Camille reflexively slapped her hand across the water in retaliation this time, spraying him with a healthy amount to his own face. His expression made her... giggle. She took another good aim, and did it again.

For the next hour they splashed about like unruly

puppies, always touching one another, as if they could not bear to part for even such a short time.

Then he pulled her under the waterfall, kissing her while the liquid pounded about their joined bodies, and finally carried her out of the shallow pond, laying her gently on the fur.

"I am even hungrier, now," said Drystan, smoothing his warm body next to hers, propping his head up with one arm to gaze intently at an empty patch of ground. His satisfied smile made her look in that direction, and she marveled at the feast that appeared on the moss.

"I could get used to this," he said, "if only I could control it."

"Then let us take advantage of it before it fades," she replied, sitting up and reaching out for a red apple. It looked real, tasted tartly delicious, and hit her belly the same way real food did.

"Ah," said Drystan, sitting so closely beside her that his hip melded with hers. He opened a silver serving dish filled with cakes laced with sugar, chocolate crumpets, and thick cream. He stuck his finger in the cream, and she obligingly opened her mouth, sucking it clean. They smiled at each other, and she could see desire flicker in the depths of those amber eyes yet again, but his expression slowly sobered.

"I shall make it my mission to feed you," he said, "for I fear you are too thin for good health. Does Roden of Dreamhame not feed his slaves?"

Camille looked out over the garden, the moving swaying riot of color, and sighed. "Enough. But the only time I had any appetite was when I cared for the children, Rufus and Laura. And then for Lady Pembridge."

Drystan stilled, his voice soothing and low. "Will you tell me of them?"

And so Camille recounted her times above stairs, leaving out any mention of the deaths of her charges, and her life of slavery, and Drystan did not press her for those accounts. Perhaps one day she would be ready to tell him those stories, but not here, not now.

And then he told her more of his life, of the fits the scepters had brought upon him, and how others had considered him mad or touched by the devil. It explained much about him. His loneliness and desire for books. The way he did not realize how utterly handsome and appealing he was.

Perhaps even his obsessive determination to chase after a dream.

Which Camille could now feel only grateful for.

He got up and pulled on his breeches, handed her his linen shirt with a smile. She put it on, rolled up the sleeves, and surreptitiously breathed in the scent of him that lingered in the fabric while he searched his coat pockets and withdrew two books.

Camille lay back with a sigh. Of course he would have some books on his person.

A cold wind swept through her hair, and she thought she saw a white haze from the corner of her eye. Then Drystan sat down next to her, his leg touching hers, and it faded. He opened the larger book and began to scratch out some notes.

Camille sat up and watched him quickly sketch the plants he had seen today, a map of the garden, and remarks beside the pictures. She offered her own observations, which he obliging wrote down.

When she began to fidget, he laid down his writing book with a smile, opened a smaller one, and read "The Passionate Shepherd to His Love."

Her eyes watered yet again when he read the last line, and he sat and waited, as if he had asked her a question. The garden chirped and clapped and rang, occasionally blew a delicious scent reminiscent of roses and spice.

Could she be his love? She did not know. But he deserved an answer, and she tried to gather her thoughts to express her feelings... something she had never tried to do before. Something no one had ever asked of her. It had been long and long since anyone cared.

"How can I explain to you what it is like to be a slave?" Camille closed her eyes. "I remember when I was little I used to fight against the way my captors treated me. As if I had no rights... as if I had become a lesser person than anyone else. It enraged me, and I would fight back. I would demand to be treated as if my opinions—my life—still mattered. And then the men would take what they wanted anyway. If I made too many of them angry or tried to run, I would be beaten. And after days, after months, after years... I fought for so long to be strong that I lost pieces of myself—of my heart—along the way."

Camille opened her eyes, gazed at his handsome face, at the sympathy etched across his perfect features. She did not want him to feel sorry for her; she just wanted him to understand. She lifted her chin and leveled her voice. "I do not know if I will ever be able to get those parts of me back—to regain what I have lost. No matter how hard I try, no matter how hard you try… I am cursed… I am not a whole woman… there are so many reasons why I cannot ever offer what you are asking for."

He picked up her hand and kissed it, his lips warm against her skin. "But you will allow me to try?"

An odd feeling swelled in her heart. Hope. He offered her hope, and she could not deny him.

She nodded.

His golden eyes darkened to brown. "In the meantime, I shall just have to love you enough for the both of us."

She reached over and smoothed his pale hair back from his temple, gently traced the tip of his pointed ear. Camille kissed him then, trying to pleasure him with her touch, since she could not hope to do so otherwise.

When she finally pulled away, he turned and stared off into the distance. "One day I shall write a poem of my love for you."

And so they talked of what they would do after they finished their task for the Rebellion—never once mentioning they may not survive it—until night began to fall, and Drystan yawned, then folded her in his arms, laying them both back onto her fur cloak. Within moments she heard the sound of his deep heavy breathing, but she fought her own exhaustion, forcing her eyes open to gaze at the sky dusky with twilight. She had never expected to have a lover. Never expected to enjoy… friendship with a man. She did not want to lose this feeling inside of her.

She tried to identify it. Not contentment. Stronger than that.

Joy. Ah, this is what joy felt like. She would tuck this feeling—the memory of this entire day—safely within her heart. For Camille knew it could not last. Not as long as the elven lords ruled their world, for only in Drystan's illusions could she no longer be a slave.

Ten

Despite her best attempts to stay awake, Camille must have drifted off to sleep, for when she opened her eyes again, the night had turned to deepest black. She tried to untangle herself from Drystan without waking him, but he sat up when she fetched her clothes.

"What are you doing?" he asked. "My magic still holds… we can stay here 'til morning."

But at his words they both felt a chill breeze and saw a hint of falling snow.

Camille had actually been surprised when she had woken to a warm summer night instead of the dead of winter. Drystan had more powerful magic than he realized, to keep up an illusion for this long. Too bad he could not seem to control it.

She slipped her chemise over her head. "I made a promise to see Grimor'ee tonight."

Drystan sat up and groaned, ran his fingers through his hair.

"I believe," she continued, "your illusion coincides with the natural world. Magic usually takes the path of least resistance, and it feels like late evening or early morn—oh, Drystan, look."

He stood and glanced around, his eyes widening. Camille felt his warm hand close over hers as they both stilled in wonder.

The waterfall glowed. No, the crystal glowed, lighting up the water as it spilled into the small pond, casting myriad sparkles of reflected light off the glassy surface. Tiny flowers had opened in the moss at their feet, each blossom containing a small spark of luminescence, the whole of them glittering like thousands of diamonds. Something similar had happened to the flowers and plants lining the gravel path, for they all sported their own phosphorescent colors of blues and reds and deep purples.

"This is not my doing," said Drystan. "I could never have imagined anything like this. I changed the garden only from winter to summer."

"Elfhame must be beautiful," murmured Camille, "and the elven lords mad to have left it."

"Indeed. Here, allow me to help you dress, my love. I am coming with you."

His casual endearments—as if they had spent years together instead of days—made her feel warm inside. As if they had, indeed, known each other all of their lives. Camille flushed, wrapped her stays around her, and presented her back. "To see Grimor'ee? I am not sure that is wise, Lord Hawkes. After all, he threatened to turn you into a toad."

His warm fingers tugged at her laces. "I believe it was a frog, but it does not signify. I do not trust that dragon, and I shan't let you meet with him alone."

Camille shrugged. She had been meeting with Grimor'ee alone for years. She had done everything alone for years. What an odd feeling to have someone who wanted to cleave to her side. It would require some getting used to.

When they finished dressing, Drystan headed off down the path, stopping to investigate an occasional glowing petal. Camille gave the waterfall one last sad glance before following him. She would never forget this place as long as she lived.

Hand in hand, they reached the building of pillars atop the rise and stopped for a moment, unable to resist gazing at the panorama below them. In the daylight the garden had been a moving, shifting riot of color and sound. Although some of the plants still continued to sway, most appeared asleep. Only their long stamens glowing with color danced above them, releasing tiny particles of sparkling pollen that littered the air like thousands of fireflies.

They left the garden wordlessly, Camille's heart sinking with each step they took. She twisted her hand from Drystan's as soon as they walked out the gate.

They had entered the real world again.

Camille took one last look behind her. The glowing colors slowly faded, snow once again covering the garden.

Night had indeed fallen outside, the horses half-asleep where they stood sheltered amongst the trees. Camille put on her gloves and cloak, wrapping the latter tightly around her against the cold, which seemed harsher now in comparison to the warmth of their summer garden. The ride back through the woods did not alarm her as much as it had before, and a full moon turned the snow into a blanket of glistening white.

When they reached the stables, a very sleepy lad took their horses, and they crossed the deserted courtyard and used the stairs that twisted outside the dragon's tower to reach Grimor'ee's perch. Camille felt the unfamiliar weight of the weapons on her hips and took comfort from it.

Drystan tried to take her hand as they climbed, but she shied away from him until he finally gave up.

A light snow began to fall when they reached the top of the tower. Grimor'ee waited for them in a patch cleared of snow, those golden eyes glowing and his tail swishing back and forth. Camille sensed something different about the dragon, but she could not tell what until she got closer to him.

The tips of his golden scales had darkened to an ugly brown, as fruit would do when left to rot.

"What is it?" she asked, bewildered by his suddenly altered appearance.

Grimor'ee shook his head like some enormous dog, opened his mouth, and dropped something gold near her feet.

Camille heard Drystan huff behind her, but spared no attention for him at the moment, her eyes fixed upon the dragon. "You look unwell."

His tail slapped the stone, spraying snow several feet into the air. "This is what happens when a dragon dares to break an enchantment that binds him." He lifted one sharp talon and pushed the gold thing he had dropped toward her. "Do not touch it. Wrap it in something before you pick it up."

Camille glanced down at the golden object near her feet. Her stomach lurched, and her knees almost gave beneath her. She tried to deny what her vision told her. "That is not Roden's golden scepter."

"It is," answered Drystan, stepping up beside her. "But at least the damn thing is quiet now."

"What do you—never mind. Grimor'ee, what have you done?"

"I have broken a spell that has bound me for centuries. I have acted directly against my master to aid a human."

"But how... why?"

He snorted, a white mist enveloping her. Within it she glimpsed several quick visions: her thin arms hugging his snout, his wing wrapping around her body, her hands stroking the fine scales along his great jaw.

"I am not the first to do so." He glanced at Drystan. "Nor do I suspect this will be the last time we dragons struggle against the enchantments that bind us. But be assured that I felt I had no other choice."

"I am sure you didn't," drawled Lord Hawkes.

The red lines separating the dragon's irises flared. "I have done more to aid her in this one moment than you shall ever do in your lifetime."

Drystan straightened his spine, his hand hovering closer to his sword. Camille glanced from one to the other in confusion and took a step half in front of Drystan to break the tension. She wished Drystan and the dragon had not taken such an immediate dislike to one another.

"Grimor'ee. Does the elven lord know you took it? Perhaps you can return it before he discovers the theft. I do not want you in danger because of me."

His snout lowered as his gaze swept to hers. "I had a vision… I could not lose you. You will need the scepter to use the key. Take it, or my sacrifice will be for nothing."

Drystan stepped forward, withdrew a large kerchief from his pocket, and wrapped up the scepter, then gave it to Camille. Her hands shook as she stared at the bundle. "What will happen to you?"

A grumble sounded in Grimor'ee's scaled throat. "I will lead Roden on a merry chase, giving you a chance to escape. It might not be enough, however, and you must fear more for yourself than me."

Camille could still not believe the dragon had betrayed the elven lord for her. The beast already looked ill from the effects of fighting the spell, and she wondered how long it would take before the rot crept over his entire scales, leaving them dead and lifeless. She stared into the dragon's golden eyes and felt her own start to burn.

"What should we do?" asked Drystan.

Grimor'ee did not take his gaze from hers. "The elven lord will march his army to Firehame tomorrow, scepter or no, although he might delay a few hours to search for it. You must leave tonight, in secret, for he will not notice your absence when he discovers I have stolen his scepter. I made sure he knew who took it."

"What will you do?" whispered Camille.

The dragon softened his voice from a rumble to a hiss. "I will go into hiding until I am… called. Do not worry for me, little one. The future of England lies within your small hands."

Camille's breath hitched.

"I must get word to Talbot," said Drystan, his mind obviously intent on concerns that did not involve the dragon's well-being.

"Tell no one," rumbled Grimor'ee. "The man can take care of himself. Your only hope is to leave now, to travel to Firehame as quickly as you can. Get the key to the pretend Mor'ded—this half-breed Dominic Raikes, and take the scepter…"

The dragon choked, a shudder running through him from snout to tail. "I must go. Now, Camille. Come say good-bye, quickly."

She handed the bundle to Drystan with nary a glance at him and ran forward, wrapping her arms around the dragon's snout, resting her cheek against his cold scales.

"I do not understand," she whispered.

"I know," replied Grimor'ee, moving his maw carefully so as not to dislodge her when he spoke. Camille felt his wings wrap around her, cutting off her sight and protecting her from the snowfall. "But from this moment on, you are free to make your own way in the world. I have watched you suffer for so long… Do not be sad, Camille, for if all goes well, we shall meet again."

"You have been my best friend."

"No, I have not," he replied. "For friends help one another." He lowered his wings and took a step back, ripping his snout from her arms. "But I am now."

He spread his wings, and Camille backed away, watched as he struggled to gain the sky. He lacked his usual grace as he launched from the tower, nor did he appear to dance so easily with the stars when he managed to lift upward. What had he done for her? She would never have thought—

"I would not have believed it if I had not witnessed it myself," said Drystan. "I discounted the rumors… can it be that living among humans have truly given the dragons a heart?" Then he frowned. "But the elven lords lack any feelings, nor will they ever acquire them. Come, my love, and let us take Grimor'ee's advice. For he has given much, I think, to see you freed."

"Yes." Camille staggered forward, her eyes blinded by tears, which she had not shed in so long she did not think she remembered how to cry. They just trailed silently down her cheeks, freezing on her skin near her jaw.

Lord Hawkes reached out a hand and steadied her, led her across the tower and down the stairs, through the courtyard and into the stables. Camille stood in the warmth and continued to stare blindly forward, aware that Drystan prepared the horses himself in quiet stealth, choosing fresh mounts.

He led the horses forward, tied their reins around a post, then touched her cheek. She looked up into his amber eyes and nodded. She would not let Grimor'ee's sacrifice go to waste.

Drystan handed her a bundle and she blanched, until she realized it was larger than the scepter. "Do not worry," he whispered. "I put *that* in my inside coat pocket—and it is jabbing me under the arm. This is the uniform you, err, acquired. Thankfully, the stableboy kept it with my saddle. It will be faster and easier for you to ride astride, and two men will gather less notice. I have already been thinking of some sort of story we can tell... here, follow me." He led her into a small supply room, and quickly unbuttoned her bodice with practiced fingers, then turned her around and untied her stays. "I am going to the kitchens to pack up some provisions. I cannot rely on my magic to provide for us. Will you be alright?"

Camille nodded and began to untie her hoops.

He gave her a sharp look, nodded back, and left the stables.

She changed clothing quickly, the tight leather gloves she wore hindering her only slightly. The soldier's uniform that Molly had stolen sagged on her, but she stuffed the breeches into her boots, and rolled up the sleeves of shirt, coat, and waistcoat as she had done earlier with Drystan's shirt, buckling her new belt of weapons around the lot. She pushed away the sudden image of an enchanted waterfall and tried to ignore the pit of dread in her stomach.

She must hide her other garments. Questions would be raised if someone found them. At the far back of the room lay tackle covered in dust, and she carefully moved a saddle to avoid disturbing the fine layer, and stuffed her clothing beneath it. She pulled her fur cloak back on, for she had no greatcoat to replace it with, and the black velvet on the outside made for good cover over the dull gold of the uniform.

If one did not look closely, her cloak could be mistaken for a man's. She had seen dandies wear even fancier.

She removed her mob cap and stuffed it in the

pocket of the soldier's coat, pulled the hood over her head, and went back to wait for Drystan by the horses. It felt odd to be free of stays once again, but she did not miss the skirts. Her legs moved more freely in breeches, although the fabric scratched her inner thighs. She had not thought to ask Molly for a man's drawers, and shuddered to think of even wearing them. She could live with the discomfort.

Lord Hawkes returned quickly enough, carrying several sacks, which he tied to the horses' saddles. Then helped her mount, Camille flushing at the position of her legs when astride. She would get used to that as well.

They rode from the stables and through the still-empty courtyard, beneath the arches and past the blooming trees. The gargoyles that decorated the palace walls bared their teeth and hissed at them, but Drystan ignored them, so Camille did not fear. Only when they reached the end of the golden road did she pull up on the reins in alarm. She had not left the boundaries of the palace since she had been captured and sent there as a child.

She turned her head and looked behind her. The road twisted and curved, shining a muted yellow by the light of the moon. The palace gleamed just as brightly, turrets and spires and towers capping the evening sky like graceful fingers reaching for the stars. The palace appeared to float above the land on a cloud of white, like some beautiful creation from a fairy tale.

"But it is not a beautiful place," muttered Camille.

"Looks can be deceiving," replied Drystan, who stopped his horse alongside hers. "You shall never go back there, Camille. Not as long as there is a breath in my body. Come."

She urged her horse forward, comforted by his words, for they rang with truth.

Despite her fear of the unknown, she could not help gazing at the city that surrounded Dreamhame Palace with anything but wonder. She had heard tales of it, of course, but had never ridden through the streets. Drystan took a path among mansions that must house the great aristocrats, for the oddly shaped marble walls and golden bricks had surely been created with illusion.

Grand facades sported golden statues with moving eyes and limbs. Mostly dragons, of course, but also wolves and lions and creatures created only from imagination. A panther with golden eyes flapped its wings at her. A creature with the head of a horse and the body of a snake hissed a warning as they passed.

And then there were those that showed a less imposing face to the world. A garden with trees laden with golden apples fronted a house made of delicate filigree work. A tower of stacked layers like golden coins leaned drunkenly to one side. Tall spires reached for the heavens in impossible shapes that appeared to teeter precariously.

But all of the structures had been colored in shades of gold, and although globes of mystical lamps also lit the streets, the glow of the homes from the reflected light of the moon made it appear almost as bright as day.

"Open your cloak and show your weapons," Drystan leaned over and murmured. "If we are stopped by the night watch, you are my escort home from a night of revelry at the palace celebrating Roden's march to war on the morrow." And with those words, he slumped drunkenly over his horse's neck, and began to slur a bawdy tune.

Camille could not help a little smile as she tossed back her cloak and displayed the weapons at her hips. To even be in disguise as someone else's protector made her feel more courageous. "What do we pretend when we reach the outskirts of the city?"

The drunken song halted. "Then you are an advance scout for Roden's army. I am one of his loyal courtiers intent on adventure and unwilling to wait for the slow crawl of the army that follows." He picked up his tune then halted again. "That's if anyone we meet on the road questions us before they start shooting."

He slumped back over his saddle, and the smile on Camille's face quickly faded. In order to discourage her from accompanying him to Firehame, Drystan had mentioned his journey to Dreamhame and the chaos that dogged England's roads. Now she would find out if he had exaggerated about bandits and wild magic let loose to devour those not wary or powerful enough to avoid it.

Even if Drystan could not seem to call his magic at will, at least he had some to protect them. Other than her enchanted sword, Camille could not offer much to their defense... except for determination. She had chosen the direction her future would take, and she would not let anything stop her from fighting for the freedom of her fellow slaves.

The yellow glow of the buildings slowly faded

behind them, and snow began to fall. Well and good, for it would hide their trail. But without the protection of the city walls, the wind tore at her cloak, making her shiver as they descended into a world of white.

At first, she could see the road Drystan followed, for other horse's hooves and carriage wheels and even footprints had turned the snow brown. But the snowfall soon obscured the tracks in the road, until they became little more than depressions.

"How long will it take us to reach Firehame?" she asked.

Drystan glanced at her a moment, then turned his attention back to staying on the road. "It depends on the weather. At least a week, perhaps less if we push ourselves."

Camille frowned. As far as that? Anxiety skittered through her, and she huffed a breath to release it. "Then we shall push ourselves."

He smiled, moonlight dancing across his pale hair and strong cheekbones. "The sooner I get you someplace safe, the better." And he nudged his horse into a trot, Camille's mount picking up the pace to follow.

Her teeth clacked together, and she found it difficult to keep her seat, until Drystan urged his steed to a gallop. Then she found the rhythm much easier, narrowing her eyes against the chill sting of the wind, her nose and ears soon becoming numb from cold.

Drystan had been right. This wild flight in the moonlight was not romantic. After a few hours, her entire face went numb and her inner thighs began to burn. Camille fell into a sort of dream state, the world narrowing down to nothing but white and the determination to hold on.

It seemed an eternity before the sky began to lighten with a new day. Snow still fell gently around them. Drystan had slowed the horses to a walk to rest them yet again and glanced at her with a worried frown. "Do you need to stop and rest?"

She shook her head.

"We will continue on until our midday meal, then."

They rode for several more hours, when the snow abruptly ceased, and the sky darkened slightly.

Drystan pulled up the reins, frowning at the trees that lined the side of the road.

"What is it?" whispered Camille, afraid to disturb the sudden silence that now surrounded them.

"It is *too* quiet," he replied, still studying their surroundings with a suspicious gaze. Then he slowly looked up at the sky, and his handsome mouth fell open.

Camille followed his gaze. A sheet of ice glowed far above them, the sun that now lay behind it reflecting off the bluish-crystal surface. "What is that?"

"Roden," growled Drystan. "He has set a barrier over the sky."

No wonder it had stopped snowing so abruptly. "He has discovered the loss of his scepter."

"Indeed," Drystan said, "and he must know his dragon stole it. Why keep a barrier over the skies, then?"

"Surely Grimor'ee has already left Dreamhame. Do you think Roden surrounded all of his sovereignty with a layer of ice?"

Drystan shrugged his broad shoulders. "We will

find out when we reach the border. It would take a lot of power to cut off his entire realm for so long, and he needs his magic for the war against the half-breeds of Firehame and Verdanthame."

"He will have to drop the barrier to let his army through."

"Perhaps. But I do not want to have to wait to meet up with them to get through. Let us hope he realizes Grimor'ee is no longer within his land before that." Drystan tapped his heels against his horse's flanks. "Come. The sooner we get this key—and this thing in my pocket—to the leader of the Rebellion, the better."

Camille glanced at the lump from the scepter in his coat pocket and winced. Yes, she wanted to rid herself of both those burdens as well.

They encountered a few other travelers, but Drystan's pointed elven ears heard them long before he saw them, and he drew their mounts behind bush or tree to hide until they passed. They stopped for a hasty meal and continued to ride until the sky darkened with true night.

"There's an inn a few more miles down the road," said Drystan. "Can you make it?"

She nodded, gritting her teeth. Food. Warmth. Sleep. She had often gone without, so the lack of it did not affect her as much as Drystan seemed to think it would. But when they finally stopped at the inn, he had to help her from the saddle.

"I am not used to riding."

He patted her shoulder. "I will see if the innkeeper has a salve we can use." And he set off and made their arrangements, acting every part the nobleman on an important mission for the elven lord.

Camille did not protest when he made accommodations for only one room. She did not protest when he stripped her down to her shirt and applied a foul-smelling concoction to her inner legs. Nor did she mind when he joined her in bed. For the delicious warmth of his body soon had her fast asleep.

Drystan woke her early the next morning, helping her to dress even though she told him she could manage quite well on her own. He still treated her as if she were some delicate lady of the court, and Camille could not find the heart to be too annoyed at him. She had never felt so cherished before. He had made the innkeeper's wife get up early to prepare them a hot breakfast of toast, tea, and poached eggs, and Camille found herself back in the now-dreaded saddle faster than she would have thought.

They rode all day, eating in the saddle, stopping only to relieve themselves. The ice covering the sky seemed to glitter a deadly warning, reminding them of the power of the elven lord, of the danger of their mission. And the importance of what they carried.

Drystan decided it would be safer to avoid all public accommodations, and when night fell he paid a few shillings for the use of a barn from an old couple on an isolated homestead. They slept in musty hay, huddled together for warmth, too exhausted to even speak.

He pulled Camille closer to him, her back to his belly, and buried his face in her hair. The stable suddenly became warmer, their bed of hay much softer. She realized his arms felt protective around her—they did not trap or confine—and marveled at how easily she had become accustomed to sleeping with him. To touching him.

On the third day, their luck ran out.

Drystan had urged Camille to eat, and their morning repast lay heavily in her stomach as they resumed their journey once again.

"We will reach the border today," he said, his golden eyes scanning the road ahead of them. They had just descended into a small valley, trees again lining the sides, hemming them in. "We will leave the main road to avoid the border patrol, but Roden has not dropped his barrier yet, and I am not sure my magic will be strong enough to break through it—"

Camille's horse suddenly reared, nearly dropping her onto the snowy ground, and she scrambled to keep her seat. Drystan's mount did the same, although he was better at getting his horse back under control. Shots rang out, shattering the stillness of the air, and men erupted from the trees, waving swords and pistols.

Drystan's horse spun in a circle as he fought the reins while pulling his sword from its scabbard. "Run!"

"No," shouted Camille, reaching for her pistol. She could not steady the weapon to aim, with her own horse panicked and stomping beneath her, and realized that's why Drystan had reached for his sword. So she just pointed it in the general direction of the group of men and fired.

A figure fell.

Drystan gave her a look of amazement, then smacked the rump of her mount.

The horse bolted down the road, completely

ignoring Camille's curses and her yanking on the reins. Somehow she managed to hold onto her pistol, and shoved it back in her holster. Damn Drystan and his attempts to protect her. He faced half-a-dozen men, with no one to guard his back—

Her horse leaped. Or tried to. For a log lay across the road. The beast had not expected it and jumped too late, its hooves scraping the bark, accompanied by the dreadful sound of tearing flesh. Camille flew through the air to land in a bank of snow.

Her vision went black, but a pitiful neighing reached her ears, and she struggled to stand, to see. Her horse lay a few yards from her, its legs twisted beneath its body, unable to rise, writhing in the snow. Heaven help her, she would have to put the poor thing out of its misery—

Two men leaped out of hiding from behind the log to face her, their dirty faces wreathed in smiles. They wore equally dirty, ragged clothing, and held dented swords that still looked quite sharp despite their battered condition.

Bandits. They had set a neat trap with the log.

Camille drew her sword.

Their smiles grew wider as they separated, coming at her from both sides.

"There's no need fer this, luv," crooned one of the men, his face pockmarked with scars. "Jest hand over yer coin, and lie still fer us a while, and we'll let ye live."

Camille's eyes widened. So much for her disguise.

"Ye curse like a girl," said the other man.

Her knuckles whitened on the hilt of her sword.

The pockmarked man swung his blade with a laugh, and her sword automatically countered.

His bushy brows rose. "Careful, Tom, she's got a—"

Camille spun. Or rather, her sword spun her around, and met the blade of the man behind her. Tom had tried to overpower her with one forceful lunge, but not only did she possess some elven strength, but her sword knew better, and parried the strike away with a twist, then swung up faster than her gaze could follow, and sliced him across the chest. He dropped his sword and clutched his hands to his wound, then fell to his knees, his mouth agape.

Camille blinked. It had happened so fast—

Back around again, to meet the blade of Pockmark. But he had come closer than she realized, and must have some elven blood running through his veins, for he struck out with his leg to trip her with a speed she could not counter. She spun and fell face-first into the snow, arms out… but she did not loosen her grip on her sword.

Camille heard snow crunch as Pockmark took a step forward to plunge his blade into her back. Her entire body cringed, waiting for the feel of cold steel breaking her skin.

Her sword spun her over, nearly tearing her arm from its socket, and slapped the other blade away, surprising the man and making him stumble.

He fell onto her blade.

Camille held on with both hands, pushing him over to her side as he fell.

She might have no magic, but she held enough elven blood to allow her body to move quickly

enough when required. She was on her feet before
Pockmark hit the snow, twirling to face the other
man. But that one blow had felled Tom. He lay on his
face in a bloody circle.

Camille's legs trembled, and she just breathed, the
sound loud in the sudden silence. She stared at her
bloody blade. The sight of it should have repelled her.

She glanced at the dead bodies staining the white
snow, walked over to the nearest, and cleaned
her sword on his ragged clothing. She should feel
horrified. Disgusted. Instead her heart soared as she
sheathed her blade. These men had wanted to touch
her, to take from her. And she had stopped them. *He*
had given her the means to not only take her freedom
but to keep it.

"Drystan," she breathed.

It took Camille two leaps, using all the elven
strength she possessed, to scramble over the log.
She blessed her breeches, for she would never
have managed it in skirts. She ran through the path
of snow her horse had already broken, her heart
pumping wildly.

He could not die...

A horse and rider appeared over the rise of the road,
and she stopped, hand on the hilt of her sword. Had
one of the bandits stolen his horse? For they had all
been on foot...

But she soon caught a glimpse of ivory hair, of
pointed ears and golden eyes. Relief swept through
her, leaving her body too weak to move. So Camille
just stood and waited for him.

Drystan pulled up his horse a few feet from her,

vaulted out of the saddle, and within a blink had his arms
around her, kissing her hair, her cheeks, her mouth.

"I saw them go after you," he said. "I fought like
a demon to follow. I feared I would be too late. My
love, my love, I thought I had lost you."

His concern for her held Camille immobile. She
could feel the intensity of his emotions, and it touched
her somewhere deep inside. Even when Molly fussed
over her after a beating, she did so quietly, without
passion. Slaves could not afford the emotion.

Drystan pulled back. "What is it? Are you hurt? Did
they touch you?"

"No, I am…" Camille took a deep breath. "The
sword protected me. They… the two bandits… they
are dead. But my horse. It is in pain."

He nodded. "Stay here."

Camille heard his footsteps crunching in the snow,
the thud of his boots as he leaped over the log. The
shot of his pistol. She mourned the loss of the beast
more than she did the two men who lay near it.

He returned quickly enough.

"We will have to ride double. 'Twas a poor lot
of thieves. They did not have a single horse among
them." Drystan took her hand and led her over to
their remaining mount. "Which was fortunate for me,
as a mounted man always has an advantage in a fight.
Are you sure you are well?"

Camille nodded. His calm, authoritative manner
soothed her.

He leaped into the saddle and held his hand down
to her, pulled her up in front of him. He felt solid
and warm against her back. She could not resist the

impulse to melt into him. He kissed her hair, the back side of her ear. "If I lose you, I lose my heart."

He spoke so low, barely a whisper. But his words rang in her head while he guided the horse around the log, having to pick their way through the trees at the side of the road before getting back on it.

They topped a rise, and the woodland faded; a vista of rolling hills covered in snow spread out before them. A smudge of gray off in the distance told of a chimney and farm. A few birds flew low beneath the ice covering the sky. A frozen pond reflected the glow of Roden's illusion above it. The peaceful view looked entirely at odds with the dangerous elements afflicting England.

Although Camille enjoyed the feel of Drystan's mouth kissing her while they rode, the cold soon made her pull her hood back over her head, wrap her cloak tighter around her body. The shield of ice hanging over the land hampered the sunlight, making the still air seem even colder.

Apparently, Drystan did not like the barrier of velvet and fur between them. He transferred his reins into one hand, removed his glove from the other, and slid his hand beneath her cloak, reaching into the baggy waist of her breeches to slide his warm palm against her hip.

"You are being foolish," sighed Camille, not really caring if a swarm of bandits descended upon them. His touch made her feel so alive.

"Perhaps. But I must assure myself that you are real. That I have not lost you. You have been only a dream for so long that sometimes I have to make sure you are truly flesh and blood beneath my hand."

His fingers gently stroked her hip.

The road forked, and Drystan took the less-traveled one, their overburdened horse trudging tiredly along. Although their mount had to break a new fall of snow on the main road, traffic had already carved paths within the underlay. Not so on this smaller road. Their progress slowed to a crawl.

Camille did not have to concentrate on staying in the saddle, not with Drystan's arms firmly about her, and lost herself in her thoughts. If they made it to Firehame, what then? She could not imagine Drystan allowing the Rebellion to decide what to do with the key, and returning with her to Wales. He would want to help, if he could. Would he try to send her away without him?

She had only an enchanted sword to aid the cause. What use would they have for her if she argued she must stay?

Camille hugged her cloak more tightly about her. It did not matter. She would convince Drystan she must stay, despite his intentions to keep her safe. She would not leave his side. Not now, when she had discovered...

What?

That she cared for him more than anyone she had ever known? That her feelings might even run deeper? Deeper than she thought they ever could?

Was this love?

She wished she knew.

"At this pace," blurted Drystan, his deep voice heavily laced with annoyance, "we shall never reach Firehame."

Camille blinked. She could still see the smudge of smoke from the farm she had spotted earlier.

"Too bad your dragon did not think to give us a ride to Firehame."

"He is not *my* dragon," replied Camille softly, "and you know he had to leave Dreamhame immediately."

"Grimor'ee could have chosen to hide in Firehame."

"I think not. He was already sickening from defying the enchantment. What might have happened to him if he helped us even more? If he went to Firehame and was forced to choose to aid us yet again? No. He had already risked too much."

"Perhaps you are right," he conceded. "I just wish I was not forced to expose you to bandits and who-knows-what-else we might encounter before the end of our journey. Time presses upon me and tries my patience, for I do not know how long Verdanthame and Firehame can withstand a siege. We must reach Firehame before Roden does. Illusions that can kill, added to the magic already hounding them, might push the scales in the rest of the elven lords' favor."

Camille could feel his frustration, and laid her head back on his shoulder, turned to look into his golden eyes. "I did rather well with the bandits, thanks to your gift. And together we shall face whatever lies ahead."

He relaxed his scrutiny of dangers hiding within their surroundings, and gazed into her eyes, a smile tugging at his lips. "You did do rather well, didn't you?" And then he leaned over and swept his mouth across hers, but quickly pulled away before the kiss could deepen, his gaze once again alert to danger.

"Still," he continued, "I would rather be on the back of a dragon instead of this poor, tired beast. I could bring you to safety—"

The breath left his lungs as their seat shot up in the air several feet, Drystan's hold on Camille tightening almost painfully. She swallowed, forcing her heart back into her chest, and looked down.

Their horse had disappeared to be replaced with… the golden scales of a dragon. Wings spread out beside them, tentatively batting the air. The long neck in front of her turned, blinking limpid golden eyes devoid of the red lines that distinguished Grimor'ee. Indeed, the creature did not come close to matching the sheer size of her friend, but it was truly a dragon, nonetheless, and much taller than their horse.

"Damn," exclaimed Drystan.

"Did you do this with your magic?"

"I… I think I did. I feel drained and exhilarated, all at the same time. I am not used to having magic, you know. It never occurred to me to try to change our mount."

Their seat wobbled as the beast took two steps forward, equaling perhaps a dozen of the horse's strides.

"It would not occur to most half-breeds, Drystan. It takes powerful magic to create an illusion this strong. It is not just a semblance of the creature. We sit upon its back. We can feel the breath of its lungs and the rhythm of its walk."

"Do you think it will truly fly?"

Camille glanced up. "It does not matter, for Roden's illusion still holds. We cannot gain the higher sky."

Drystan grunted.

The dragon continued walking, trudging along as the horse had done, but covering much more ground. Camille adjusted to the rolling gait of the larger beast much more easily than she had to the horse's shorter one. She relaxed against Drystan's warm chest, his hand on her hip making her feel connected to him despite the silence that fell over them both.

It seemed as if the land held its breath as they traveled through it.

The dragon's head almost reached the top of the trees. Its legs had little difficulty treading through the snow, and a slight vibration shook the ground from their passage. They saw neither man nor beast, and Camille imagined that the sight of their mount would send anything running in the other direction.

They had finally gained some measure of safety for their journey, so it surprised her when she felt Drystan's muscles tense.

"What is it?" she murmured a bit drowsily.

"Do you hear that?"

Camille stiffened and cocked her head. A slight tinkling sound met her ears. The trees began to thin, steep snow-covered cliffs replacing their evergreen branches. Then short pillars of ice grew alongside the road, rising in height the farther they progressed.

"Wild magic," whispered Drystan.

The pillars grew until they seemed to almost reach the sky. Then they curved overhead, meeting at their tops, creating an archway over the road. A layer of crystal ice stretched from one to another, forming a canopy of what looked like translucent lace. Icicles dripped down from that canopy, making them duck their heads more than once to clear some particularly large ones.

The vibration from the dragon's gait shook the ice and made it chime like tiny bells.

"Danger?" hissed Camille.

She felt him shrug, look up. "We might want to avoid any loud sounds. Those icicles look pretty sharp."

She nodded. They could fall upon them like a million sharp daggers. Indeed, one broke off just to her right, plunging into the snow point-first.

The dragon's stride shifted, as if it too sensed the danger. If a dragon could tiptoe, their mount surely did.

Camille narrowed her eyes at the pillars lining the road. It seemed as if... yes, odd creatures had been encased within the ice. A scraggly-haired beast with red eyes and matching claws. A man half-covered in green rot. A woman with a tail and wings, emaciated arms and legs ending with pointed barbs.

"Drystan, do you see them?"

"Aye. They cannot hurt you."

"Indeed? What if they break through the ice imprisoning them?"

"It looks like they have been here for a long time. There is no reason to suspect—"

The icicles shuddered behind them, and they both turned to see the end of the dragon's tail bounce off one of the pillars. A crack zigzagged its way up the icy surface.

"Damn," said Drystan, leaning forward toward the dragon's head. "Have a care with your tail, beastie!"

The dragon turned its head, those golden eyes blinking innocently at them.

"How much of it do you control?" asked Camille.

"What do you mean?"

"It is your creation. Surely it would respond to your will, like Ann's little golems respond to hers."

Drystan's beautiful eyes widened, and he cocked a grin. "My tutor said something of the sort—blast my inexperience with magic! I fear Giles may have been right. I am ill prepared for this world of enchantments."

"Giles?" prompted Camille. Drystan had mentioned him before.

"My foster father in Wales. He fell in love with Lady Cecily, and the two of them stole her father's blue scepter and brought it to the orphans' castle."

Camille frowned. "You say it so casually, Drystan, as if stealing a scepter was a commonplace event. Yet now I see where you received your passion for the Rebellion. Perhaps you were destined to take the golden scepter. I think your foster parents would be proud of you."

He seemed to garner some confidence from her words, for he firmed his mouth and narrowed his eyes. The dragon swung its head back around and picked up its pace.

"You are right," he said, a touch of wonder in his voice. "It responds to my commands."

Camille glanced over her shoulder. The dragon's tail no longer swayed from side to side, instead it stuck out behind them as straight as an arrow. She looked at Drystan and gave him a smile. "Well done."

He dipped his head as if he meant to kiss her, and she frowned when he froze, his eyes shifting to glance at the road ahead of them.

Now what?

Camille turned. A sliver of ice burst through the snow on the road in front of them, bringing the dragon to an abrupt halt. The beast veered to go around it.

Another sliver broke through the crust. Drystan cursed. The beast dodged it, but another grew, seeming to pierce the sky. And another, and another...

"This is no wild magic. It is a purposeful trap."

Drystan did not reply. She could almost feel his concentration as he sought to direct the dragon around the growing obstacles.

But soon, the road ahead became a prison of upside-down icicles, with a hairsbreadth between the soaring columns.

He leaned forward, pushing her flat against the golden scales as the dragon attempted to fly. Drystan must be using magic to keep them anchored to their seat; otherwise the beast's attempts to fly over the imprisoning bars of ice would surely have thrown them. Camille felt the wind from the beat of its wings, but it could not easily take flight from a standing position. Still, it managed to launch itself forward and up, shattering the ice, shards of crystal peppering their heads and shoulders.

More icicles grew, and the dragon plunged through them as well, until their progress became a jumping, lurching, crashing journey of falling ice. Their horse never would have made it this far, but Camille prayed they had a chance of breaking free on the back of a dragon.

She had shielded her eyes, but at Drystan's sudden shout, she uncovered them.

They had reached the border. Roden's spell extended from sky to land, for a sheer wall of ice plunged downward several miles in front of them, like some enormous bubble surrounded the sovereignty of

Dreamhame. And in front of that barrier gaped a deep and dark chasm.

Icicles no longer blocked the road. For the road had disappeared into that miles-long gap. The dragon teetered on the brink of it, wings backpedaling as it tried to prevent them from falling over the edge.

Drystan sat very still as the dragon swayed, and Camille could almost hear him thinking.

"What is it?" she asked.

"I have noticed my magic comes to my aid when I desperately want something for *you*."

The dragon swayed back on its haunches. She prayed it would win its battle against gravity, and spoke to distract herself from the panic that threatened to overwhelm her. "W-what about when the bandits attacked?"

"I did not think to use magic. As I said, I am not used to having it, to calling it at need. I have relied upon my sword for far longer. But all of the other powerful illusions I have created—the demons, the Arabian tent, springtime in the garden—have all been to help you. When the elven lord threatened *me*, I could not gather a shred of my magic."

The dragon tipped forward yet again. Camille could not help the shrill tone of her voice. "And?"

"And you reminded me that my tutor told me the creation of any spell required strength of will more than anything else, which is why powerful illusions take more energy. Where you are concerned, my willpower knows no boundaries."

They swayed backward as one. "Where are you going with this, Drystan?"

"I can break through Roden's illusion."

His voice rang with confidence. He believed he could do it. And she trusted him with her life. As they swayed forward yet again, the dragon's wings beating ferociously at the alarmingly new perilous angle, Camille said with forced bravado, "There is only one way to find out."

And then she closed her eyes and hoped his unpredictable magic would continue to hold if the dragon actually managed to fly.

Eleven

DRYSTAN KNEW HE COULD DO IT, AS SURELY AS HE knew his own heart. But Camille's voice held a hint of doubt.

She was the bravest woman he had ever known. Even though she had scared him witless, he felt glad she defended herself against the bandits. It changed her. A new confidence lay in the set of her mouth, the slope of her shoulders. Her eyes sparkled with an inner dignity.

She had learned not to fear him. Perhaps now, she would no longer fear any man.

They toppled over the cliff, and Drystan's stomach rose up into his throat.

He looked at the dragon's leathery wings, willing them to beat faster.

They did.

He tightened his grasp on a golden scale with one hand, his other still holding Camille's hip. Fie! He had finally thought to untangle his arm from beneath her clothing, but he could not quite manage it, for the dragon took to the air, a sudden lift that pushed the breath from Drystan's lungs.

He felt a moment of jubilation at the wondrous freedom of flight, but it quickly faded as they bobbed across the chasm. The dragon struggled to keep them aloft, and although Drystan had read about the principles of dragon flight, he lacked any experience to guide the beast in the proper way to manage it.

It appeared the dragon had an instinct for flight, however; otherwise they would have already plunged to the bottom of the gap.

Drystan glanced down into an abyss that appeared to have no end and quickly looked up. The view improved only slightly, for he faced the solid wall of ice cutting Dreamhame off from the rest of England.

He had read that dragons used air currents in the higher skies to allow them to coast for long distances, for the sheer size of the beast made staying aloft difficult. Granted, the dragon he had created looked puny in comparison to Grimor'ee, but the concept still held. So Drystan willed the dragon to fly higher, for it did not matter whether he broke through the barrier ahead or above them.

If he failed, it would be a disaster regardless.

As they climbed upward, he tried to imagine a hole within that barrier of ice, but could not envision it. The ice looked too solid, too real. He already felt the drain on his strength from maintaining his illusory dragon and keeping them glued to its back, and did not know if he had enough magic left to summon even a small crack in the elven lord's enchantment.

The wall grew closer. He felt Camille tense.

"For her," he whispered, his words tossed away and

over his shoulder from the wind of their flight. "I will do this for Camille. I must."

He felt a burning sensation from his pocket but ignored it, his entire being focused on breaking a hole through that ice.

And a small crack appeared.

Too small for their beast to fly through.

Drystan gritted his teeth. The break must widen enough to allow them through. It would. His world narrowed to that small crack, willing it to melt about the edges. To widen.

The dragon let out a scream, the sound of it very close to the one in Drystan's mind as they flew into the break. The tip of a wing slid along the ice, disturbing the balance of the beast, who overcompensated, causing its other wing to slide along the glassy surface. They bounced back and forth as if in some wild gale of wind, until Drystan worried that despite his magic, they would be flung from the golden scales to fall far, far down, beneath the earth into the blackness of the chasm.

How thick was the damn ice?

White abruptly clouded his eyes. Drystan shook his head to dispel it, realized the dragon's flight had just as suddenly become a smooth glide.

They broke through the mist. No, a cloud, for now he looked down upon a fluffy layer of what he had before seen only *above* his head. Then the white shredded to a fine layer and disappeared, and he saw the sheet of ice below them, and then that, too, vanished from view.

Drystan went over the mental map in his head, trying to adjust it to the actual view of England's landscape.

They had left the sovereignty of Dreamhame, also leaving Stonehame, Bladehame, and Terrahame behind, which lay to the east of Roden's realm. They briefly passed over Dewhame. Even in the dead of winter, water trickled a path through the snow. To his right lay Bath and the palace of Imperial Lord Breden, although it was too far for him to see the mad elven lord's palace of steaming water and fountained hills. But they soon left the land of the blue scepter behind, and flew into the realm of Firehame. Drystan caught a glimpse on his left of the forest within Oxford, called the Seven Corners of Hell, where Viscount Thomas Althorpe had discovered the source of magic and a doorway into the fabled land of Elfhame.

A maelstrom of magic sundered Oxford's forest, shooting flames into the sky, waves of water, volcanic ash, and colors of green, silver, gold, and lavender sparkles. All seven of the elven lords' sovereignties met within that mad forest, the conflicting magics resulting in a chaos that Giles and Cecily had barely survived.

Drystan made sure to guide the dragon far away from the sky above it.

Then they flew over a land riddled with pockets of fire, trees of flaming leaves that melted the snow around them into pockets of brown. A journey that would have taken them days would now take them only hours.

Drystan relaxed, rubbed Camille's hip, which would surely carry bruises from his hold upon it during their crazed flight.

She leaned back against his shoulder, the tips of the fur of her hood tickling his chin, and said, "I am free." Only the wind of their flight brought the words to his ears.

Drystan gave her a gentle squeeze. He had been so focused on gaining their bearings that he had not thought of how Camille must be feeling. Leaving Dreamhame must have been a liberating experience for her.

"You will never be a slave again," he swore, leaning close to her ear so she could hear him.

The dragon climbed high enough to catch a current, creating a smooth ride for its passengers, but the chill of the higher skies near froze the moisture in Drystan's eyes. Feeling a confidence in his magic he never had before, he created enormous fur blankets to wrap around Camille, to half-lay over his face against the frigid air.

Drystan had not been aware of her trembling until she stopped.

"It smells different up here," she shouted against the wind.

It did. A sharp odor that stung his nose.

She glanced down. "We are in Firehame already?"

"Aye. We should reach London in a few hours."

"And then it will begin."

Begin? For Drystan, it started the moment he had first dreamt of her.

He longed to tell her about the land of Firehame, and what he knew of the half-breed General Dominic Raikes, who had killed and taken the elven lord Mor'ded's identity, and who had fooled the other Imperial Lords for years. About his secret wife, Lady Cassandra, and their son, Alexander, who had seduced

Imperial Lord Lan'dor's champion, Wilhelmina, and stolen the silver scepter of Bladehame.

When they reached Firehame Palace in London, they would meet the living legends behind the Rebellion. Drystan's curiosity flared with excitement about meeting the people he had only read about.

But the pounding wind did not make for easy conversation, and his desire to educate Camille about the people she would be meeting would have to wait.

So he pulled the fur lower over his face, trying to get some feeling back into his nose, the tip of which had gone numb several hours ago, and occasionally glanced down at the snow-covered land, making sure the dragon kept to his bearings.

He held Camille tenderly, relishing the feel of her in his arms. They had become even closer over the last few days. The danger and their reliance on one another cemented the bond between them. Drystan just wished he could banish the niggling doubt that ate at him. In all of his dreams, it had never occurred to him that she would not eventually fall in love with him. That she would think herself incapable of doing so.

Would the bond he had tried so hard to develop between them hold until she—?

Something large flew straight up past them. He caught a glimpse of brown wings from the corner of his eye. Drystan directed his dragon to a circular pattern, slowly climbing higher up into the ether.

Camille tensed at the same time Drystan saw them. A flock of brown dragons just ahead, on a straight course to London. They did not have the size and power of Kiz'rah, Annanor's dragon-steed. The elven lady must have created them with magic, like the one Drystan rode. They would act on instinct or the instructions of their master. So if Annanor had sent them to Firehame while she waged her siege against Verdanthame, her attention would be divided, and her beasts would serve only to harass Firehame. Until Verdanthame fell.

Drystan urged his dragon to go faster, to keep up with the flock ahead of them, but not to overtake them. What would they find when they reached London? And how did Verdanthame Palace in Norwich fare, under the rule of the half-breed Dorian? What other magical forces had Annanor already launched against them?

He could only guess Verdanthame's fate, but at their speed, it did not take long to discover how Firehame Palace prospered.

Not as badly as Drystan feared.

From their vantage point, he could tell that Breden's water magic struck at both Firehame and Verdanthame from the sea on the south and east. Waves jetted in the air, a blue haze off in the distance. Verdanthame Palace lay too far away to see if it still withstood the siege, but Drystan could see a wall of seething green off to his left, an occasional crack of brown running through it as Annanor of Terrahame used her power of earth to break through Dorian's verdant defenses. It appeared that the half-breed still managed to hold his territory against the elven lady.

But the land of Firehame had been ravaged by Breden of Dewhame's water magic, and some of

Annanor's earth ruptures also spread into the sovereignty. Ponds of water replaced the pockets of fire that had formerly marked Firehame's lands. The pristine snow began to blacken the farther they flew toward London. Drystan could see the blue-uniformed soldiers of Breden of Dewhame's army destroying farms and villages, and as they neared their destination, the swell of the army grew larger, ringing the outskirts of Firehame Palace.

Drystan could smell the blood and death, even at this height. The images the scepters had sent him in his dreams became real.

He felt tempted to turn the dragon's head back around, to take Camille away from danger. But she had sworn herself to the cause, had made her own decision regarding her destiny. He could do naught but support her, and ignored the impulse.

Besides, the freedom of England may very well depend upon the knowledge they carried. When the three other elven joined their magic and army to the battle, Firehame would fall. And then Verdanthame would no longer be able to hold.

Drystan slowed the dragon as they neared London. The brown dragons had already joined the ranks of the beasts that circled the sky. They dipped into a lake near Breden of Dewhame's war banner, and rose with a bubble of water clutched in their talons. They dropped it upon the ring of fire protecting the city, but only a brief flash marked the spot where it splattered. General Dominic Raike's magical warding of fire still held.

Camille turned, her eyes wide with fear and dismay.

"Will your spell of concealment hold until we enter the palace?"

"My…?" Drystan snapped his mouth shut. He had been so concerned about what lay below them that he had not considered how they would cross the battle lines to reach Lord North. They now flew over Breden's army, and no call to arms had been raised against them. Perhaps the elven lord thought they were allies, since they rode on a golden dragon from Roden of Dreamhame's sovereignty.

Or perhaps Camille was right. Drystan had been thinking only of keeping her safe, and perhaps his magic responded to his will by concealing them. He'd had the knack of making himself almost invisible in Wales; indeed, he thought it proof of the power of his magic. But he did not hold as much of the gift as he would have liked. It had been proven to him time and again since entering England.

Unless he used his magic for Camille's sake. Perhaps it had risen to her aid once again.

"Do not worry," he finally replied. "I will get us into the palace."

She nodded with complete confidence and turned back around. Drystan smiled weakly. Despite his bravado, he couldn't really be sure of anything. If Breden of Dewhame thought them an ally, Dominic of Firehame would as well, and launch an attack against them.

Drystan feared his magic could be no match for Dominic's.

As they neared the heart of London he could see Firehame Palace, the yellow flaming walls a beacon of refuge for the Rebellion. Dominic's winged fire-lizards protected the skies against Breden's water dragons and Annanor's creations. Although the lizards might lack the glittering scales and more fearsome countenance of the illusory dragons, they spat liquid fire that ate through scale and turned water to harmless mist.

The elven lords had not sent their true dragons into battle, so their creations did not have the power to be much more than a nuisance to Dominic's own lizards or the black-coated soldiers of his army below them.

Drystan wondered if the elven lords would eventually send their dragon-steeds into battle. If they did, all would be lost, unless some of the true dragons came to the Rebellion's aid in turn. Surely Firehame's black dragon, Ador, would join in the effort to protect his own palace? But perhaps he had chosen to avoid the sickness that afflicted Grimor'ee from breaking the enchantment laid upon him. Perhaps Ador had chosen to huddle in a tower somewhere, refusing to aid either side.

One of Annanor's illusory dragons flew straight toward them, trying to avoid a blast of fire from one of the lizards pursuing it. Drystan hurriedly willed his dragon to dip, pulling Camille down as he ducked, the sharp talons of the beast barely missing their heads and the following crackle of heat forcing them even lower.

They flew straight for the red-flaming turrets of Firehame Palace.

A barrier of some sort shivered around them. It looked and felt like the waves of heat that form close to a flame. Dominic must have used another form of magic besides the fire lizards to protect his skies—a spell to serve as an alarm for any enemies approaching too closely from above. Drystan expected to hear an outcry from the soldiers below them, but his pocket burned once again, and they flew nearer to the court-yard without anyone the wiser.

Drystan frowned. He had noticed the burning once before. It came from the pocket where he kept the scepter. Yet for most of the journey, the golden rod had lain quiescent, like nothing more than a lump of coal. Indeed, it had not attempted to hum or commu-nicate to him in any way since Grimor'ee stole it from Roden. But it had sparked to life twice now, as if it expended some magical energy. If Drystan did not know any better, he would think the scepter aided his own spells. Surely that could not be, for he did not carry enough elven blood within his veins to wield the thing. He had felt the promise of death when Roden threatened to touch him with it.

But Drystan did not have time to wonder about it, for the ground rushed at them too quickly, and he did not have any idea how to land a dragon.

They rocked back and forth on unsure wings, abruptly descending into the largest courtyard in the middle of the palace. Red bricks paved the square and the walls, and warm yellow flames danced along the towers and turrets. They flew too close to one wall, but the yellow flame did not burn, and although Drystan had heard of the degrees of Dominic's magical fire, Camille let out a little bark of surprise.

One did not need to fear the yellow fire, but the red burned powerfully, and the black perhaps the worst, for it burned in the mind. Dominic had used it to kill his father, Mor'ded, and take over the elven lord's sovereignty.

Drystan forced himself to concentrate, for he could not keep them on a steady landing course.

After colliding with another wall, he decided it might be wiser to allow the beast's instincts to take over. Camille screamed as the dragon bobbed erratically across the cobblestones of the palace courtyard.

"Damn," growled Drystan.

The dragon's talons toppled over two carriages and a pile of boxes.

A knot of Firehame's soldiers split apart and drew their weapons, shouting in confusion.

Drystan willed the dragon in the direction of a cart overburdened with stale hay. If they had to crash—

He had not once loosened his hold upon Camille during their chaotic flight, but the impact of their landing tore her from his arms. A wild jumble of images flashed before his eyes. Camille's fur cloak as it fluttered about her gold uniform. The shimmer of fading magic as dragon turned back into horse. The face of a soldier with sparkling silver eyes, mouth open in astonishment. And then a yellow mass of twigs.

Drystan grunted from the impact, then rolled, brushing aside the hay that clouded his vision, looking for Camille.

She lay a few feet from him, atop the pile of hay now covering the completely smashed cart. The horse landed a few feet from her but stood upright soon enough, apparently unharmed, but snorting and stomping in fear.

Drystan crawled over to Camille, the hay puffing

up dust that made his nose itch. His back ached with bruising, and his head felt like an anvil sat upon it, but he ignored his pains as he patted Camille's cheek.

He could not have harmed her. So foolish—

"Don't move," shouted a voice ringing with command.

Drystan turned and looked up into the same silver eyes he had glimpsed earlier, but now realized they belonged to a female soldier. Her white elven hair sparkled with a matching silver color, testifying to the healthy dose of elven blood flowing in her veins. He envied that sheen.

"I am a member of the Rebellion," he panted. "I have come to see Lord North." Then Drystan turned back to Camille, completely dismissing the female warrior. "My love, please wake up."

Apparently the silver-eyed woman was not used to being ignored. "Get up," she snapped. "I do not care who you say you are. You have invaded the palace, and if you do not want to die in the next few seconds you will submit to your arrest."

Camille's lashes fluttered, and Drystan breathed a sigh of relief. He turned back to the woman. "My lady is hurt, and if you do not fetch someone to see to her this instant—"

Those silver eyes narrowed, and the woman drew her sword, effectively cutting off Drystan's flow of words.

"You have five seconds," she hissed, pointing the blade at Camille. "Your *lady* wears one of Roden's uniforms."

"Hold!" shouted another voice from within the doorway of the palace.

Drystan did not take his eyes off the soldier. He tried to fling a spell at her, something to push her away, but his magic had gone back to evading his will once again.

"Drystan? Is that you? Thank all of the saints!"

Drystan glanced over the woman's shoulder. Giles. His white-blond hair blended with the half-breeds surrounding him, but Drystan would not mistake those human green eyes for any other than his foster father.

"General… Wilhelmina," said Giles soothingly, "this is Drystan Hawkes. Stand down."

She arched one silver brow, but lowered her weapon.

"I need a healer," said Drystan.

Giles nodded, but before he could dispatch a soldier to fetch one, Camille sat up, brushing hay from her ivory hair.

"I am fine," she wheezed. "Just a bit addled from that landing."

"I am sorry," replied Drystan. "Getting a dragon down is much harder than keeping it aloft. Are you sure you are well?"

At her emphatic nod, Drystan turned and looked back up at the female soldier. "*The* Wilhelmina?"

Her silver brow rose slightly higher, and she shrugged.

Damn. Drystan should have guessed. With those silver elven eyes that bespoke of Bladehame, and the magical sheen of her sword along with her imposing physical stature, it could be none other than Lan'dor's former champion. Her height topped that of the man standing next to her, who caught Drystan's attention as well. If not for his pointed ears and fine features,

Drystan would not have guessed him to carry any elven blood, with those human brown eyes and hair.

"Alexander?" breathed Drystan.

The man dipped his brown head in acknowledgement, a smile playing about the corners of his mouth.

"What's the matter?" murmured Camille.

Drystan stood up, bringing her with him. "Miss Camille Ashton," he pronounced, "may I introduce you to Wilhelmina, the Duchess of Chandos, who was once Lan'dor's champion, but gave it all up for the love of the man beside her: Alexander, the Duke of Chandos, a skilled sword-dancer, son of General Dominic Raikes and Lady Cassandra. The two of them together... *acquired* the silver scepter for the Rebellion."

"I see." Camille gave a hesitant smile. "I am pleased to meet you."

The duchess managed to soften her stunning face with a little smile, but the duke now grinned broadly.

Drystan frowned. Camille did not sound as impressed as she should. Did she not understand the perils these two had undergone for the Rebellion's cause? Or did shyness hold her back? They might be legends in their own time, but Camille was now a free woman, and should consider herself as an equal. His foster father rescued him from his conflicted feelings.

"Now I know how I rate," said Giles, "when you introduce your lady to strangers before the man who raised you."

"Forgive me." Drystan flushed, guided Camille down from the pile of hay to his foster father. Then found himself blinking in surprise, unconsciously lifting his hand toward Giles's cheek. Giles said he had been marked by wild magic, but until now, Drystan had never seen the proof of it, for the blemish faded in mundane Wales.

Giles's hand rose as well, fingering the livid green mark on the left side of his face. "Aye, it came back the moment I passed the magical barrier into England."

"You should wear it proudly, Father."

He shrugged, and Drystan realized how foolish he had been to become enthralled over meeting Alexander and Wilhelmina. The perils Giles had endured surely equaled any others'... except, perhaps, General Dominic Raikes. "Camille, allow me to introduce you to Giles Beaumont, my foster father."

Giles crossed his muscular arms over his chest, his four-and-sixty years not reducing his prowess in the least, thanks to his elven blood. He tapped one booted foot impatiently on the red cobblestones.

"Giles and my foster mother," Drystan rushed on, "discovered the source of magic in the Seven Corners of Hell... which is where he acquired the green mark upon his face. It is from wild magic." He glanced at Giles, who still tapped his foot. "Which dangers he fought with valiant bravery, helping Lady Cecily to escape. At great peril to his life." Drystan waited. Had he apologized enough? The foot still tapped a steady rhythm. Apparently not. "Because of my foster father's heroic deeds, Lady Cecily managed to wrest the blue scepter from Breden of Dewhame, and they both escaped to Wales, where they raised the orphan children saved from elven testing. As you already know, I was one of the lucky recipients of his training and guidance. He is a master swordsman. And a brilliant

scholar of elven lore. And—damn it, Father, if I go on
at length any longer, I shall—"

Giles laughed and stepped forward and hugged
Drystan. "It's good to see you, Son."

Drystan hugged him back, measure for measure,
until Giles set him aback and cocked a smile. "You
have come into your full strength, I see. It's difficult
to believe you were once sickly."

Drystan flushed again. The problem with one's
parents, he decided, was that they always viewed one
as still a child. He quickly changed the subject. "What
of your sword? When you entered the realm of magic
again, did it go back to its bloodthirsty ways as well?"

"Aye. Damn thing keeps whining for me to take
it into battle. I haven't had a lick of rest since we
got here."

"Lady Cecily came with you, then?"

"Of course."

"And what of… what of the three?"

Giles gave Wilhelmina a pointed look. She and
her husband had been listening to their conversation
intently, Dominic's son still wearing that broad grin.
With some dismay, Drystan suspected it had widened
on his behalf.

Wilhelmina turned to her men, who milled about
with curiosity. A few of them still held sword or pistol
in hand. She frowned at them. "Did you honestly
think I could not handle these two by myself?"

Heads immediately shook, and weapons were
hastily sheathed.

"Back to your drills," she commanded.

Alexander spun to follow the rest of the men.

"Not you," she groaned with exasperation suffusing her voice.

Alexander turned around and winked at Drystan. For some reason, that small gesture made him feel more at ease.

Giles leaned forward and enfolded Camille in his arms. "Welcome, child. I hear you may bear a mark as well."

She caught her breath, then nodded against his chest.

Drystan reached out and towed her back to his side. Giles frowned, and then suddenly his face cleared. "That's the way of it, then? It seems Lady Cecily was right. She will be pleased to hear it." He studied Camille thoughtfully. "She is beautiful, Drystan, this lady of your dreams. And what remarkable eyes! I think I see every color of the seven sovereignties within them. And unless these old human eyes of mine have deceived me, you rode in on the back of a dragon. You must have powerful magic, my dear."

Camille shook her head. "I have no magic at all, Mister Beaumont, despite my elven blood. 'Twas Drystan who changed our horse to dragon, and who concealed us well enough until we landed."

"Call me Giles. You shall make me feel old, otherwise." He glanced back at Drystan. "It seems you have come into your magical powers as well, my son. I am glad for you. I just prayed you had brought some hope for us."

"But we did."

Wilhelmina gasped, and her husband threw an arm about her waist to steady her.

"Camille may not have any magic," continued

Drystan, "but she held the key, *and* was clever enough to decipher it."

Giles's handsome old face split into a radiant smile, one that made many a young woman swoon, despite his advanced years. "It existed then? I had prayed... come; we will talk inside, where it is safe. There are more spies among these walls than even we can guess."

Drystan glanced at Camille. "It has been a long, difficult journey. She must eat and rest first. And she will need a change of clothing."

"Of course," said Giles.

"I am fine," interjected Camille. "Besides, we carry important news. I will not be able to rest until we deliver it."

Drystan sighed, but understood exactly how she felt. Too many of their countrymen were dying outside of these walls.

"I will call a meeting," offered Wilhelmina. "We shall gather in the blue salon." And she strode away.

Her husband followed her with his eyes, turned and grinned at Drystan when he noticed him watching. "We'd best hurry. My wife and Lady Joscelyn will have them assembled soon enough."

"Lady Joscelyn," repeated Drystan, striving to keep the eagerness from his voice. He would not act like some awestruck schoolboy yet again.

"Indeed. Ever since Beaumont brought the lavender scepter from Wales, she has been enchanting gems for the soldiers to carry into battle. She despises using the thing almost as much as Lady Cecily despises using the blue scepter, so I imagine she will welcome a break."

Drystan turned to Giles, who easily read his expression.

"Your foster mother has been trying to slow the advance of the rest of the elven lords. She sent a blizzard to Dreamhame, but Roden managed to shield his sovereignty from the brunt of it, and his army steadily marches. She has managed to slow La'laylia of Stonehame and Lan'dor of Bladehame, but not as much as she hoped. She fears to harm the humans in their armies."

Drystan read the worry in the older man's face. Using the blue scepter must be taking a toll on Lady Cecily, who feared the scepter's ability to beguile her to use all of its devastating power.

They could do nothing about his foster mother's struggle with temptation; she would have to fight that internal battle on her own. Drystan quickly tried to divert Giles's thoughts elsewhere. "I suppose General Samson Cavendish is here, as well?"

"Of course," replied Giles, his strong chin lifting slightly. He slapped Drystan on the back again, and led him forward into the palace. "Besides Verdanthame, this is the last bastion of the Rebellion. Soon you shall meet many of those you have read about, for they will wish to hear your news firsthand. And if you hadn't noticed, we are running out of time."

The mention of their current predicament sobered them all, and it was a quiet procession that filed into the palace hall. Drystan stared at their surroundings, having only read of Firehame Palace. It looked much like Dreamhame, but with less gold opulence, and more magical creations of fire. Fountains of yellow flame spilled into marble bowls; eyes within portraits followed their movements as they passed. The statue of a flaming griffin snapped at them, and fiery strands of tapestries rewove themselves into one dreadful scene after another.

Drystan did not release Camille's hand. If he was feeling a bit overwhelmed by the company and their surroundings, he could only imagine what she might be going through. But she only clasped his fingers tighter, her face betraying none of her emotions.

"It is best not to wander the halls," said Giles. "Dominic did not change Mor'ded's decor for fear his charade would be discovered, and he did not have the time to concern himself with such matters when the elven lords suspected him and attacked."

"Of course," murmured Drystan as they followed his foster father into a withdrawing room with watered blue silk covering the walls. Blue carpets lay scattered about the floor like puddles of water, and blue fire swirled from silver urns and blue crystal vases. Even the ceiling had been painted blue, with white clouds to relieve the color, giving an eerie likeness to true sky.

Drystan froze, bringing both Camille and Giles to an abrupt halt. Alexander bowed deeply, then continued into the room and pulled up a chair, watching Drystan with that indulgent smile still on his face.

Alexander, the Duke of Chandos, must be near fifty years old, although he possessed enough elven blood to make him appear much younger... and carried himself with enough poise to make Drystan feel even younger than half of those years.

But Drystan could not help his astonished stare. For Lord North, the leader of the Rebellion and Prime

Minister to the king, sat in a chair near the window, the yellow flames of the outside walls occasionally flickering over the thick glass. Next to him sat a handsome blond man of middle years. If the crown circling his brow had not already told Drystan he faced the king of England, the protruding eyes, straight nose, and small mouth of the Hanoverian line would have.

Giles bowed as deeply as Alexander had, jolting Drystan to do the same. Camille gave the king an elegant curtsy, and his heart soared with pride for the grace of his lady.

"Your Majesty," said Giles. "May I present my foster son, Viscount Drystan Hawkes—"

"That is my brother's title," whispered Drystan.

"No longer," answered Giles, "since you are returned home. Indeed, should we survive this war, I think you will find your brother happy to give over the inheritance to his long-lost brother."

Camille gave Drystan a worried frown, but quickly turned back to the king when Giles introduced her as well. She curtsied once again, her cheeks pink when she rose. Giles had introduced her as Drystan's lady. To his chagrin, Drystan couldn't tell if she had been pleased or embarrassed by the introduction.

"So," said King George, "we now have two more heroes to add to the Rebellion's roster."

Drystan tried to resist the urge to deny the king's words. One did not disagree with a king. But he could not rank himself with the likes of Giles and Alexander. "I did nothing to deserve such an honor-ific, Your Majesty."

The king waved his hand dismissively. "That is

precisely what they all say. Did you or did you not, bring us the key?"

"I... yes, Camille—Miss Ashton—has the key, and a theory to decipher it."

"And we are sure you braved perils—just like all the others—to bring it here. No, do not dispute it again. We heard about your efforts to land a dragon. You still have hay in your hair."

Drystan reached up to the pale strands, which lay about his shoulders in wild disarray.

Alexander snorted with suppressed laughter.

"Take a seat, Lord Hawkes," suggested Lord North, breaking his silence for the first time. Although he might be the undisputed leader of the Rebellion, he obviously deferred to the presence of the king. "His Majesty understands you have rushed to bring your news, and that your appearance shows no disrespect."

But Drystan worried about more than his disheveled state. Did the king truly think that he and Camille were some kind of heroes? Would folk tell tales of their adventures with the same wonder in which he had listened to those of Alexander and Wilhelmina? It seemed so improbable. They had done only what had been needed...

Giles led Drystan and Camille to a blue silk settee, and then pulled up a carved wooden chair beside them for himself.

Lady Cecily entered the room, hastily dipped a curtsy to the king while her brilliant elven eyes stayed fixed on her foster son. All of the gentlemen save the king had risen on her entrance, and Drystan leaned down a bit to return her hug.

"You are safe," she breathed.

"Aye. And I have brought a gift."

She released him and turned to Camille. "I see. Welcome, Camille Ashton. I have so many questions to ask you that I do not know where to begin."

"Your curiosity will have to wait," interrupted Giles with a gentle smile. "For our son has brought us the key to England's freedom."

"We do not know that for certain, Father."

"Aye, that is true. But we still have more important matters to discuss than your love life."

Drystan grimaced and sat down, avoiding Camille's gaze. And Alexander's soft laughter. Heaven save him from loving parents.

Giles pulled up another chair for his wife, Cecily, and by the time she had settled her azure skirts about her, General Dominic Raikes and his wife entered the room. Alexander greeted his mother warmly, and extended the same to his father, although the impassivity on the older man's face would have prevented Drystan from it. Lady Cassandra resembled her son, with her human brown hair and eyes, and the way she moved with the grace of a trained dancer, although she did not dance with swords as her son did. She smiled and laughed almost as much as her son, Alexander, making Dominic appear even sterner by comparison.

Dominic Raikes, the man who had killed his elven lord father and stolen his identity, walked a bit stiffly with age, but looked no more than five-and-thirty, his white-blond hair lacking any gray, the silver sparkles within it still gleaming with the vigor of youth. Drystan glanced at the ring on Dominic's finger: a pale amethyst stone set in a thick band of gold. Cecily's father had been sent on a mission to find that ring, although Cecily and Giles had been the ones to return with it. Crafted by the powers of three scepters, it had the ability to hide Dominic's true age, for his human blood threatened to reveal his disguise as one of the near-ageless elven lords.

Dominic suddenly turned and stared at Drystan, those black-faceted eyes fixing upon his. At first, the other man's gaze seemed remote. Emotionless. And Drystan struggled with hero worship. This man, this half-breed, was the epitome of a legend. Dominic and his Lady Cassandra had become the true force behind the Rebellion. Dominic Raikes had fought like no other to gain his freedom. And would continue to fight with untold valor to gain the freedom of all of England's people.

Then those midnight eyes changed. And Drystan caught a flicker… of pain. Of suffering. What Dominic had accomplished had come at great cost. And the strength in his face told Drystan he would be willing to pay even more to reach his final goal.

Perhaps it had been building ever since he left Wales and experienced his own adventures, but in that moment, Drystan understood. He did not gaze at a legend, but at a man with a strength of will matched only by the brown-haired lady at his side. His awe of the company slowly began to fade as they filled the room.

General Samson Cavendish entered, his suffering more visible in the scars on his face and hands— scars which could be given only by repeatedly cutting the same area, for those of elven blood held extraordinary powers of healing. He escorted his wife, Lady Joscelyn, to sit next to him. Her lavender eyes matched the scepter she held in her hands—the scepter she and Samson had stolen from La'laylia of Stonehame. Wilhelmina followed, taking her place by her husband's side. And Drystan no longer gazed at a warrior-woman of legend. But at a middle-aged lady who had spent most of her life fighting for what she believed in.

Alexander still continued to watch Drystan, but the smile on his face had died. He nodded, and Drystan returned it, a silent communion of understanding.

Drystan had become one of them. He understood his own worth to the company. He was no longer the child of Giles and Cecily, but a man who had fought his own battles, who had struggled for the love of the woman at his side, and would continue to do so. They were not heroes in a storybook. But people who shared a common purpose, and would fight and die to see it accomplished.

Twelve

"WE ARE ALL GATHERED, THEN?" SAID KING GEORGE.

Dominic nodded. "Except for Dorian of Verdanthame and his lady, Aurelia. I shall speak to them after our discussion."

"How?" whispered Camille.

She had been so quiet that Drystan felt grateful she had finally spoken. He hoped she had become to feel as he did. An equal in this company.

Camille's voice had carried, and Drystan's foster mother answered her. "La'laylia of Stonehame made a crystal for each of the elven lords." She held up the blue scepter. "When their scepters are placed inside of it, they can communicate with one another. But five of them no longer possess their scepters."

"We have accomplished that much with our thefts, at least," said Giles.

"Not that it has made much difference," interjected Dominic. "They did not communicate with each other much anyway."

Lord North leaned forward. "We know we miscalculated the importance of the scepters."

Drystan watched the king settle back into his throne-like chair. Ah, the power had shifted. The king's advisor would primarily hold sway over this meeting, allowing his prime minister to do what he did best. Plot and scheme.

"Perhaps not," offered Drystan.

Giles's eyes widened at his son's temerity to speak a contradiction among the leaders of the Rebellion. His foster mother just smiled.

Dominic cocked a pale brow and fingered the black lace at his throat. "Perhaps you should tell us about this key of yours, Lord Hawkes."

A moment ago, Drystan might have flinched at that cold black stare. Now he only gave Dominic a grave nod, and began to speak. "As you know, the white witch of Ashton house witnessed the arrival of the elven lords. She placed a birthmark on her child as to what she saw, and it was passed down among her descendants. I searched the archives for years, trying to find some trace of the lineage. I did not know if it would aid us in our quest to free England, but all knowledge is power."

"But you had help," interrupted Lord North.

"Yes. Yes, I did." If the man thought to rattle him, he would have to try much harder. Drystan was no longer the young man who had lived in Wales. His fits were a part of the same suffering that joined this company, and they would no longer demoralize him. "The scepters spoke to me of a key to open the doorway to Elfhame—and that the white witch's descendant held said key."

"And this is where I get concerned," growled Giles. "Do we trust these devil-wands to aid us in any way?"

"It is interesting that they chose to speak to you, and no other," added the king.

Drystan frowned. Did the king doubt his story in some way?

"I have seen him suffer through the fits caused by the scepters," avowed Lady Cecily. "Trust me, no one would welcome such... communication."

All eyes fixed on Camille. She flushed and leaned closer to Drystan. He shifted so she sat slightly behind his shoulder. "The scepters sent me dreams of her, as well."

"And you fell in love with a dream," sighed Lady Cecily.

"Indeed. She became my heart's desire, and I knew I would do anything to free her from Dreamhame Palace."

"And a life of slavery," muttered Dominic.

"Yes."

"Then perhaps that is why they chose you," said Lady Cecily.

"I have heard whispers from my scepter," said Dominic, "and can only imagine what their actual voices might do to a human's mind. As for the scepters' intentions... Ador has told me often enough that they want to go home."

"Firehame's dragon?" scoffed Lord North. "I hear he has gone missing."

Dominic shrugged. "My understanding is that all the dragon-steeds have disappeared. At least they will not aid the elven lords in their war against us."

"They would not survive it," whispered Camille.

Drystan's foster mother gave her a surprised look. "Indeed. To aid a human sickens them. The elven lords bound them with an enchantment to ensure their loyalty."

Drystan rubbed at his forehead, which still ached from their tumble.

"You are ill, Lord Hawkes?" asked Dominic.

"No. I just do not know how to land a dragon properly."

Dominic's lip twitched. "So I heard. It takes a powerful illusion to construct a dragon that can fly passengers, and it can sap your energy for days. It appears that Lord North underestimated your magical abilities."

"Nay, he did not." Drystan glanced at Camille. "Unfortunately my magic is most… unpredictable."

"Which may be a result of your absence from magical influences since childhood. I am more surprised that Miss Ashton possesses no magic, what with those unusual eyes of hers. But I sense none at all. It is astonishing you both managed to make it out of Dreamhame in one piece." Dominic raised the black scepter. "I will take care of your injuries myself, then. It will help if you close your eyes."

Drystan remembered the brilliant healing fire of the little old woman who had tended to his injuries in Dreamhame Palace, and complied. Blue light shone behind his lids, and he felt the same healing magic, only so much more powerful it made him gasp. He had not realized how badly his head and back hurt until the pain faded. Even the slight ache of his old injury disappeared.

It was as if Dominic's healing fire cleansed him of all wounds, making his body as whole as it had been at birth.

Camille gave a deep sigh, and Drystan's eyes flew open, watching the blue fire dwindle away from her as well.

"You told me you were unhurt," accused Drystan.

"It was nothing."

He lowered his voice and whispered in her ear. "Don't you know my love for you means you must tell me such things? Your every breath is important to me."

Camille colored yet again. Lady Cecily huffed, and Giles grunted in approval. Drystan did not care that they had overheard his words.

"Will you just tell us of this key?" blurted Lord North into the sudden silence. "Then we shall make our own decision on what to do about it."

Drystan nodded. "Miss Ashton is the descendant of the white witch, and she carries the birthmark."

Camille obligingly leaned her head and pushed the hair back from her ear. Everyone craned to get a look at it.

"The birthmark is partly beneath her hair," said Drystan, "and difficult to make out. May I have quill and paper?"

Giles brought it to him, with a look that made Drystan wonder at the newfound respect he saw in those human green eyes. And then he understood. His foster father no longer saw him as a child he must protect, but as an equal. More than Drystan's own perceptions had changed from this gathering.

"Thank you, Father."

Giles chest swelled and he nodded, then returned to his seat.

Drystan drew the outline of the mark as he had done in Dreamhame, and held the paper up for the company to study. "As you can see, it is in the shape of a seven-pointed star. I could not fathom its meaning, not until Miss Ashton drew the individual shape of each point. Besides being an extraordinarily intelligent woman, I believe she held within her very blood the means to decipher the brand that her family has carried for generations."

Drystan could hear the breaths of each person in the room, the scratch of quill across paper as he drew. For the first time, he became aware of their mingled scent: lavender, roses, and spice, with a hint of elfweed. He fancied he could feel the expectation of his fellow compatriots. He held up the drawing when he finished.

"As you can see, the shape is similar to—"

"A scepter!" blurted the king. "I am right, am I not? But how is this a key?"

Drystan looked at Camille, willing her to speak, to indeed stand as an equal in this company. He shifted his gaze to the enchanted sword that lay on her hip, trying to remind her of her bravery when she confronted the bandits, of how she had defended and protected herself. Of the new strength he hoped she had found.

Something sparked in her rainbow-colored eyes, and Camille glanced around the room and spoke, her voice getting stronger with every word. "I believe this is what my ancestor saw when the elven lords entered our world. She saw all seven scepters joined to create this star, a combining of all their magics, creating a spell powerful enough to open a doorway between Elfhame and England."

"It makes sense," offered Lord North, with a glance at the king to make sure he had permission to preside over them all once again. At the king's nod, the heavy man continued. "But I am also afraid it raises more questions than answers."

"For example," said Dominic. "Why didn't the scepters just send you dreams of this key? Why the journey to Dreamhame, and the involvement of Miss Ashton? It would have been much… simpler."

"Would we have listened to the dreams of an untried youth?" asked Giles. "I am sad to admit that even though I witnessed Drystan's… communications with the scepters, I doubted the existence of this white witch and key."

Dominic's fingers tightened around the black scepter. "Ador has often said humans must help themselves. That we must earn our freedom."

Giles snorted. "A convenient excuse to do nothing."

"I disagree," said Camille. "Grimor'ee looked quite ill when he helped us. I do believe an enchantment discourages them from plotting against the elven lords."

"Perhaps the scepters are under the same enchantment as the dragons," offered Lady Cecily. "Perhaps that is why they can help us only indirectly."

Dominic focused his midnight gaze on Drystan's foster mother. "That makes sense. But I still think there is more to this than we know. Why, indeed, involve Miss Ashton? If she carried the white witch's power—any power, it would make more sense to engage her in the fight to free England."

"I would not have pursued the key if not for her," stated Drystan. "And no one would else would have believed in my dreams."

"We have argued in a circle," said Lord North. "Let us assume for the nonce—"

"Forgive me," interrupted Cecily, "but, Camille, you have referred to Dreamhame's dragon offering you aid. I think we all assumed he helped you to escape. May I ask specifically what Grimor'ee did to defy the enchantment binding him?"

Camille licked her lips, glanced at Drystan. He slowly withdrew the bundle from his pocket and carefully unwrapped it, making sure he kept the cloth between his naked skin and the golden scepter. "He gave Camille this."

Everyone gasped.

"He said we would have need of it," said Camille, as if apologizing for having it in their possession.

"But you cannot wield it," pressed Dominic.

"No."

"And as evidenced by his careful handling, Lord Hawkes fears to even touch it."

"Then it cannot offer us much help in our war against the elven," said Lord North.

Drystan studied the golden scepter. "It *has* been very quiet."

"What do you mean, Lord Hawkes?" asked Dominic.

"Even after I left Wales, I sometimes heard the voices of the lavender, blue, and silver scepters in my head. Not just in my dreams. When I was in Dreamhame, I heard the golden one as well, but only a murmur. It has been quiet since then." He did not mention the odd burning sensation when he worked magic, for he could not be sure if he had only imagined it.

"I have never heard my scepter's voice, just a humming sort of whisper," mused Dominic. "Lady Joscelyn, Lady Cecily. Do you experience the same?"

"Yes," admitted Drystan's foster mother, glancing down at her blue scepter. "It coaxes me to use the greater power of the sky."

Lady Joscelyn nodded. "The lavender scepter whispers to me at times."

"I hear them quite clearly," said Drystan. "Or at least, I used to. It changed when I entered the barrier of magic."

"More puzzles we cannot solve," sighed Dominic. "Since you cannot wield a scepter, it is most unusual that you have such a connection to them."

"Perhaps it has something to do with the natural magic that exists beyond the barrier," said Lady Cecily.

Lord North scratched at the white wig upon his head in frustration. "We stray from the most important subject. The key. If we join the seven scepters, they will open the gateway to Elfhame. If not, we shall lose the battle against the elven lords anyway. Perhaps Grimor'ee gave Roden's golden scepter to Miss Ashton for that very purpose. Let us put our minds to how we might accomplish the task."

A sudden deluge of blue sparkles drifted down from the ceiling. They imbued Drystan with a calm, refreshed feeling. And judging by the expressions on the other's faces, it produced the same sort of effect on them. Apparently, the blue withdrawing room had been chosen on purpose for its enchantment.

"First," said Dominic, "we must form this star. I can wield the black scepter, and Dorian's overthrow of Verdanthame proves he possesses enough elven blood to wield the green. Lady Cecily commands the blue scepter of Dewhame, and Lady Joscelyn the lavender of Stonehame. Although we possess the silver scepter of Bladehame, and now the golden of Dreamhame, we have no one who carries enough power to actually wield them. And Annanor of Terrahame still holds the brown."

Lord North smiled his cherubic smile, obviously pleased to finally discuss what he thought most important. "We still have spies in Terrahame. Malcolm has long been a trusted consort of Annanor's. I hesitated to ask him to risk stealing it, as the information he provides of the elven lady seemed more crucial. But now—"

"Can this Malcolm wield it?"

"Ah, I do not know, Dominic. He has wisely refused to touch the thing."

Dominic scowled. "You know it is but a carefully cultivated rumor of the elven lords that if anyone touches a scepter they are destroyed."

"I have touched the silver scepter," offered Wilhelmina, the warrior-woman from Bladehame, "and it did me no lasting harm."

"No *lasting* harm," repeated Lord North. "I will not risk my spies unless I am forced to. And more than one human who lacked enough elven blood in their veins to touch it *has* died."

Drystan focused his gaze on the golden scepter in his hand. "It is possible to touch the scepter, then, but not necessarily have the power to wield it."

"Absolutely. It depends on the level of elven blood and magical powers one inherits. But it is risky, since one can never be sure they possess enough until they attempt it."

Drystan nodded. His own magic had proven to be erratic. But strong. When Roden of Dreamhame tried to touch him with the scepter, Drystan had felt the threat of death from the thing. But perhaps the elven lord's ill will lay behind the destructive power Drystan had felt. Since Grimor'ee had given the scepter to Camille, he felt nothing evil from it. Indeed, it now sat quietly within his hand. As if it slept.

Or tried to fool him into believing it was harmless?

"So even if we acquire the brown scepter," continued Dominic, "we must still find someone to wield it."

"And the silver and gold," added Lord North.

Drystan set the golden scepter on his lap and removed his one remaining glove. Camille clasped Drystan's upper arm, those rainbow-colored eyes searching his face, as if she read his very thoughts.

"No," she whispered.

Giles glanced at them distractedly, then turned back to Lord North quickly enough. "What of your attempt to find orphans powerful enough to wield the scepters?" he asked.

"We have found several who appear to carry a healthy amount of elven blood." North's heavy features sagged. "But I fear that, like Lord Hawkes, they have lived beyond the barrier of magic for too long. Even if they have the power to wield a scepter, their magic may be too erratic. And they would have to touch a scepter first. We have no sure guarantee it will not kill them, and some of them are so very young... The risk is too great."

Drystan took a deep breath. Now or never. He turned and looked into Camille's eyes, his heart swelling with love for her. Did he love the Rebellion more? Could he risk leaving her to face the world on her own, in the hope he could free thousands of slaves just like her?

Again, it appeared as if she could read his thoughts. Fear still shimmered in her eyes, but Camille gave him a slight nod and gently squeezed his arm. She did not like it, but she understood.

"You have no right to make such decisions for others," said Drystan.

And he wrapped his bare hands around the golden scepter.

Dominic nodded, but the rest of the circle startled at his action. Giles erupted from his chair, a strangled sound catching in his throat as he stared down at his foster son.

The room fell silent, the muted sound of dragons battling overhead filtering past the flame-covered walls.

The golden scepter felt warm in Drystan's hands, and for a moment he felt the thrum of powerful magic, heard a faint whisper in his head. "It did not kill me," he breathed.

Camille let go of his arm, sagged back against the cushions of the settee.

Giles opened his mouth as if to yell, but quickly snapped it shut and collapsed back into his chair, the green mark upon his face livid against his paled skin.

General Dominic Raikes leaned forward and raised a pale brow. "But can you wield it?"

Drystan squeezed his fingers around the scepter, which now felt cool against his palms. "I… I think I felt the power for a brief moment."

"Close your eyes. Feel the smooth weight of it in your hands. *Will* its magic to come to your call."

Drystan complied with Dominic's instruction, a part of him idly thinking about such an astonishing turn of events. At one time, he would have given anything to *not* hear the voice of a scepter. But now…

Drystan gripped the wand even tighter. His heart rose. He had dreamed of having enough power to make a difference in the fight for England's freedom. If he could actually wield the scepter, and not just hold it in his hands, his dream could actually become true.

But of course, now that he wanted a scepter to speak to him, it refused to do so.

Dominic shook his head in resignation. "You hear nothing… feel nothing."

Drystan nodded.

"Ah, well. Bravo for taking the risk, Lord Hawkes."

"But does it follow," mused Lady Cecily, "that one must be able to wield the power? Would it still be possible to open the doorway by just joining the seven together? As long as we can find someone to hold them, we might still be able to open this portal."

The room grew quiet once more.

Lord North turned his sharp gaze on Wilhelmina. "Would you be willing to hold the silver scepter?"

She winced, and then gave a negligent shrug. "Of course."

The leader of the Rebellion rubbed his hands together. "Then all we will need is for someone to hold the brown. Events force me to ask Malcolm to try. As Drystan has so dramatically pointed out, it is not my right to make the decision for him. Even if he cannot wield it, he can hopefully carry it to… where?"

"The Seven Corners of Hell," said Lady Cecily. "For that is where the opening to Elfhame is located. If we lack the full combined power, at least we will have a better chance of success if we stand near the doorway."

"That makes sense. What do you all say?"

Giles stood, the sword at his side shivering in his scabbard. Drystan gazed at it warily. All his life, it had been an ordinary sword. But Giles had told him often enough of its magical properties, and he did not doubt it still thirsted for blood.

Giles laid a hand on Cecily's shoulder. "We have been to the Seven Corners of Hell, and it is a mad place, with a chaotic clash of power we barely survived. And even getting there will not be easy. We have to get through Breden of Dewhame's and Annanor of Terrahame's armies, and I do not doubt the other three elven might also stand in our way by the time we manage to make it to Oxford. Or am I the only one who will point out our ages? With the exception of Drystan and Miss Ashton, we are all past our prime."

"Which means I am doddering," snapped Dominic, "since I am older than all of you."

Giles shrugged.

"But your elven blood makes you all look and act much younger," soothed Lord North. "And your powers can ease the journey."

Dominic ignored him and stood and faced Giles, his black scepter clenched in his hand. Red fire curled from the tip of the wand, dancing around the half-breed's body, twisting about his arms and legs. He glowed with power, with the might of his elven blood.

King George gaped, and Lord North coughed.

Lady Cecily intervened. "This display is not necessary, General Raikes. You know very well my husband is protesting only because he fears for my safety. I have tried to break his habit of protecting me, but it appears it has become ingrained in him. No one here has any doubt you are up to the task."

Camille squeezed Drystan's arm and murmured, "So, that is where you get it from."

Giles glanced down at the two of them as Drystan shrugged in resignation, and his foster father's bluster abruptly faded as he thumped back into his chair. "I still say it is a mad venture. We have no guarantee we will even open this doorway… and only a guess about what might happen if we do. The dragons say Elfhame is a peaceful place, and the elven lords breached the barriers between the worlds because they longed for power and glory and chaos. But what if they are lying just to return to their home? What if all elven-kind are as evil as the seven who conquered our world? We shall not be able to stand against them."

"Then we shall close the door," replied Dominic, the red fire still curling about his body fading to a glowing white. "Besides, what is our alternative? Sit here and wait for the other three Imperial Lords to join the army already waging war against us? We have no chance of defeating them. I would rather grasp at even a slim hope, than none at all."

Lord North cleared his throat, his intelligent gaze

turned inward, as if he were only partly paying attention to the disagreement. "There are many things that could go wrong. Which means we shall have to plan carefully. Malcolm may not be able to steal the brown scepter, so I will have to send more spies with an affinity for Annanor's powers of earth to aid him." He glanced up at Drystan. "I will ask for volunteers among the orphans."

"And Dorian of Verdanthame must agree to the plan," said Dominic, sitting next to his lady again. "But I have no doubt they will think the venture worth the risk. And I daresay they will have a much easier time of it reaching Seven Hells, for they both are nearer to Lord Hawkes and Miss Ashton's age." He shot Giles a disgruntled look.

Giles rolled his eyes.

A ghost of a smile flitted across Dominic's face before his usual mask of impassivity replaced it. "But we shall leave Verdanthame vulnerable, without Dorian's scepter to defend it. And Firehame, as well. We must travel quickly, for if we fail to open the doorway, we must return to defend our people."

Drystan swallowed. He could guess the direction of Dominic's thoughts, and the means he intended to propose for their journey. Besides the elven lords' dragon-steeds, England's skies had remained relatively clear over the years. The elven preferred the humans to do their fighting, not their magical creations. But with the war, and the scepters in the hands of half-breeds, it seemed the skies would now be teeming with flying beasts. Drystan glanced at the quiet golden scepter in his hand. "I do not know how I managed to keep my illusory dragon long enough to get here, and I do not know if I can create such a being again."

"Do not worry, Lord Hawkes. We shall not rely upon an unpredictable spell… or luck, which is surely what aided you across the battle lines. You may have concealed your entrance to Firehame from most, but the elven lords cannot be fooled by a spell unless it has been cast with the power of three scepters. Fortunately, we have three to wield."

"I can create our dragon-steeds," offered Lady Cecily. "With my affinity for the sky, they should fly true… and perhaps be easier to land." She gave Drystan a gentle smile.

Joscelyn gripped the lavender scepter a bit tighter. "And I can enspell them with a gem which will cast an illusion to hide us from the Imperial Lords."

"And I can forge them in fire to combine our magics," said Dominic, "and give our beasts the gift of fire's breath. We have our mounts… now to our route." He gave Wilhelmina and Samson Cavendish significant glances. Since they were former champions, Drystan assumed they both had kept the same positions as generals in Firehame's army. Samson's next words proved his assumption. His gravelly voice rang with authority.

"We shall have to get through Breden of Dewhame's army to get to Oxford, but since we're flying, we need only worry about his water-dragons, and although they cannot compare to our mounts, it would be best to avoid conflict."

"I daresay I would not want to try and fight on dragonback," agreed Lord North.

"You are staying here," growled General Cavendish.

"Now see here—"

"He is right," interrupted Dominic. "You and the king must stay. You must coordinate your spies, and the people will need the king for support. And it will help conceal the fact of our departure. If Breden of Dewhame and Annanor of Terrahame become aware of our absence, they will not wait for the other elven lords to join the war. They will attack with full force."

Drystan blinked. He had been wrong about who presided over this meeting, for both the king and Lord North offered no further argument.

General Dominic Raikes turned his midnight gaze back to the other generals. "We stay sharp, avoid any flocks sent to patrol the skies. It should take less than a day to reach Oxford, if we fly high and fast. I believe I can keep some of my magic focused here at Firehame, and I believe Dorian can keep his own greenery animated to hide his absence from Verdanthame. We will leave on the morrow. Will you bless our mission, Your Majesty?"

The king gave a regal nod. "I pray you will be able to open this doorway, but if not, may you all return safely home." His lip quirked. "If this fails, we will need all of you to devise another wild scheme for England's freedom."

Drystan smiled, just as they all did, save Dominic, who appeared to rarely smile at all.

But Drystan's smile abruptly faded as he realized perspiration had started to bead his brow, and he glanced down at the golden scepter in his hand. It still seemed lifeless, but he could sense the enormous power it could command. It reminded him of his past life. Of his fits. And of his current failure to possess enough power to wield it. With a grimace, he wrapped it back up and stowed it into his pocket once again.

Wilhelmina rose in one fluid movement. "I need to prepare my men. A surprise attack in the morning might help distract anyone from our departure."

"Same here," agreed Samson. "I also have a few men who will be eager to show their prowess, and I have my own orders to give. There are always fools seeking glory."

Dominic stood. "We must create our dragons at once, so I can send one to Verdanthame for Dorian and Aurelia."

"And one to Malcolm in Terrahame," added the king, rising to signal an end to the meeting.

Drystan frowned as he watched the company leave the room. Despite Dominic's display of power, he had to agree with his foster father. Most of them were past their prime, and he wondered if this mission might truly be their last. It did not occur to him that he might not survive it as well, until Camille turned her rainbow-colored eyes upon him, and he read the concern in her gaze.

"You do not have the power to wield Roden's golden scepter," she said, keeping her voice low as most of the company left the room. "When it is joined with the power of the others, the magical backwash could kill you."

"Wilhelmina is taking the same risk with the silver, Camille. I can do no less."

"But surely they can find another to carry the gold. You do not have to prove yourself by holding it."

"Is that what you think? That I am trying to prove myself?"

"I know you have spent your entire life reading about the adventures of others, and I worry that you are not thinking your decisions through."

Drystan tore his gaze from hers, his jaw rigid, aware that, less than an hour ago, some truth might have lain in her words. It had been a risk to touch the scepter, and he had done nothing but read about adventures... until he dreamt of her. But he now knew his own worth. "On the contrary, Camille. My strength is in my intelligence—in my knowledge of the elven lords I have gleaned from years of pouring through the archives. My magic is erratic, and there are many who can beat me with a sword. But my decisions are something I will never doubt."

"I just... I just wish you would not go."

He lifted her hand, brought it to his lips. "I think you are afraid for me. Is it possible?"

Her forehead wrinkled as she nodded.

Drystan felt his heart soar. "Fear not, my love. My choices are sound. Did they not bring me to you?"

Thirteen

CAMILLE ENVIED DRYSTAN'S CONFIDENCE. INDEED, even when Lady Cecily took her to one of the guest chambers in the palace to rest before dinner, she could not stop thinking about the bold way in which he had pressed his naked skin to the scepter.

She meant to close her eyes only for a few moments, but she fell asleep, and dreamt of Drystan shattering into a thousand fragments. Of alighting in a blaze of fire. Of crumbling to blackened ash.

Camille awoke to a knock on the bedchamber door, and it took her a moment to control her panting and trembling. What would she do if she lost Drystan? He had somehow become the center of her world, and she did not know how to process this realization with her perceptions of her everyday life... and yet, her life had not been familiar to her since she met Viscount Hawkes.

Another knock, this one a bit more forceful than the last, and Camille dragged herself out of the enormous four-poster bed. Lady Cecily called it the burgundy chamber, and it had obviously come by that name for the dark red silk covering the walls and upholstery and bed coverings. It rivaled Drystan's family chambers in opulence, with gilt decorating the edges of every surface, the soaring ceiling supported by flame-shaped columns, and a massive fireplace surrounded by intricately carved marble statues.

Camille ignored the staring eyes of cherubs and fauns as she crossed the room and skirted a fountain of white flowing fire to open the heavy door.

Lady Cecily stood outside, wearing a gown that matched her large blue faceted elven eyes. Her black hair had been swept up in elaborate braids, the ribbons threaded through it hiding the gray strands. Her slightly pointed elven ears peeked through the hairstyle.

"Where is Drystan?" asked Camille before Lady Cecily had a chance to speak.

The older woman started, and then smiled. "I made him rest, as well. He is not used to wielding magic, and does not realize how draining it can be. We will need his powers, erratic or no, and despite his youth, his body needs time to recharge."

Camille frowned. "Then your husband was right?"

"About our age and endurance?" Lady Cecily shifted the bundle in her arms. "I admit it takes us longer to recover from using our powers, but we have had years to hone and perfect the craft. We expend our energy more wisely. Do not fear, my girl, we are up to the task, and have been waiting for years for some hope. My thanks for bringing it to us."

"It was not I, but Drystan. Which room did you say he was in?"

"I did not. But he is just across the way. He did not

want to be too far from you. Dearest, this is getting rather heavy. May I come in?"

Camille's face heated. "I am so sorry, yes, please do come in." And she opened the door and stepped back, mentally chastising herself for her rudeness.

"I brought you some clothing," said Lady Cecily, dumping her burden on the bed. "The king insisted we all join each other for dinner this evening. To discuss any last-minute plans. We are *not* to consider it as a last supper or anything." She made a face.

Camille stared at a white iridescent gown spread across the bed, avoiding Lady Cecily's gaze. "You are all so... comfortable with each other."

"We have adjusted to our circumstances as best we can, and I rather fear we must seem like an odd group to outsiders."

Camille winced.

"Not that you and Drystan are outsiders," Lady Cecily hurried to say. "It is just that we have become perhaps *too* comfortable with one another over the past few weeks. The threat of death has a tendency to do that. And I expect you and Drystan will soon become comfortable as well—" She threw up her hands and collapsed in a silk-upholstered chair. "I am making a complete muck of this, aren't I? Drystan will never forgive me."

"On the contrary." Camille could not help smiling. "You have made me feel more at ease."

"By my complete lack of finesse?"

"Yes. I mean, no. I mean—"

They stared at each other for a moment, and then burst into laughter.

"I like you very well," said Cecily. "At first I feared for this dream woman of Drystan's. I was afraid you would not be what he expected. That you would hurt him. But now I see my fears were groundless."

Camille's smile faded as a trickle of guilt rushed through her. Could she give Drystan the love he needed? How could she explain her lack of certainty to his foster mother? "I have been a slave, my lady, and I am not used to any sort of an equal standing among such peers."

"The barriers of social status—fie, that is an old familiar tune, and I am sad to hear you sing it." Lady Cecily sat up and folded her hands in her lap. "Sit down, my dear, and I shall tell you of my courtship with Giles Beaumont, a journey of magic and adventure, and of needless personal strife. For the darling man worried that my title did not make him good enough for me."

Camille sat on the bed, fingering the fine fabric of the gown the older woman had brought her, and listened intently as Lady Cecily, wielder of the blue scepter of sea and sky, without a doubt the lady of the storm, told her of Drystan's foster father, and the man's stubbornness to do what he thought was right, instead of what his heart bade him.

"And so you see, my dear," said Cecily when she finished her tale, "worrying about titles and other's opinions is only a screen to hide behind because you are afraid. Never allow fear to keep you from your heart's desire. It is a difficult lesson to learn, and one I am most qualified to give you advice on. Although I suppose Giles is the true expert."

Camille nodded. "I do understand how he might have felt. But I also see how Drystan may feel. I shall try not to let my fears get in the way of my feelings for him."

Fie, she had so many things she feared to tell him. Could she truly find the courage to make herself that vulnerable?

"Excellent, replied Lady Cecily. "I never truly expected Drystan to marry so young; he was always such a bookish lad—good heavens, what is it?"

"Marriage?" breathed Camille. "His lordship wants to marry me?"

"Well, naturally. Drystan loves you, my dear, and he is an honorable man. What else did you think we were talking about?"

"I-I just did not think…" Camille twisted her fingers together. "I am a *slave*."

"Not any longer. Not ever again. We shall succeed in opening the doorway to Elfhame."

"But if we are successful, and free England, and Drystan is reunited with his family and his title and lands… how will his family and retainers feel about me? I cannot hide what I was, nor the treatment I received. In many people's eyes, I am a soiled woman. How can I ever be wife to a viscount? How can I ever make Drystan proud?"

Shadows created by the firelight danced across Lady Cecily's sculpted cheekbones. "I can tell you what I have seen in Drystan's eyes. He is already proud of you. Proud to call you his lady. He has never been concerned about what other people think, for the other orphans thought him touched by the devil, and how ridiculous is that? I cannot speak for Lady Hawkes, or Drystan's brother, but I can tell you that Giles and I have been the only real family he has ever known. And we both highly approve of you. If that should bring you comfort when facing your new position, allow it to do so."

Camille blinked against the burn beneath her lids. Lady Hawkes? Drystan's mother? She now wondered how that lady might feel about having a slave for a daughter-in-law, much less a woman who… "But you see, that is not the only obstacle I would be facing."

Cecily cocked her head, and waited.

Camille swallowed. She had never thought to discuss this with anyone. Indeed, she had never considered it… until now. "The elven lord put an enchantment on his slaves. One that prevented a nuisance."

"Nuisance?"

"Yes." Camille colored. Best to put it baldly. "The nuisance of little bastards running about the slaves' quarters. You see, Lady Cecily, I… I cannot have children."

That took the lady aback. "Have you told Drystan?"

"I told him I was not a whole woman, but there was no reason to elaborate on all of the ways I was not… suitable for him."

"I see." She frowned in thought. "It would probably take the power of another elven lord to remove the spell… or perhaps that of a very powerful half-breed." Then her brow cleared and she rose in one elegant movement. "The entire purpose of opening this doorway is not only to rid our lands of the elven lords, but of their magic as well. Otherwise, we would just hope to kill the lords off one by one. It is entirely probable that all of their spells will fade along with their magic. And when the spells fade, you will be able to have children again."

Camille felt dizzy with hope. "Do you think so?"

"I do. But if we should fail in our task, or if the spell cannot be removed, you should still not consider this as an obstacle to your love for Drystan. Giles and I never had children, and yet we have been most happy raising hundreds of orphans as our own. I may not have given birth to Drystan, but he is my son." She shrugged. "And besides, Drystan has a brother who can provide an heir."

Camille studied Cecily's face, and saw a hint of doubt on those perfect features. The lady was not as confident as she tried to pretend. Drystan had the responsibility of a title. And it would not be the same as if his own son inherited it.

But Camille dared not love Drystan anyway, so Cecily was right. She need not worry about a future with him.

"Now then," said the lady, crossing to the bed and picking up the iridescent gown, "let us see about getting you into this lovely dress. Did you notice it is rather like your eyes, with all of the colors of the rainbow shimmering within it? You shall look positively elegant, and an equal to every lady in the room."

Camille breathed deeply, and allowed the other woman to transform her into a woman a viscount would be proud to call wife. During their preparations, Drystan knocked on the door, but Lady Cecily shooed him away, telling Camille she wanted them to make a grand entrance into the salon.

And when Camille finally looked into the mirror, she admitted that Lady Cecily had done a fine job of making her look presentable. The soldier's uniform had been replaced with yards and yards of the silky fabric that shifted colors whenever she moved. The mantua wrapped in front, falling in graceful folds to the floor, with a short train behind. A stomacher of glittering stones peeped through the crossed front, each stone a different color representing each of the sovereignties. A silver girdle cinched her waist, and her white hair had been braided up in a circular crown, pinned with tiny sparkling stones.

Next to Lady Cecily's vibrant color, Camille looked like some glittering ghostly dream.

"Perfect," announced the older woman, guiding Camille through the door and down a hallway blazing with Dominic's magic. Columns of yellow fire flanked them as they strode across a floor glowing with radiant stones. They traveled down the stairway and crossed the great hall into a dining room laden with silver and crystal. Lady Cecily pulled Camille up short just beyond the threshold of the massive double doors.

They both curtsied to the king, who nodded regally to them.

As one, the occupants of the room turned to follow the king's gaze. To stare at Camille. But they did not gaze at her as if they thought her eyes peculiar, or as if they wondered what a slave might be doing dressed up as gentry. Indeed, the ladies smiled as if she did them proud, and the men gave her looks of admiration... except for Drystan.

He had risen with the gentlemen, one strong

hand on the back of an empty chair beside him. His golden eyes widened, grew heated as he raked his gaze over her from head to toe. Drystan wore a coat and breeches of dark brown velvet, with a white shirt ruffled at neck and sleeves, giving the skin of his hands and face a golden tone. His wavy white hair had been pulled back from his face by battle braids woven at the sides and secured to the back of his head. The style made his cheekbones more prominent, exposed the pointed tips of his ears.

He stared at her with an intensity that made a shiver of anticipation rush through her body.

Camille felt drawn to him as if led by an invisible string. She had not thought it possible that Drystan would find her heart, and feared he had managed to do so.

No one spoke a word as she crossed the room, and then curtsied before him. "My lord."

Her words seemed to jolt him aware, for he took her hand and lifted her upright, brought her satin-gloved fingertips to his lips. "You are too beautiful for words. There is not a line of poetry I can recall which would do you justice."

"And that's saying quite a bit," said Giles Beaumont, striding forward to escort his wife into the dining room, breaking the quiet that had fallen. "I do not know of a man who knows poetry better than Drystan."

"It would not harm you to learn a bit yourself," replied Lady Cecily. "A line or two might do you in good stead."

"Indeed?" mused Giles with a leer.

Soft laughter flew about the table, and Camille felt

the piercing gazes fall away from her as Drystan settled her into the chair beside him. He moved his chair closer before he took his seat, his thigh touching her silk skirts.

Liveried servants brought in trays laden with decanters of wine and burgundy, silver bowls of savory soup thickened with spices that teased Camille's nose. The company must have worked hard this day, for they all fell quiet as they ate with hearty appetites, only the king and Lord North speaking quietly through the first few courses.

Camille paid only half-attention to their conversation of fortifications and battle plans. Although the meal tasted delicious, she did not seem to have much appetite. She felt keenly aware of Drystan's body sitting next to her, and every time she glanced at him beneath her lashes, her stomach would flutter.

Conversation finally began to flow among the company somewhere between the baked cod and roasted beef.

"You have hardly touched your food," murmured Drystan beneath the flow of talk. "I hope you do not feel intimidated by our fellow conspirators."

Camille glanced about the table. In their silks and satins and jewels, the assembled heroes of the Rebellion now looked the part, and had she been paying the slightest attention to them, she might have felt a bit in awe.

"They do not unnerve me, Drystan. They are all too… human. Despite their elven blood."

"Then what is it?"

"You."

He dropped his fork. "Me?"

"Indeed. I cannot explain it. I know we have traveled together, have gotten used to each other's company. I usually feel quite at ease with you. But tonight... tonight there is something in the air. Can you not feel it?"

A slow smile spread across his face.

Dominic and Lord North discussed the magical properties of the scepters held by the half-breeds, versus the powers of the full-blooded elven lords. Whose would prove the strongest in a direct confrontation?

With their hands clasped together, Lady Cecily and Giles discussed the dragons she had created, with Lady Joscelyn adding comments about the gems she had crafted in the creature's breasts, and how they would aid the beasts. Samson idly traced a finger along the back of his wife's neck, making her blush and forget her words more than once.

Alexander teased Wilhelmina until she laughed, and begged Lady Cassandra to save her from the twisted humor of her husband.

Cassandra appeared too intent on playing with her husband's long battle braids to pay much notice.

Drystan abruptly rose, tossing his embroidered napkin upon his plate. "Lords and Ladies. Will you kindly excuse us? I feel the need for a walk in the clouds."

Camille's mouth dropped open at the outlandish statement, but not a one of the rest of their party even blinked.

"Before dessert?" asked the king, his eyes twinkling.

"Ah, youth," said Giles, cocking a teasing grin at Dominic.

Drystan took her hand and guided Camille out of the chair.

"Thank you so much for the lovely dinner," she said as Drystan ushered her from the room.

"It was a pleasure to have you," said Lady Cassandra, her voice trailing after them as they walked through the double doors of the dining room into the hall.

"Drystan," murmured Camille, "do you not think that was a little rude?"

He shrugged broad shoulders beneath chocolate velvet. "They understand. And do not doubt they will make their own departures soon enough. I am surprised we all got past the fifth course."

Camille smiled up at him, and he stopped in the middle of the flame-shrouded hall, his amber gaze searching the walls. He dragged her behind a pillar into the shadowed alcove just behind it, and enfolded her in his arms. He lowered his head and kissed her, swallowing her gasp of surprise. His mouth tasted of wine. Warm and sweet. His arms felt like steel bands encasing her, but he held her so gently she felt protected, not trapped. The shiver just beneath her skin, which had stayed with her since she had first laid eyes upon Drystan, suddenly blossomed into a rush of giddy excitement. She melted against him, into him, until she forgot to breathe.

The world stopped. Time hung suspended. And all she could do was experience Drystan.

He broke the kiss, placed his forehead against hers, his breath warm on her face. "I have wanted to do that all evening."

"I have waited for you to do that all evening."

"Indeed?" He pulled away, looked deeply into her eyes. "My foster mother came to see you tonight."

"Yes."

"What did she say?"

Camille squirmed. She had no reason to feel guilty. "She told me about her courtship with your foster father."

"And?"

"And… what did you mean by a walk in the clouds?"

He cocked his head, his smooth forehead marred by a slight frown. "If I show you, will you tell me your secrets? Have I not proven you can trust me?"

Camille closed her eyes, took a breath. She had told Lady Cecily she would not allow her fears to conquer her. She did not feel ready to share the truth about her barrenness, for tomorrow it may be moot. But there were some truths she must share with Drystan, or it would prevent her from getting closer to him. And she wanted that now more than ever.

"Show me," she breathed.

Drystan took her hand, led her around the pillar, his brow furrowed in concentration. For a moment she saw the flaming walls of Firehame Palace; then they dissolved into a world of soft color. An enormous full moon glowed softly in the distance, nothing but clouds before and below it. It resembled the sky they had flown through to reach London, but in a fantastical way, the fluffy whiteness as iridescent with color as her gown, the moon a golden gem of shimmering warmth.

Drystan took a step forward.

"No," cried Camille, pulling back on his arm. The

instinctual fear of falling she had felt on the back of his dragon made her throat tighten once more.

"I control this illusion, my love," he soothed, gently pulling her after him. Camille wrapped her arms around his neck and looked down. But she could not see the ground far below, only the thick blanket of clouds.

"As much as I enjoy your arms about me, my love, you must know I would never let you fall."

Camille loosened her hold and stepped back, held just his hand. She must stop being foolish. Of course Drystan would not allow any harm to come to her. She rocked from heel to toe. "It feels like pillows. Not like the clouds we flew through over England."

"They were naught but a wet mist," said Drystan, his face alight with pride. "But they gave me the inspiration for this spell."

"But you will need all your magic on the morrow. Is it wise to drain your resources?"

Drystan ran his hand across her cheek, frowned at his gloves until they disappeared, and then she felt the warmth of his skin. "If we are successful tomorrow, and the elven lords are sent back to Elfhame, we shall close the gateway firmly behind them. I do not think the Rebellion would risk another invasion. Right now, the portal leaks magic into our world, and it pools against the barrier created by the elven. If we close the door, the magic will fade... and I wanted to give you this gift while I am still able."

Alarm flared within Camille as she suspected another meaning beneath his spoken words. Even if the Rebellion succeeded in their task, Drystan might not survive it. He was not as confident as he would have her believe—

"You really must feel this," he said, glancing down at his feet. Camille followed his gaze. His shoes and stockings had disappeared, his fine calves rippling with muscle as he walked through the downy whiteness. He pointed at her satin shoes. "May I?"

Camille nodded. Her footwear disappeared as well, and she sank her naked toes into the clouds. Soft, buoyant, like lamb's wool but not itchy. Although part of it felt solid, some of the whiteness puffed and swirled, creating a path of new shapes behind them. And now that she noticed, the white landscape shifted with different forms that grew and then altered to something new.

She pointed. "What is that?"

Drystan narrowed his golden brown eyes. "I do believe it is an elephant."

"A what?"

"I saw it in a book once. That long tube is his nose, and the big flaps are his ears."

Her finger shifted. "And that thing?"

"A giraffe. Faith, it is like true clouds, only better. As soon as a shape reminds me of something, it forms into what I imagine, only more accurately." His voice lowered. "Magic is a grand thing, Camille. Now that I have known it, I will miss it."

She shuddered. "Not I. You craft spells of beauty and wonder. But I have seen too many of Roden's creations to regret the loss of magic."

They walked in silence for a time, as shapes continued to form and shift around them. Camille recognized some of them, and marveled at those she could not. "Your books are like magic, Drystan. Taking you to new places and sights. You shall never lose them."

"No." His fingers tightened on her hand. "May I remove your gloves?"

She nodded, and they disappeared.

"You owe me a secret, Camille."

She knew he would not allow her to evade the subject, and did not even try. Drystan had revealed all of his secrets to her. And now... well, now, she would have to tell him the most damning one of her own.

"I am cursed," she blurted.

He did not scoff. Just turned and looked at her, concern etched in his handsome features. "Why do you believe so?"

"It has happened too often for me to doubt it. Perhaps my odd eyes should have warned me, but since I have no magic, I did not think I could possess something *other*."

White fluffy flowers with long petals grew above and beside them in an arch that created a private tunnel. Camille suddenly felt sheltered and safe, and it allowed her to continue her confession.

"I discounted it the first time," she continued. "With Rufus and Laura."

"The children you took care of?"

"Aye. For the Earl of Ailesbury and his countess. They were good children, and too easy to love. I would have been happy, caring for them until they were grown, and then perhaps their own children." Camille shook her head at her old foolish dreams and plans. "But Roden called them for testing..."

"They showed too much promise for magic?" he prodded.

"On the contrary. They showed little affinity for magic. Laura could barely conjure a decent illusion, and Rufus, none at all. But when Roden of Dreamhame crafted a nightmare to threaten them, they fought back with a creature that defeated his, and then in the blink of an eye, they were ripped from my arms and taken away. Lord and Lady Ailesbury were so distraught they could not bear to look at me or the governess, and dismissed us both, sending me back to the slave quarters."

Drystan frowned, and Camille could see him thinking hard, as if he sought to piece together some sort of puzzle. But she already knew the answer. Besides the key branded on her body, the white witch had also cursed her to lose anyone she ever loved.

The flowers faded from the archway and shifted into a white rainbow speckled with bands of glittering color.

He gently squeezed her hand. "How long did you care for the children before this happened?"

Camille breathed a sigh of relief. He took her seriously. "A few years."

"And were you with them when they were tested?"

"Yes." Faith, how the memory hurt. She had buried it for long and long, but now those dreadful feelings felt as fresh as a new wound. She could feel the children trembling in her arms, hear their cries to save them as the elven lord's soldiers dragged them away.

Her breath caught on a sob, but Drystan squared his shoulders and continued to walk her through the clouds, and she knew he would hear it all.

"And then I managed to find a position with Lady Pembridge. Such a sweet soul, who loved nothing more than gossip and a new gown. I tried not to love her, and managed to avoid it for a time, but I still possessed a heart back then, and after several years of her kindness and generosity, I could not help myself." Camille kicked at the clouds beneath her feet, sending up a swirl of white puffy balls. "She had become a bit absentminded, a bit silly, her tired old mind no longer making sense at times. I tried to stop her from challenging Roden—no one challenges an elven lord. Still, there should have been little danger, for she had no magic to speak of to pose a threat to him. But somehow she managed to conjure a dragon to defeat his... and Roden killed her. I... I can still hear the snap of her old neck bones."

"Camille, Camille." Drystan stopped and pulled her into his arms, his chest so warm against her cheek. "At one time I thought I had been cursed, for I did not know about the scepters, and I believed the worst that people thought of me... that my fits were brought on by a demon, by an affinity for evil. But Giles and Cecily believed in my goodness, and they helped me to discover the truth." He gently pulled her away by her shoulders, waited until she looked up at him. "My love. You are no longer alone. You have *me* to believe in you."

Camille blinked. He understood. Perhaps he was the only man in the world who truly could. "But... what if I *am* cursed? Too many coincidences throughout my life have convinced me of it."

"There is something..." He shook his head, stray tendrils of pale curls sweeping his forehead.

Perhaps Drystan's curse had been revealed to him as brought about by the scepters. Camille did not know what caused hers, but until she found out the truth of it, she could not be sure that loving him would not cause him harm. "You have volunteered to hold the golden scepter, even though you lack the magic to wield it. You will be tested with elven magic. Do you not see the pattern here? You will die like all the others."

"Camille—"

"If I love you, you will die."

Drystan gently squeezed her shoulders, stared deeply into her eyes. "I see you believe that as surely as I once believed I was touched by evil. But there may be another answer, Camille. For it always comes down to the scepters, does it not?"

"I… I have no idea what you are talking about."

Drystan dropped his hands and put some distance between them. She felt oddly bereft, for she had grown used to having him as close to her as possible.

They stood there for a time; the only sound a soft whisper as the clouds undulated about them.

"No change," murmured Drystan, "but I have been close to you for some time now. It is possible our bond has become strong enough to withstand separation."

Camille did not know what he meant by that, but watched him think, her heart rising with hope. Drystan was the smartest man she had ever known. If anyone could manage to uncover the truth of her curse, he would.

"If you had not told me about the deaths of your loved ones, I might not have put this together. But you are right; there have been too many coincidences for me not to question… especially after today when I touched the golden scepter." He withdrew it from his pocket, and unwrapped it. Camille took a step back. "Let us try an experiment, shall we?"

She shook her head. "That scepter is too dangerous, Drystan. Please put it away."

"You must trust me, my love. It is worth some risk to discover the truth of your supposed curse, is it not? For I do not think you will allow yourself to love me until I do."

"I would rather not love you, than put your life at risk."

Drystan wrapped his bare hand about the golden scepter. "And I would rather die than live without your love."

Camille held her breath. Despite her nightmares, he still did not shatter into a thousand fragments, or burst into a ball of flame.

"I do not think I could have done this a few weeks ago," he mused. "I thought I was just developing my powers, but now I have to wonder." He held out his other bare hand. "Touch me, my love."

Camille had promised Lady Cecily she would be brave. Her hand trembled, but she held it up and stepped forward. How many times had she seen the scepter kill? How many times had she felt the promise of evil from it as Roden of Dreamhame used it to threaten and cajole? But if Drystan had been brave enough to touch it, she could do no less than hold him while he did so.

At least if the scepter turned on him and he died, Camille would go with him.

She clasped his warm fingers.

"Ahh," breathed Drystan. He closed his eyes and threw his head back. "I can feel the power now. I can hear it sing to me." He lowered his head, his golden eyes now glowing as brilliantly as the moon in front of them. "Look around you, Camille."

She did as he asked, astonished to see the illusion he had crafted for her now sparkling with clarity. The edges of the clouds now appeared sharp and defined. The moon as real as the one that hovered in the true sky. Stars sparkled in the heavens, and lights twinkled below their feet through the breaks in the clouds. She could pick out the glowing flames that marked Firehame Palace far below.

"I do not understand," she breathed. "How can my touch affect your magic? I have none."

"Which is why it never occurred to me that you affected mine. I had thought my magic worked only for you, because my love for you made my will stronger. But when I think on it now, I always managed to craft a spell when you were near. And even stronger ones when I touched your bare skin. You do not just hold the key to opening the door to Elfhame, Camille. You *are* the key."

Her heart raced. Could it be possible? Could she hold no magic of her own, but be the catalyst for others' magic? "You are saying that the longer I am close to someone, the more I affect their powers. And that touching me increases the effect twofold?"

Drystan loosened his hold. "Let go of my hand."

Her fingers dropped to clutch at her skirts. The glow dimmed in his eyes, although his illusion still held strong.

"I cannot feel the power of the scepter anymore," he said, his handsome face alight with the joy of discovery. "Although I believe the effects of your gift take longer to fade once you have influenced them."

"Gift?" blurted Camille. "You call it a gift? If not for me, Rufus and Laura would not have shown enough magic to threaten Roden. Lady Pembridge would not have been able to craft a dragon strong enough to fight Roden's."

Drystan wrapped up the scepter and pushed it back into his pocket, his face now creased with concern. "You did not kill them, Camille. Roden did." He picked up her hands and brought them to his lips. "Many have suffered and died at the hands of the elven lords, and so will many more, until we free England from their rule. And without you, we would never be able to do that. Don't you see? We can now wield all seven scepters to open the doorway."

To be able to help in such a significant way... then her curse would indeed be a gift. Or at least, she would finally be able to use it as such. "Do you believe this curse can allow others to wield a scepter?"

"It is a logical assumption."

And Camille suddenly realized something else. With her help, Drystan would be protected from any harmful magical backlash when the scepters were joined. Instead of being his doom, she might be his only salvation.

Her legs gave way beneath her, and she collapsed into a puddle of skirts and cloud, Drystan following to kneel in front of her, bringing her hands again to his lips. Her eyes, those strange multicolored eyes, with all the colors of each sovereignty... no, each scepter, within them. They were not just some strange accident of birth. They held meaning. A connection with each of the scepters' powers.

"Can it be possible," she whispered, "that I can truly love you without bringing you harm?"

He kissed the back of her hands. "I promise you, Camille. Your love will not kill me, but the lack of it surely will."

His words pierced her soul.

He dropped her hands and leaned forward, his mouth covering hers, blanketing all thought. His hands swept through her hair, and Camille felt it tumble down her back and over her shoulders. The world shuddered, and it took her several moments to recognize the sound of thunder. Her soft bed of cloud began to sway, and Drystan pulled away from her, sat back on his haunches.

A roof of white cut off the glow of the moon, sheltering them and casting Drystan's face in shadow as rain began to fall from the higher clouds above them. Camille could smell the fresh moisture, could hear the gentle patter of the drops atop their roof, and marveled at Drystan's illusion.

Clouds formed fantastical shapes around their shelter, protecting them from the glistening curtain of rain. Flowers from the garden of Elfhame spiraled from a bud and grew into brilliant blossoms. An English rose bloomed, a hint of red within the petals. Sprays of white buttercups and pansies and marigolds—and other flowers she could not identify—shimmered with opalescent color. White swans entwined their necks around each other, and pairs of doves flew across the fluffy ceiling. Gemstones sparkled within the creations, casting specks of glitter on her satin skirts.

She looked up into Drystan's golden eyes, at the half smile curving his lips.

"Love me, Camille."

She let out a rush of breath. "It has been so very hard to stop from loving you, Drystan." And leaned back into the soft whiteness, holding out her arms to him.

His smile spread, changing his already handsome face to near poignantly beautiful. Her brave, bookish, brilliant Drystan. He had saved her life in more ways than one.

He lowered his body over hers and gently smoothed the hair back from her forehead, kissed her brow and then her lips, with a confidence and reverence that shook her to the core. She wrapped her arms around him, pulling impatiently on his velvet coat.

He laughed, a low raspy sound, and his clothing disappeared, and she felt the smooth heat of his skin beneath her palms. His shoulders bunched with muscle, velvety rounds of steel, and she swept her hands down and across his back, marveling at the new contours she felt.

Drystan traced a path from her mouth to her chin, down to lick the smooth hollow of her throat, before continuing his parade of kisses to one shoulder. Then the other. His mouth moved lower, down to her bodice, and the fabric disappeared at his touch. He still held his body above hers, and she wished he would make her entire dress disappear, and press himself against her, so she could feel the silky heat of all of his skin.

But Drystan had other ideas.

He kissed her left breast, starting at a circle from the outside and taking his sweet time to reach the peak of her nipple. By the time his warm lips touched one, she had built up such anticipation that she cried out from the shiver that went through her when he opened his mouth and suckled. He repeated the same torture on her right breast, until she arched against him.

"Drystan. Please."

But he would not be rushed. His mouth moved down to her waist, fabric fading, until her entire upper half lay naked to his gaze.

Drystan took a moment to stare at her. He did not need to say the words. His eyes told her he thought her beautiful.

He leaned down once more, fabric fading as he kissed her stomach, then each hip, Camille now trembling with desire.

She could not remember a time before Drystan. A time when love was not a glorious sharing of tenderness and sensibility.

He kissed her thighs, her knees, her calves... until she finally lay naked beneath him, on a bed of clouds amid falling rain. Tendrils of white swirled up to cover his back, his legs, encasing them in a cocoon of pale mist, hiding and revealing a flash of skin, a curve of waist.

Drystan gently spread her legs, his eyes glazed with passion, the pupils large and black.

Camille's breath hitched.

He kissed a path back up her inner thighs, mumbling nonsense words of love, until he reached her core and the syllables stopped, and she could feel nothing but his mouth, his tongue, stroking and caressing, building her anticipation higher. And higher.

Until she cried his name again and again.

In one elegant sweep of motion, he drew her upward, his mouth stopping her cries, his hands on her back. He pressed her closer to him, cradling her chest against his, until she sat atop his kneeling body, her legs draped over his thighs.

Mist swirled about his angular cheekbones, across the rugged contours of his chest. He swept her ivory hair over her shoulders, while she explored his chest, the smooth expanse of it, the muscles that rippled with her every touch.

His hands slid off her shoulders and all the way down her back, until his big hands wrapped around her cheeks. And he pulled her bottom closer. She felt the velvet skin of his desire touch her throbbing center.

Camille ran her hands up his shoulders, cupping his neck, her thumbs playing with the lobes of his pointed ears. He stared into her eyes, waiting.

"Now," she pleaded.

He lifted her up, and then ever so slowly down, sliding his velvet heat into her wet core.

He growled something inarticulate, a vow, a promise, an exclamation. Then squeezed his fingers, driving her in deeper and deeper, until Camille threw her arms about his shoulders and buried her face in his hair. He smelled of spice and the indefinable scent of Drystan.

She could only hold on while he rocked her in

a gentle rhythm that swept her away, narrowed her concentration to the feel of him inside of her. To her body's awareness of the smooth friction he created against her nub as he pressed her tightly to him. His elven strength allowed him to hold her sure and strong for a length of time that stretched to infinity.

Sometime during that glorious joining, Camille threw back her head, Drystan leaning down to suckle her neck. He did not build their desire to a frantic peak. He did not struggle and pull them toward their pleasure. Instead, when it came, it washed over them at the same time like a gentle wave, Drystan moaning against the pulse in her neck, Camille sighing with openmouthed delight.

When his tremors eased, Drystan pulled away from her neck, his mouth sweeping a kiss across her own.

"I love you," she said. With conviction. With wonder.

"I have waited long and long to hear you say that." He hugged her gently to him, still rigid inside of her, and Camille wished they could stay joined like this forever.

But Drystan frowned, ran his fingers down her shoulder. "Allow it to strengthen you tomorrow, my love. For I fear we will both have need of it."

Fourteen

A POUNDING AWOKE CAMILLE THE NEXT MORNING. She lay in the bed of the burgundy guest room, tangled within Drystan's arms and legs. She had fallen asleep on a bed of clouds, Drystan reciting poetry in her ear, and wondered that his magic had brought them both to her chamber. And felt supremely grateful for it.

Another knock at her door, and she sat up, blinking in the gloomy light. It felt as if she had barely slept a few hours. Her gaze narrowed at the clock styled with flaming torches that sat on the mantle. It was hours before dawn, when the company planned to ride to the Seven Corners of Hell.

Whoever stood on the other side was obviously too impatient to wait for her to answer it, for it flew open.

"Drystan?" called Giles.

Camille yelped and drew the covers over her as Drystan's foster father entered the room.

"Ha," said the older man, strolling over to the bed. "I knew I would find you here. Get up, Son. We have a bit of a problem." And then rather belatedly to

Camille, "My apologies, dearest Camille, for barging in on you like this. But as I said—"

"We have a problem," finished Drystan, sitting up and blinking at Giles. "What is wrong?"

"Our plans have been discovered. Bless Lord North and his distrustful nature. Even his spies have spies." A muffled boom shook the walls of the palace, and Giles scowled. "It has already begun. We must fly. Now." He tossed a bundle of buckskin on the bed.

Drystan leapt from the bed in one fluid movement, pulling on the buckskin breeches before his feet barely touched the floor. "Camille, did Cecily bring you a riding outfit?"

She blinked at the pile of clothing the lady brought her last evening, now draped over the top of a satin couch. "I am not sure."

Giles halted in midstep, threw a startled glance at Drystan. "You are bringing her?"

Drystan nodded.

"You were going to leave me here?" huffed Camille.

Drystan pulled his shirt over broad shoulders, and shrugged. "I wanted to keep you safe. And besides, you would have been of little help."

"And what has changed overnight?" demanded Giles.

"We made an astonishing discovery, Father." Drystan grunted the words as he pulled on his leather boots. "It appears that Camille carries more than just the key to opening the door to Elfhame."

Another boom shook the walls, rattling the crystals in the chandelier.

Giles glanced up, and then toward the door to the hall, his feet shifting restlessly. "What do you mean?"

"She *is* the key."

"Dammit, Drystan."

"It is difficult to explain. She has no magic, but she is a catalyst for it. Watch." He withdrew the scepter from the pocket of his discarded velvet coat. It lay quietly within his hand, until he reached out with his other and clasped her shoulder. Camille still felt astonished when she saw the scepter immediately begin to glow as Drystan called to the magic within it. He created an illusion of a golden unicorn, complete with horn and flowing mane and tail. The creature tossed its head, pawed the marble floor with a clopping sound.

Giles's human green eyes widened to almost elven proportion, glancing from unicorn to scepter to Camille. "Can you do the same for the other scepters?"

"I do not know. I-I did not know I had such an ability until Drystan discovered the truth of it." She clutched the covers more tightly. "I do not feel the magic. I feel... nothing."

A great roar of sound swelled, and a force shook the palace. Water pounded the glass of the window, threatening to break it in, briefly extinguishing the glow of fire that covered the outside walls. But Dominic must have rallied his magic, for soon the liquid cleared and yellow flames danced around the ledge once again.

Giles spun on his heel. "Cecily. She will be out there, helping Dominic—hurry, both of you!"

Camille sprang from the bed, mentally blessed Lady Cecily when she discovered a brushed woolen riding coat and skirt, both of sturdy design, and a quilted petticoat. Drystan helped her finish dressing, his fingers gentle and calm, despite the increasing noise of battle. He wore no gloves, and insisted she do the same, tying the string of a rabbit muff to her waistband in case she needed to keep her hands warm.

He buckled on her sword belt and tugged her toward the door.

"Drystan? The unicorn?"

Those golden eyes glanced at his creation, and with a flick of the scepter, the illusion disappeared. "I am not used to this," he muttered.

"If we send the elven lords home, you will not have to get accustomed to it."

They entered the hall.

"That is some consolation," he replied, before grabbing her hand and urging her into a fast walk. "However, it would be helpful if I knew more about Roden of Dreamhame's magic. I am sure there is some spell that would allow us to reach our destination faster, but damn if I can think of a way. I can will only the most basic illusions."

"Perhaps we could fly on the back of a cloud?"

"We weren't really up in the sky." His brow furrowed for a moment, then cleared. "Besides, it would be too slow."

The interior walls of the palace lacked their usual fiery decorations. The fountains lay empty, the chandeliers dark, the walls but blackened stone. Servants scurried about with candles in hand, on tasks for their masters that Camille could only guess at. Soldiers lined the main entrance, but Drystan took the back one, through the kitchens that reminded Camille too strongly of Dreamhame's, and past another knot of soldiers guarding the doorway.

Wilhelmina detached herself from the group, gave Drystan a nod, and Camille a startled glance. Alexander joined his wife's side, his mouth curling into a smile as the duke addressed Drystan. "Couldn't leave her behind, eh?"

"We need her."

Alexander raised a brow, but his wife only shrugged. "The rest are outside. We have deployed enough soldiers to distract Breden of Dewhame for a while, and his daughter—Lady Cecily, has managed a defense that should exhaust him for a time. We must leave now."

She spun on her heel, and they followed the tall woman outside into the courtyard. The fiery walls of the palace still lit the area, and Camille gaped at the chaos. Seaweed hung from wall and window, blanketing the yellow fire with occasional dark splotches. Fish flopped on the ground, soldiers using the butts of their muskets to stun them. Piles of loose brick lay alongside sea anemones and translucent jellyfish, and when Camille raised her eyes, she saw that several portions of the palace towers had crumbled.

"Did the elven lord dump the entire ocean on Firehame?"

"Just a few waves," replied Alexander, who stood on her other side. "Lady Cecily managed to repel most of it."

"I must speak with Dominic," said Drystan.

"He is right in front of you... ah, but I forget." The duke raised his voice. "Lady Joscelyn, these two need gemstones."

The lavender-eyed woman appeared in front of them out of thin air, making Camille start. Unlike Wilhelmina, who wore breeches and a sword, Lady Joscelyn wore a riding outfit much like Camille's, but of a darker color that made the silver sparkles in her white hair appear to glow in contrast. Joscelyn carried the lavender scepter in one hand, and opened her other to reveal two amethyst stones.

"Take them," she said, holding out her palm. "They will allow you to see past the spell of hiding we have placed on the dragons, and make you a part of it."

"Will the spell truly hold against the elven lords?" asked Drystan as he took a stone.

"We are not sure. But are we sure of anything, when it comes to this fey magic that has altered our world? The ring of youth Dominic wears was crafted by three elven lords wielding scepters, and therefore has the power to fool just one. We hope the same holds true when half-breeds attempt the casting. Oh, do not fear, Camille, the stone will not harm you."

Camille fought down the urge to tell her she did not fear the stone. She just did not wish to see what it would reveal. But she took the gem, and the moment she held it, her sight was opened to Lady Cecily, Dominic, and Joscelyn's creations.

Like Lady Joscelyn, they appeared out of thin air. The dragons' blue scales shimmered in the firelight, the beasts more than twice as large as the golden one Drystan had created. They also looked fiercer, with the horny faces of some water monsters. They smelled like metal and smoke. And five of them milling about in a circle, occasionally snapping at each other's tails, or belching a stream of fire, made Camille's legs go weak at the thought of mounting one of them.

Her last adventure aboard a dragon's back had not ended well.

General Dominic Raikes and his Lady Cassandra had already mounted one of the dragons, and the beast kept stomping its legs, impatiently scanning the dark sky. Dominic held his black scepter aloft, his face wan and his dark eyes narrowed in concentration, apparently still using his magic to defend the palace. His wife held him about the waist, and Camille feared Dominic would fall over if not for her support.

Lady Cecily and Giles also sat atop a beast, and it appeared that Giles did the same service for his wife that Cassandra did for her husband. Lady Cecily's scepter glowed a brilliant blue, and a whirlwind of water beyond the castle walls seemed to dance with her every movement. Giles supported her as she swayed, turning briefly to make an impatient gesture at them, the green mark on his face lurid in the firelight.

"Have the other elven lords joined Breden's attack?" asked Camille as Drystan led her toward Dominic's dragon. She had to raise her voice as they neared the circle of beasts, for they made a racket with their stomping and hissing.

Alexander shook his head, brown battle braids dancing against his angular elven cheekbones. He raised his voice to a near-shout to reply. "No. Which concerns us, for they know of our plans."

Camille wondered if their attempt to open the door

to Elfhame was indeed futile, if the elven lords did not even bother to stop them.

"My father," continued Alexander, "is reinforcing the protective fire around the palace, and Lady Cecily is controlling the beasts and helping Dominic defend us against another assault. And they are both still weary from Breden's surprise attack. They tried to protect the humans in our army—and Breden's, against the magical forces the elven lord summoned. Breden of Dewhame does not care if humans are slaughtered in this war."

Drystan halted near Dominic's mount, careful to maintain a good distance from the lethal claws and fluttering wingtips. He threw back his head, waves of white hair nearly reaching the bottom of his back with the gesture, and shouted, "Dominic Raikes. I must speak with you."

Camille noticed that Samson and Lady Joscelyn had mounted their beast, and the eagerness to fly had it stomping and clawing up cobblestones as well.

"He will never hear you over this din," said Alexander. "Whatever you need to say can wait until we reach Seven Corners. We must fly." He turned to join his wife on their dragon, the beast growing still as he approached. Camille watched with interest as he used the dragon's long tail to climb up onto its backside, his skill as a sword-dancer apparent in his graceful moves.

"This is too important," growled Drystan.

Camille squeezed his hand. "We are not even sure what to tell him, for we do not know if this strange ability of mine will work on the other scepters. Perhaps it would be best if we found out now."

"What do you—?"

Camille released his hand, gathered all the courage and elven agility she possessed, and leaped upon the tail of Dominic's dragon. The beast rolled an enormous blue eye at her and stilled his appendage, allowing her to run up the scales of it like a set of stairs. Rickety and irregular stairs, to be sure. But she managed the feat, albeit a bit breathlessly, and crossed the dragon's back to where Dominic and Lady Cassandra sat.

"What is it?" asked Cassandra.

Camille crouched. "Drystan can wield the golden scepter."

Lady Cassandra's brown eyes widened. "He developed the power overnight?"

"No. Drystan discovered that I am apparently some sort of strengthener of magic."

At her words, Dominic turned to look at her, his midnight eyes dull with fatigue, but his seamed face alight with interest. His chest rose and fell with small rapid movements, and judging by his haggard appearance, Camille realized she had done the right thing. The half-breed would never make this journey without her help. The use of his magic to protect Firehame had drained him, and his body no longer held the resilience of a young man. He had to assert too much of his will to call on his magic, and his strength already threatened to desert him.

"I do not know if this ability will work on others," she said. "But I would like to try."

Dominic shrugged wearily.

Camille reached out her bare hand. Lady Cassandra eyed it as if it were a striking snake, but she allowed Camille to touch her husband's shoulder.

Dominic trembled beneath her touch, a man near total exhaustion. And he continued to tremble.

"You feel nothing?" she asked, her throat tight with disappointment.

"Touch the hand that holds the scepter," said Drystan's voice behind her, and she turned to see his handsome, most welcome face. "The effect is most powerful skin to skin. And put some will behind it, Camille. Is that not what you did with Lady Pembridge and the children?"

She nodded. Yes, she had wanted to keep them safe. Her intentions had gone awry, of course, but only because of her ignorance. Camille fought her fear of the black scepter and reached out and clasped her hand around Dominic's. She ignored the flush of anxiety that flew through her body, the rapid pounding of her heart and the rolling of her stomach, and closed her eyes and willed him to have enough magic to sustain him.

And the scepter glowed. And Dominic quit trembling. "Astonishing," he commented. "It is as if the scepter has become more powerful. Or as if I have. The magic comes to me much more easily now."

"Camille is the key," said Drystan.

"The key to a way to open the door," finished Cassandra. "I grasp the meaning. Can you help Lady Cecily? I fear she is drained as well."

"I shall try," said Camille, a rush of satisfaction spreading through her. Perhaps Drystan was right, and she had not been directly responsible for the deaths of the children and Lady Pembridge. But she still felt a stain upon her soul, and her heart soared at the knowledge that she now possessed a way to avenge their deaths.

Perhaps she would become worthy of Drystan's love after all.

Camille felt grateful for her elven strength and speed as she made it down one dragon's tail to another, Drystan hard on her heels. Giles nodded when she reached out to clasp Lady Cecily's hand, knowing her intent, and the blue scepter glowed just like the black. Cecily looked up at her from where she sat perched on blue scales, with such a look of gratitude and relief that Camille felt her eyes burn.

"For the first time," said Cecily, "I feel like we might have a chance at accomplishing our task."

"Guard her well, Drystan," added Giles.

Cecily rolled her brilliant blue eyes at Camille.

She smiled in return, and then a rush of air made her sway on the dragon's back. Drystan caught her about the waist. They both looked up as Dominic's dragon launched into the air, quickly followed by Samson and Joscelyn's.

"The beasts feel the rush of power," said Lady Cecily. "They are eager to fly."

Drystan nodded, pale hair whipping in the breeze, and quickly led Camille down the dragon's tail. They managed to settle themselves on the back of their own mount just as another dragon took to the air.

"Giles and Cecily will take the rear," shouted Drystan, as he wrapped his arms about her waist. "Hang on, love."

And Camille's stomach flew up into her throat as the beast fully spread his great wings and heaved

upward. It did not feel like riding the golden dragon
one bit. Indeed, it felt like the entire world moved.

The golden glow of the palace's fiery turrets faded,
and darkness surrounded them like a cloak. Camille's
eyes slowly adjusted, the moon and starlight providing
just enough illumination for her to make out the
shapes of the four dragons surrounding them. One in
front, one at right, one at left, and one in the rear.

They climbed higher and higher, until the tip of
her nose frosted and she began to shiver. She dared
to release her hold from the blue scales and stuff her
hands into the rabbit muff. The air smelled sharp and
clean, but threatened to sear her lungs if she breathed
too deeply.

"Watch this," shouted Drystan against the roar of
the wind.

He removed one of her hands from the muff and
held it in his. A golden light surrounded them, and
the air grew warm and still. Camille looked over her
shoulder at Drystan in astonishment.

He gave her a lopsided grin. "My foster mother
showed me how to do it. She uses a similar spell to
create a bubble of air underwater. We had to modify
it a bit, but I think it is better than the furs I used on
my dragon, don't you?"

Camille nodded, although she had not minded
snuggling so closely to Drystan beneath those furs.

"It is odd," he mused, "how magic is shaped by
will, and yet you must know what you wish to shape
it to in order for it to work. And why does *will* sap
physical strength? It is almost as if one must pay a price
to work the magic."

"In my experience, nothing comes without a cost."

"Which concerns me, Camille. This ability of yours. What cost will you pay?"

"If we manage to free the world of the elven lords, it will be worth any price."

His arm tightened around her. "Not if it means losing you. I plan on living a long life with you, my love."

She sighed and leaned her head back against his strong shoulder.

Drystan's warm mouth moved at her ear. "You will marry me, Camille. After this is all over. Will you not?"

The dragon swayed as if dancing a minuet with the wind, and she clutched the blue scales again. If she refused him now, they would argue in circles. She would tell him she could never be a proper wife to a viscount, and he would tell her he did not give a damn what anyone thought of her. And then she would have to admit she did not know whether she could have children or not.

She cringed to think of the look upon his face.

No, it would be best to wait and see. And then... then, if she could not provide him with an heir...

She loved Drystan too much to make his life miserable. He would never admit to his disappointment. But a man with a title wanted children above all else. And Camille could only imagine what his mother would think, when her long-lost son returned home with a barren former slave.

No. She did not relish a future filled with silent reproach.

But she knew he loved her just as much as she loved

him. After all their time together, she had little doubt of that. They could not live without each other. Unlike Giles, she admitted that much to herself very quickly.

So, Camille had come up with a plan. She would be his mistress. No one would raise an objection to Drystan's having a former slave for a lover, not even his mother. He would have to set aside his honor, but it would be a small price to pay to insure he had a proper family.

"Yes," she finally said. "After this is over, we shall be together forever."

He did not seem to notice she had not agreed to marry him. Drystan nuzzled her ear and she turned, allowing his warm lips to cover hers. She did not know if they would survive the day. If they would manage to save England. If the enchantment the elven lord put upon her would ever be lifted.

Camille sighed and wrapped her arm around his shoulder, stroked the soft skin on the back of his strong neck, and for a time, forgot about the future, and just allowed herself to drink in Drystan's strength and love. No matter what happened, she would always be grateful for the time they had shared together.

Drystan recited poetry to her between kisses, and Camille marveled at the sheer beauty of words. She would never have discovered such a thing without him.

He had just finished reciting *Love's Secret* when a shout sounded from behind them.

Camille blinked. She had forgotten their companions. Forgotten that she rode a terrifying dragon high above the earth, on the way to a terrible place called the Seven Corners of Hell. Such was the power of Drystan.

They turned to look behind them. A golden predawn light had just begun to illuminate the sky, and Camille could see Giles gesturing wildly toward the rising sun. A small dark shape came into view.

"What is it?"

Drystan stiffened. "Another dragon. I cannot tell whether it is friend or foe—wait. Do you see the sheen of blue scales?"

"Yes."

"Then either Malcolm or Dorian has managed to join us."

They waited until the dragon came into full view. At first Camille could tell only that two people rode the beast, but as they neared, she could see the sheen of white hair, and red.

"Dorian and Aurelia," pronounced Drystan. "Unless this Malcolm fellow managed to find another redhead."

Then the spark of a green scepter glinted in the hazy light, and Camille knew Drystan had guessed right. The usurper of Verdanthame, Dorian Ward, and the Rebellion's assassin, Aurelia Lennox, had managed to escape the siege and join them. A cheer sounded from the company as the sixth blue dragon flew into their formation.

"By damn," muttered Drystan. "We may have a chance after all."

"But we still need Annanor's brown scepter," said Camille.

"One hurdle at a time, love." Drystan kissed her brow. "We have six. Let us rejoice in that for a while."

Camille nodded and turned back around, melted

into Drystan's comforting arms. They would succeed. Malcolm would steal the brown scepter and join them. He must. She had little chance of happiness otherwise.

As the sun continued to rise, Lady Cecily began to circle the dragons down through the clouds, until the white vista of a snow-covered England began to appear. Far ahead, Camille glimpsed an area of darkness. An emerald canopy of forest that no snow appeared to touch.

"The Seven Corners of Hell?"

"Indeed," replied Drystan. "We will wait on the southern border of the forest for Malcolm to join us."

He did not voice any doubt that the half-breed would also manage the feat of joining them, and Camille did not have the heart to. All their plans now hinged on the Rebellion spy stealing Annanor's brown scepter and escaping with it.

Lady Cecily landed her blue dragons with much more skill than Drystan had managed to land his golden. Camille felt nary a jolt as the large beast settled to ground. Drystan helped her to stand, and they stretched a moment, flexing cramped muscles.

The dragons formed a rough circle around their riders, and the entire company met in the middle, all eyes fixed upon the forest before them.

"Now what?" asked Dorian.

Camille turned to stare at their new member and his companion. Dorian resembled the elven lords, with the silver sparkles in his hair and his large green faceted eyes. But Aurelia was a surprise, for other than her uncanny beauty, she possessed no elven traits. Red hair, gray human eyes, and freckled skin. She threw back her fur cloak to reveal an assortment of daggers hanging from her belt, like so many pointed teeth. "Now, I suppose, we will have to wait."

"Aye," said Dominic, his midnight eyes focused on the evergreens. "And we cannot wait long. If Malcolm does not manage his end of the bargain, I will have to return to defend Firehame."

"And I must return to Verdanthame," added Dorian. "Annanor of Terrahame is tearing up my forest by the roots."

"We must wait as long as we can," said Lady Cassandra. "But I fear we make ourselves vulnerable, with so many scepters in one place."

Giles stomped the snow beneath his boots. "I still think it is madness to go in *there*." He stuck his chin up at the forest, the mark on his face glowing a livid green.

Samson and Alexander walked a restless circle just behind the dragons, scanning everything but the forest.

"They expect an attack," said Wilhelmina, giving her husband a nod of approval. "The elven lords have been too quiet for my liking."

"Did Lord North know anything more than that our plans were exposed?" asked Drystan.

"They do not know what the elven lords' plan, if that's what you mean," replied Dominic.

"It is starting," interjected Lady Cecily, taking a step back from the line of trees.

"What is?" asked Camille. But she did not receive an answer, for the forest suddenly erupted into a fountain of black flame, reaching far up into the sky. The dragons hissed; heads turned toward the sound of the seething flames. As one, the company moved back, even General Samson Cavendish and Alexander, distracted from their patrol of the snow-covered meadow surrounding them. The black fire blanketing the forest shivered, and red glowing stone slithered between the flames. Soon, a wave of blue water covered both, the sound like a thousand steaming kettles. The earth split, swallowing the chaos, and huge spires of jagged quartz grew upward, metal spikes sticking out from them, tearing apart creatures conjured of golden illusion.

Camille covered her ears against the sound of their screams.

How could they enter that madness to reach the source of magic? Surely they did not have enough power amongst them to survive in such chaos.

Giles turned and gave them all a look that screamed, "I told you so," and then his eyes drifted beyond them to the meadow, and his sword trembled and literally flew into his hand.

Camille turned, and at the sight of the army facing them, suddenly felt her own sword to hand.

"No," shouted Drystan, the forest still making creaking, groaning, ugly sounds behind them. "My scepter will do more than your sword. Take hold of my hand, Camille."

She did, but still kept her weapon to hand. Drystan was probably right, but she did not want any of their enemy to get close to them without some defense. For other creatures besides humans comprised the army bearing down on them. Golden demons and ogres, and monsters from nightmares, with gemstones embedded in their foreheads. Camille had the fleeting thought that Ann would be amazed by the earth golems facing them. Far larger than her doll-like figures, they swung clubs made from gnarled branches, and wore nothing but stick and mud. Other creatures made of metal screeched and groaned as they charged, swords and pikes raised high.

"There are too many of them," said Camille, her legs frozen with shock and terror.

Drystan held the golden scepter before them, the tip of it glowing like a miniature sun. "All the elven lords save Breden have sent their creatures against us. The advantage of the Rebellion was in our ability to work together. If the elven lords have joined forces—"

Camille tried to twist her hand from his. Her every instinct told her to run. Drystan turned and stared into her eyes, his golden irises shining with sympathy... and an inner strength she had glimpsed more than once. "I need you, Camille. Stand firm."

And she did. How could she not, when he needed her? She had been stronger than her fellow slaves, always striving to better her position. But Drystan gave her even more strength. As if the two of them together could conquer the world.

Or an army of the elven lords.

"How is it possible they see through my gems' spell of invisibility?" demanded Lady Joscelyn.

"I believe the elven lords are working together," shouted Dominic, confirming Drystan's worst suspicion. "The power of three elven, or in this case, at least four, can break through the spell of three half-breeds."

Camille's world narrowed to Drystan's hand in hers. A distant part of her watched Lady Joscelyn use the lavender scepter to control the dragons. They spit gouts of flame at the advancing army. She watched the soldiers burn and fall, to form piles of black within the snow. But they kept coming, and many made their way past the circle of dragons. Dominic used gray fire to create a wall of flame about them, but it did not hold back the magical creatures, who plunged through the wall. Lady Cecily called to the snow and ice, and formed another wall just behind Dominic's.

But the creatures broke through that, as well.

Dorian tried his green scepter, calling up hibernating roots from beneath the snow, weaving them together to form another wall behind the first two.

Drystan conjured an illusion of a golden wall just behind the green. Morning had broken, and the bricks sparkled in the new light.

For a moment, silence reigned.

"Our defenses will not hold against the creatures," said Dominic. "The elven lords are somehow strengthening them."

"And we cannot attack with our magic," added Lady Cecily.

"Why not?" asked Camille.

Alexander turned and gave her a crooked grin. "My dear, we risk hurting our fellow Englishmen. What good is it to conquer the elven lords, if we have no countrymen left to turn the land over to?"

"Of course. I did not think… what are we to do?"

"My dragons have fallen," interrupted Lady Joscelyn, lowering her lavender scepter.

Camille turned to her with a frown. "How do you know?"

"I can feel the death of my gems," she explained.

Drystan turned and nodded in the direction of the forest. "The creatures may follow us in there, but humans will not, no matter what enchantment the elven lords try to coerce them with—their fear of the place runs too deep. We will have a better chance to fight back."

"I hate it when you're right," said Giles. Then he spun, for one of the creatures had already managed to break through all of their defenses. A hideous beast with wicked claws and a horned head. Giles's sword curved in an arch, decapitating the creature. Camille watched in horrified fascination as his sword began to absorb the blood of the dead body.

Samson and Alexander spun in slow circles, watching the walls for any more breaches. Wilhelmina joined them, grinning as she drew her sword. "I suggest you make a decision soon, or it is liable to get rather bloody."

Samson raised his voice over the sound of grinding metal. "If we are lucky."

And a creature of iron burst through Drystan's golden wall. Composed of squares of metal and barbs of steel, it swung a long chain with a bladed ball at the end of it. Wilhelmina ducked and swung her sword, catching the creature on the leg. A loud clang made Camille grit her teeth, and Wilhelmina cringe from arm to toe. Alexander screamed a battle cry and launched himself at the creature in defense of his wife.

Camille forced herself not to blink. Alexander,

the Duke of Chandos, was indeed a sword-dancer. He spun about the metal creature with deadly grace, avoiding the hundreds of wicked blades by twisting his body in amazing configurations. The duke's sword flashed in a blur of silver shadow, penetrating the seams that held the pieces of metal together in parody of a human shape. Within moments, the individual parts separated, and a pile of metal rubble lay on the snowy ground.

"No blood," growled Samson.

"Indeed," panted Alexander.

Dominic raised a pale brow and faced the four other half-breeds wielding scepters. "Lady Joscelyn, now that your dragons have fallen, add a bit of stone to our barrier, will you?"

She nodded, and the ground shivered, enormous columns of crystal sprouting from it to cover Drystan's golden bricks. The space inside their circle became very close.

"On my count, lower your walls to the forest. One, two, now."

Color flashed: blue, green, lavender, black, and gold. An opening formed in the wall, and Camille could see the forest through the tunnel. "The storm has passed."

"Indeed," agreed Dorian, his green faceted eyes directed at the trees. "It will allow us to enter."

He spoke as if the wood communicated with him. No wonder people called him forest lord.

"It will not last for long," warned Giles. "The seven powers will clash again."

"Is there any regularity to the occurrences?" asked

Drystan, as if he discussed a theoretical problem from one of his books. Camille admired his calm manner. It made their situation seem somehow... less frightening.

"No," answered Lady Cecily, as she lifted her skirts and walked quickly toward the tunnel. Giles mumbled something and followed her. Dominic intercepted them at the entrance, and as always, he and his lady took the lead.

Camille walked over a layer of crystal, golden brick, and dry vines. A shout rang out just as she raised her foot to place it on a layer of ice. She looked up, but could not see past the broad shoulders of the men in front of her.

"What is it, Drystan?"

"Monsters," he replied. "They are blocking our way to the forest."

Fifteen

DOMINIC SHOUTED SOMETHING, AND CAMILLE COULD see a sudden flash of heat and light. Drystan clasped her hand tightly and his scepter began to glow, shaping itself into a golden sword. "We will have to fight our way through."

Camille swallowed. Drystan held her right hand, and so she held her sword in her left. She could barely use the blade with her left, but as they ran forward, she realized she needn't have worried. Her enchanted blade did all the work; she only had to be brave and hold on.

Which turned out to be harder than she would have thought.

Dominic fought his attackers with short bursts of flame, avoiding humans whenever he could. Humans had been forced to fight in the elven wars, and even now, it became apparent their hearts were not in the battle. Very few of them fought alongside the monsters.

Lady Cassandra moved as gracefully as her son, both of them wielding their swords as if they danced to some wild tune. Lady Cecily called forth whirlwinds of blinding snow while her husband's sword drank blood time and again. Dorian and Lady Joscelyn's scepters had transformed into swords like Drystan's, while Alexander and Wilhelmina and Samson wielded ordinary blades of steel with much more skill. The redheaded assassin, Aurelia, threw blades that had been enchanted to return to her hand like loyal hounds.

They were the best the Rebellion had to offer. The monsters did not stand a chance against them.

Camille might have felt in awe, if she had not been so busy with her own sword. At first, she could not distinguish one attacker from another. Beings made of fire and black ooze, of sticks and mud, of horns and decayed flesh. She winced when her sword cut them down. But then she noticed their eyes. Inhuman eyes, filled with madness and a gleeful desire to see her dead. She had never felt such hatred directed at her before. It frightened her… and then made her determined to rob them of the satisfaction of her death.

By the time they reached the relative safety of the forest, blood and gore spattered the front and side of her riding dress. The rest of the company looked no better, and a silence fell among them. The forest now seemed quite at odds with the maelstrom of magic Camille had witnessed earlier. The massive trunks and undergrowth muted the sound of the army beyond them. A gentle breeze shushed through the canopy of leaves, and although the temperature still made her breath frost, no snow reached past that shady barrier.

"They shall gather the courage to follow us soon

enough," said Dominic, his face now as haggard as it had been in Firehame. Indeed, most of the company looked drained, and Camille wondered if she should volunteer to touch them.

How odd, to think she could make a difference.

"We had best move," he continued. "Lady Cecily, which way?"

The blue-eyed woman shrugged. "My father, Viscount Althorp, led us to the source of magic. I know only that it lies within the center of the forest."

"Next to a large lake," added Giles. "Sense the direction of the water, my dear, and we shall find it."

She gave him a tired nod, clasped her scepter a bit more tightly, and led them forward on a rough path through the trees. Camille stripped branches bare of leaves as she walked, and used them to wipe at her gown, trying to remove the worst of the gore. Drystan noticed her distress and used his magic to help, as did the rest of those holding scepters, each in the manner of their particular magical skill.

"Keep your eyes upon me," warned Cecily, "and not on the trail. It will trick you to another path, and you shall be lost."

"Why am I not surprised?" said Samson in that gravelly voice of his.

"Lady Cecily," interrupted Dorian, "we were given only a brief explanation of our mission. Perhaps you should describe this source of magic to us. What, exactly, are we looking for?"

She spoke over her shoulder as she led them forward. "It appears to be nothing more than a natural spring sheltered by crystal rocks, with small streams flowing from it. It does not reveal its true nature until the black fire comes with the maelstrom. That's when my father witnessed the doorway to Elfhame."

"Tell them how he managed to survive to witness it," said Giles, a hint of vindication in his voice.

"He was suspended in crystal at the time. It somehow kept his essence alive when his body died."

"You might have mentioned this earlier," snapped Wilhelmina.

"It changes nothing," interrupted Dominic, his voice low with some deep emotion. "I can protect us from black fire, long enough to open this doorway, if we can. This is our only chance. We shall succeed."

Camille took heart from his words, as did the rest of the company.

The feeling lasted until the sound of breaking branches and bloodthirsty growls grew behind them.

"The monsters have finally found their courage," said Alexander, an odd hint of amusement in his voice. Camille glanced at him. She could not understand him, for he appeared to view everything with some degree of humor.

"Shall we fight, or run?"

"Dominic is too old to run," teased Giles, as if Alexander's cavalier manner had infected him. "And my sword still thirsts for more blood."

Dominic turned and scowled at him, and with a flick of his black scepter, created demons of fire. Lady Cecily managed to add some vicious-looking water nymphs, Lady Joscelyn some creatures made of shimmering stone, and Drystan added some golden demons. After they dispersed their creatures, Dorian turned and wove the trees of the forest behind them into a seemingly impenetrable wall.

"That should keep them away for a while," said the forest lord.

"Why did you not create such beings before?" asked Camille.

"It is... distracting," answered Drystan, with a tug on her hand as they made their way through the gloomy forest once again. "I must keep half my will trained upon them, or they shall go their own way. It is difficult to do while trying to defend yourself, although I imagine the others are better at it than I, having more practice."

"Any use of our magic is draining," said Lady Joscelyn. "We are trying to conserve our strength for opening the portal, for we have no idea how much power we will need to accomplish it."

The forest suddenly opened up into a wide meadow. The snow had managed an entrance here, for the ground lay covered in a sheet of unbroken white. Camille followed in the deep footsteps of those in front of her, suddenly realizing how very tired she felt. And she had no magic to drain her. She could only imagine how those who wielded the scepters must feel, although Drystan looked alert. Perhaps because he still held her hand.

"Shall I offer to help them?" Camille murmured.

Drystan glanced up at the gloomy sky, the sun hidden behind gray clouds, and then around at the rest of their fellows. "Dominic is aware of your gift, Camille. He will ask you if he thinks there is need... but I believe he will wait until we join the scepters. All of our strength must go into that moment, for whatever happens before then will not matter a whit unless—"

"Look," cried Lady Joscelyn, her lavender scepter held up to the skies. "It is one of mine."

They followed her gaze and saw a small dark speck circling above them. A flash of lavender sparked, an answering reflection in Lady Joscelyn's scepter.

"It is one of my dragons!"

"Malcolm," breathed Lady Cecily, and at his name, a sigh of relief seemed to envelop the company as one. "Our odds of triumphing keep increasing."

Smiles wreathed the faces of those around her, and Camille could not help but feel hopeful for the first time. All of their plans hinged upon Malcolm, and he had come!

They all watched as the dark speck grew larger, into the blue scales and wide wings of a dragon. It circled lower until Camille could see it carried one rider, a man with flowing white hair and the silver sparkle of a rich heritage of elven blood.

He lifted a hand and waved at them.

"Thank providence for this clearing," said Drystan. "Or he would not have found us beneath the trees."

"It is probable he has been circling for some time looking for us," mused Giles. "And only now has dropped lower to—"

A bolt of murky color shot from a group of trees beyond the meadow, striking the dragon squarely in the chest. Lady Joscelyn cried out and fell to her knees, her skirts a puddle in the snow. Samson knelt at her side. "Jo!"

She shook her head. "Do not worry. I just need a moment… to recover."

But Camille had no time to be concerned for the lady, for the dragon's wings had crumbled to ash, and beast and rider separated, the man windmilling his arms as he fell. Within moments, the blue dragon burst into a flame of multicolored fire, and only a thin streak of black testified to the creature's existence.

"Damn," muttered Drystan, and he held up his golden scepter before anyone else had time to react. The snow within the meadow suddenly erupted into puffy balls, and Camille could not help smiling. When the man reached the earth, he fell into a soft pile of golden-edged cloud.

"Quick thinking," said Dominic.

"Well done," echoed Giles.

Drystan only gave them a nod before dispersing his illusion, then towed Camille forward behind Dorian, who reached the man first and helped Malcolm gain his feet.

"Softest snow I ever landed in," muttered Malcolm.

"You have Lord Hawkes to thank for that," replied Dorian.

The half-breed sketched a wobbly bow, his white hair near disappearing into the snow at his feet. When he rose, he studied the company, most of whom had walked over to join them. Camille tried not to stare, for Malcolm resembled the elven lords too much for comfort. She saw little trace of his human heritage, and if she had not known that an elven lady held the brown scepter, she would have thought him to be an Imperial Lord.

Malcolm flashed them a crooked grin. "Do not let my looks fool you." He dug inside his pocket, and pulled forth Annanor's brown scepter. "I can hold it, but I cannot wield the magic within. I had a devil of a time stealing it and bringing it here, but I am afraid I bring you poor hope for the success of your venture."

"On the contrary," said Dominic. "You were our best hope, and now we may have a chance." He turned to Camille. "Perhaps we should make sure you can influence the earth scepter as well?"

"What are you talking about?" demanded Wilhelmina, and Camille realized the duchess had not been privy to her secret.

"Perhaps I should try them all, just to be sure?" suggested Camille.

She loosed her grasp from Drystan, who scowled but allowed her to separate from him. She noticed that his golden scepter still glowed, and wondered that he might have been right. The longer one stayed close to her, the longer her gift appeared to influence them.

She clasped her hand around Malcolm's, and the brown scepter in his hand glowed with a light she saw reflected in the half-breed's eyes. Wilhelmina did not spare any more words. She withdrew the silver scepter from her coat pocket and held it out to Camille. Her silver eyes widened when Camille wrapped her fingers around the tall woman's hand.

"Such power," murmured Wilhelmina. "It frightens me. Give me my sword over this, any day."

"You possess a unique talent," said Malcolm, his face alight with admiration. "I have never heard of such magic."

Drystan stepped forward and towed Camille back to his side. "Because it is not magic. We can sense none on her person at all. She is some sort of catalyst for power. Perhaps a gift given to her by her ancestor. Perhaps gifted to her line by what they witnessed so long ago."

"The opening of the gateway between worlds. Damn, is it possible?"

"We shall soon see," said Dominic.

Malcolm frowned, a marring of his perfect skin. "I had expected to find you waiting for me at the border of the forest, but when I saw the army, I hoped you had made it within, and searched for you there." His brown faceted eyes studied the company. "It appears you made it through at great cost."

"As did you," said Lady Joscelyn, who seemed to have partially recovered from the destruction of the gemstone the dragon had carried, and now joined their group, Samson holding her upright with a strong arm. "Does anyone know what destroyed my dragon?"

Without asking, Camille stepped over to Joscelyn's side and touched her hand. The lady's lavender eyes widened nearly as round as Wilhelmina's, and she took a deep breath, standing up straight and strong. Camille turned toward Dorian, but Dominic waylaid her with a gesture.

"I think," he said, "we can now assume your gift works with them all."

"All of what?" demanded Joscelyn.

"All of the scepters. Camille is a catalyst for their powers—"

A crackle drowned out his words, and as one they turned to look behind them.

"At least we shall not have to worry about the army of monsters anymore," said Alexander.

Samson paled, the scars standing out on his perfect features in vivid relief. "Now we have only the maelstrom to worry about."

A wall of black fire engulfed the forest behind them, and raced at an uncanny speed to their meadow.

"Come on, old man," said Giles, turning to Dominic. "Use that elven blood of yours to run." And he grabbed his arm, urging him forward. Dominic shrugged him off with a scowl, but leapt ahead with elven grace, his lady at his side.

The rest of the company quickly followed as the sound of destruction grew louder behind them.

"I still want to know," shouted Joscelyn, leaping over a fallen log, "what the hell shot down my dragon."

"Stubborn," grunted Samson, who ran so fluidly he appeared to glide over the ground.

"Not what, but who," replied Dominic, his breath coming in shallow gasps. "You should all know. I fear I know why the elven lords themselves did not stop us from entering the forest—"

They burst through the trees. A calm lake lay to their right. Another snow-shrouded meadow sat before the next line of trees, a layer of white covering a jagged hill of crystal near the middle of it. And just beyond that bubbled a small spring surrounded by large crystal stones, with unfrozen streams flowing away from it.

And five elven lords waited for them in front of the source of magic.

Lan'dor of Bladehame, with his silver eyes and

broad shoulders. La'laylia of Stonehame, with her lavender eyes and sharp beauty. Breden of Dewhame, his faceted blue eyes cloudy with madness. Roden of Dreamhame. And even Annanor of Terrahame, who must have used her own magical steed to reach the Seven Corners of Hell before her consort, Malcolm.

Dominic took several deep breaths, and finished, "It is because they are waiting here for us."

The elven lords stood in a half circle, ominously still and silent. Camille's knees trembled, and if not for Drystan's warm hand in hers, she would have bolted. Despite their beautiful faces and perfect forms, she knew the elven were evil. And would not hesitate to unleash their powers upon them. Roden's sharp gaze flicked over her, his eyes widening in surprise. Camille lifted her chin and suddenly stopped shaking.

She was no longer a slave. She had the power to help banish him. And she would not allow fear to stop her from what she needed to do.

Dominic walked forward with an arrogant stride, his face devoid of emotion, and the rest of the company followed.

"But why here?" murmured Giles.

"My guess is that their powers are strongest at the source of magic," whispered Drystan. "The scepters might just be a conduit for the power that flows from Elfhame, allowing them to tap into it. By making a stand this close to the source, they might rival half-breeds wielding their very own scepters."

"Well done, human," said Roden of Dreamhame. "Lord Hawkes, is it not?" Dominic had halted their group with a third of the meadow still separating them from the enemy, but with the elvens' keen hearing, they did not miss a word. "We are pleased to see you fell for our little trap."

"I'm sure that's what you would like us to think," drawled Dominic. His voice usually lacked inflection, but now it sounded almost... bored. It frightened Camille more than if he had shouted, for then she would have had proof he still harbored some human emotion.

Lady Cassandra stood close to her husband, rocking back and forth on the balls of her feet, as if she listened to some silent tune.

"Well, by all means," replied Roden. "Please attempt to do what you came here for. By allowing you to steal our scepters, you have provided us with an entertainment we could never have devised for ourselves. We shall show you our gratitude after we watch you struggle. If the depth of grief from your failure amuses us enough, we might even save some of you." He gestured behind them. "Besides, I do not know how long we can hold off the maelstrom. It would be a pity to see it destroy you before the game is even begun."

Camille realized the crackle of the black fire had indeed slowed. So the elven lords could watch the foolish humans construct the star from the scepters? Good heavens, what would they truly unleash when they opened the doorway? Her gaze met Drystan's, and he shrugged.

"They could be bluffing," he said, "but if it is a trap... if it is just another one of their games... if they allowed us to steal the scepters and gather together to make one devastating blow against the Rebellion..."

Dominic turned. "Then they have underestimated us. Their arrogance has always been to our advantage. Let us use it now."

"But we cannot be sure—" started Giles.

"I am sure we cannot use the scepters to fight them. Or should we so easily allow them to take back what they lost?" Dominic's midnight gaze narrowed on Giles.

He shook his head, the blemish on his face a dull green in the dawn light. "They would not stand and watch if they thought we had a chance of succeeding. You heard them. They want to wallow in our failure."

"My love," said Lady Cecily, "we must try. We cannot give up just to prove our defiance, now that we have come this far."

"Besides," breathed Drystan, keeping his voice so low Camille could barely hear it. "We have the key."

A cackle of laughter sounded from the group of elven. Breden of Dewhame grinned maniacally, nodding his head at his daughter.

"The key, the key," sang the elven lord. "Form the star to open the door but it is stuck stuck stuck." He bent over and whooped, slapping his knees. The rest of the elven lords ignored him, calling to the river of magic leaking from the spring, the illusory water suddenly changing direction and flowing toward their outstretched hands. Except for Roden of Dreamhame. He stared at Camille with a frown upon his handsome face.

The elven lords thought Drystan had referred to the mark upon her neck, and not Camille's gift. Since it was not magical in origin, Roden had never sensed it.

But Roden possessed a quick mind, and if he should puzzle it out...

"Hurry," she commanded.

The half-breeds holding the scepters formed a rough circle. Dominic held the black out first, quickly met by the edge of Dorian's green. A glow of dark emerald fire swirled above the two. Lady Cecily's blue scepter met the edge of Dorian's, and Joscelyn's lavender scepter joined hers. The glow now coalesced into a color reminiscent of the Seven Corners of Hell when consumed by the maelstrom. Only three more scepters remained to form the star, but those who could not harness the power held them. Camille must help them withstand the energies the key had already created.

Wilhelmina traded glances with Malcolm and Drystan. Camille squeezed Drystan's hand and he calmly nodded at the duchess, took a step forward, and placed the top of the golden scepter alongside Joscelyn's.

Something odd happened to Camille, and she did not have time to decipher the feeling before Wilhelmina leaned forward with the silver scepter, reaching out her other hand to Camille.

When Camille grasped those strong fingers, another tremor ran through her, and she wavered on her feet.

"What is it?" demanded Drystan.

But she ignored him, trying to maneuver her body past the taller woman as Malcolm stepped forward to finish the star, a frown on his face as he reached out for Camille.

"Wait," she told Malcolm, releasing Wilhelmina's

hand and grabbing his, stepping in front of the taller woman. "Duchess, place your hand on my neck," she said. "Your skin needs only to touch mine."

Camille felt the brush of the woman's callused fingertips near her pulse, which now beat with a frantic measure. Camille had never felt anything like this before. But she had never been so close to such powerful magics before. She now understood what wielding magic must feel like, for she felt a drain not only on her body, but on her inner strength as well.

Yet it also felt as if the scepters drew energy from her very soul, and Drystan never mentioned that in relation to using magic.

Camille's stomach lurched. Perhaps that feeling was unique to her gift. Perhaps she had found the answer to Drystan's question. The price of using her gift would be her very soul.

"What is that girl with the ugly eyes doing?" demanded La'laylia, the elven lady of Stonehame.

"Interesting," replied Roden. "She is making a connection with the three half-breeds who lack the power to wield a scepter. And yet, the slave girl has no magic to aid them, for I have tested her myself. Several times. Because of those odd eyes of hers. They appear to possess all the colors of the scepters..."

Wilhelmina pressed the top of the silver scepter against Drystan's gold. With a hastily muttered prayer, Malcolm quickly inserted the brown between the black scepter and the silver, completing the shape of the star. The glowing color intensified, all the colors of the seven scepters swirling like a small tornado above the star. Camille felt her chest contract, and then shatter, as if her heart had been ripped out and now mingled with the colorful dance of conjoined power.

"Fie!" sputtered Roden, taking a step forward. "The girl—do you feel it? Stop them!"

A rush of sound pounded Camille's ears as the elven lords unleashed their hold on the black fire and it threatened to envelop their company. Dominic held up his free hand, an answering rush of gray fire surrounding them and the five members who did not hold a scepter. Aurelia, Giles, Samson, Alexander, and Lady Cassandra pressed closer to their mates while the column of power grew above the star. It did not look like smoke, or mist, or anything Camille had ever seen before. The power whirled and swelled and grew, until it formed a column that pierced the smothering black fire to reveal the blue skies above.

The ground trembled, and she could not hear the elven lords' cries any longer. For a timeless moment chaos surrounded the companions, as once again the full fury of the maelstrom shook the Seven Corners of Hell.

Dominic's face paled; his teeth gritted against the power he summoned. Camille wished she could reach him, to give him some of the strength from her gift.

Instead, the other six added their own power to his. When the black fire pushed at the gray barrier, Lady Cecily called forth a wall of icy water to quench it. When the earth split, Dorian called to his green growing powers to weave a tangle of roots to bridge the gap. Malcolm made a fist and calmed the raging earth, letting loose a whoop of triumph when the earthquakes actually ceased. Lady Joscelyn shattered the quartz that heaved upward. Drystan sent a rain of golden arrows against the beasts emerging from the fire. And Wilhelmina spoke to the iron ore, cooling and coaxing it back into the ground.

A silence descended, and it felt as if they floated in the blackness for a moment, before plunging back down to the meadow. They stood in a circle of daylight, the column of magic still piercing the clouds like a beacon.

"We did it," breathed Drystan.

"We are alive, at least," added Giles, his arm about the waist of his wife.

"Light," gasped Dominic, and white fire lit the rest of the meadow.

Camille blinked, trying to make sense of her surroundings. They did, indeed, still stand in a meadow, but it looked like nothing she had ever seen before. The snow crawled across the landscape as if it held a life of its own, and the streams, which once flowed like ordinary water, now sparkled with a brilliance rivaling the tornado of power they created with the scepters.

"What is happening?" she whispered.

"We are in the eye of the maelstrom," answered Lady Cecily.

"I told you," laughed the melodic voice of an elven lord. "It is stuck stuck stuck." They turned as one to see Breden dancing a jig in front of what once had been the crystal stones of the spring. But the stones had grown into glowing columns surrounding a shimmering translucent portal.

"The doorway to Elfhame," murmured Drystan in wonder.

Sixteen

CAMILLE COULD GLIMPSE ODD SHAPES JUST BEYOND the shimmering door. Plants, perhaps, or distorted trees, reminding her of Dreamhame's garden. And tall figures with flowing robes and pale hair.

"Breden is right," said Dominic. "We are not strong enough to open it."

Apparently the elven lords did not wish to indulge their human playthings any longer. The fresh power that flowed from that opening into England coalesced about the five elven, and they shaped it in their hands. Lan'dor of Bladehame crafted a sword of silver that matched the color of his eyes, glanced from the portal to the group of humans, and let out a war cry that made Camille flinch.

Lan'dor leaped toward their group, but before he could swing his blade, Lady Cassandra danced forward, a swirling mass of skirts and lethal intent. Her son, Alexander, leaped in front of her, his sword parrying a blow that would have taken off his mother's head.

Wilhelmina jerked.

"Stand firm," warned Dominic, his eyes on his

wife. Although the man did not flinch, Camille could see the fear for Cassandra in that black gaze. "The magic of our star is countering the chaos of the storm. If we falter, we all die."

Lady Annanor called to the powers of the earth, the ground near her feet rising upward to form the shapes of monstrous golems. Flashes of silver passed by Camille, and she realized the assassin, Aurelia, had launched an attack with her daggers. The flying missiles managed to distract the elven lady, but no matter how accurate the aim, they kept missing their true target. Instead of returning to Aurelia's hand, the blades shot point-first back at her, until she could no longer dodge them. One pierced her shoulder. Another lodged in her leg.

Camille heard Giles's sword singing in anticipation as he engaged with Breden, who had stopped laughing long enough to shape whips of liquid that twisted so furiously they gained solid force. Those flails reached past Giles's guard more than once.

Samson attacked La'laylia with grim determination, grunting as the elven lady struck him with one spell after another, lines of blood sprouting on his handsome face.

Lady Cassandra broke away from Alexander, who appeared to be holding his own against Lan'dor, and tried to harass Roden. But the elven lord of Dreamhame created golden harpies with wicked claws, and Cassandra soon found herself dancing for her life while her gown was ripped to shreds, crimson showing at each rent.

"They cannot hold for long," snapped Joscelyn,

turning her gaze upon Dominic. "Do you expect us to just stand here and watch them die?"

"Do not be overly concerned," answered Lan'dor as he countered Alexander's whirling sword as if he swatted away a pesky fly. "We shall not forget you." And with two prodigious leaps, he crossed the distance between them, appearing just behind Joscelyn, and ran his blade almost lovingly down her back before turning back to Alexander, who had tried to follow. Lan'dor cut him as easily as one would carve a mutton roast, and after two strides, Alexander's legs collapsed beneath him, a look of astonishment on his comely face.

Lady Joscelyn sucked in a breath, her face turning white as snow, and only Lady Cecily's steadying hand prevented her from collapsing.

Lan'dor laughed, and Camille stared in horror as he raised his silver sword to plunge it into Alexander's chest.

Wilhelmina opened her mouth to scream, but a sound like a thousand trumpets cut off her cry.

The elven lords froze, and looked up at the opening in the sky above the star's column of magic.

"Ador," breathed Dominic.

A black dragon circled that beacon of power, and then dove toward them, followed by a green, then a blue, then a silver. A brown dragon flew before a lavender and gold. The last two beasts landed with unsteady wobbles in the meadow, their scales dark with decay.

"Midaz," gasped Lady Joscelyn, her eyes filling with tears. Camille did not think it was because of the pain of her wound, but her love for the dragon. Because

Camille then saw her dear Grimor'ee, and felt her own eyes burn.

Ador, the black dragon of Firehame, picked up Lan'dor with a delicate baring of his teeth, and tossed the elven lord back toward the other four.

Alexander lurched to his feet, wobbling crazily but sword at ready, glancing between the elven and their dragon-steeds, as if unsure which insurmountable battle he should tackle first. Then he turned and motioned to Giles, Samson, and his mother, and they all staggered back to join Aurelia, who had taken up a defensive position just in front of Camille's scepter-wielding companions.

Roden of Dreamhame tossed back his sparkling white hair and looked up at the group of dragons. "Where the hell have you been?"

"Said just like a human," replied Ador, who seemed to be the leader of the scaled flock. "Careful, Roden. You are resembling the animals you so despise."

"Never," answered the elven lord. "And you are a little late. We can handle this group of rebels ourselves."

The shiny black scales above the dragon's brow lifted slightly with a scraping sound. "You misinterpret our appearance."

Dominic of Firehame made a strangled noise, which oddly enough resembled laughter. The dragon ignored him.

"You see," continued Ador, "it is time for us to go home."

"Madness!" shouted Breden of Dewhame, his whips twining about him like liquid snakes. "You cannot disobey us; we ensured it with a spell."

"Ahhh," replied Grimor'ee, turning his liquid gaze upon Camille for a moment. "The enchantment has weakened over time. You laugh at the human concept of love, mad lords, but it has proven more powerful a weapon than you know. It chipped away your spell, bit by bit."

"And although we have suffered for it," added Midaz, his violet gaze fixed upon Joscelyn, "we do not regret it."

The green dragon of Verdanthame gave a negligent stretch of his wings. "Besides, the humans have earned their freedom. Have fought for it. And they discovered the key." He lifted an olive talon and scratched his massive chest and added, "The scepters want to go home."

Roden's slim body vibrated with rage. "The humans may have discovered the key, but they cannot open the door. And the scepters do not matter. They act only on instinct."

"Nevertheless," replied Ador, "we shall give the humans a chance to succeed."

Lady Annanor held out her hands in entreaty, power dripping through her fingers like shimmering grains of sand. Her bronze gown shifted with the movement, outlining her generous breasts, her long legs. Her brown eyes opened wide, reflections of amber and sienna in their depths. "Ador... my dearest Kiz'rah... blessed dragon-steeds of beauty and might. You know what will happen to us if we return to Elfhame. Our people consider us mad, and will cleanse our minds. They will take away that very essence which makes us unique."

After one calculating glance, La'laylia copied Annanor, raising her own hands, her gown of jewels shimmering like a blanket of stars. She stepped toward Ador, pale skin revealed in tantalizing glimpses with every move she made. "You cannot truly wish to return to Elfhame. Have we not been happy, here? Such adventure, such chaos! We shall shrivel and die if we return—"

It happened so quickly, Camille barely saw the exchange. Lan'dor, Breden, and Roden raised their hands along with the two elven ladies, and launched a bolt of power straight at Ador's massive jaw. Kalah, the blue dragon of Dewhame, let loose a roar punctuated with a great blast of lightning straight at the elven lords. Both Grimor'ee and Midaz moved in front of the group of humans to protect them, while the rest of the dragons launched molten metal and roars and snarls of magic-imbued smoke at the elven lords.

But after that first attack on the black dragon, the elven ignored the beasts and moved as one, directing their power toward the star of scepters. The blast hit Dominic squarely in the back, and he let out a startled oath of surprise before his eyes rolled back in his head.

Mother and son caught him in their arms before he had a chance to break the pattern of the star. Lady Cassandra held Dominic's hand around the black scepter, and looked up at the startled faces of the company.

"Open that damn portal," she shouted over the cacophony of battling magic behind her.

"We were not strong enough to do it with Dominic," Wilhelmina countered. "How do you expect us to manage it now? I have never wielded a damn scepter before, and I do not know what I am doing—"

"Be calm, Duchess," soothed Lady Cecily. "Look, Dominic is already regaining consciousness. Do not underestimate us as the elven lords have done."

Malcolm shook his head. "I fear the warrior-woman is right. We do not have the strength."

Camille felt her heart drop as she looked around the circle and saw despair reflected in every set of eyes. They could not falter now. They were so close…

She recognized Grimor'ee's particular roar amongst all the others, and cringed at the cry of pain in it.

"We must do something, quickly," exclaimed Lady Joscelyn. "They are killing Midaz!"

Camille glanced at Drystan. His golden eyes mirrored the other's—pain and despair in their depths. He had shown her such strength. Had championed and protected her. And now his dream of freeing England would die with him. He was her hero, and he would die a failure.

"No," she said, not realizing she spoke aloud. "Love weakened the enchantment on the dragons. Perhaps it can strengthen our magic as well."

"What do you mean?" asked Wilhelmina, her breath stirring the hair on the back of Camille's head.

Camille ignored her and turned to Malcolm. "Let go of my hand."

The beautiful man frowned, fear in his eyes.

"Do not worry. As long as I stay in the circle, the scepter will not harm you."

He nodded and let go of her.

"What are you doing?" demanded Drystan.

Camille maneuvered her body sideways, between Wilhelmina and Drystan. "I am the key, is that not what you said? I am the key to your strength... and to that of the scepters."

His amber eyes widened. "No. You do not know what it will do to you."

"Wilhelmina. You may release me."

Without another word, the woman allowed her hand to drop.

Camille leaned forward and kissed Drystan's furious mouth. "You have taught me self-sacrifice... you have furrowed out the best in me. Do not allow your love for me to weaken that."

And Camille pushed her way between the gold and silver scepters, to the center of the star where magic still twisted and roiled in a tornado of sparkling power. Dominic had opened his eyes, and although his hand shook, he held the black steady. As one, the seven half-breeds of the Rebellion allowed her to break into the circle, pressing their scepters against her waist.

Camille had never touched a scepter before, much less seven of them at once. She felt them each as individual entities, with a distinct personality and will. They shouted incomprehensible words in her mind, the syllables blocking out the sound of battle, consuming her with such force she forgot where she was, *why* she was.

The swirling power devoured her, made her a part of the whirling, glowing force. Her heart still flew within the tornado, and now her soul joined it by bits and pieces. The column bent lower and lower, until it angled toward the portal, until the top of it pierced the shimmering doorway between the crystal columns. A sound rent the air, as if the very heavens opened, and for a moment the meadow lit with an unnatural display of fireworks. Colors of green, blue, violet, and gold sparked and danced. Silver, black, and brown exploded in dazzling accompaniment.

Camille kept her eyes fixed on Drystan, the prismatic lights playing across his smooth skin, as she lost her memory of him.

Until she wondered at the look of sadness that crossed the handsome stranger's face.

The roaring finally ceased.

Quiet descended on the little meadow in the Seven Corners of Hell.

"Hush now," murmured Camille to the singing, crying voices in her head. "We have opened the door."

The portal shuddered, a round opening forming in the middle of it, which expanded like the pupil of a dragon's eye. Camille glimpsed a land lush with color, of castles nestled into enormous trees, of creatures wild and free grazing on lavender grass. A wondrous place of peace and harmony.

The five elven lords standing in front of the portal backed away.

"Fie," breathed the man with the midnight eyes. "They are afraid." He spoke as if he had never expected to ever see such a thing.

A scent reminiscent of elfweed wafted through that doorway, and two beautiful beings stepped out of it, their glowing eyes sweeping over the scene before them. A sadness crossed their delicate features, not marring their perfection in the least.

They each wore a crown of odd gemstones that blazed like the sun, the man's slightly larger than the woman's. They resembled the elven lords who had invaded England, with their white-blonde hair sparkling with silver, their pointed ears and smooth pale skin. But the king and queen of Elfhame held a beauty and peace inside that reflected in their calm expressions, the warmth in their clear faceted eyes.

Their beauty shone inside and out, transforming them into beings who rivaled the angels.

"Thank the Lord," murmured Lady Cassandra. "We did the right thing."

Camille knew the angels. The scepters told her their names. "King Dremen. Queen Sarsha. Welcome to our world." She bowed her head, the tornado of power following her movements, a glowing crown all her own.

The king raised his pale brows, throwing a glance at his wife. Queen Sarsha nodded regally at the humans, but quickly turned her attention to the five elven lords.

"So," she said, her voice rippling like clear water over crystal stone. "Our errant lordlings have finally been returned to us." She stepped away from her husband, the folds of her gown moving with a life of their own. "We have missed you sorely, my little mad elflings."

Roden curled his long graceful fingers into fists. "We won't go back."

King Dremen spoke then, his voice like thunder from a cloudless sky. "You will not be difficult, will you?" He smiled, and his beauty made Camille want to weep at the sight of it. "You have harmed this world so badly, that I am sure the council will not blame me for snuffing you out of existence, right here, right now. If not for my queen's pity of your demented state, I would have done so already."

Roden cringed, his bravado disappearing as swiftly as it had come. With nary a glance at his fellows, he strode into the portal. Lan'dor sheathed his silver sword and followed, La'laylia and Annanor right behind him.

Breden stood with arms crossed, his foot tapping a mad rhythm against the smoking scale of a fallen dragon. "You cannot make me go. I like it here."

Queen Sarsha's sensuous mouth fell in a frown. "My poor Breden. Look at what this primitive world has done to you. Come, my dear one. I have hot chavi waiting for you, and freshly baked nardo. And sweet music to soothe your nerves, and caring hands to tend you."

"Peace is boring."

"Perhaps. But now that we know of your illness, I think you will find Elfhame more to your liking."

Breden huffed, but allowed the lady to lead him into the portal. She watched him disappear behind an enormous scarlet flower, and shook her head before turning back around.

A half circle of dragon-steeds awaited her, like a band of hungry hounds. Three of the beasts still lay upon the ground. Unmoving. Unbreathing. The king and queen approached them first, their sadness nearly palpable.

"Ador," said the queen, bending to stroke a smooth black scale. "The memories of the mad elflings have told me your fate. Have shown me you stood as leader against them, to find your way home. And now it shall never be." Her voice hitched, and she bowed her head. "We cannot even ask for your forgiveness."

Camille glanced at the man who held the black scepter, for he made a choking sound. As if he just now realized the fate of the dragon and grieved for his death. Indeed, she felt an odd sort of twist in her chest when the queen approached another fallen dragon. This one with golden scales, blackened about the edges from something other than battle.

"Grimor'ee," breathed Queen Sarsha, stroking the fine scales of the beast's snout, "Tender one. Whose heart allowed you to love a human and weaken the enchantment upon you. Look how your scales have blackened from illness—Dremen! He still breathes!"

The King of Elfhame quickly strode forward, glorious and lithe, and placed his hand upon his wife's shoulder. They both glowed as softly bright as the moon, and the queen's hand sparkled with a power that encompassed the beast, changing the blackened scales to a newly burnished gold.

The dragon opened one eye, and Camille thought his jaw curved in a smile. When the beast rose to his feet, she wondered why her lips curved in a reflection of that smile. Wondered at the way the dragon turned to stare at her.

"She is the one," said the queen.

The beast bowed his head. "Yes. She captured my soul... but she does not know me now. She is fey from the scepters. No human can endure what she has— aah, how I had hoped to bid her a fond farewell."

Queen Sarsha's clear crystal eyes fixed upon Camille, who did not particularly like such attention.

"The key—" began the queen, but she did not finish, for the woman who held the lavender scepter quickly spoke up.

"There is another," she said, "Midaz. Perhaps he breathes as well?"

The queen stared at the woman for a moment, understanding flashing within her gaze, then strode over to the dragon who had such decayed scales that Camille could not tell what their original color had been.

"He has been suffering from breaking the enchantment much longer," said the queen.

"Too long," echoed the king, who joined her side. "He was near death before the battle. Perhaps it is a mercy he took a killing blow."

At his words, the lady with the lavender eyes moaned, tears flowing down her cheeks, her fingers tightening around the scepter she held. She shook with silent sobs, and the half-breed with gray-black hair and bloody face gently stroked her arm while she mourned.

The king of Elfhame raised his voice. "My faithful dragon-steeds."

As one, the beasts bowed their heads to the king.

"You shall be rewarded for your deeds this day. And the sacrifices of those who have fallen shall be remembered for all time in songs from the king's bard at my very table. Go home, brave knights, and take your brethren, so we may build them shrines of crystal and sori'eth. We shall follow soon."

A round of sighs shook the dragons from snout to tail, and they beat their wings, clasping Ador and Midaz in their great claws before launching at the portal. Camille blinked, for surely they could not fit their massive girths into the opening. But the moment their scaled snouts touched the glowing doorway, they disappeared, and she could see them flying in the skies of Elfhame, above azure lakes and crimson mountains.

The king turned toward the small group of humans, his wife laying a gentle hand upon his arm. "I believe you have suffered much under the madness of our kind, and we ask your forgiveness. Had we known such an illness afflicted some of our people…"

"But we have had peace for time beyond remembering," continued the queen. "We grew complacent. The barrier between our worlds has been closed for so long we forgot you even existed… until our mad elflings breached it."

"We thank you for returning our people," said the king. "And will be vigilant in protecting the portal until the end of our days. We cannot make recompense for the damage our kind has done you, without changing your world even more than it already has been." He raised a hand toward them. "But this much, at least, I can do."

The half-breeds who had defended those in the star-circle closed their eyes as the sparkle of power surrounded them. It grew to include the lady with the lavender eyes, and the man with the black, who both looked as if they no longer had the strength to even hold up their scepters. Within a heartbeat, all their injuries disappeared, although oddly enough, the damage to their clothing remained.

The king continued to speak as if he had not just performed a miracle. "But I think some good may have come of this, for I see our blood within each of you. The gifts you inherit from our race— that of strength and grace and wit and beauty, and whatever mundane creations already forged from magic—will forever be with you. Even when we close the doorway."

Camille could not believe the temerity of the black-eyed man when he spoke up. That wash of healing power had put the strength back in his limbs and a determination in his refined features.

"It will be over then," he demanded. "England shall be free."

The king frowned. "Yes, but… I owe you an honest answer. The scepters are the most powerful talismans of our magic, and as such, they carry within them the ability to… evolve. I can feel their connection to your world, and your people, and this concerns me. You must know they are the only way to breech the barriers between worlds, or we would have fetched our mad elflings sooner. Although we will guard them more closely to prevent any more incursions from our world, we cannot know if the scepters will sever their connection with you."

"What does that mean?" growled the man with the green blemish upon his face.

The queen faced him, her lovely eyes searching the warrior's features. "It means that although that mark of yours shall fade, a bit of our magic may still leak into your world. We shall try, but we do not know if the scepters will close the doorway completely."

The woman with the blue-faceted eyes quickly spoke up. "Thank you for your honesty. Now we may be vigilant in watching for any sign of magic... and take the necessary precautions."

The queen gave one regal nod. "You may release your burdens, now."

"No!" blurted Camille, who could not be sure if that protest had come from her, or the seven who crowded her head.

"What will happen to the key?" demanded the man with the golden eyes.

"Do not fear, our magic will keep the star bonded—ah, you mean the girl." Queen Sarsha stepped closer to the circle of humans, her gaze fixed upon Camille. "Grimor'ee was right. The girl is fey, and once we sever the scepters' connection to her..."

"They have been in my head," continued the man. "I know what she must be going through."

"But you did not give up your heart and soul to the scepters."

"I will not lose her."

"No, Lord of Illusion, perhaps you will not. For there is more that binds you together than you know." She shook her pale hair, dazzling flashes of silver in the movement. "We cannot be sure what may happen to her. Ahh, my heart aches at the sacrifices you have all made for your people, but it seems she had the strength to make the most difficult sacrifice of all. Can you do the same?"

He stared at Camille, this man with a face more

handsome than King Dremen's, and she frowned in confusion, for she thought she should know him. But the voices in her head drowned out her own. They wanted to go home. They rejoiced at the thought.

They wanted her to go with them.

But she could not look away from those golden eyes. They held her more surely spellbound than the ring of scepters around her. She did not know what it meant when they filled with tears as he continued to gaze at her, his face taut with indecision. And then one tear escaped the rim of his dark lashes and slid down his sculpted cheek unheeded, and he tightened his jaw, and loosed his hold on the golden scepter. It hung suspended in midair, as did the rest of the scepters, as one by one, the half-breeds released them.

The king and queen of Elfhame joined their magic with the swirling power of the scepters, and Camille felt their souls for a brief moment.

Like diving into a pool of crystalline water. Clean and true and glorious.

And far too brilliant for her mind to encompass.

Camille's legs gave way beneath her, and she collapsed to the snowy ground.

The scepters snapped together just above her head, forming the star once again. They began to spin, copying the movements of the tornado of power they had formed, and rose in a wild dance, as if they sought to join the true stars in the heavens. But at a motion from the king and queen, they settled above the two crowned heads, a whirl of color and brilliance.

Camille felt a strong pair of arms pull her closely

to a warm chest, and she did not need to look at him to guess who held her. She continued to watch the star and the two elven, for her heart and soul went with them. The king and queen of Elfhame turned one last time, waved a farewell at the half-breeds, the gesture conveying a respect and gratitude more surely communicated than any words could have done.

And then they stepped beyond the threshold.

The star winked at her. *Come. Come.*

But the man with the golden eyes held her firmly, whispering her name over and over.

And the doorway to Elfhame shivered to a close.

The pillars flanking the sides of it withered to small crystal boulders, and a dry spring appeared, furrows branching from it which suggested streams had once flowed across the small meadow. The blackness that had surrounded them abruptly lifted, and a silence descended on an ordinary forest of tall evergreens.

"They are gone," whispered the black-eyed man, as if he could not quite believe it.

"We have done it," echoed the lady at his side. "The magic is gone."

The younger man who resembled her so strongly nodded his head. "I do not hear the music anymore. But my body recalls the moves. Perhaps I can learn to dance with swords without the magic."

A tall woman patted the hilt of her sword. "I relish the challenge of wielding an ordinary blade for once."

"As do I," echoed the man who had once possessed a green mark upon his face.

The lady who leaned against him smiled. "I, for one, feel free in the knowledge that I will never be asked to wield magic again. The power of the storm calls to me no longer."

"I have not wielded a scepter long enough to notice the lack," said the man with eyes the color of new earth. "But I once shared the bed of an elven lady. I doubt another will suffice."

"You would be surprised," said the scarred-faced man, hugging his lady tightly. She looked up at him, a smile tugging the corners of her mouth.

The redheaded girl shrugged. "Dorian, you can still feel the forest, can't you?"

"Aye. How did you know?"

"I think there are many things we will not lose."

"And our freedom to gain," said the man with the midnight eyes. "Damn, does not the air smell sweeter? Does not the earth feel lighter?"

A swell of sound interrupted him, and they all turned to look through the trunks of the trees.

"What is that?"

"Another storm?"

He held up his palm to halt the flow of questions, a slow grin crinkling the lines on his face. "It is the army. It is the sound of thousands of humans cheering."

And then it seemed as if they must all join in, and Camille sat and watched the half-breeds shout their own joy and triumph. She should feel the same. She should know why they rejoiced. But she did not. For she still heard seven voices in her head. Still heard them calling to her. And her mind joined them, until the world she sat in began to darken, to fade, until she could no longer feel the cold snow beneath her or the warm arms around her.

"Camille."

She turned and looked into the golden eyes of the stranger just before her vision darkened to solid black.

"Do not be afraid," he said. "I will wait for you. No matter how long it takes."

She could not find her own voice among all the others in her head. And she had no idea what he might be waiting for.

Seventeen

DRYSTAN SAT WITHIN THE KING'S PRIVATE STUDY IN Firehame Palace. Well, he supposed it was now called the Houses of Parliament, but despite the lack of fire on the walls and throughout the rooms, he still could not think of it as anything other than Firehame.

King George sat behind an ornately carved desk, his blond hair tousled from constantly running his hands through it in frustration. "How am I supposed to take a small mock government and expand it into a functioning decision-making force for the entire country?"

Drystan glanced around the mahogany-paneled study. Save for a few, the same group who had met once before to plot the overthrow of the elven lords occupied this room.

"You are doing well, Your Majesty," soothed newly titled Lord Dominic Raikes.

"Fie, 'tis easy for you to say. You are off to live an easy life in the country." The king scowled. "Had I known bequeathing you a title and lands would absent you from court, I would not have done it."

Dominic smiled, something he did rather often,

lately. Lady Cassandra sat as close to her husband as propriety allowed. They would leave today, and Drystan would miss them. But they had stayed to support the king for longer than agreed upon, and he knew they were anxious to settle in a new home.

Far from Firehame Palace.

"It would not have mattered," replied Dominic. "Or do you not recall that my wife has her own title and lands? Do not begrudge us a life of leisure, my king, for you know we have earned it. Besides, I shall leave you in good hands. Is that not right, Alexander?"

The Duke of Chandos, resplendent in coat and breeches of chocolate satin, bowed his head. Only the points of his ears peeking from the gathering of his brown hair gave away his elven blood, a fact that aided the king enormously. A tide of hatred toward anything elven had swept the country, and although Drystan understood it, he feared what it portended for half-breeds.

"My father is right," said the duke. "You have a roomful of advisors you can trust to the death. It is a rare man who can say that."

The king sighed. "I suppose that is true. But must you leave on the heels of Sir Giles and Lady Cecily?"

Drystan smiled at his foster father, who flushed at the new honorific. Giles had never expected to hold a title, and it flustered him to no end. He grew even more discomfited when Lady Cecily reminded him he had always been a brave knight to her.

Giles straightened in his chair. "You know it is imperative we return to Carreg Cennen if we are to preserve the history of the elven. I already have two carriages full of artifacts and records, and it will take me most of a year just to sort through those. Especially when I must train a new curator."

Drystan shrugged off the remark. "I will not leave until she is well."

Lady Cecily quickly intervened, before the argument could start anew. She knew Drystan would not live in Wales, for he had an estate in Herefordshire to run one day—although he had yet to see it. But Giles wanted him back, and Giles could be stubborn. "Drystan is right to keep Camille here, with people she knows. And as soon as she is feeling better, he shall visit our little cottage by the sea. Is that not right, love?"

"Of course," replied Drystan. "After I see my mother. Her letters are getting rather persistent."

The king cleared his throat. "I received another missive from Lady Hawkes a few days ago."

Drystan scowled. Since she did not appear to be getting anywhere with her son, his mother had resorted to appealing to the king. Drystan understood her eagerness to see him. But he would not attempt a journey that might jeopardize Camille's fragile state.

He glanced out the window into the garden, a riot of red roses and flowering trees. As soon as Captain Talbot and his new wife, Augusta, had shown up in London and asked to remain in Drystan's service, he had sent them directly back to Dreamhame, to fetch Molly Shreves and Ann Cobb, hoping the two former slaves might jog Camille's memories. They sat near her now, no longer slaves but paid companions, idly chatting and throwing crumbs to the songbirds. But

Camille stared off into the distance, her mind and thoughts unaffected by the presence of the women.

"Apparently," continued the king, "the dowager viscountess decided she would not wait for you to come to her. She insists she has the right, given the circumstances. I rather imagine she will reach the palace today."

Drystan returned his attention to the king's words, taking a moment to comprehend them. Odd, but he felt no leap of excitement. After years of yearning to be a part of his true family, he found it did not matter. Not without Camille as a part of it.

"That is wonderful news," said Lady Cecily. "Now I can leave you in good conscience, knowing that she will be here to help Camille."

Drystan nodded, turned away from the window to grant his foster mother a smile, albeit a forced one. As much as he would miss them, he could not regret their leaving. Giles beamed with happiness, and Lady Cecily glowed from within. They could not wait to return to Wales and live a life without fear for their charges. Although most of the orphans had been returned to their families, some had lost their parents, or they could not be located. The children needed the goodness and kindness of Giles and Cecily's fostering.

He glanced at Giles. "I will send you my observations of the gardens as I write them."

Giles nodded, but he hardly needed the reassurance. Although the creations of the elven lords had vanished with them, those natural things of the earth wrought with their magic still remained. Drystan had taken it upon himself to continue to study and analyze the gardens of Elfhame, for Camille seemed happiest among those altered plants.

Lady Cecily rose, a rustle of indigo skirts, and her husband rose with her. "By your leave, Your Majesty. If there is nothing else you require of us, our carriages await."

The king gave a disgruntled sigh, but nodded, and rose to clasp hands with Giles, and accept an informal hug from his foster mother. Lord North and the rest offered their farewells, but Drystan had already said his good-byes privately last evening. With Camille standing vacant-eyed by his side.

If only he could manage to get her to speak. Surely that would bring her back to him—

His foster mother hugged him one last time; Giles shook his hand and told him to have faith. Drystan felt a sudden urge to demand that they stay. Not for his sake, but for Camille's. Her glorious rainbow-colored eyes always seemed more alert when Lady Cecily spoke to her.

But he knew they had an important task for the king, in preserving the knowledge of elven magic. In case that door had not sealed shut. And he of all people knew they deserved their happiness.

Dominic and Cassandra took their leave next, the petite lady granting hugs as enthusiastically as Lady Cecily. But the new Lord Raikes only nodded his farewells, reserved as always.

Drystan nodded back. "Thank you."

The older man did not ask him what for; he only raised his brows.

"For teaching me what courage is, without ever having to say a word."

Dominic still looked confused. Lady Cassandra hugged Drystan and whispered in his ear, "I shall explain it to him later."

They left in a swirl of velvet and lace, the couple who had dealt the first fatal blow for the Rebellion.

Silence fell over the room.

"Well then," said the king, "I will have to rely on the rest of you. Lord North, what news do you have of Lord Dorian and his lady?"

The heavy man blinked, then shook his jowls. "They are near to completing their mansion in the Seven Corners of Hell, thanks to the generosity of Your Majesty. Lord Dorian is quite content among the trees, and reports that there has been no… unusual activity in the area. He does suggest sending a few more troops to guard the spring. Too many curiosity seekers."

Drystan snorted. The tale of the final battle with the elven lords had been told all across England. And still there were those who would see the proof of it.

He hoped never to get near the damn place again.

"What say you, General Cavendish? Can you spare the men?"

Samson nodded, the scars on his face now even deeper than before. But he had enough elven blood to counter the effect, and it did not detract from his handsomeness. The deeper slash marks made him look only more dangerous. "I have called several in from the field. Order has been restored to England much more quickly than we had ever hoped for."

"Indeed," agreed Wilhelmina, who had also insisted

on keeping her title as general, although she did not mind being referred to occasionally as the Duchess of Chandos. Especially when Alexander was about. "I believe it is because you have given them a fresh purpose, Your Majesty. Despite our elevating slaves to lost ranks, and demoting followers of the elven lords to commoners, we did not have as much resistance as we expected."

"Plans for sending a representative from both lords and commoners have met with approval, then?"

"Indeed. They embrace your new—old government. And the abolishment of slavery is met with relief on all sides."

The king picked up a quill, drew the feather across his cheek absentmindedly. "I am more concerned now about the world beyond our borders. With the barrier gone, foreign ships are landing on our soil, and I fear we must control trade if we are to recover financially. And then there is the threat from other lands that may see England as ripe for the picking…"

Alexander spoke up, revealing his art for diplomacy once again. He had been more help as the king's representative than Lord North, for not only could he charm a smile from the surliest of the aristocracy, but he'd also had a direct hand in the freedom of the English people. And it helped that he looked more human than elven. "We must face one challenge at a time, Your Majesty. I have already discussed the matter with my duchess."

"My suggestion," said Wilhelmina, "is that we build up our naval armada, which has been sorely limited to a few vessels of trade. We can use the additional ships in that capacity, of course, for there is an even higher demand now for elven-wrought goods, and our neighbors will not worry over our activities. But we need to train officers in wartime skills and battle tactics. Just in case."

The king glanced back and forth between husband and wife. "You make a formidable team."

"Thank you, Your Majesty," said the duchess with a grin.

Wilhelmina and Alexander had adjusted well to their life here, as had Samson and Joscelyn. No, they had done better than adjust. They were happy, in love, eager to see the new world they helped to create set to rights.

Drystan wished for his own happily ever after. Just like in his books. Granted, he was no longer the dreamy romantic who had first set off to find the woman of his dreams. He knew love, like freedom, took great sacrifice. It humbled him that Camille made the greatest sacrifice of all. But it had never truly occurred to him they would not eventually live happily together.

Although he had found her, and saved her, he had failed her when it counted most of all.

He felt Lady Joscelyn's eyes upon him, and turned to meet her gaze. Her happiness was tempered by her sorrow for Camille, and it warmed him to the lady even more.

Joscelyn leaned her head closer to whisper to him, while the rest continued to discuss shipbuilding and finances. "Camille has still not spoken a word?"

Drystan shook his head.

"Does she… does she know?"

He tamped down his frustration. He had no earthly idea what filtered into Camille's confused mind. Or if she had a mind left at all. He knew what three scepters had done to him, but seven in full possession of their power? He shuddered to think. "She will do what she is asked, and she takes care of her private needs. Beyond that, I do not think she is aware of the changes to her body—"

The doorman stepped into the room. "Lord Malcolm Reese requests an audience, Your Majesty."

"Ah, the restless one has returned. Show him in."

The doorman bowed, the curls of his wig flopping over his shoulders, and stepped back so the young man could enter. As a latecomer to the company of the Rebellion, Malcolm did not have the stronger ties they all seemed to possess. Or perhaps his restless nature made him seem ill at ease, his feet constantly shifting and his brown-faceted eyes always looking through one, as if he sought some far horizon.

He bowed his white-blond head, the silver sparkles in his hair making each individual strand glow. Besides Dominic, Malcolm resembled the elven lords the most. Drystan still thought he might have truly loved Lady Annanor, despite everything, and it had hurt the young man to banish her.

Malcolm appeared constantly surprised by their new world. And accepting the guise of the king's personal emissary, seemed to constantly be seeking something he had lost.

Drystan hoped he would find it, one day.

"I have news from Northern Verdanthame—err, Norfolk. Many of the plants twisted by elven magic refused to be tamed with scythe or fire, and the locals swear the woods are haunted, and will not work near them. I doubt there is anything more to it than superstition… but have you news from Lord Dorian? Is the… spring still dry?"

"It is," answered Lord North, a frown between his sharp eyes.

"Hmm." Malcolm collapsed into a nearby chair. "Perhaps we should send him to Norfolk to take a look? He still has an affinity for the woodland that may help the situation."

Drystan sighed, turned back to look out the window once again. He had promised to advise the king, but sometimes he regretted the necessity of these meetings. It took him away from Camille, and he constantly worried about her while he was gone, for although she did not know him, she seemed most calm while in his presence. It was why Ann and Molly had taken her to the garden, so he could look out for her himself to make sure she was well.

Camille still sat quietly on the marble bench, surrounded by her ladies, and looking like a goddess. She wore a white mantua loosely belted, with a stomacher heavily embroidered with gold dragons. Her ivory hair glowed white in the sun, strips of gold ribbon woven in her elaborate coiffure. Her eyes glowed as if she carried a true rainbow within them, the specks of gold and silver glinting like polished jewels.

Faith, how he loved her.

Molly suddenly looked up, giving Ann a sharp elbow to the ribs. A woman in a striped satin traveling gown with a matching umbrella bore down on them.

Drystan frowned. The staff had strict instructions in regards to Camille's privacy. Strangers agitated her. Ann and Molly quickly stood, creating a barrier in front of Camille, and halted the woman's progress.

Molly gestured wildly while Ann scowled. But the woman was obviously intent on speaking to Camille, and somehow managed to get around the two ladies by using her umbrella as an offensive weapon.

Drystan jumped to his feet and sprinted for the door.

"I say—" sputtered Lord North, but Drystan had already reached the door, flying past Talbot with all the elven speed he possessed.

"What is it?" asked his captain when they reached the side door.

"Camille."

"Of course."

The door opened onto a walkway lined with white rock, surrounded by a swath of grass. Drystan ignored the meandering path and sprinted across the green straight toward the garden of roses, a raindrop striking him squarely on the nose.

By the time he reached Ann and Molly and the stranger, Camille had run away.

At the sight of the three ladies, Talbot sheathed his sword with a self-mocking grin. Drystan had not even realized he had drawn it.

The stranger in the striped gown turned to face Drystan, and her face brought him up short. She had his nose. His chin. And although her eyes lacked the faceted shimmer of his own, they glowed a golden brown. And abruptly filled with tears.

"Drystan?"

"Mother?"

She dropped her umbrella and threw her arms around him. "At long last! They told me you were in a meeting with the king and could not be interrupted—"

Drystan gently grasped her shoulders and set her away from him. "What did you say to Camille?"

Lady Hawkes appeared confused. "I—I just introduced myself to her. I swear, that is all. I have waited so long to meet her, to see *you*—"

Drystan blew out a breath. He could not blame her. He should have arranged to meet her sooner, should have told her more about Camille's condition.

Her shoulders shook with impending sobs.

"Mother, please, it is all right."

"But she looked so frightened when I told her my name! And then she ran—"

"Frightened?" Drystan's heart stopped. Camille would get agitated, would flutter her hands and wander in circles around strangers. But she had not shown any true emotion in so very long. "Are you sure? You saw the emotion in her eyes?"

Lady Hawkes frowned. "I am quite sure, although I cannot imagine why—no one has ever been frightened of me in my life."

Molly strangled a cough while Ann raised her ivory brows nearly to her hairline.

The lady spun to face them. "Besides obstinate maids with foul tongues," she added.

Drystan swept his fingers through his hair, felt the tie binding it back loosen even more. Thunder sounded overhead, punctuated by a sudden breeze laced with more rain. "Talbot. Take the ladies inside.

I must go find Camille. Mother, do not worry. I shall be back soon." Drystan turned to Molly. "Which way did she go?"

When Molly pointed toward the forest at the far grounds of the palace, Drystan felt little surprise. That's where he'd found Camille when she had wandered off before—although it had taken him the entire day to locate her, and he had never been more frightened in his life.

He started off in an easy lope, and then doubt began to assail him. What if she had gone somewhere else this time? What if she stumbled into some nasty surprise the elven lords' magic left behind? England was still riddled with the mundane aftereffects of their spells.

Drystan broke into a run just as the skies opened up in a downpour. The cool wind rose to a healthy gale, and he heard the garden before he reached it. Like the forest of Dreamhame Palace, an elven garden grew within Firehame's woods. Many of the alien plants within it had faded with the magic, but the natural flowers and plants of the earth altered to resemble Elfhame appeared to flourish.

Drystan stepped through the gate to a cacophony of sound, the garden at Firehame somewhat resembling Dreamhame's in volume and color. But here, rain beat on drum-shaped flowers, wind whistled through tubelike petals, and the tinkle of chimes sounded from blossoms shaped like bells. He walked past neat rows of peculiar bushes and trees shaped into perfectly round circles, heading for the pavilion.

She sat on the steps just beneath the shelter of the

roof, her arms folded about her knees, gazing out into the far garden.

Drystan sat next to her, loosening his shoulders with relief, and listened to the melody of the flowers. He had no idea why his mother might have frightened her—she appeared to be a harmless lady, although perhaps a bit imperious. But the fact that Camille had shown some type of emotion heartened him. Perhaps with time, she would eventually come back to his world. The scepters would stop filling her head with their voices, and drowning out her own thoughts. He would not believe they had taken her heart and soul back with them to Elfhame for good.

If naught else, he had learned to trust in Camille's love for him.

The rain slowed to a sprinkle, and the song of the garden changed to a quiet sigh of a tune. Over the past few months, Drystan had written the love poem to her he'd promised, and he recited it now, the rhythm a match for the garden's melody.

He sighed when he finished, hoping some small part of Camille's mind and heart had heard it. He supposed he had best take her back to the palace. His coat stuck to his shoulders in a soggy weight, and she looked half-drowned herself. He would not want her to catch cold in her—

"Drystan," she said, "I have something I must tell you."

She spoke! As if she had not been lost inside her head all these months. He took a breath. Another. He must go easy. "What is it, love?"

"We can never marry."

He reached out and clasped her hand, laced his fingers through hers. Instead of laying lax in his grip, she gave him a squeeze.

His heart raced. "And why is that?"

"Roden put an enchantment on me. He did not want his slaves having children. I am sure you want an heir to pass your title on to, so I am afraid I shall just have to be your mistress."

He fought down a laugh. A shout of joy. Despite his best efforts, his voice shook when he spoke. "But the elven lords are gone, dear."

She turned and looked at him. Truly looked at him, for the first time in months. "Gracious, do you think I am daft? I know they are gone. I... I remember bits and pieces. But I do not know if Roden put an enchantment upon me, or used his magic to alter me physically. If he did, your mother will not approve of our marriage."

Bless his mother.

Camille sighed. "She is here, you know."

"I know. And she quite approves of you. In fact, it is her fondest wish that we marry at once."

"Good heavens. Why?"

Drystan reached out his other hand, covered the slight bulge beneath her loose stomacher. "Because she wants our first child to be legitimate."

She glanced down at his hand. "Our child?"

"You are five months pregnant, Camille. That is how long it's been since we sent the mad elven lords back to Elfhame. When we stopped the magic from flowing into England."

She frowned, and he could see her trying to process some connection. "I don't understand."

Drystan sighed. He feared for her, afraid that too much of her memories rushing back at once might send her away from him again. But she had a right to know. "Do you remember when I landed my golden dragon?"

She made a face. "Rather badly, if I recall."

"Indeed. And do you remember Dominic healing us with blue fire? Well, whether Roden put an enchantment on you, or altered you physically, Dominic's power was strong enough to heal you of either."

"Dominic," she breathed. "Yes. He always had the power to rival an elven lord's. And that means our baby was conceived..."

"On a bed of clouds, beneath a golden moon."

"Oh, Drystan. Thank you for that last gift of magic for me." Tears swelled in her eyes and covered her cheeks. "It feels as if I have been gone, my mind and soul joined with the scepters in Elfhame. It is so hard to explain. The scepters kept shouting in my head, until nothing remained but their voices. Yet I felt you, always. Sometimes I even thought I could hear your voice." She lifted her head, gazed into his eyes, her hand replacing his over her womb. And he saw the bright warmth once again. Camille had truly returned to him.

"You are right," she continued. "I can feel... gracious, it feels like a butterfly is dancing inside me."

Drystan kissed her then, and when she returned it, his heart exploded. It had been so very long. He groaned and deepened the kiss, until he did not know where Camille began and he ended. Until she wrapped her arms around his shoulders and melted against him. Until a fire flared between them, and she stole his breath.

"Camille," he gasped, "you are cold and wet."

She tried to press his face back down to hers. "On the contrary."

As much as it killed him, he stood, dragging her up with him. "I will not allow you to get sick. Not in your condition."

She frowned. "Of course. I did not think. I am not used to…"

"I know." Drystan paused, allowed the joy and excitement he felt to well up within him. "Isn't it grand?"

Her smile lit his world.

Drystan lifted her off her feet and carried her through the garden, thanking his elven strength. The king and queen of Elfhame had been right. Some good still came from the elven lords, for he barely broke a sweat as he carried her through the forest and back to the palace, half-running in anticipation.

Talbot opened the door they had left through before Drystan even reached it. The silver specks in his eyes flashed. "You look like a drowned rat. Is Camille all right?"

"She is better than all right—she has come back to us." Drystan gently set her on her feet. "I need you to hurry, Edward. You must go after Sir Giles and Lady Cecily. And send another man to stop Lord Raikes and Lady Cassandra's carriage."

"To give them the good news, my lord?"

"Yes. And to invite them to my wedding. I am getting married today."

Talbot grinned and spun, running for the stables.

"Today?" squeaked Camille.

"I should say so," said Lady Hawkes, who had apparently been waiting with Ann and Molly at the window overlooking the garden, for they approached from the nearby withdrawing room. "My dearest Camille, I am so sorry if I frightened you earlier. You must forgive me for being anxious to meet my son's future wife."

"Please do not concern yourself—I wasn't truly frightened. You just reminded me of something I urgently needed to tell Drystan."

Drystan leaned over and pecked his mother on the cheek. "And I shall be eternally grateful for that."

His mother's face flushed pink, and then she smoothed the folds of her skirts. "Well. Well. At least allow me to make it up to you. I brought along my seamstress, and I just happen to have Drystan's great-grandmother's wedding gown in my trunks. I thought it would require only a few alterations, you see."

"Astounding," remarked Drystan.

"You will find, my son, that I am ever prepared for any situation, especially those of the domestic kind. I hope… I hope you shall give us the opportunity to get to know one another better, and come home."

"Of course. I am sure Camille is just as curious about my estate as I am. That is, if my brother welcomes me?"

"Oh, yes! He is so anxious to meet you, and to formally hand over the title. He has always yearned for the priesthood, you see, and now he shall be free to follow his calling." Her face crumpled for a moment, and Drystan glimpsed the years of sorrow she had suffered. Then her spine stiffened. "I never gave up hope you would come home one day, and planned accordingly."

Drystan suspected he would find his mother to be more amazing than he ever could have wished.

"Now, off with you both, before you catch the sniffles. I shall take care of all the arrangements."

"Arrangements?" echoed Drystan. He had thought only to find a priest, gather his friends, and say their vows. After having waited so long, he did not doubt that the king would give them a special dispensation.

Lady Hawkes gave Camille a conspiratorial smile. "Just like a man, to think these things are just thrown together. I must make arrangements with the Abbey, and then there are the flowers, and the ring—oh, will this one do? It belonged to Drystan's great-great-grandmother." She held up her hand to Camille, displaying a sapphire ring surrounded by diamonds and filigree.

"It is lovely," she agreed.

"Good, then. Morning weddings are more in vogue, but I am sure those involved will understand the necessity of an evening service. Will that suit, Drystan?"

Camille answered before he could. "That will suit us just fine, Lady Hawkes." Her face shone with a strength Drystan had not noticed before. He imagined that after saving an entire country, his wife would manage a new mother-in-law.

The dowager viscountess blinked, studied Camille, and nodded. "We shall suit exceptionally well, you and I."

"Indeed. I am touched by your efforts to make

our marriage memorable." Camille turned to her two
ladies. "Ann. Molly. Please assist Lady Hawkes with
anything she might require."

Ann nodded mutely, her eyes wide. Molly threw
Camille a wink.

She ignored it, and held out her arm to Drystan.
"My lord, I do believe we should follow your mother's
advice and remove our wet things. Shall we?"

His mother swallowed. Loudly.

Drystan could not help the grin that curled his mouth,
and led his lady through the corridor, up two flights of
stairs, and into the long hall of guest chambers. As they
progressed, they drew speculative stares from gentry and
servant alike, but no one spoke a word to them.

"Yours, or mine?" he murmured, pausing in the hall.

"Mine."

Drystan opened the door to the burgundy chamber
and ushered Camille inside, closing the latch firmly
behind them. He had just turned about when Camille
pushed him against the wall and began to unbutton the
front of his coat.

"I suppose it would be proper to make you wait
until after the ceremony. But apparently the damage
has already been done."

Drystan barked a laugh, his fingers busy with the
fastening of her girdle.

"It is rather a shame," he replied, struggling with
the wet ties of her stays. Thank heavens they had been
fastened loosely because of her condition. "I would not
mind creating another little Hawkes tonight. It would
be a perfect way to remember our wedding day."

Camille did not reply, too intent on removing his wet

clothing. They both huffed and tugged, until Drystan mumbled, "'Twas much easier when I had magic."

And this time Camille laughed, the sound like the chiming of bells.

Magic or no, they eventually managed to strip completely, and Camille glanced down at her swollen stomach. "It is true, isn't it?"

Drystan caressed her rounded flesh, so smooth, so soft and perfect. That touch made him long for the rest of her, and he curled his arms around her, pressing the length of her to him. They warmed their chilly skin against each other, until Camille lifted her face and he kissed her. Long and hard and sweetly.

Camille broke the kiss and clutched his shoulders. "Faith, we must hurry, Drystan. Molly will not be able to delay your mother for long, and she will be at our door with yards of lace to fit me in."

He lifted her bottom, and when she wrapped her legs around him, he had a sudden inspiration. He turned, putting her back against the door. "Demanding wench."

"Yes, I rather like this new me."

"I am afraid to hurt the babe."

Camille reached down and curled her fingers around his shaft. "You will not. You shall only make the mother very happy."

Drystan sucked in a breath. "I have missed you so much."

"I can tell. Fie, quit talking, Drystan, and show me."

He held her up with one arm and touched her where she needed it the most. Camille groaned and leaned her head back against the polished oak door.

He could not resist the vulnerable lure of her neck, and sucked and nuzzled the skin there, stroking his fingers slowly back and forth. Damn, he wished he had the time to take it slow. To savor his Camille.

But they would have a lifetime together, and the thought made him flush with anticipation.

Camille sucked in a breath, went rigid, then exploded in tremors of pleasure. As soon as Drystan felt the wet warmth of her drench his fingers, he guided himself into her. A bit at a time. Still fearful of the babe, despite her assurances.

She lowered her head and kissed him, looping her arms beneath his, around his back, and pressing him more tightly against her.

Drystan obliged. He would make it his mission to oblige her for the rest of his life.

He kept a fast but gentle rhythm, allowing his need for her to overtake him, until she cried out, deep shudders wracking her body, and he could not help his own response to her bliss, releasing his rigid control and allowing his pleasure to join with hers.

They sailed away together, taking a very long time to settle back down to earth.

Drystan cradled her in his arms and carried her to the bed, and she kept her body twined around his as they settled onto the linens. He felt Camille's sigh sweep from her head to her toes, and she whispered, "See, Drystan. We do not need clouds of gossamer or Arabian tents to feel the magic between us."

And when she wrapped her fingers in his hair, and tucked her head beneath his chin, Drystan knew he had been given his own happily ever after.

Read all of Kathryne Kennedy's
Elven Lord series
Now available from Sourcebooks Casablanca

THE
FIRE LORD'S LOVER

THE LADY OF
THE STORM

THE LORD
OF ILLUSION

THE
FIRE LORD'S LOVER

London, England, 1724

THE PEOPLE LINING THE STREETS OF LONDON CHEERED while General Dominic Raikes rode to his doom. Not that they had any idea what awaited him at Firehame Palace, and if they did, he doubted they would care. He resembled the elven lord too much for that. Yet he had won the final battle and they hailed him as their champion despite his elven white hair and pointed ears.

Young women threw flowers from upper-story windows, the petals flickering through the air like snow and coating the dusty streets with color. Gray skies covered the sun and in some places the buildings nearly met above the streets, further shadowing the riders' passage with gloom. The glass-fronted shops had been locked up as their owners joined the throng in the streets: painted harlots, street urchins, costermongers, servants, and the occasional prosperous Cit, distinguishable by his white wig. The fishy smell of the Thames overlaid the stench of the streets as his troops approached Westminster Bridge.

Over the murky waters the flaming turrets of Firehame Palace beckoned Dominic onward.

He shook back his war braids and straightened his spine and glanced back at his men. They had cleaned their red woolen coats as best they could, and lacking wigs, had powdered their hair to resemble the elven silver-white. They had polished their boots and buttons, brushed their cocked hats. Despite their stern faces, Dominic could see the glitter of pride in their eyes and nodded his approval at them. They returned his gesture with wary respect.

Dominic turned and sighed. They were brave, good men, every one. Some he owed his victory and life to. He would like to oversee their promotions himself but it would be too dangerous. He didn't know the personal life of a single man, nor did they know of his. Dominic had grown used to his solitary existence, yet sometimes he regretted the necessity of it.

The hooves of his horse met the road at the end of the bridge with a crunch of pebbles. The noise of the crowd faded as they neared the open gates of Firehame Palace. Red flame jutted from the top of the stone pillars flanking the entrance, danced along the outlying curtain walls. Dominic halted his mount for the span of a breath, studying his home with the unfamiliar gaze of one after a long absence. Elven magic had tinted the stone walls a glossy, brilliant red. Warm yellow flame slithered up the stone, whorled over the buttresses, making the entire structure shimmer in his sight. The towers soared above the three-storied palace and

Dominic's black eyes quickly sought out the tallest, looking for a flicker of wing, a jet of red fire. But he could see no sign of the dragon and so flicked his reins, urging his horse into the courtyard.

Dominic wanted nothing more than a bath and then the quiet of his garden or the sanctuary of the dragon's tower. He knew he wouldn't manage any of his comforts until he'd been tested in fire.

He thrust away the memory of pain and dismounted, feeling his face turn to stone, his body conform to rigid military posture as he crossed the paved courtyard and ascended the steps into the opulence of Firehame Palace. Several of his officers followed, although many decided to forgo the privilege of coming to the attention of the Imperial Lord of the sovereignty of Firehame.

The back hallways they marched through displayed the magic and wealth of the elven lord. Delicate tapestries that rewove their pictures every few minutes covered the walls, and thick rugs of rippling ponds and bottomless chasms carpeted the floors. Dominic breathed in the scent of candle wax, perfume, and elfweed, ignoring the portraits framed in gold with their moving eyes that followed his passage. At the end of summer the air in the corridor still felt chill against his cheeks. His ears rang from the silence.

Then Dominic opened the door leading to the great room and the thunder of applause broke that brief moment of quiet. He paused, waiting for his men to compose themselves, then started down the middle of the enormous room through the crowd of gentry that awaited them.

Fluted columns lined the sides of the hall, capped with ornately carved capitals that supported archways even more ornately carved with golems, gremlins, and gargoyles. Courtiers milled between the stone supports, a riot of colorful silk skirts and gold-trimmed coats. Full court wigs of powdered white sparkled with the addition of the ground stone the nobles used to imitate the silver luster of elven hair. Buckled shoes flashed with diamonds; ceremonial swords sparkled with ruby and jet.

The smell of perfume became overwhelming, and Dominic suppressed the urge to sneeze. He kept his gaze fixed on his goal, the dais of gold where the elven lord Mor'ded waited, but he caught the faces of the courtiers from the corners of his eyes. The lustful gazes of women—and more than a few men— followed his every movement. Despite their fear of the elven, humans could not resist their beauty, and Dominic had inherited more elven allure than his half blood warranted.

When he reached the Imperial Lord's throne, Dominic stared at Mor'ded for longer than he intended. Silvery white hair cascaded past broad shoulders in a river broken only by the tips of the elven lord's pointed ears. Black, fathomless eyes stared coldly into Dominic's own, the expression robbing them of their almost crystalline brilliance. Smooth, pale skin glistened like the finest porcelain over high cheekbones and strong chin. A full mouth, straight nose, high brow.

When Dominic looked at the Imperial Lord, he might as well have been gazing into a mirror of his future, for although his father must be over seven hundred years old, he did not look a day over five and thirty. And despite the thickness of his elven blood, Dominic aged at a normal human pace. In ten years, Dominic would look like the man before him.

Dominic dropped to one knee and bowed his head, war braids dangling beside his cheeks and eyes fixed on the marble floor. A wave of silence rolled across the room until he could hear nothing but the breathing of his men and the rustle of the ladies' silk skirts. "I have won the king, my lord."

At his words, the room erupted in applause again and Dominic stood, gazing at his father, hoping to see a glimmer of pride in those cold black eyes. He had fought for years to achieve such acknowledgment.

Imperial Lord Mor'ded smiled, revealing even white teeth, and cut his hand through the air, signaling the court to silence. He stood with a grace no human could possess and stepped down from the dais, one hand wrapped around the black scepter that enhanced his magic. Dominic's eyes flicked to the rod, the runes carved on it swirling momentarily in his sight before he quickly looked away.

As a child he'd been constantly hungry. He'd been stealing food off the sideboard in the grand dining room when his father and court had entered. He'd hidden under the table and his father had sat, the triangular-shaped head of the scepter jutting beneath the crisp white linen. Dominic didn't know what made him reach out and stroke the forbidden talisman, for everyone knew only one of true elven blood could hold it without being flamed to ash. But he hadn't tried to wield it, had only touched it, and since then he couldn't look at it without feeling strange. As if the thing possessed a conscious awareness of him. It bothered him that he had such a fanciful thought.

Mor'ded reached his side and placed his other hand on Dominic's shoulder. The chill of his long fingers penetrated the heavy wool of Dominic's coat. "After a hundred years the king will finally be returned to his rightful place. Thanks to my son, the champion of all Firehame."

Applause thundered again. The elven lord's words echoed in Dominic's ears. His father had publicly acknowledged him as his son. Fierce pleasure rose in Dominic's chest and he had to force himself to concentrate on Mor'ded's next words.

"General Raikes has defeated Imperial Lord Breden's forces, and we have won the ultimate trophy—King George and his royal court. London will again be the center of taste and fashion. The sovereignty of Firehame will house the man who decides what color breeches you wear."

A ripple of excited pleasure ran through the court-iers, and Dominic stared coldly at the assemblage. Did they not hear the disdain in his father's voice? Did they not understand the mockery toward the king who should be their rightful ruler?

Mor'ded's fingers tightened on Dominic's shoulder, and the elven lord's magic shivered through his spine. Dominic forced himself to relax under the painful grip. It did not matter if the ton understood or not. They could do nothing about it, anyway.

"Tonight we will feast in my son's honor."

His fingers gave Dominic one last painful squeeze before he released his grip and climbed back up on his dais. With a flourish of his scepter, Mor'ded filled the long great room with sparkling white fire, the flames harmlessly bouncing off the wigs of the men and the silk skirts of the ladies. The courtiers laughed and wove their bodies through the magic, and Dominic watched them with hooded eyes until his father grew tired of amusing his playthings.

When Mor'ded swept the skirts of his red silk coat through the door behind the throne, Dominic followed, resisting the sudden urge to draw his sword and run it through his father's back.

He'd tried it once. It had cost him the life of his best friend.

FROM

THE LADY OF THE STORM

Devon, England, 1734

GILES BEAUMONT HEARD THE SOUND OF BATTLE COMING from beyond the rocks in the direction of the village at the same moment Cecily emerged from the waves of the English Channel. His magically cursed sword flew from its scabbard, smacked the palm of his hand, and it took every ounce of Giles's considerable strength to shove it back into the leather sheath. As much as his blade longed to be finally used, the years of training to protect the young woman held firm and he ran away from the village to the beach.

He'd removed his stockings and half jackboots after the first hour of waiting for Cecily, and now his toes dug through the hot sand while broken seashells stabbed his heels. But the elven blood that ran through his veins allowed him to reach the tide line soon enough, his feet now slapping on wet sand, the spray of the crashing waves cooling his face, the ocean breeze billowing open his half-buttoned shirt with even more welcome relief.

He kept his gaze fixed on naught but her.

Cecily Sutton, half-breed daughter of the Imperial Lord Breden, elven lord of the sovereignty of Dewhame, did not look like a direct descendant of the elven royal line. At least, not at the moment. She had one arm wrapped around the fin of a dolphin, the creature propelling her through the water at wicked speed. Her black hair gleamed in the sunlight, her luscious mouth hung wide open with laughter, and she'd half-closed her eyes against the spray of flight.

A wild magical woman, indeed. A mysterious creature whom he'd been assigned to protect since she was nine years old—and Giles himself only fifteen—in hopes that she would be of use to the Rebellion some day. But a daughter of those cold, reserved elven lords? No, she did not fit that mold.

She swam by herself the rest of the way to the shore, with a wave and a last caress for her dolphin-steed. Her magical affinity for the water made her look one with it, her swimming near effortless as she crossed the final distance to the beach. Giles waited for her, waves lapping about his ankles, watching as her eyes grew round with surprise when she recognized him. With her large inhuman eyes, he could not deny her birthright to the elven lord. They glittered in the sunshine, twin jewels of blue, with a crystalline depth that bespoke the enormous power the young woman could summon.

Although she'd managed to keep that power well hidden through the years.

"What are you doing here?" she said, her gaze flicking away from him to stare at her abandoned clothing on the beach. Cecily kept her body hidden in the water, but the motion of the waves occasionally revealed the swell of her breasts. Giles made sure his gaze stayed fixed on her face, but despite his efforts to appear unaffected by her nudity, the warmth of a flush crept over his cheeks.

For he'd been ordered to protect her but keep his distance. Thomas had warned him that the girl was destined to marry a great lord. And in more subtle terms, that Giles would never be good enough for her. So by necessity he had spied upon her from a distance for years. Many times he had damned her for her magical affinity to water, for scarcely a day went by without her sneaking off to this private cove where she stripped and flung herself into the ocean. Perforce he'd watched her body develop from skinny youth into the full curvature of womanhood.

Now her curves rivaled those of any woman he'd bedded; indeed, once she'd matured, he would often dream of those perfect features while he made love to one girl after another.

Many times he had fancied himself in love with one of the village maidens. For a time he would feel relieved that he had been able to put the forbidden girl from his thoughts. But thoughts of Cecily would always intrude yet again. He would find himself comparing those vivid blue eyes, that heart-shaped brow, the lilt of her laughter, with every girl he met. And would find himself dreaming of her once again, chiding himself for a fool.

"There's something wrong in the village," he managed to say. "I want you to stay hidden in the water until I return."

As usual, she avoided looking into his eyes, her gaze fixed somewhere around his nose. "How did you know I'd be here? How did you manage to climb the rocks? No one knows about my secret place—" A more urgent question suddenly halted her flow of indignation. "Has Thomas returned?"

He shook his head. "No, but I fear that your father may have something to do with it."

"With what? What is happening?"

"I'm not sure, and I don't have time for this. Just stay here!"

Giles spun, raced back to his hiding place, struggling damp skin into woolen hose, sandy cloth into leather boots. He pulled his sword from the scabbard, the greedy thing ringing with delight, eager for the taste of the blood Giles had denied it for so many years.

A thrill went through him from hilt to hand and he fought it with a clench of his muscles. "You devil," he murmured. "If I could have gotten rid of you, I would have. Father's gift or no."

The sword answered him with a tug in the direction of the village, where the sounds of battle had grown louder. Giles took one last glance over his shoulder...

The little hoyden had ignored him. Cecily stood next to her clothing, her net with her day's catch abandoned in shallow water, flopping fish and scuttling crabs quickly making their way back to ocean. Giles would have cursed if he'd had the wits to, but the sight of her bending over to pick up her chemise near knocked the power of speech completely from his head.

He sprinted back to the water, his sword resisting him all the way. Giles should have known she wouldn't listen to him. She treated him like all the villagers did, as if he had nothing between his muscled shoulders but his fine elven features. He had carefully cultivated that impression of course, assuming the quiet manner of a humble blacksmith, in spite of how much he despised the role. But Cecily's attitude had surpassed his assumed disguise. After the night she offered herself to him and he gallantly refused her, she'd avoided him with a disdain that bordered on contempt.

By the time he reached her side Cecily had pulled on her chemise, struggled into her stays. Her fingers fastened up the front-lacing stays most working women wore, and she pulled on her jacket and skirt without benefit of her quilted petticoat.

Giles found it easier to speak once she'd covered that glorious body. "I told you to stay in the water."

She did not answer, pulling on stockings and shoes.

Not for the first time, he mentally cursed the task of having to protect this young woman. "I cannot keep you safe while fighting."

She straightened, her eyes widening at that. "Why would you care—what in heaven's name is wrong with your sword?"

The damned blade kept twisting his arm around, pointing at the village like a dog scenting a hare. Giles's boots began to slide across the sand, little furrows left in his wake. "It smells blood—"

About the Author

Kathryne Kennedy is an award-winning author acclaimed for her world-building and known for blending genres to create groundbreaking stories. *The Lord of Illusion* is the third book in her magical new series, *The Elven Lords*, following *The Fire Lord's Lover* and *The Lady of the Storm*. She's lived in Guam, Okinawa, and several states in the United States, and currently lives in Arizona with her wonderful family— which includes two very tiny Chihuahuas. She loves to hear from readers, and welcomes you to visit her website where she has ongoing contests at: www. KathryneKennedy.com.

In the Heat of the Bite

by Lydia Dare

Chivalry is far from undead...

Matthew Halkett, Earl of Blodswell, is one of the few men in the *ton* who can claim to be a knight in shining armor—because that's precisely what he was before being turned into a vampyre. When he spies a damsel in distress in the midst of a storm in Hyde Park, his natural instinct is to rush to her aid...

But not every woman needs to be rescued...

Weather-controlling witch Rhiannon Sinclair isn't caught in a storm—she's the cause of it. She's mortified to have been caught making trouble by the imposing earl, but she doesn't need any man—never has, and is sure she never will...

But when Rhiannon encounters Matthew again, her powers go awry and his supernatural abilities run amok. Between the two of them, the ton is thrown into an uproar. There's never been a more tempestuous scandal...

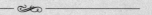

"Heartwarming romance, engaging characters, and engrossing plot twists...fast becoming 'must buy' books. I recommend them all."—Star-Crossed Romance

For more Lydia Dare, visit:

www.sourcebooks.com

Never Been Bit

by Lydia Dare

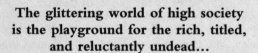

The glittering world of high society is the playground for the rich, titled, and reluctantly undead...

Alec MacQuarrie's after-life has become an endless search for pleasure in an effort to overcome his heartbreak and despair. Wandering through the seedy world of London's demimonde, he's changed into a dark and fearsome creature even he doesn't recognize until he stumbles into a magical lass he knew once upon a time and sees a glimpse of the life he could have had.

But the ton is no match for one incorrigible young lady...

After watching each of her coven sisters happily marry, Sorcha Ferguson is determined to capture a Lycan husband of her very own. When she encounters Alec, she decides to save her old friend from what he's become, all while searching for her own happily-ever-after.

Over his dead body is Alec going to allow this enchanting innocent to throw herself away on an unworthy werewolf, but that leaves him responsible for her, and he's the worst monster of them all...

For more Lydia Dare, visit:

www.sourcebooks.com